Visiting Vati

Library of Congress Number: 2001118365

This book was printed in the United States of America.

Heckner Press
www.hecknerpress.com
www.visitingvati.com

ISBN: 0-6156-7478-X
ISBN-13: 9780615674780

Visiting Vati

Ingrid Wiegand

My thanks: To my editors: Judith Lillard, who helped me tighten up my sprawling original, and Deborah MacLaughlin, who helped me give the book its final shape;

To Terry Eisinger, who took time from his busy life
to correct my inadequate German;

To my son, Peter, who designed and produced the perfect cover;

To my daughter, Indira, who provided necessary encouragement;

and *in memoriam* to my friend, Irene Towbin, for her warm-hearted support.

Chapter 1

I had given up all hope in my small heart one late afternoon as the train that was bearing my mother and myself away from my father's final farewell was slowly picking up speed as it rumbled over shunt after shunt out of the city, the tracks at each shunt spreading away to my left to other destinations, a web of tracks flowing away faster and faster, so that when I finally said to myself, "*Ich werde meinen Vater nie wiedersehen*.... I will never see my father again," the train picked it up and repeated it only a few times before we were going too fast to hook the syllables onto the clack of the wheels on the rails. As my mother leaned forward to take off my coat I looked up to see the magnificent black-and-silver uniform of a tall SS officer who told my mother to give him her papers, before he passed on to frighten other refugees–because that is what we now were–and dazzle other children.

I had said goodbye to my father at a railroad station on my way to Paris with my mother, getting out of Germany just before World War II was legally declared. They were divorced; he had terminated an unsuitable marriage, one which had tainted his Aryan ancestry with my mother's Jewish blood. It was a gross oversimplification, but one which served him, although the marriage was unquestionably a disaster on a lot of other, more mundane grounds. Nevertheless, I adored him then, as I adored *meinen lieben Führer*, whose picture, supplied by my school, hung in my room without protest from my mother, who knew better.

Now twenty-three years later, I was making my first visit to my once-beloved Vati, as well as to his third wife and several step-brothers. Like the small child I still harbored rather than the relatively sophisticated New Yorker I had become, I came to this visit with the assumption that if you approach someone with good will they will respond in kind, ignoring at my peril very different agendas that were already in play in my father's household.

I arrived at Frankfurt Airport from Paris, where I had spent a week on the town with my boyfriend, Jack, who had business there. I found my father in the crowd. Age had loosened the folds of his face, emphasizing the obligatory dueling scar of his university years. He was no longer—but I had not expected him to be–the dashing blonde man with the face of a 'Twenties film star as he had appeared in the only picture my mother had kept of him as I grew up American. But he was still slender and tall, now dressed in English tweeds rather than the uniform of a dueling fraternity. He seemed glad to see me, but it was hard to tell.

Although I found out that he spoke French fluently and Italian well, his English was on a par with my college-learned German, my native tongue which, like many small children in new countries, I had once discarded as inoperative. He had asked me to fly to Frankfurt, almost 300 miles from Mannschweig, the big city to which my old home town of Stammbüttel was a suburb. Clearly, Hanover, only fifty miles away, would have been nearer, but I think he wanted the time to tell me something. I was listening as hard as I could, but I didn't hear what he was trying to say—though later I came to understand that even he didn't grasp the whole situation–the complex web of relationships into which I was stepping. After all, his family had been around for centuries; the family business predated the discovery of America. I had left before I was old enough to remember who was who. I was prepared to be sensitive, responsive, and ready to learn. All I really wanted was to have a picture of my father that hadn't been retouched by an abandoned child's fantasies. I was not fine-tuned for other information, no matter how pertinent it might have been.

We went out to his car: a new, dark blue Audi, clearly an item of pride and joy, not, it seemed, because it had cost a lot, but because he was an admirer of beautiful machines. As we drove through the town on our way to the Autobahn, Germany's main no-limit speedway at the time, he talked about its various bells and whistles. This wasn't too difficult for me to follow: being scientifically minded, I knew a fair amount about cars–enough, anyway, to make appropriate noises at the right times. When he wasn't talking about the car, he was pointing to large excavations and piles of rubble, remnants, he said, of the war and the Allied bombings. To me, it looked like the usual scattering of construction sites you find on any old day in New York City, which at the time had never seen anything bigger than a pipe bomb sent as a goodbye gift from one Mafioso to another, but I was being too polite to say so.

Before we reached the Autobahn, however, my politeness was severely tested when he said, "*Aber das Bombardment von Frankfurt*.... But the bombing of Frankfurt was nothing like the bombing of Dresden. That was the most terrible thing in the whole war. Terrible." And he shook his head tragically as he negotiated a turn on an access road. "*Armes Dresden*.... Poor Dresden," he said, mournfully.

The most terrible thing in the war? I mean, yes, it was terrible. I knew we had incinerated several thousand people in a single night like moths in candles. And they were civilians. But the Germans had not been dropping candy canes on London at the time. But mostly I thought, what about Dachau, Treblinka, Auschwitz, and the concentration camp where my grandmother had died—Theresienstadt?

What should I say to him? There was a silence. Then I said–not very coherently "*Aber ich glaube dass Leute*.... But I think people think there were some other things that were more terrible, like the concentration camps."

"*Ach ja*," he said, nodding and shaking his head sadly again. "*Das war auch schrecklich*.... That was terrible too. A tragedy. But of course we knew nothing about them until after the war."

How could he say that? I thought. Was it a kind of self-protective amnesia, an ignorance precluding guilt? But then I remembered that my mother had always made it pretty clear that my father had not been a Nazi; in fact he had been a member of some left-wing organization that the Nazis later destroyed. He had gotten away with it because my grandfather was a member of the German Parliament–the one that elected Hitler. In the end, my father was just another German who was drafted into the *Wehrmacht*, the German army. I knew that very few of the people who didn't have to leave put up a fight, and almost none of those who did, survived. My father was definitely not a hero, or he wouldn't have let us go into such a precarious situation without a cent of his family's substantial money.

We pulled onto the Autobahn and drove in silence for a while. "You know that I have remarried," he said.

"Umhm," I said. "*Ich weiss*.... I know."

"She was my secretary." I didn't know.

"Really," I said.

"Yes. Her name is Ilse." There was a long pause. "It was many years after Adele died—that was my second wife, the mother of Hans and Gustav, your half-brothers. It was very sad. Very sad." And he looked very tragic again, much as he had about Dresden.

"How old are Hans and Gustav?" I asked. I didn't know the Göring family timetable. Göring was my father's family name and had once been mine, until my mother dropped it when we settled down in America. Then it was also the name of the head of Hitler's Air Force, the *Luftwaffe*, and the object of hate when it wasn't the name on a fat, uniformed German in the political cartoons of the day.

When he told me Hans was thirteen and Gustav was twelve, I started calculating. Hans was probably conceived when he got back from the French P.O.W. camp where he had reportedly spent the last year of the war. My mother had managed to pick up this item about father's end-of-the-war from some mutual friends with whom she had made postwar contact. She had passed it on to me with the implication that he had somehow engineered this cushioned denoument–cushioned, compared with service on the Russian front in 1943, when the Russians and their local winter sent what was left of Germany's "Eastern Front" back West.

Naturally I did not lay out any of these indelicate thoughts at the time, even though I had always thought of my father as a rather randy guy. My mother had made it clear–with a good deal of invective–that the ostensible reason for the divorce was not the real one. He had left her for another woman. He had had an extended affair with "an actress"–my otherwise liberated and bohemian mother said it as if she had been a street whore–who he had the nerve to see with me in tow. Although my mother said that I spent a lot of time with him, to this day all the real memories I have of him are from this visit, and earlier memories remain as they were: a faded, featureless but essential presence, like the trace of a ghost in a photograph of a haunted house.

He glanced at me and then with his eyes on the concrete belt rolling us north, he said, "My wife is young. She is not much older than you. I hope you will be friends." The idea appealed to me. Things would be much simpler if his wife and I could be friends, or at least friendly. I said "Yes. That would be really nice," and I meant it. I assumed friendly was possible.

My father and I talked about a lot of other things. He was still living in the house where I had once been a small child. It was, he told me, actually a couple of adjoining town houses dating from the fifteenth century which served both for living and for his publishing business. To his chagrin, all of them had been declared part of the town's historic district, which had prevented him from enlarging a window in his office. "Do you understand," he said, throwing his arm up with a gesture of indignation, "*meine eigene Haus*.... my own house, that belongs to my family for over four hundred years, and they tell me I cannot change my windows?"

I agreed. "*Schrecklich!*" I said emphatically. "Terrible."

"Of course," he immediately added, "Stammbüttel is a beautiful town. The old part, where my house is, is still as it was, and the old *Schloss*–the Castle–is still there." The Count, an old school friend of his, still lived in it, he said.

"My half-brother's family and two half-sisters also live in Stammbüttel." I knew his mother had died when he was quite young. "Oh," I said. "Then your father remarried."

"Yes," he said with a diffident smile. "Twice. I am following in his footsteps." Then his face became somber, and his voice softened. "Unfortunately," he added. "It is for the same reason. As I told you, my second wife–Adele–she also died."

"What happened?"

"She became very sick." It still seemed hard for him to talk about it.

"What did she die from?" Even though I had come from the Land of Euphemism where people never die, they only "pass away," I wanted to know.

He was silent a moment, and then shook his head. "*Sie hatte eine Art*.... She had a kind of influenza."

"*Was meinst du*.... What do you mean by a 'kind of influenza' mean?"

"*Sie war krank*.... She had been ill for several weeks when suddenly she got much worse and was gone." From the tone of his voice he seemed on the edge of tears. "It is almost six years since she is dead."

"How terrible. With the boys so young."

"Yes. But fortunately, my old nurse, Anni, who had brought me up, was their nurse too, and she lived with us. She lives with us now, and takes care of..." He stopped. After a while he continued. "You have another half-brother: Helmut. He is Ilse's son."

That was the first I heard of what I later decided was my family's version of Damien, a little boy who was the Devil's spiritual son in a movie of the same name. Helmut, of course, had no special powers, and his bent for mischief came from being wildly indulged by his mother rather than through his paternity. "How old is he?" I asked.

"He is three, but he will be four next week. You will be here for his birthday party.

"That will be nice," I said, but my mind was working. I had first thought that for all his show of grief, my father couldn't wait to get remarried after his second wife died, but I had it wrong. After his wife died, he had an affair with his secretary, and she had become pregnant. I understood that in a small town almost anywhere, if you are not married, you marry the Devil's daughter rather than have her running around pregnant with what everyone knows is yours.

After a minute he spoke again. "My brother also has died, but there is my brother's wife and son, your cousin Rudi. My sisters are alone. They never married. They both depend on me. There is also a very old aunt. My stepmother's sister. There are many people. It is a small business..." his voice faded.

I knew my father had a publishing business of some sort, but aside from the fact that the family had been putting out a local paper for several centuries, I didn't know anything about it. "*Erzähl mir davon....* Tell me about the business," I said. "What do you publish?

"Ummm," he said and cleared his throat. "I publish the *Stammbüttler Zeitung*. What I call '*mein Käseblatt*'..." he waved his right hand in small, explanatory circles, "...the paper that the grocer uses to wrap cheese in." He laughed, very pleased with the modesty of his description. I liked it too, and I understood what he meant. "I am joking, of course," he went on. "It is a very good paper. It is not only about Stammbüttel; we publish news of the whole world. Everybody reads it. You will see. I will show it to you."

"How old is the *Zeitung?*" I asked.

"My great, great, great grandfather–that is from my mother–started the *Zeitung* in the year 1487. That was almost five hundred years ago. His name was Wilhelm Graben, and Graben Verlag has been publishing ever since. But I have brought it into the twentieth century. After the war, when I became head of the Verlag, the type was still set by hand." He shook his head. "I brought in linotype machines and an offset press. You will see it. When you see the house, you will not believe that such a machine is in it!"

I was impressed. Perhaps it was childhood memories, but I wouldn't have been surprised to see little old men hand-setting type in dusty little rooms. I knew what such print shops looked like. As a teenager, I had a part-time job with a local printer who did things like handset invitations and business stationery. I remember how I loved the smell of printers' ink.

"I used to work in a print shop," I said.

"What is a 'printshop'?"

I explained. He was amused. "*Komisch*," he said, shaking his head with a smile. "*Sehr komisch*." Very funny."

"Why? Why '*komisch*'?"

"That my daughter would work in a 'printshop.'" He said the word as if it were something just one notch above a whorehouse.

"But," I said, feeling offended, "If I had grown up here, wouldn't you have let me work in your...printshop?"

"That is possible," he said thoughtfully. But it would have been only for amusement. In our family, women do not work in the Verlag. And none of them have ever worked with their hands for another!" He shook his head.

I realized he thought it was a *declassé* thing to do. "Look," I started, and stopped. How was I going to address him? "*Vater*," I said. "In America most teenagers have jobs, even if their parents are middle-class. Almost all the girls I knew did babysitting, and the boys also had jobs after school..."

He threw me a suspicious glance. "What is this 'babysitting'? Did you do it?"

His concern confused me; I didn't want him to disapprove of anything I had done. "Yes. No. I mean, yes. You take care of other people's children for an evening while the parents go out."

"You mean," he said, "that even doctors and lawyers hire young girls, who they do not know well, to take care of their children? Why do they not hire a nurse? Do they not have servants?"

"Not servants who live in the house. Only rich people have live-in servants."

Now he looked really worried.

"Rich people. You think only rich people have servants?" He shook his head again. "So you must think I am rich."

I shook my head. No. I didn't think he was "rich." Just very well-off, which was different. So I said, "Not rich. Just...comfortable."

"Com-for-ta-ble." He pronounced the word slowly. "Hmmm. *Tröstlich*. Hmmm." My father liked his 'Hmmm.' It came from deep back in his throat and made him sound much larger and fatter than he was. It reminded me of the way a dog will ruff up his neck when threatened, or a pheasant his tail feathers–to look larger than it is. It held you off and gave him time to think. Finally he said, "Ach! *Ja. Bequem. Bequem wohnen.*" I didn't follow, but then he said, "Comfortable. Very interesting," with a satisfied smile. I understood that he had just discovered the right word. At heart, I decided, my father was a writer. For writers, the right word, the right verbal connection, is the wine drinker's Chateau Mouton Rothschild, Cartier-Bresson's "perfect moment," and a truly thin slice of Schaller and Weber's hard salami. I gave him a big smile, but he was watching the road.

We had been driving for a couple of hours now and it was getting on to three-thirty. At the next exit, my father turned off and we drove into a town. "Here is a very good coffee house," said. We went in. It was half-empty and we were seated immediately, the maître greeting my father with familiar courtesy. Without taking an order, the waiter brought a plate of different small pastries, covered with powdered sugar or filled with whipped cream. I didn't eat a lot of this kind of stuff, but I wasn't about to turn my nose up at the first thing my father offered. He selected a substantial cream tart covered with a mound of fresh raspberries. I took a piece heaped with whipped cream. My father smiled. *"Ach, Sahne!"* he said approvingly. And *Sahne* it was, as our coffee arrived, also *"mit Schlagsahne"*–a large topping of whipped cream.

The waiter seemed to know him, and a man who may have been the owner came over and made a point of greeting him, eyeing me curiously. I wasn't a great beauty, but I had my good points and I had dressed to impress. I had worked on my wardrobe for this trip for weeks: the suit I was wearing, like most of the clothes I had brought with me, was a really good knockoff of a current French couturier at a time when there really wasn't any American or Italian competition, although Halston and Schiaparelli were already in the wings. My father followed his eye and said, *"Herr Lachsober, das ist meine Tochter,* Helene."

The surprise on the man's face surprised me, and it wasn't until afterward that I realized he wasn't expecting me to have that kind of relationship to my father. But he recovered immediately and bowed. *"Ach, wunderbar,"* he said, beaming, and bowed to me. *"Gnädiges Fraeulein,"* he murmured as he genuflected, with just a hint of heel knocking. I like *"gnädiges."* It means "gracious" and is merely a formal term of polite address to one's elders and betters, but it felt like a plus. I noticed that my father introduced me by only by my first name, but I assumed that got him off the hook from explaining why I had a different name but was still a *Fräulein.* I was tempted to say "Gelbart," as if he were waiting to hear it, but I kept my mouth shut. As it was full of whipped cream, I would not have done myself credit.

When we went out to the car, my father surprised me by suggesting that I drive. He was tired, he said, and he thought I might enjoy driving the Audi. I wasn't going to say no. I loved to drive, anytime, anywhere, and his car, though a conventional family sedan rather than the sportier models I favored, would be a treat to drive. On the other hand, I wasn't too eager to be entrusted with one of the family jewels on such short acquaintance.

We started off all right–more or less. My father seemed pleased with the decision to let me drive, and I assured him that I was a good driver, which was more or less true. I had certainly avoided any significant damage to persons and property, although friends who drove with me tended to sit with their feet braced against the front of the passenger foot space and one arm pressed against the dashboard. They often started pumping their right foot aimlessly, well before I hit the brake myself. But I didn't mind. I always delivered them safe and sound, if a bit nervous, to their destination.

The Audi was a stick shift, but that was not a problem. One of my early boyfriends, who had taught me how to drive, had been an autophile who I left when I realized that I rated far behind anything on four wheels. I put the key in the ignition and turned, waiting for the sputter and roar of my trusty old Merc back home, and held it until I heard a small grinding noise. The engine had turned over so quietly that ignition had taken place before I was aware of it. I threw a corrugated, cartoony grin at my father, who returned an equally short nervous smile to me. I took a deep breath, slipped the gearshift into what I presumed to be reverse and lurched forward, managing to avoid knee-capping another patron only by a fast foot on the brake. The zig-zag smile of the misbegotten seemed pasted on my face as I shot another apologetic glance at my father and checked the gear shift pattern on the handle, something I could have done earlier if I hadn't been so determined to look wonderful. We moved out of the parking lot and onto a side road without further incident, and reached the Autobahn.

He settled down and I relaxed slightly, admiring the clean and well-tended margins of the throughway and the seamless, wide-laned road as it flashed under me. Although I occasionally reminded myself to look and see the country of fields and still-quaint hamlets glimpsed through fences and green trees, it wasn't high on my agenda. Even the Hartz Mountains, which reminded me of the Presidential Range in New Hampshire, only somewhat more rugged, didn't hold my eyes. Whenever I looked, my attention was drawn back to the man beside me, this stranger who nevertheless had the most basic relationship to me, my blood-parent whose DNA had come down to me through generations, who I had once addressed in a little-girl voice as my "Vati"—my Daddy. I sat there, wanting so much for him to like me, to think I had turned out all right after all. At the same time I was aware of (and avoiding) the fact that if I was okay, it was no thanks to him.

After dozens of Autobahn kilometers had slid away to the motor-hummed sound of the long, smooth road, my father cleared his throat, and said, "We must go faster."

"How far do we have to go?" I asked.

"It will be another hundred kilometers to Stammbüttel," he said and sighed noisily. But then he settled down again and my mind drifted back to the road, and to Paris, and to Jack, who had put me on the plane to Frankfurt. I liked to think of Jack as my kind of guy–although my mind immediately countered that assertion with a number of qualifying "buts." He was funny and very smart, and a nice mix of bawdy and tender where sex was concerned, but out of bed he had very finite ideas about everything else–business, politics, social life, women–attitudes I wasn't prepared to deal with.

Although he hadn't asked me outright, I knew he was toying with the idea of asking me to marry him, and the "if" was beginning to sound like a condition I was not prepared to meet. I was doing well as a free-lance science writer. I had a good reputation for what I did, I had a good time, I traveled around working on different projects, and at a time when most professional women didn't do all that well, I was already as well paid as most men. I wasn't about to become somebody's Mrs. and stay at home while my husband led an interesting life and I didn't. I pulled my shoulders back and arched my back to stretch.

"*Bist du müde?*.... Are you tired?" my father asked.

"No, no. *Nein, nein. Nur...*" I didn't know the word for stretching.... "stretching?"

"Ach, ja. Ausstrecken. Almost the same. Yes." He nodded. "Some words are almost the same. But when we get home, it will be easier. Ilse speaks very good English. She worked for the Americans after the war. At Nürnberg."

"At the Nürnberg Trials! What did she do?"

"She was a secretary, and worked for the Americans. So her English is very good. She will be happy to have someone to practice with."

This was not welcome news. Even though I wanted to be friendly with my father's wife, I really didn't want her to be the main channel to my father. We weren't doing too badly working the territory between our two languages, and I had figured it could only improve over the week I had planned to spend with him. I saw that this could be a problem, and it was coming up quickly as we passed a sign that said "Mannschweig–2km." At that moment my father said, *"Recht! Recht!....* Right!" As I turned into an exit, my father pointed imperiously toward a landscaped pullout, where I stopped. He got out and strode purposefully around the front of the car while I slid over to the passenger seat. My father got in, adjusted his jacket and put the car into gear.

We passed from farm country to the typical outskirts of a town until we entered a truly ancient part with wood and stuccoed houses which I had only seen on film sets. We stopped in front of one of these buildings. My father opened a beautiful wrought iron gate and drove into a widening courtyard running the length of three houses and lined with rosebushes about to bloom. A door in the back opened and a tall, somewhat heavy, awkward-looking boy in his teens, dressed in *Lederhosen*–traditional short pants of heavy leather held up by brightly woven suspenders–came out and walked toward us.

"Here is Hans," my father said.

"Grüss Gott, Vater," Hans said as he stopped short and gave a short bow. It surprised me to see him bowing to his own father, so that I was standing there looking vacant as my father introduced me.

"Deine Halbschwester.... your half-sister, Leni," he said, using the familiar form of my name. Hans not only bowed in my direction, but clicked his heels with a sound like a pistol shot. It was disconcerting. I said, "Hallo," making it sound as German as possible. He gave me a dour half-smile, said "Hallo" back and extended his hand limply. I shook it.

Hans stood there eyeing me with a less than a welcoming gaze until my father brought him to with an imperial gesture toward the open gate. Hans turned and rushed to close it. Then father took my bag out of the trunk and we entered the house: I following my father, Hans bringing up the rear. I had arrived at my ancestral home.

Chapter 2

We entered a small low-ceilinged room, with several dark wooden doors. The room was lined with very old wood paneling to a height of about four feet, with a rough stucco above that and a polished stone floor. One of the doors was open to the kitchen, and as my father stopped to take off his trench coat, a small gray-haired aproned woman with a big smile came out and said, "*Grüss Gott*, Herr Franz." She looked at me shyly with her head tilted slightly down.

My father gave her a big smile back and said "*Grüss Gott, Anni.*" As he hung up his coat, he gestured toward me and added, "*Erinnerst du dich an Leni....* Do you remember Leni?"

Anni gave me a shy smile before she said, "*Nein. Ich erinnere mich nicht an diese Dame....* No. I don't remember this lady."

"*Aber sie ist ebendieselbe Leni....* But she is the very same Leni that you knew when she was a child." Anni shook her head and continued to smile as my father motioned me to follow him through another door that Hans was holding open. It led directly into the dining room, where a long dark table was laid for six, with plates and soup plates, very plain but heavy-looking silver, and a variety of napkin rings holding tightly-rolled table napkins beside each place. The late-day sun came in through two mullioned windows, and between them stood a large armoire filled with glasses and stacks of an elaborate dinner service. There was a long, low sideboard where a platter of cold cuts sat beside a napkin-lined basket of bread. I remembered that dinner was at midday; the evening meal would be a light supper.

As I stood taking all this in, Hans pointed to a stairway that came down at one end of the dining room and said in lightly accented English, "Perhaps you would like to wash your hands?" and then looked down at his feet and grimaced–I assumed it was because for him, as for most adolescent boys even in less repressed societies, directing a woman to a bathroom was fraught with sexual overtones.

"Yes. Oh, yes. Sure," I said and headed up the stairs. As I reached the top, he cleared his throat and said, "To your right, please."

I opened the door and stepped into an immaculate bathroom out of the Twenties, with a large claw-footed tub and a pedestal sink. Only the toilet, in an adjacent room, was of relatively recent vintage. A small, glistening white folded hand towel with a thin blue line across each end was there for my use.

As I washed my hands, I looked into the mirror above the sink. I was only occasionally pleased with what I saw in mirrors, and this was not one of the occasions, but I had felt worse about the image. I could never decide whether what others saw as attractive–even occasionally, beautiful–was anything other than merely healthy and vaguely interesting. I confined myself to looking for familial likenesses and could find only one–the bump in my nose which I had always assumed to be from the Jewish side was clearly from more Aryan genes; Hans's masculine version matched mine in everything except scale: his was bigger. As my father's nose was perfectly straight, I had to assume the nose I shared with Hans went back a ways. I wiggled it at the mirror and took it down to join its kin for supper.

When I got back down to the dining room, Hans was standing expectantly by one of the chairs, as was a slightly smaller and thinner version, also dressed in *Lederhosen.* This had to be Gustav, who Hans introduced somewhat protectively as Gustl, *his* brother. Before I could do more than acknowledge Gustav's formal bow, we were interrupted by a scream appropriate to a disembowelling or similar excruciation. The sound introduced a small, exquisitely beautiful, pale blond boy who was pulling a slightly over-weight but pretty woman into the room. She was making coy but ineffectual protestations as she permitted herself to be borne in like a caveman's hunting trophy. Her hair was disheveled and her blouse was partially pulled out of her skirt. When she saw me she stopped, yanked her hand out of the little boy's, brushed back her hair, and tucked in her blouse with a single dexterous movement.

The face she turned to me after these lightning maneuvers was friendly. "You must be Helene," she said in lightly accented American English. "I am Ilse," she added and shook my hand in a surprisingly American way. I shook hers, and opened my mouth to speak, but instead I jumped back from a sharp pain in my shin and hollered. I grabbed my leg and looked down to see the small angelic blond face configured into a perfect mask of hatred, his small hands knotted into little fists as he took aim with his thick-soled shoes for another hefty kick.

"Hey!" I yelled and reached out to hold him away from me, when he was snatched to a safe distance and held there by Ilse's strong grip.

"*Geh weg*!" he shrieked, struggling to get at me. "*Geh weg, du verdammte Hexe!*" I got the gist, even though I was stunned by his righteousness and wondered what I could have done to make him so angry. It was one of the few really honest expression of feeling I was to get, although I would have rather done without it.

In the face of this, Ilse was *magnifique.* If a child of mine had put on this kind of act for anyone (never mind somebody you'd rather had no clue to your feelings), I would have been completely rattled, but not Ilse. I would have had to admire her even if she hadn't given me such a friendly welcome just a moment earlier. Holding him tightly by the collar as he struggled to get at me like one of these nasty small dogs that show their teeth and snarl believably, she smiled again and said, "You must forgive Helmut, Helene. I have read him a book about a wicked witch and I think it scared him."

I was so ready to overlook this and get on with relating to everybody that I was only too happy to accept her explanation. She laughed and bent over him as she said, "*Helmut, Helmut, das ist nicht die böse Hexe....* This is not the wicked witch. She is your older half-sister, Helene, from America." He looked from her to me and back again. "Helene is a *good* sister, Helmut," she said in English–for my benefit, I thought–but he seemed to understand as he looked at her doubtfully. "Nein," he said, and shook his head. "*Sie ist die Böse,...*She is the wicked one," he said and stamped his small foot.

Ilse looked down at the boy fondly, and then shook her head with a disarming smile to me. "Don't mind. He will get over it. Let us have supper," but I was grateful to see that she kept a tight hold on her son, whose look at this point had subsided to a glower. She glanced around and as she looked at Gustav and Hans, her face shifted subtly from a glow of maternal affection to that of command, like a sergeant addressing her platoon. "Where is your father?"

"Washing for supper," Gustav answered in English. I understood that both of them would be learning English in school as a matter of course. I assumed it was for my benefit, but he said it without any change of expression or glance in my direction, just with his eyes on Ilse, as if it only had to do with them. It was one of those clues to the family puzzle that I would have to decipher like a crossword, from other clues as they became available.

Everyone arranged themselves behind their chairs and Ilse showed me to mine, mercifully down and across the table from little Helmut. I was about to sit in it when I noticed that everyone had remained standing. I understood: nobody sat until Father did. As a the very model of a modern American, I found it strange, but as I wanted to fit in with the family, to be a part of my father's world for a little while, to see how it fitted me and how I might have fitted into it, I retreated to a standing position.

Out of the corner of my eye I could see Helmut looking down and kicking his chair desultorily. I became aware that my shin was aching. I was not off to a good start with Helmut, and I wasn't so sure where I stood with the two boys either. Every time I caught them looking at me, they would immediately look away. A couple of times they would look at each other with what seemed to be significant glances. It reminded me of what it had felt like when I was the new kid at a school, about to be subjected to various rites of passage. I stared at my silver napkin holder with its simple, elegant design around the crisply ironed linen napkin with the blue woven border, and told myself that I was a grown woman and didn't have to put up with anything from anybody, including half-grown half-brothers.

Then my father came in and nodded pleasantly at Ilse. As he pulled out his chair and sat down, everyone followed as if we had all come to life again. Anni appeared from the kitchen bearing a large, handsome white lidded tureen with a long, thin, delicately branched gray crack on its side, and placed it in front of him. She stood for a moment as he lifted the lid and a cloud of steam rose. He breathed in its aroma and turned to her. "*Ach, Anni! Erbsensuppe mit frischen Erbsen!*.... Pea soup with fresh peas! My favorite!" and gave her a warm smile. She smiled as if to herself and left the room.

As we passed the bowls at our places to him and he ladled out the pale green soup dotted with bright green peas, he acknowledged the boys, asking Helmut if he had been good. "*Ja, ja, Vati*," the little boy lied, waving his spoon and looking like an angel again.

"*Nein, nein*," said Gustav coyly, smiling and wagging his finger playfully at Helmut. "*Nicht die ganze Zeit*.... Not all the time. He..."

"Gustl!" Ilse's voice cut across the table. "*Stör deinen Vater nicht*.... Don't bother your father with these little things." Gustav promptly directed his eyes to his plate and kept them there. My father wanted to know, What little things?

Nothing, Ilse told my father. Just a boy will be a boy, or something to that effect. She leaned over and patted the small monster's blond head. "Helmut is a good boy," she said coaxingly. Helmut gave her a complicit look from under demurely lowered lashes and shot a triumphant glance at me as she shifted the conversation away from the forbidden topic. "What took you so long from Frankfurt?"

Now it was my father and I who exchanged glances. He spoke deliberately, firmly. He spoke in German, but I followed most of it. It had been a very nice drive. We had stopped and had coffee at the Weiss Cafe. Herr Ober sent her his regards. Ilse looked pleased to be remembered until she asked how he could have remembered her when she hadn't been there for two years. He always asks after you, my father reassured her with a smile so charming I could see some basis to my mother's claims that he could be an incarnation of Don Juan. Ilse looked pleased again. He continued talking. He didn't mention that I had driven the car. Gradually the conversation shifted to other matters.

The boys listened attentively, but Helmut kept a concentrated interest in his soup when he was not checking out his mother's expression. He only stopped, spoon in mid-dip, when she said *"Gott im Himmel!"* at the mention of some accident we had passed on the road, of which I had not taken much note. *"Was? Was?"* Helmut said anxiously. *"Nichts. Nichts,"* she said, *"Alles in Ordnung*.... Everything's all right." She reached over and patted his head. *"Iss deine Suppe, Liebchen,*...Eat your soup, darling, and afterward, mama will give you something good." He wanted to know what good thing she would give him later. It went on for several minutes, while my father, the patriarch before whom no one sat first, nevertheless sipped his soup and kept his peace. The boys kept theirs, exchanging occasional cryptic glances.

Even though the boys didn't seem to be very friendly to me, it was nice the way they were so tight with each other. It must be very hard for them, I thought, to have lost their mother and then find yourself moved further away from your father by a new wife who didn't seem to care much for you. But like any family, there seemed to be a lot of other things going on too. It was going to take some time to figure things out.

When everyone had finished their soup, Ilse got up and took two of the plates to the kitchen. I started to rise, but she told me to sit down. "Anni will do it," she said over her shoulder as she headed through the kitchen door.

She was barely through before Anni hurried out and started to collect the rest of the soup plates. "*Ich kann das tun*.... I can do that," she said angrily. "*Ich kann das noch tun*.... I can still do that." and hurried, laden with the four other plates, back into the kitchen as Ilse was heading out. "*Ich kann das tun*," she said again to Ilse as she went in. Ilse shook her head and smiled as she walked back toward her chair, picked up the platter and basket of bread from the sideboard and put it in the center of the table. Then she sat down and said to me, "Anni is always thinking that if I help, I am saying she is too old. But she *is* old and she needs the help. I don't know what I am going to do with her." Just then, Anni came in, looked at the sideboard, saw the platter gone to the table, turned on her heel and went back to the kitchen, shaking her head and muttering. Ilse smiled triumphantly. "If I let her, she will try to do everything herself. She has to learn."

"Ilse," my father said. "*Bitte. Ich weiss dass Anni*.... I know that Anni is sometimes difficult, but she has run the house since I was a little boy. You will not find another servant as good as Anni." It was clear that this was an ongoing argument. My father protecting his old nurse; Ilse protecting what she saw as her turf. I wanted to sympathize with Ilse, my contemporary and my hostess *and* my father's current wife, but I found myself leaning toward Anni. My money, nevertheless, was on Ilse.

As we assembled our own open-face sandwiches from the makings on the table, Anni brought my father an ancient stein, a tall, decorated pewter mug with a hinged top shaped like a Chinese coolie hat. He gestured toward it and said, "It was my father's, and his father's also. When I am at home, I always drink my beer from this stein." The fact appeared to give him great pleasure, and he demonstrated by lifting the top with his thumb and taking a long drink. He looked so solid when he did that, so established in his world, so essentially *German* to me–sitting there at supper in his tweed jacket and tie, in this antique room, with the last sun fading through the mullioned windows.

As I was thinking about this he asked me if I would like some. I was amazed that I was so caught up with the rightness of my father drinking *his* beer that it had not occurred to me that I wanted some too. "Yes," I said, "I'd love it. *Das hätte ich gern*." This pleased everyone. Ilse rang a bell, Anni came in and returned with classic tapered glasses filled with beer. "*Deutsches Bier*," my father said, raising his stein. "The best in the world."

"*Sehr gut*," I said.

But drinking beer focused attention on me. Did I drink beer often? I said that since college, I drank wine more often than beer. What college? What had I studied? Journalism? Well not exactly, although I sometimes I wrote for trade journals for electronic equipment. Mostly I worked for the companies that made the equipment, writing manuals and technical proposals. Very interesting. Not always, I said, but often enough to keep me working at it. Did I live with my mother? No, I had my own apartment. Wasn't that very expensive? Somewhat. But then, I made good money. Very interesting.

We finished with a homely bowl of lightly stewed fruit, with whole cloves and thin slices of lemon still visible. The adults had coffee and smoked. After desert, Anni came and got Helmut who was sleepy but held out until Ilse promised him a story when he was in bed. He gave me one direct, questioning look, but there was no feeling in it. Not only was he tired, I thought, but perhaps he was no longer so certain that I was the enemy–at least I hoped so.

The talk was about family things in a crazy mix of English and German that was to continue throughout my stay, the German mostly for my father's benefit and the English for everyone else, to practice. I of course had come hoping to practice German, but Ilse translated a lot of it for me. It was like trying to learn a foreign language by looking at films with subtitles; the subtitles always win. However, my father often spoke slowly for my benefit and I understood a lot before it was translated.

The boys were talking about a hiking trip they were going to take next week with one of their teachers when my father interrupted them. "*Ist das wahr?*.... Is that true?" he said with real surprise. "Herr Gross is taking you?"

The boys exchanged glances. Then Hans looked down at the table and said with a satisfied smile, "*Ja, Vati*.... Yes, father. He has to. He is our teacher."

"*Ja*," my father said. "*Aber nach*.... But after the last time, I am surprised that he has agreed to let you go." Nobody was translating now; I was barely keeping pace.

"*Er hatte es nicht vor*.... He wasn't going to," Hans said, "but Tante Ilse spoke to him and he..." He threw a sly glance at Ilse. "He changed his mind."

My father frowned and looked at Ilse. "*Was sagst du*.... What did you say to Herr Gross?"

Ilse shrugged. *"Ich brauchte nicht viel sagen....* I didn't have to say very much. I just reminded him that they were *your* sons, and..."

My father suddenly hit his hand on the table and spoke very quickly. English and I were forgotten. The gist was that he did not want the Göring name used to get the boys off. It sounded serious, although I wasn't sure until my father almost shouted, *"Gott im Himmel! Der Bub ist fast umgekommen....* The boy was almost killed!" I looked at the boys. They had their heads down and their eyes were swinging from Ilse to Father and back. Finally my father said angrily that if the family name was so important to her she should see to it that the boys didn't sully it. He shook his head. I caught up with the whole sentence. *"Morgen....* Tomorrow," he said finally, "you will call Herr Gross, thank him for his courtesy and tell him they will not go."

Ilse frowned. "Franzl," she said coaxingly, throwing a collusive glance at the boys. *"Franzl, du weisst....* you know they did not mean to harm the boy, and they apologized to everybody. We cannot continue to punish them forever."

My father shook his head. *"Das Ende von....* The end of one term is not forever." The boys sat absolutely still: this was between Ilse and their father, and they were not sure of the winner. He would not ask Herr Gross for 'favors', my father said, bringing his hand down on the table again as I caught up with the German. Hans and Gustav had always been good boys. He didn't know what had happened with them. At this point the boys were sitting with downcast eyes, their expressions blank. There was a long silence. Finally, my father heaved a big sigh and said, *"Ich gehe jetzt in mein Arbeitszimmer....* I'm going to my study." He turned to me. *"Gute Nacht, Leni,"* he said in a tired, kindly voice. "Tomorrow I will show you the Verlag, Yes?" he added in English, and left.

For a moment, no one moved. Then both boys smiled at Ilse, who looked at her hands with a fairly pleased expression. I wasn't sure what everyone was so pleased about, but I was beginning to consider the possibility that I had watched an uneven contest, and that my father may have had less to say about things that went on in the house than it appeared. Both of them said goodnight, mostly to Ilse, and went upstairs.

"We go to sleep early on weekdays, when the boys go to school," Ilse said, "although tomorrow is a holiday. Franz goes to sleep later, but he stays in his study. Come, I will show you your room." She got up and went to a door at the far end of the dining room near the stairs and opened it.

I got up and followed her into a plain, pleasant room where a large bed with a carved headboard took up half the space. A wide old mirror, engraved with an intricate floral border and set into a dark and massive Art Nouveau frame, hung over it. The bed was made up with crisply ironed monogrammed linen sheets and an eiderdown. There were several plump pillows, monogrammed with the same intricate "G." A small, spindly-legged night table next to it held a tall lamp which lit the room through a yellowed parchment shade. Under the lamp, the table was covered with a small embroidered cloth. Against the far wall, another mirror over a bureau reflected me as I stood in the door. My suitcase was already there, set down on a fine, well-worn oriental rug, under the dark window on my left. "It will be quiet," said Ilse modestly, "I will see that the boys don't wake you when they come down for breakfast. Franz has early coffee and eats a little later. You are on vacation. If you want to sleep late, you can have your breakfast when he comes for his coffee break." She said "coffee break" with special emphasis. I smiled appreciatively and nodded. "Perhaps you would like to unpack. I will go and read Helmut his story if he has not fallen asleep. When I am finished I will come to the living room and we can talk."

Chapter 3

After I unpacked, I put on a sweater–the late-June evening had become very cool–and went into the living room. It was a room that resembled all the living rooms of my mother's peers and family who had fled Germany in haste and finally settled comfortably in the States. There were white walls, simple furniture somewhere between Bauhaus and Swedish modern, and oriental rugs. A large worn brown leather couch dominated the seating, with a coffee table surrounded by various chairs and lamps. A large leather armchair to the left of the couch surveyed the room; I guessed it was my father's. A table in a corner by one of the two windows held a serious Bosch-Fernseh stereo system with a record player and a rack of LP records on a shelf below. Several bookcases held books of various vintages. A pair of modest paintings of flowers hung over the couch. A copy of my father's paper, *Die Stambüttler Zeitung*, lay on the coffee table. I sat down at one end of the couch and picked it up.

The front page was national news. Conrad Adenauer's meeting with Willi Brandt, then the Mayor of Berlin. An article on Krushchev's threat to turn East Berlin over to East Germany. Another article on Secretary of State Herter telling Krushchev he better not. Someone making it through the Iron Curtain, and several others not making it. That was a big article, probably because the border–the Iron Curtain between East and West Germany was only twenty miles–or was it kilometers?–away. I remembered my mother telling me that part of the province was supposed to go to the Russians when Germany was carved up after the war, but the local Count had called on some old prewar British connections dating back to his schooldays and managed to get some less well-connected land, with less lucky inhabitants, ceded to the Russians in exchange. When I thought about that, my mother was right: my father was a lucky man.

My father's "*Käseblatt*" was very respectable for a small-town paper. It was tabloid size, but that was all that was tabloid about it. It wasn't until several pages in that the articles started to focus on the town, and most of that was civic stuff–new housing, sewers. I was looking for the social section when a small headline over a small paragraph caught my eye: "Professor Gross ein Held.... Professor Gross a Hero." I was about to get my trusty *Deutsch-Englisches Wörterbuch* to translate the story when Ilse came in.

"What do you think of your father's newspaper?" she asked, sitting down at the other end of the couch from me, next to my father's chair. She took out a piece of embroidery about a foot square with its center stretched over an embroidery hoop. It looked like it was destined to be a pillow cover, similar to those I saw scattered about. As she waited for me to answer, she picked up a threaded needle that had been left in mid-stitch and started to sew.

"It's very impressive," I said, truthfully. "I don't think a lot of American small-town papers give as much space to national news. But I didn't get to the local news yet."

"Well, there is not much of it–the 'local' news. Just the usual things." Suddenly she put her embroidery down on her lap, sat up and pursed her lips, batted her eyes and raised her chin. She lifted one of her hands, and waving it beside her shoulder as she spoke, she said in an approximation of a British plummy tone laced with acid: "Yesterday Frau Gräfin Holstein gave a tea for the Stammbüttler Cultural Society and they all ate cake." Then she paused and looked at me out of the corner of her eye. I was so surprised by her try at humor that it took me at least two seconds too long to laugh, but then I did. She laughed too.

"I guess social notices are the same all over the world," I said. "But in the States," I added, smiling at her with my best tell-me-about-yourself interview approach, "the wife of the publisher of the local paper–especially when his family has been around for a few hundred years–would be in the paper herself."

Her face fell. I had said the wrong thing. She looked down at her hands and then gave me a hard and powerful look. "She would be if she came from the same..." she hunted for a word "...kind of family," she said coldly. "But not if her father had been a grocer and she had been the publisher's secretary." She stopped and waited.

"Well." I said, finally. "I don't see what is wrong with being a grocer or a secretary. In the States, running a store doesn't disqualify you from being President. President Truman..."

She spoke disdainfully. "In theory, a grocer can be President here too. But his daughter does not have tea with the local countess and her friends."

She narrowed her eyes and dropped her voice. "But I did not marry your father so that I could have tea with those ladies."

"Oh, I'm sure you didn't," I said, trying to be helpful.

"No, I did not. But my children will go to school with their children, and my grandchildren will marry their grandchildren. They can...how you say..." I suggested 'snub.' "Yes, they can snub me, but they will not snub the whole Göring family." She looked at me the way my cat back home watches a fly she is about to catch and added, "No one is going to stop that from happening."

The conversation had such powerful over and undertones that I was sure I had missed the main theme. "Of course not, Ilse," I said as placatingly as I could. "Why would anyone want to?" The cat-to-fly look persisted, as if I should know what was going on, but I didn't. I certainly had no desire to prevent her children from having tea with their children. I didn't give a damn who had tea with who–anywhere, including Stammbüttel. I began to wish I had stayed in my bedroom, but couldn't think of any excuse to leave; it wasn't even nine o'clock. My "Why would anybody want to?" seemed to irritate her even more. There was a significant social silence.

"People," she finally said, "have their own reasons. But they will not triumph over mine."

I had run out of platitudes. Finally she dropped her eyes, picked up her embroidery and said in a perfectly pleasant tone, "Your father will be at work most of the day and we do not want you to be bored. Tomorrow we will go with the children for a walk in the woods."

I was ready to go along with anything that take me out of the unknown territory we had traversed. "That would be terrific!" I gushed. "I love to walk in the woods. I really enjoy being out of doors. It will be a nice way to get to know the children. How far away are these woods?"

"It is about half an hour to drive. We are near the foothills of the Hartz Mountains. They are very beautiful. You will enjoy them."

"Oh, I'm sure I will. I will love it. I love mountains. In the States, I used to go hiking in the White Mountains. They are in New Hampshire. In the north. The Northeast."

She ignored my babbling. "We have had some quite damp weather recently, so that there should be many mushrooms." She was stitching deftly. "Do you like mushrooms?"

"I love mushrooms. There is a German restaurant in New York that serves Pfifferlinge and I always order them. A whole dish of them. I can eat mushrooms anytime."

"Pfifferlinge!" she said and laughed. "We have much better mushrooms than that! Pfifferlinge are ordinary mushrooms here. You will see. We have some wonderful mushrooms that you cannot find anywhere else."

I had a thought. "Isn't it rather dangerous to pick your own mushrooms? Some of them are so poisonous."

She shook her head and smiled in a friendly way, so that I almost felt forgiven for bringing up the painful subject of the ladies of the town. "Oh, don't worry about that. Mushrooms were one of my father's 'hobbies'–we have the same word, 'hobby'–and he often took me into the woods with him, so that I learned to know most of the edible mushrooms–and," she chuckled in a playful way, "and some not so edible." Then she added archly, wagging her finger, "But we do not pick those."

"That would be really interesting for me. I've never picked wild mushrooms because I don't know anything about them," I said, flatteringly and plunged on. "Does your father live near here?"

"My father is dead."

"Oh, I am sorry. I didn't know."

"Yes. He is dead. He was hanged at Nürnberg."

My mind felt like it had run into a well-built masonry wall. I gave Ilse credit; she could be very direct. Not for her the sorrowful glance with a reference to the beloved's "passing away." No. He was dead. He had been hung. My mind started to poke at what this meant. He was hanged at Nürnberg, where the Nazi war criminal trials were held, and a number of those found guilty were hanged shortly thereafter. But I knew they only hanged the big ones–except for Hitler, of course, who managed to give himself a *Götterdämmerung*-type funeral under what he had left of Berlin. Clearly, Ilse's father had not been some ordinary army man, most of whom were sent back to what remained of their homes after the war. He had done something really nasty. I decided to play it as straight as she had.

"Why did they hang him?"

"They held him responsible for the massacre of some people in a little village in Poland," she said, stitching away calmly. "It was, of course, ridiculous. Whatever he did, he was just following orders. It was not right."

This seemed a little dense. A lot of the people tried at Nürnberg were just sent to prison for various terms. Many of them had already served their sentences by this time, and were forgetting they had ever been Nazis. And the "just following orders" defense...Well, she had been there. I decided I had to say something.

"But Ilse," I said as if she might have forgotten some obscure fact, "the judges at Nürnberg decided that even men and women under orders were supposed to follow their consciences." I realized that I sounded overly righteous, but I felt I had to plow on. "I mean, you weren't supposed to kill an entire village of women and children and old men, which I assume it was, even if the commanding offer said to." I was pretty clear about it.

Ilse was not so clear about it. She laughed coldly. "I know what the judges at Nürnberg said. But they were the victors judging the defeated. It is very well to say that you should not obey 'unethical' orders, but in the army, a soldier does not try to decide which order is ethical and which is not. My father did what he was ordered to do."

"What rank did your father have?"

Her needle paused above the embroidery. "He was a general," she said. I remembered that a minute ago, she had said he was a grocer, and that grocers were low on the German totem pole as far as social tea parties were concerned. I had read enough about Germany and about armies to know that you didn't make General in any army on merit alone. Many of the German generals of The War were old upper-class buddies, just as they were in the British army. If her father had been a grocer before the war, her father must have been an old Nazi Party member to get such a high rank in the *Wehrmacht.*

"A general!" I said. "In the *Wehrmacht?*" She nodded. It could have been the SS–Hitler's death-head-insignia elite which included many rank-and-file hoodlums and sadists–but it wasn't. So it was impressive: grocer to general. "Well then, he'd have been giving orders instead of taking them, wouldn't he?"

She gave me a dismissive look and went on sewing. "That was what the Court said. But he was–what do you call it in English?–like a 'brigadier' general. He gave orders, but he had to take them. And what he did was under orders." She was silent a while. I didn't say anything. "It is very easy to say, 'He should not have done that. He should have said no and let himself be shot for disobeying orders rather than do what he did.' It is easy to say that now. But one day you will see that one of your soldiers will do something like that–and you will not find it so easy to judge him." She stopped. I was fortunate then, of course, that we hadn't yet had to deal with the vision of Lieutenant Calley and the massacre of Vietnamese villagers at Mylai. Even though Mylai made me think the whole business over, it didn't change my mind from what I was thinking then as I sat and watched her sew.

Yet, I understood that we were not talking theory; we were talking about her father. "It was not right to hang him," she said in a tight voice. And I remembered that I had come all this way to see my father, who was in the house and alive, and I let it go.

I sat there uncomfortably. Every time I opened my mouth it was as if I had opened the kind of letter bomb that blew up in your face and left you with–at the least–singed eyebrows. It still felt too early to retire gracefully. As I looked around, the stack of records caught my eye.

"Would you mind if I put on some music?" I asked.

"Oh, yes. Certainly." She gestured with the hand holding the needle. "Play anything you like."

I looked over the records. There were all kinds of classical pieces–a lot of Beethoven, Brahms, Mozart, a few operas (plus a big section which looked like most of Wagner's Ring cycle), and this was a surprise–a fair amount of American music, especially big bands like Benny Goodman and Artie Shaw, and some Dixieland. I tried to think what Ilse would like. I passed over a couple of recitals of German Lieder which would have bored me and found what looked like the covers of pop records–lots of top hats and champagne glasses–that I thought would be a safe bet. One in particular, almost at the bottom, looked well-worn, like a favorite, and I put it on.

A woman with a nice full voice and an easy delivery, sort of like a German Barbra Streisand with a Lotte Lenya edge, sang standards of love, loss and maybe revenge–I couldn't follow. I looked and saw that Ilse was nodding along with the beat. I finally seemed to have done something right.

"That is an old song," she said. "I think it is from before the War." She frowned slightly. "Who is it that is singing?"

I picked up the record cover and read, with my very best German accent, "*Die Liebeslieder von Herbert Brockmann.*"

"Yes," she said, nodding over her embroidery. "But who is singing?"

In smaller letters at the bottom, I saw and read it out: *"Gesungen von Adele König."*

The effect was electrifying. Ilse dropped her embroidery frame and hit both her knees with her fists in a gesture of total vexation as she stamped her foot. "Take it off. Stop the music. I will not have that record played! I do not want to hear it! Turn it off!"

I leapt up and tried to comply. I did not want to scratch the record by grabbing the stylus with my hands, and was looking down trying to find the reject button, but all I ended up doing was hitting some kind of skip-track switch, so that it raised up and settled down in the next track. Ilse started up as if I had poked her. I hit another switch. The arm lifted off and I smiled at her reassuringly, but then it went back down and started at the beginning. I finally managed to grab the stylus and put it on its hook. I took the offending record and slipped it quickly in its cover and tucked it somewhere, anywhere. "How about a little Wagner?" I said.

She sat there looking straight ahead with her hands, still in fists, resting on her knees. She stared across the room as if someone were standing there. I stood by the record player. I looked where she was looking, but there was nothing there. Finally I asked, "Who is Adele König?"

"She was..." She seemed to have difficulty with the words. "She was... your...she was married to your father."

Although I knew my father's second wife was called Adele, I would not have connected her name with that on the record cover if I had seen it. My mother had referred to her as an actress, not as a singer. In any case, Adele certainly sang, and someone had spent a lot of time listening to the record. Suddenly Ilse leaned back, picked up her sewing and said, "Play Brahms' Fourth. I know it is there, because your father likes to play it." I found it and put it on, getting the levers right. As I sat down and listened to the opening passages I remembered how much my mother used to enjoy it.

I was just starting to get into the music when Ilse said, "I knew Adele quite well. Not the 'great' singer, of course. She sang often for your father's guests, but she did not sing for the employees."

Ilse seemed to specialize in collecting personal slights. "You worked for Father when she was alive?"

"Oh, yes. I was your father's secretary for almost two years before she died."

"What was she like?"

"She was quite tall, and pale. Her skin had no color at all. She never looked well. And she did not live a healthy life. It was all parties and going out. She was not a Hausfrau. Annie took care of everything. When she was here, the house was always full of all kinds of people." She made a face.

"What kinds of people?"

"Her kind. You know what I mean. Singers, theater people, people like that. A strange lot of people. Before she married your father, she traveled all over Germany and outside, too. She led a very strange life." She pursed her lips and shook her head.

I couldn't help saying, "It sounds interesting. You mean she toured as an actress?"

"I think that was what she did. I, of course, did not ask for the details. I was not interested." Like my mother, she made it sound as if Adele had spent time in a whorehouse.

"She seems to have settled down after she married Father. She had Hans and Gustav."

"She worried more about herself than about the boys. It was not surprising when she died."

"What made you think that?

"She often claimed she was 'not well,' and everyone would make a big fuss. So when she got sick just after a visit from a friend who had been traveling in Africa, the family was not unusually concerned. But the friend had just recovered from a serious illness; he had almost died. When she died, the family always thought she might have caught it from him."

"If they didn't know, didn't they do an autopsy?"

Ilse became very indignant. "An autopsy. Of course not. She was ill, she died. One does not do an autopsy and upset the family for no reason. It was a natural death."

"I gather you didn't get on," I said.

She gave me a sharp glance. "We got on well enough. It was not important that I like her or that she should like me. I was always polite."

"And she was not?" I was beginning to get the picture of a class-conscious secretary and a narcissistic artiste-boss' wife. They must have been as chummy as a pair of porcupines. She crumpled her lips into a tight moue, closed her eyes and shrugged her shoulders dismissively as she continued her embroidery. "She was not impolite. She did not call me names, or say "du" to me. It was always *'Fräulein Winnig hier,'* and *'Fräulein Winnig da.'* She never spoke to me except when she wanted something done. Otherwise, I was... invisible."

"It sounds like she was a snob," I suggested helpfully.

"If that was the case, why did she spend hours in the kitchen talking to Anni? To Anni, *ein Stubenmädchen*–an ordinary servant, who had not even finished grammar school–while I had graduated from the *Gymnasium.* But I was good enough to make her appointments, arrange her train tickets, even when I was busy with your father's business. If I objected, your father would not hear of it. Madame Adele could do no wrong."

I thought about that. Perhaps my father had really been serious about Adele, had really cared for her and had not just substituted my mother with a more convenient wife. But, Oh, I thought, she had certainly got herself into Ilse's black books–although from the way I seemed to bring up sore points like a suicide virtuosa, I was concerned that I might soon rank among the Top Ten on her "Destined for Hell" list. But after what she had told me, I wondered why Ilse had lasted. If I had been Adele, I would certainly have asked my husband to get rid of a secretary who must have been such a royal pain to deal with. But I was talking to the other side of the war–the victor, as Ilse had just put it. So I asked, "Why didn't you just leave and get another job?"

She laughed derisively–a cackle of superiority: how little I knew! "You could not have said that if you had any idea what it was like in Germany then. The country was...destroyed. Even several years after the war, it was still very hard to find work, especially if one had any kind of education. Being a secretary to your father was a very good job. Many people would have given much to have a job like that. And your father was always kind to me. He gave me food sometimes to take home to my sister. There were food shortages often."

"Really?" I really didn't know.

"Yes. But it is not something you Americans would know much about, would it? You were not touched by the war, not one bomb fell on you."

It was my turn to give her a long look. "I would hardly," I said in my best disparaging tone, "say that I was not touched by the war. My whole life was changed by it." But even as I said it, I thought that to Ilse, my 'facts' could look very different from the way they had to me.

She shrugged. "To grow up in America, without the bombing and the destruction. What happened to you was...an inconvenience. Here, it was a nightmare. You missed your father and your place in the world, but while you were well fed and warm and safe, people killed each other for a few potatoes, a few pieces of coal, for a warm coat. It was *shrecklich, schrecklich.*" She shook herself at the memory. "Terrible. Terrible."

"That was after the war," I said, getting up. I couldn't go over it again. It was late enough, whatever time it was. But I couldn't entirely let go of it. "During the war, it was the other side that had the hard times and the Germans who were well fed and warm and safe."

She shook her head. "We were never safe. America is safe." She took a hard poke at her embroidery. "That should have been enough for you."

I didn't get it. "Enough of what?"

She gave me another look that I couldn't fathom and then shook her head and smiled. "I am sorry. I should not bring up all these things. Why are we arguing? You cannot know all these things. You must be tired. It has been a...big day!" She was almost beaming at me.

"Yes," I said lamely. It is hard to dance when your partner keeps changing the steps.

"Yes. You are tired. You must sleep. We will have a good time tomorrow."

I hesitated. "I'd like to say goodnight to my father..."

"Oh, that is not possible. He does not like to be disturbed. Even I do not go into his study except when it is absolutely necessary. You will see him in the morning before we go to the mountains."

I was too tired to argue, and went to bed.

Chapter 4

When I got up the next morning, my father had already gone to his office–next door, but in another world, and therefore unapproachable. At the table, Hans and Gustav were both mounding red jam onto the bottom halves of some oblong rolls. As I entered, they grunted, "*Morgen*," and went on eating.

The moment I sat down, the kitchen door opened and Anni darted through it with a pot of coffee, like a figurine from a Bavarian clock.

"*Guten Morgen, Fräulein Helene, wie geht es Ihnen?*...How are you. Did you sleep well?" Anni said quickly as she poured coffee into a white oversize cup at my place. I barely had time to give her my best "*Sehr gut, danke*," before she was back in the kitchen, to appear a moment later with a basket in which some fresh rolls were neatly wrapped in a white napkin. She reached over and brought the ravaged butter and jam over to me, shaking her head at the boys. She raised her hand with an affectionate look to give Gustav, who was nearest to her, a pat on the head, but he shook it off and she let her hand fall to her side. I could see she felt bad about it, and I knew she must remember when she helped raise them from the time they were little boys. But even then I understood: they were teenagers, and even blood mothers who try to pat those in that humanoid stage of development lose a finger from time to time.

She turned to me. "*Essen, essen*," she urged, as if I were not likely to see food again soon, and returned to the kitchen. I broke open one of the rolls and buttered a piece as I thought about Anni. Although she used the formal *Sie* to me, she had coupled the *Fräulein* with my first name, indicating a familiar relationship. Perhaps she hadn't remembered me when I arrived, but how well she must have known me when I was little, during the four or so years my parents spent together. I made a mental note to talk more with Anni soon, remembering to bring my dictionary; as far as I knew, she spoke no English at all.

Suddenly there was a clatter on the stairs and Helmut shot into the room. He stopped when he saw me and I braced myself, but he only said a polite "*Guten Morgen.*" I *Guten-Morgen*ed him back, but he was already speaking excitedly to Gustav and Hans, who ignored him. He was urging them to hurry up and finish, when Ilse entered.

"Oh, you are awake," she said as if I were Sleeping Beauty, while Helmut started to do a war dance around her, circling her with his arms raised, chanting "*Wir fahren in die Wälder, wir fahren in die Wälder....* We're going to the woods." Despite the din, he looked angelic.

"Have you finished breakfast?" Ilse spoke loudly over Helmut. I nodded.

"Then let us go," she said, motioning to the boys, who stuffed the last of their rolls into their mouths, rolled up their napkins and put them through their rings. "All of you, some jackets. It will be a little cool." As she spoke she deftly maneuvered a jacket onto Helmut's still-waving arms. As I came out of my room with a sweater, Gustav came out of the kitchen holding a large, flat lidded basket.

"It is our 'picnic'," Ilse said as we followed Helmut out the back where a black Volkswagen beetle awaited us. With the hamper under the hood, and after some jousting with Helmut who was apparently accustomed to occupying the front seat next to his mother and unaccustomed to sharing the rear with his half-siblings, we were off–with a wild lurch into first which shot us out the gate past the elderly man who shut the gate behind us.

Ilse hugged the wheel like a drowning person with a life preserver, her hands together at the top of the wheel and her forearms lying down across it. She overcorrected constantly, so that we *wädeled* our way down the road, veering slightly from side to side to the clear dismay of other drivers. We were heading for a stretch of "highway"–a four-laner without shoulders and no dividers. After a long wait, Ilse entered the right lane with a lurch and a crunch of gears and slowed down, almost setting off a chain reaction as another VW coming along swerved to avoid her, narrowly missing the car in the left lane which it displaced. Other cars quickly took their distance from her, passing us only with a dash which reminded me of the way a school of fish will open around a cruising shark. But now in addition to the side-winding movement, Ilse added a pulsing motion, alternately letting the car slow to about sixty kilometers and then gunning it until it hit 110, so that at one moment we were speeding toward the grass or rocks on our right; at the next we were sidling into the speed lane.

I looked back at the boys. Helmut was in heaven, following each lurch as if he were on a Coney Island ride. The boys saw me looking at them with what was probably an expression of something approaching terror. They exchanged knowing glances. Then Hans smiled and shrugged his shoulders, opening his hands much as Pontius Pilate must have opened his to say that it was none of his doing. "Do not worry," he finally said in a low voice, "Ilse always arrives." I prayed it would be in one piece.

Unaccustomed as I was to prayer, I thought about whom I should address. I remembered an old boyfriend of mine used to say of an unknown, unmitigatable aspect of the future that it was "In the eyes of the Buddha." That seemed as good as any place to leave it. Certainly no Jewish god had had any recent influence in this part of the world, and Christ hadn't done so well either–which was a disappointment, considering that I had been baptized in my father's family church in Stammbüttel. Although I knew the Buddha mainly as the hero of Herman Hesse's *Siddhartha* and not at all as a refuge of desperate automobile passengers, I asked him to keep his eyes on the car and the car as much on the road as possible.

After about half an hour Ilse made what felt like an unintentional exit with a sudden swerve to the right, taking a thirty-mile-an-hour turn at a wavering fifty and stopping with a burnt-rubber screech at a red light. I braced myself against the dash; seatbelts in cars were still unknown. As the light changed, Ilse turned right into light local traffic and snaked slowly down the road. It was such a relief to worry about mere fender-bending as opposed to dismemberment that I began to relax and look around.

We were in farm country interspersed with woodland. There were wooded hills in the distance and the sun shone, reflecting brilliantly from a few scattered, very white clouds. I had not noticed it was a nice day, having been too concerned about the likelihood of not living to enjoy it. As we wove along, the road pitched upward and the woods at the sides became thicker. We turned into a narrow road at a sign that said "*Hochwälder Tor*." The paving was rough and broken, which slowed Ilse down, and it soon gave way to a graded dirt road. After about a mile, we turned into a small area where two other cars had already been left, and parked.

My legs felt weak as I got out of the car, but I forgot that quickly as I stepped into a wonderful scent of woodland, of leaf mold and pine needles and loam and damp bark on an easy breeze. It was that soft edge of time between spring and summer when all the buds have unfolded into leaves, but their green is still delicate and bright. The trees in leaf were shouldered by huge pine trees with great hanging boughs of dark pine needles endlessly branching into rows, fringed by new growth in a fragile green.

Ilse handed the picnic basket to the Gustav with a warning to be careful, took Helmut's hand and headed for a path at the edge of the wood. At first glance, the wood looked dark compared to the sun that flooded the parking area, but when we stepped into it, the warm gloom under the leaves was broken by a million small shifting shafts of brilliant sunlight that confused the path pleasantly as we walked. Ilse let go of Helmut's hand as he danced before her, occasionally rushing to catch up with him. Behind us, Hans and Gustav walked noisily, horsing around and jostling each other in a good-humored way.

The path was an old one and easy to follow. It grew slowly steeper, so that we had to climb over rocks and an occasional fallen tree. It was steep enough so that I started to sweat, but Ilse didn't seem to flag at all and kept up with Helmut. She was much stronger than her soft, round figure implied. As we continued, the land fell off more and more steeply to the right, and glimpses of sky and other hills started to appear between the branches. Then all at once we stepped into a beautiful open grassy space ringed by trees on three quadrants. On the fourth, the hill fell away slowly and then disappeared, opening a great view over the landscape. At the far end, the trail entered the woods again and continued upward. I heard the sound of rushing water. "There is a stream with very good water, a little bit into the woods," Ilse said and took the basket from Gustav.

She opened it as Helmut looked on curiously. It held a complement of an elegant picnic: tablecloth, napkins, silverware. The main concession to contemporary life a large flat plastic jug, which she took out. "We will get some water," she said and put her hand out for Helmut. But he wasn't there.

It is always alarming when a small child is not where you expect it to be, but Ilse's look was close to terror. "Helmut," she screamed and rushed toward the open side of the clearing. I ran after her. The edge fell away into a jumble of rocks that became steeper and steeper as we scrambled down them, falling finally away into a deep ravine whose bottom was hidden below the tops of tall trees. Just as we were getting to the point where I started to worry about sliding into the ravine myself, I heard a small cry of "*Mutti, Mutti*," and looked up to see Helmut's tiny figure perched precariously on a rock, waving his arms like a bird preparing to fly.

Ilse looked up and a series of intense emotions moved rapidly across her face. The sight of heaven opening was followed by rage, and that was followed by fear. The fear stayed so long that I looked back at Helmut and saw a large figure behind him. It was Hans, who was reaching out toward the boy–to draw him back to safety, I understood. But Ilse seemed to see it differently. *"Geh weg!"* she screamed. *"Geh weg!*...Get away!" She waved her hand sharply. *"Du, Hans! Steig herunter vom Felsen!....* Get off the rock! Off the rock!" Hans hesitated. I couldn't see his expression, but he stepped back. Ilse was ahead of me, scrambling back up the slope. Helmut was now standing with his arms down, watching. I was close behind Ilse. As we got nearer, I saw that Helmut was smiling.

Ilse worked her way around the rock and up to him with me close behind her. We were both panting and sweating now. When she reached him, she stretched her hands out and grabbed him by his arms so that he flew to the ground, where she started to shake him, screaming words that I couldn't follow. I couldn't blame her, but since I hadn't been as scared, I wasn't angry, so when he started to cry, I said, "Ilse, he didn't mean it." It took me a couple of "Ilses" more, but she finally let him go and we walked back to the clearing.

Hans and Gustav were watching the whole scene with calm interest. Ilse ignored them. She took out a handkerchief, dried Helmut's tears and said the things mothers say. She picked up the plastic jug from where she had dropped it, took Helmut's hand and went up the path to the woods. I stood there and looked at the view, across miles of German forest dotted with lakes and small towns, with a larger town–maybe a city–sulking under a pall of smog to my right. The sun was too high and I was too unfamiliar with the area to figure out directions. It was enough that it was beautiful, the sun warm and the breeze cool, and to hope that the rest of the day would be empty of small disasters.

Ilse came back and we all sat down to drink the sweet, slightly metallic water she brought back from the brook. As we rested, she identified some of the towns below us. The city under the smog was Salzgitter. Stammbüttel was out of sight around the bend to our right. Helmut was subdued, but as soon as Ilse said it was time to start looking for mushrooms he revived. The boys protested. It was time, they said, for lunch. Ilse said it was too early;

it was not yet twelve. A compromise was reached: a half-hour of mushroom hunting and then, *Mittagessen....* lunch. Hans and Gustav picked up small stones and threw them over the rocks into the ravine.

I followed Ilse and Helmut into the woods. The change was abrupt: one minute we were in sunlight; the next step we were walking soundlessly on pine needles through a dimly lit forest, where the lower trunks of great pine trees, stubbled with the remnants of lower branches, stretched into the soft gloom around us. Except for an occasional fragment from a songbird, the woods were silent, and even Helmut became quiet. The sound of water was louder, and in a few minutes we came upon a small waterfall which ran over reddish rocks and fell several feet to the rocks below, running on down in a narrow bed to where the land fell away. As the water fell, an imperceptible breeze occasionally blew a soft veil of moisture to the side away from us, and Ilse pointed silently to an embankment on which it fell, for us to follow her.

We crossed the narrow stream easily and walked to the other side of the falls. I could see nothing, but Ilse stooped over and lifted a clod of humus and leaves, and there below it was a small carpet of mushrooms, fat, white and pale. She picked one, broke off a corner and handed it to me. I tasted it. It was good. "This is an ordinary *champignon* that you can buy everywhere," she said. "We are looking for more interesting ones."

She crossed to the other side of a tree and cleared a small area of pine needles to expose a clump of scruffy looking mushrooms that were more stem than head. She worked so intently that I assumed this was a major find. "What are they?" I asked. "Morels," she breathed reverently. "They are in very good condition." She carefully cleared away the debris that had partially covered them, and took from her pocket a neatly folded paper bag, examining each morel closely as she put it in. Then she pulled out a handful of silvery thread that unfolded into a string bag, which I offered to carry. Helmut protested: it was *his* job. I yielded gracefully, and we went on.

In this way we collected a variety of mushrooms. There were some more morels, some Pfifferlinge–picked, I was made to know, as a concession to me–and several other varieties whose names I forgot as soon as she uttered them as I had never even seen them on menus. There was one large one that looked like something from a fairy tale illustration: it was at least six inches across with a reddish top sprinkled with white flecks. It was handsome, but didn't look particularly edible. Ilse assured me it was and popped it into its own paper bag. She seemed to have a substantial supply folded in various pockets.

But there was one group of very handsome mushrooms that I do remember–one that we left where we found it. "Amanitas," Ilse said solemnly. "Very poisonous." Helmut of course immediately reach to pick one and she gasped and pulled his hand away. "Nein!" she said breathlessly. "Nein, nein, *Liebchen. Berühr den nie....* Never touch that one. It is very, very poisonous." Helmut looked at her and reached out his hand again. This time she slapped his hand and pulled him away, speaking sharply to him.

Back at the clearing, the boys had ingeniously devised some sort of checker-like game using sticks and stones. Their behavior had been so peculiar that I had not even considered that they were probably quite intelligent. Even when Ilse spread a tablecloth and set out an array of sandwiches and pickles and hard-boiled eggs, it took them a few minutes to wrap up the game to a point where they would leave it. Then they ate like stereotypical teenagers, casting lots over the last half-sandwich as if they would not eat again. We drank the water we had brought back from the stream and ended up with some large yellowish grapes–from Greece, Ilse said. "A luxury. Fruit out of season is very expensive." I told her I appreciated eating them.

The warmth of the sun had brought a haze over the distance, so that the landscape softened in the light. Helmut leaned sleepily against Ilse. I spread my jacket, lay back on it and closed my eyes.

When I opened them again, Ilse was gone and the two boys were sitting on a couple of rocks below the edge of the clearing tossing stones. I looked at my watch. It was one-thirty and I had slept more than half an hour. I asked where Ilse was. Hans said she had gone for a walk with Helmut. I stood up. "Which way did she go?

Hans pointed up the mountain. "That way," he said.

But before I could turn, Gustav said eagerly, "There is another path, too. Would you like to go walking with us?"

"Sure," I said. "I'd like to. I would really like to," and meant it. Despite everything, I felt for them. Their mother was dead; their stepmother didn't particularly care for them; my father didn't seem to know what to do with them, and Anni, their only ally, was not much help. Asking me to go with them was, I felt, an olive branch of a sort.

Hans nodded curtly and said, "Good. We go this way. He waved his arm toward an opening in the uphill side of the clearing I hadn't noticed before. Gustav was already walking into the space between two trees. "*Bitte*," Hans said, motioning me forward. "I will walk at the end."

Once we stepped into the woods, the path went up a short way before it started angling downhill, toward the ravine. I looked questioningly back at Hans. He was a way behind me, but moving much more light-footedly than I would have expected, since he was so stocky–almost, but not quite, fat. When I stopped and looked at him, he stopped and frowned. Then he smiled–not very warmly, but the first smile he had granted me. "We go to see a beautiful view," he said.

"Okay," I said, and walked a little faster to catch up with Gustav.

The path broke more and more into the open, but there was no sign of Gustav. The view had shifted, leaving the town under the smog cloud behind and opening up to new country with mountains in the distance. The sun shone warmly in the fresh air and glistened on the pretty-looking villages surrounded by neat fields scattered among openings in the green woodland lying below. After we had walked another ten minutes or so, we climbed over an outcrop of rock on the slope and came out onto an entirely different aspect of the country. In the blue distance there were mountains higher than we could see before. There were fewer towns, or rather those that you could see were more buried in the mountains, as if the land had folded them into itself. As I looked, I finally saw Gustav. He waved to us from a large rocky outcrop about a hundred yards away that thrust out from the side of the mountain like a great shoulder. We waved back and continued walking toward it. About half-way there we started to climb steeply up the side of the mountain, because the rock rose sheer for a hundred feet or so from its base in the side of the hill, though earth and boulders from the mountain above had filled in both sides.

When we got to the top, the approach to the rock was wide and easy. From it, you could see even further to the south, to even higher mountains. I was all set to sit down take a rest and take in the country from where we were, but Gustav waved to us to come on. He was out on the rock itself where it formed a flat ledge that speared into space. He stood near the edge where it dropped away. I looked back at Hans. He gave me a big, fast smile and motioned me on.

I walked about halfway out and stopped again. The view was as impressive as any I'd seen and I wanted to take it in. Gustav hailed us again. I turned around to Hans. He was directly behind me, so close it gave me a start. "Go," he said urgently. "You must see the view."

"I see the view, Hans," I said. "It's wonderful."

"No," he said. "You must go where Gustav is."

I turned back to Gustav. He took a step toward me, motioning me on urgently. I hesitated. The ledge was rapidly getting narrower. A few yards ahead, the slope to my right became a sheer drop. To my left, it narrowed more gradually, but I could see that that side ended in a jumble of rocks and fell away too. I didn't like it. I'm not one of those people who faint when they look down more than three stories, but I can think of a lot better places to be than looking down over the edge of that cliff. But Gustav called to me. "Leni, come," and held out his hand. He looked so eager that I said to myself, "Oh well," and walked on out toward him.

The space he was standing on was a big ledge about five feet across. Behind him a rock rose about three feet and narrowed to a point, like the prow of a ship–but there were no railings on this deck. I sidled to the left as I walked toward him and looked down. The rocks below looked hard and jagged before they ended in air. I walked slower, but I could hear Hans getting closer behind me, and that pushed me on.

When I had almost reached him, Gustav suddenly stepped forward, his arms extended before him and fell directly in front of me on all fours. Without thinking, I threw myself to the right to avoid tripping over him, and missed landing hard on the rock only because I fell across his feet. Before I could pick myself up I heard a loud scream and turned my head just in time to see Hans flying over Gustav's back head first, his arms outstretched before him like a figure in a Chagall painting. I screamed too as I watched him go over the edge of the rock. His hands hit the first boulder he reached and then he did a sort of cartwheel and fell heavily on another rock several feet below. He didn't move, but lay with his head and one arm hanging over the edge of the big flat rock. His left leg was folded under him and the right leg hung over the other edge. There was nothing below but space.

"Hans! Hans! Hans! Hans!" Gustav was shouting his name over and over. I looked around. I saw no way I could get down to Hans in one piece, let alone get him up. I didn't even have any rope to secure him if I could have reached him. Then, for a second, Hans seemed to move.

"No!" I shouted. "Don't move, Hans. Keep still!" The moment I spoke, Gustav turned to me, his face in a rage.

"Halt's Maul! Du bist schuldig!...Shut up! It's your fault!"

"Gustav," I said, getting up and backing away from him. "It's nobody's fault. He fell. We've got to get help."

It didn't reach him. He was still on all fours, and his face was contorted with hate. *"Halt's Maul!*.... Shut up, you greedy bitch. Helmut was right: you are a witch." I didn't get it all, but I got the gist. I started to run away from the outcrop, away from the emptiness on either side.

I was almost to the woods when Gustav caught up with me and grabbed my arm. I stopped and held his arms, but he managed to hit me a couple of times. Luckily he was a little smaller than I was, and not the athletic type, but he was strong enough to hurt me. "Gustav," I shouted. "Stop it Stop it! We must help Hans!"

At the mention of Hans, he stopped for a moment and then he hit me again. *"Hans ist tot! Hans ist tot*!...Hans is dead," he wailed, and suddenly he let go and sank to the ground and started to cry.

"Nein, Gustav." I said. "No. *Hans ist nicht tot*.... We must get help." I wasn't sure Hans wasn't dead, but I thought he would be if we didn't get him out of there.

"*Wenn er nicht tot ist*.... If he isn't dead he will fall."

"You must stay and watch him," I said. "I will run and get help. You must stay and talk to him so that he does not move. *Er darf sich nicht bewegen*.... He must not move! Do you understand that?"

Finally he nodded. I set off, moving as fast as I could. The trail wasn't hard to follow, and in about fifteen minutes I was edging between the two big rocks and running up to the clearing. Ilse was sitting there, peeling an apple. Helmut was asleep with his head in her lap.

"Where have you been?" she asked peevishly. "Where are the boys?"

"Hans fell off a rock," I said between panted breaths. "We must get help."

For a moment she just looked at me. "Hans has fallen? Where?"

"Over there." I waved my arm. "A big rock." She looked at me suspiciously. "They wanted to show me the view. Hans fell off. I think he is alive."

"You *think* he is alive? You are not *sure*?" Helmut woke up. He started to whine.

"No. I am not sure. He is about...three meters below the edge. We need men with ropes!"

Ilse got up. "There is a *Förster*..." A forester–a ranger. I picked up the basket, and we hurried back along the path, Helmut trotting silently behind Ilse.

We weren't as far from the car as I had thought. As we got into it I thought idly about how the first time you walk a distance it always seems longer than it does when you walk it again. We drove further down the road and in a few minutes we drew up in front of a rough Swiss-chalet style house with a big rustic porch. A tall thin older man in *Lederhosen* and big boots came down the steps toward us and introduced himself as Ulrich Hügler. Ilse talked quickly to him and then called me over with an impatient gesture.

"He wants to know where they are."

"It is a big rock, like a shoulder." Ilse was translating, but he looked blank. I started to describe the rock and the two close rocks on the path. Then he nodded. He looked at Ilse and shook his head. "*Das ist sehr gefährlich*.... That is very dangerous. I must have help. One moment." He turned back into the house and came out with a good-looking man of about twenty, who he introduced as Stefan, his son. Stefan fetched a couple of coils of some professional looking rope and a folded stretcher. The older man pointed to a truck and told Ilse to follow.

As we got back to the car, Helmut was just about to get out of it and didn't want to be put back in. Worried as I was, I couldn't altogether blame him. I could remember the feeling but not the specifics of being a child among adults who were excited or scared or worried about something and telling you nothing.

By the time the three of us got out of the car in the parking lot, the men were already set with the rope, the stretcher, and a wooden box the size of a small suitcase with a big red cross on it. Ilse wanted to wait, but Herr Hügler asked her to go to the local hospital and have them prepare for Hans. After he gave her directions, he told her that we should be there in less than an hour. "*Wenn Gott will*.... God willing," he said.

Chapter 5

The three of us headed into the woods, Herr Hügler ahead, Stefan behind me. It reminded me of my earlier walk. I thought of the stupid joke about "lucky Pierre, always in the middle." I reprimanded my mind for not being serious enough at such a serious moment. The more serious I thought I should be, the sillier I felt and the more I felt like laughing, the feeling fizzing up in me like soda in a bottle that's been shaken too much. I was flirting with hysteria. I made myself think of poor Hans who might be dead, or at the least, suffering from multiple injuries. And of poor Gustav, worried about his brother, his only real ally in his very cold world. Thinking about Gustav sobered me up.

But my calmer mind had questions. I could understand why Hans had fallen. After all, I had stopped very suddenly. Hans must have tripped over Gustav when I fell to the side. He did just what I had tried to avoid doing when Gustav fell in front of me. After all, there was Gustav on all fours...But why had Gustav fallen? I ran the scene over again in my mind. I saw Gustav calling me forward. At the time, I thought he was eager to show me the view, but now I remembered that he seemed impatient with me, as if I wasn't moving fast enough. Maybe that was why he took that step forward–to come toward me–and that was when *he* must have tripped and fallen. It was the only possible explanation. Maybe his shoe caught on some little crevice. But when he fell, he wasn't looking at me; he was looking at Hans, or at least, he was looking over my shoulder. In fact, I remembered that I was about to look over my shoulder to see what he was looking at. It was a good thing I hadn't done that, or it would have been me that took that dive–and it was a dive, the way Hans fell, with his arms stretched out before him.

Suddenly we stopped walking, and Herr Hügler asked me, "*Welchen Weg?*...Which way?" He pointed to a fork in the trail. I looked around. I didn't remember a fork; I had just been following Hans and not paying too much attention to the way. I couldn't afford to pick the wrong one. I tried to think. "*Wie lange*.... How much time would it take?" I asked for each path.

The right one would take another ten minutes; the left would take half an hour. We took the right one.

Ten minutes later we were clambering up the side of the rock. Gustav was nowhere in sight. He still wasn't visible when we got to the top of the rock; I was getting worried. The old man threw me a questioning look. "*Da,*" I said pointing. "*Auf der anderen Seite....* On the other side." He looked over, but the rocks were piled in such a way that you couldn't see the lower rocks from the back of the formation. We walked quickly to the end, where Hans had fallen and looked again. Hans was still there, but he had moved away from the edge. Next to him, we saw Gustav's head. He must have made his way down from the back over the boulders to the rock where Hans had fallen and dragged Hans back from the edge. Hans' shoulder and arm and Lederhosen were visible beside him. "*Helf mir! Helf mir!...*Help me." Gustav was crying.

The man told Gustav not to move. When he had secured one end of the rope, Stefan used it to rappel directly down the first steep rock. After a minute, he hollered, "*Er lebt!*" So Hans was still alive! When Stefan lifted Hans onto his shoulder in a fireman's carry and secured Hans' hands and feet to his body with a small rope, I felt so relieved, so grateful that he was all right after all. But as he was climbing back up the rocks to us, moving only a little more heavily than he had without Hans' weight, I saw Gustav climbing after him.

Herr Hügler yelled at Gustav. "*Nein! Nein! Wart auf Stefan. Er wird dich abholen!*" Stefan would fetch him. But Gustav wouldn't listen. He kept trying to follow Stefan with a fanatical look on his face, although just kept slipping between rocks. Finally, he fell down between a couple of rocks, let out a long wail and stayed there.

As Stefan got back up to the ledge I ran and got the stretcher and we lowered Hans down onto it. He looked pale and wasted. I looked up to Herr Hügler but he was watching Stefan going down to get Gustav.

I looked at Hans again. Actually, considering his fall, he looked amazingly intact. I bent over him. Suddenly he sat up like Dracula in his coffin and grabbed me by my shirt. His eyes were only half open. I tried to pull back, but he hung on. He said something slurred that I didn't understand. "*Was ist, Hans? Was ist?*"

"Du Hexe!...You Witch!" he hissed. Then he let go and fell back. His head hit the rock under the stretcher. It didn't sound good.

I looked up. Stefan had just reached the ledge and was letting Gustav slide off his back. When his feet touched, Gustav just followed them down until he was sitting. I offered Gustav some water, but he shoved it away with his free hand. The man remonstrated with him, took the water from me and handed it to him. Gustav drank.

I felt sad and I felt angry. The boys were blaming me for what had happened.

After Herr Hügler got Gustav to his feet,he and Stefan picked up the stretcher, and we headed down the slope in silence. It was getting late and the shadows were getting longer. As we passed the clearing, I stopped to look down into the ravine; it was dark and deep, although the sun was still angling through the trees where we had picnicked.

At the parking lot, they put the stretcher with Hans in the back of the truck and Herr Hügler got in the back with him. Stefan told Gustav to get in the front, but Gustav ignored him and hauled himself into the back too. Stefan shrugged and smiled at me. *"Bitte,"* he said, and motioned me gallantly into the truck as he held the door open. I was so relieved to get a smile from somebody that I fairly beamed back at him. He beamed back at me. I tried to think of something funny and faintly flirty to say that would acknowledge our common view of all that had happened, but I couldn't find the German to say anything.

When we parked at the local hospital, Stefan ran in and came back with a couple of men with a hospital stretcher, but they gave up on it because Hans had begun to wake up and was thrashing around a bit. Even on Hügler's stretcher they almost lost him over the side, and they finally strapped him down over his protests. Gustav kept talking to him, but that didn't seem to do much good either.

I was watching all this from the parking lot, not quite sure what to do, when Ilse came out of the hospital scowling. I couldn't tell whether she was worried or angry. She stopped and looked down at Hans, who had given up the struggle to get up and was mumbling something which everyone was ignoring. Then she looked at Gustav, and I heard her ask him what happened. He gestured helplessly with his free hand, and then dropped it and shrugged. *"Hans ist herunter gefallen.* Hans fell," he said sullenly, but Ilse was insistent.

They were almost at the door, and I couldn't hear what she said, but suddenly Gustav stopped. He shook his head and I heard him say, "*Wir wollten nur Vati helfen....* We were only trying to help Daddy." Ilse threw up her hands and they disappeared into the hospital.

It didn't make any sense at all: "Trying to help Daddy." I thought I must have got it wrong. I went into the hospital to look for Ilse and find out what was going on with Hans, but a man at the front desk insisted that I had to sit and wait. When he left the desk after a while, I went down the corridor and found Ilse. She was listening to the doctor, who was telling her that Hans, amazingly, hadn't broken anything. He was generally bruised and scraped, but the most serious result of his back flip was a slight concussion. They wanted him to stay overnight to keep an eye on him. We could pick him up tomorrow.

As Ilse and I walked out into the hall, she asked me where Helmut was. I didn't know, because I'd assumed he was with her. It turned out she had left him at a child's table in the waiting area near the desk with a coloring book and an order to stay put. In retrospect, this was on a par with Moses expecting God to part the waters, but without the right connections.

The people at the reception desk hadn't seen him go anywhere. Ilse started to walk in several directions at once like a pigeon among scattered crumbs. I looked around. Helmut would have gone either out the door or down the hall. Out the door looked uninviting. The hall, however, had elevators. I pointed to them. Ilse nodded and we headed for the nearest one. The door opened to reveal a smooth wood-grained formica interior. I pressed "2".

The elevator was very slow. By the time the door opened, Ilse was standing with her nose almost against it. We burst directly into a nurses' station. No, they hadn't seen a small blond boy, or anything else for that matter. We thanked them and headed for "3."

"3" was something altogether different. The desk was empty and noise was coming from the long right-hand corridor, out of sight around a bend which seemed to act as a megaphone for a volley of anxious screams. Ilse and I exchanged a fast glance–Ilse's was frantic; mine was merely anticipatory: the screams were definitely not Helmut's, and how much damage could a little boy do? We ran down the hall. As we turned the corner, we saw two large women in white nurses' uniforms and headdresses moving as fast as they could, yelling "*Nein, nein!*" and "*Halt!*" The screams came from the far end, and were accompanied by a loud clattering. I broke into a run and as I edged around the wide nurses I saw what the trouble was.

Helmut was running down the hall, pushing a large wheelchair from which the screams were coming. It must have taken him some time to get it up to speed, because it was one of those old wooden types that weigh a ton. All I could see of its occupant were two hands ending in long, extremely red fingernails. One hand was waving wildly in a futile effort to reach behind the chair and grab Helmut. The other clung desperately to a tall wooden stand resembling a hat rack on casters, from which hung a bottle half-filled with a clear liquid. The stand was bouncing from caster to caster like a demented dancer, the liquid was sloshing around, and the whole assemblage was heading straight for a door at another turn in the hall. As I rushed toward them, the door opened and a tall, serious-looking man in a hospital gown stood in it with his jaw set and his eyes open so wide that they looked like those sewn on stuffed toys.

With a last-minute lunge I managed to reach over Helmut's head to grab the back of the chair and hold on, but the momentum was too great: its occupant, who proved to be a large woman with improbably brilliant red hair, flew like a flaming statue into the arms of the tall man and the two of them went down, their hospital gowns flying.

The stand took the turn like a pro and danced on down the hall, where I lost it as I went over backward with the suddenly empty chair, straight into the arms of the just-arriving nurses, who broke my fall with theirs. The din, however, didn't diminish. The red-headed woman's screams were now augmented by Ilse's, who was scrambling among us shouting Helmut's name. When I looked up it was straight into Helmut's eyes, which gazed over the fallen chair onto the heap of us with nothing more than gratified interest.

For a second after I stood up, I couldn't decide whether to help the nurses or the patients. One look at the patients, who were still nudely entangled, made up my mind that they were a job for the nurses. But I couldn't do much for the nurses either: with their age and heft it was like trying to right two giant turtles–both of them snapping mad. Once they were up, they headed straight for the patients, but as soon as they got the woman to her feet, she fainted.

The man seemed to be in better condition. As soon as he was out from under his burden, he rose, wrapped himself in what dignity his hospital gown provided and stood watching with more amusement than concern. When the nurses righted the chair and maneuvered the woman's inert body into it, he bowed slightly, murmured an ironic *"Gnädiges Damen....* Gracious ladies," and closed the door firmly, as one of the nurses called to him that she would be right back. With a stern glance at Helmut and a disapproving frown at Ilse and me, they wheeled their now-reviving patient down the hall and into one of the rooms. I thought this would be as good a time as any to leave: Ilse agreed, and with an unprotesting Helmut trolling along between us, we hurried to the elevator and back to the emergency room.

The Herr Doktor, who sported an enormous reddish brown, bristly mustache, kept telling Gustav that Hans would be better tomorrow, but Gustav still looked very upset and demanded that he be allowed to stay with Hans. Ilse scotched that, thanked the doctor, signed some papers, and we left.

Hügler and son were gone. The sun cast a golden afterglow over everything, although the air was already tinged with a twilit coolness. As we drove off, there were no sounds from Helmut and Gustav; they had both fallen asleep almost immediately. I closed my eyes too: I didn't feel like watching Ilse drive. When I opened them again we were heading into my father's driveway.

As she shut off the engine, Father stepped out of the doorway and hurried to the car. He opened the car door for Ilse as I went to shut the gate behind us, and came back to see them coaxing Gustav and Helmut out of the back seat. Ilse walked ahead with Helmut. Father put his arm around Gustav's shoulder and followed her in. It was the first affectionate gesture I'd seen since I arrived, and I was glad to see it even though I wasn't included; Father hadn't even said "Hello," to me. But then, I thought, it was natural. He'd probably been worrying about the boys.

Anni was standing by the kitchen door as we entered, her hands clasped in front of her chest in an anxious gesture. I went to my room to get cleaned up and glanced in the mirror: I looked like I'd spent a week rather than a day in the country. I needed a wash, a comb, a change; my nails ended in grungy arcs.

When I got to the table later, Father and Gustav were already eating. My father gave me a smile which made me feel better. "Ilse is with Helmut. She will come soon," he said, and went back to his soup. I served myself from the big tureen which held a rich meat and vegetable soup adrift with a flotilla of tiny dumplings. It was just what I needed, and I took a second helping without thinking about it, as if I belonged to the house.

By the time Ilse joined us, we were working on a bowl of fresh fruit and some slices of *Honigkuchen*–a honey loaf cake. Gustav was fading visibly and Father told him to go to bed. He looked like he was about to protest, but then he just got up and went. As he passed by him, Father said warmly, "*Schlaf wohl, Gustl.*" Gustav stopped and raised his sleepy eyes. "*Ja, Vati, das werde ich,*" he said and headed out the door. I was just thinking how nice my father could be, but the moment Gustav left the room, he turned to Ilse and said sternly, "*Ilse und Lene, was gibt's hier?...*What's going on?"

Ilse had just finished her soup. She glanced at me. "*Frag die Lene....* Ask Lene."

My father looked at me sternly, and it was as if all the years between had never happened; I was a very small girl again. I felt both guilty and relieved. I wanted to tell him what had happened–to tell him everything, to make him understand. I opened my mouth to speak, and said, "*Vati...*" and stopped. If I were five years old, I would have told him in German, but I didn't have nearly enough German to tell him what was on my mind. There was a long silence, and then he said in a nice voice, "*Was ist los?....* What's the matter?" I considered the question: what *was* the matter? He just wanted to know what happened in the afternoon. I felt like a fool. I was twenty-eight and I had enough German to give it a try. Besides, I thought, Ilse would help me.

"*Hans and Gustl wollten dass ich mit ihnen komme....*" I began tentatively, but before I could continue, Ilse took over and started to tell him about things she wasn't there to see. I managed finally to interrupt. "*Sowie ich in die Nähe von Gustl kam,....* When I came near Gustl, he suddenly fell in front of me." I put my hands out to show how that happened. "I fell down too," I said, "to save myself from going over. Before I could get up, there was Hans flying over both of us, and..." As I stumbled through the story, my father started to look at me rather strangely, as if he didn't believe me, which made me feel more like a small child who is telling the truth but has no power to convince anyone at all.

Then my father said something I didn't understand. Ilse translated: "Gustl says you tripped Hans."

I looked at my father trying to communicate total disbelief. A sense of righteous indignation rose and snapped me out of my five-year-old mindset. "*Aber wir sind beide über Gustl gefallen*!.... But we both fell over Gustl! First me, then Hans."

Ilse and Father exchanged significant looks that I didn't like at all. My father looked down at his plate intently. Then he looked at Ilse and said, with a puzzled look on his face, "*Es ist genau so wie beim Schulausflug!*" The same as the school trip? How the same? Ilse focused on an apple she was peeling.

"*Aber wieso*.... But why did Hans fall when you didn't," my father asked. I told him as best I could how I remembered falling away from the edge, over Gustav. "*Gustl ist zuerst gefallen!*...Gustl fell first! Before me!"

"*Aber wieso*.... But why did Gustav fall?" my father asked. I shrugged.

"*Ich habe mich auch darüber gewundert*.... I had wondered about that too. I was still wondering. He must have tripped. Father shook his head and looked confused. Then he asked me why Gustav said that *I* had made Hans fall. I was about to tell him I didn't know that either when an idea came to me.

"*Weil es ihm sehr leid getan hat*.... Because he felt very bad about what happened to Hans," I said, "because, in a way, it *was* at least partly his fault. He was so upset, it was really terrible. So it made him want to blame somebody else. He needed a..." I turned to Ilse. "A scapegoat." "*Einen Sündenbock*," she said curtly.

"*Er hatte einen Sündenbock notwendig*,...He needed a scapegoat. There was no one else but me."

My father studied his plate again for a couple of minutes. If it had any answers, it would have reminded him that Germany had developed scapegoating to a science only very recently; as a disposable Jew, I was a logical candidate. Finally Father said, more to Ilse than to me, "*Ja. Das klingt richtig*.... That makes sense–more sense than Lene pushing Hans." Ilse shrugged. He turned to me. Would I like to join him in "*einen kleinen Schnapps*.... a little brandy.". It was a peace offering. I certainly would: Ilse would not.

He went to the sideboard and returned with a pair of small silver goblets and poured from a bottle of brandy. It was old and smooth and very good. After we had both sipped it in an appreciative silence, he said to Ilse, "*Also, wir werden Pilze bekommen?*...So we will have mushrooms? What kind?"

Ilse shrugged again. She seemed to be in bad temper. Several kinds, she said. Father looked at her, and then his mouth moved into a half smile and his eyes narrowed slightly into a glint of mischief. Ilse didn't look at him, but gathered her apple parings, cleared her place and announced she was going to bed. But Father was up to something.

"Komm, komm, Ilse," he said. He continued about how she knew how much he liked wild mushrooms, how he liked to know about the ones she found. Ilse didn't get up, but she looked like she might be getting annoyed. He went on to how she was a *"Pilzfachmann."* He waited for me to react, but I didn't know what a *Pilzfachmann* was. I looked at Ilse.

"Pilzfachmann?" I asked.

"A mushroom expert," she said curtly, but a small smile started to creep across her mouth.

My father turned to me. She had, he said with mock-seriousness, *"die heimliche Wissenschaft des Waldes....* the secret knowledge of the woods." She gave him a long look. This was clearly some sort of game between them. He continued to speak to me, but his eyes were on hers. *"Ilse weiss immer....* Ilse always knows where to find the best mushrooms. She is *"die Königin des Pilzenreiches....* the queen of the mushroom kingdom." He grinned and leaned back as if he were waited for her to say something. Ilse looked pleased, but she wasn't ready to give in yet. I sensed a joke, but I wasn't sure. I like a good laugh, but I'm not to keen on ganging up on someone–I had too much of that done to me while I was growing up a stranger. And although I really believed that Ilse knew her *Pfifferlinge* from her *Morchels,* I thought that calling her the Queen of the Mushroom Kingdom was edging into a really big tease.

She arched her eyebrows, looked down at her nails, and said in a mock-threatening way, *"Wenn ich du wäre....* If I were you, it would be better not to offend the Queen of *your* mushrooms."

*"Du hast recht!...*You are right!" my father said with a smile, slapping the table with his hand in emphasis. Then he put one hand on his chest in a gesture of sincerity. *"Gnädige Königin meiner Pilze....* Gracious queen of my mushrooms," he began, and went on to say he would eat any mushrooms she prepared for him, even if sometimes, they were *"ein bisschen giftig....* a little poisonous." That got my attention. It got Ilse's attention too.

"Yes," I said stupidly trying to participate. *"Ilse zeigte mir....* Ilse showed me some *very* poisonous mushrooms."

"*Ach*," my father said, looking ruefully at Ilse with a half smile, over whom a small private storm cloud appeared to be coalescing. "*Nicht für die Suppe*.... not for the soup, I hope."

Ilse didn't move at all. She sat there with her eyes locked to my father's, and as I watched, a large, pretty tear gathered on the lower lashes of each eye and glistened there for a long moment before it fell daintily on her cheek.

Their fall pulled the smile from my father's face. "*Ach, Ilse*," he said, leaning slightly forward. "*Nein, nein. Keine Tränen, bitte*.... No tears, please."

"*Es war ihre eigene Schuld*.... It was her own fault," Ilse spoke with a small sob, like an accused child. "She is always meddling in the kitchen."

My father leaned forward, one elbow on the table, and said sternly, "*Ihre eigene Schuld?* Tante Therese?...But you have never told me why there were poisonous mushrooms in your kitchen at all!"

I looked at them playing their game, Ilse walking through the part of guilty child. She seemed to be taking it very seriously, although it looked like my father wasn't.

As my father well knew, she said, she had just brought home a sample of this kind of amanita to show her friend, Trude, and how she–Ilse–had sorted them *so sorgfältig*–so carefully. And how Tante Therese must have mixed them up and gotten a piece of one in her soup, and how, if Tante Therese *hat sich immer sehr lästig gemacht*.... always made a nuisance of herself, it wasn't her fault.

At this point, my father's tone became even more inquisitorial. "*Aber Ilse, ich hab's immer*.... I have always found it interesting that only my poor aunt had a poisonous mushroom in her soup." He shook his head and turned to me and said, "*Ilse und meine Tante Therese*.... are not the best of friends. *Ist das nicht richtig, Ilse?*.... Isn't that right, Ilse?"

Ilse was on her feet, still clutching the plate of parings, but throwing looks that if they could have would have killed my father where he sat. He backed off immediately with a look of such innocence that only guilt could have produced it. Ilse had stalked out of the room and after a brief stop in the kitchen headed noisily up the stairs, when my father smiled a self-satisfied smile, and said, only half to me, "*Sie ist sehr beleidigt*.... She's really miffed. Later I must make up with her."

It is interesting to visit your aging father and find him not only married to someone near your own age but still sexually interested in her, however unexpected the form his approach may take. I was thinking such thoughts when my father leaned over, refilled my little silver glass, raised his and said "Prost." Then he leaned back and said, "*Warum hast du gelächelt?*...Why were you smiling?"

I hemmed around a little and said, "*Ich wunderte mich*.... I was wondering why your aunt didn't like Ilse." Once I said it, I wasn't sure that that was a reason for smiling, but he smiled back.

"*Ach*," he said, waving his hand dismissively. "*Ilse und meine Tante*, they are always fighting." He went on to explain that his Aunt thought that Ilse married him for his money, and was always critical of her. Ilse, on the other hand, bitterly resented his Aunt's attitude and wouldn't humor her in any way. Father felt in the middle, because Therese, his mother's sister, had virtually brought him up when his mother died, and had always looked on him as her *Liebling*, her favorite. And it was true that she would go into the kitchen, and of course, she and Anni were old allies. I understood that Ilse had a bona fide in-law problem.

I asked what happened to his Aunt when she ate the poisoned mushroom–how did they know that was what it was? My father said that under the influence of the mushroom, she started addressing everyone by the names of people whom she had known socially many years ago, when her husband was some kind of high government official. My father thought–they all thought–she was having some kind of nervous breakdown. My father got up and offered her his arm. She addressed him as "Graf Wilhelm.... Count Wilhelm," and they swept out of the room directly into what was now my room, where she acknowledged she was tired, lay down on the bed and passed out. They called the doctor. When he found out she had eaten mushrooms, he had her taken to the hospital and had her stomach pumped out. She woke up there with complete amnesia from the main course on. They got the doctor to give her a story about some sort of flu, but Tante Therese hadn't set foot in the house again, although he visits her often in hers.

"*Glaubst du*.... Do you believe that Ilse gave her the mushrooms..." I didn't know the words for "on purpose," but he got the idea, and laughed.

"*Nein, nein*," he said. "*Es ist nicht möglich*.... That is not possible. It happened just as Ilse said. My good aunt mixed up the mushrooms and got a piece of Ilse's specimen. That is all."

And tomorrow, my father had said as he went upstairs, he would show me some of the old home town.

Chapter 6

When I got up the next morning, I had the table to myself even though I was early–or at least, eight-thirty in the morning has always seemed pretty early to me when I wasn't working. I have friends who like to get up and watch the sun rise; I like to see the sun rise only *before* I go to sleep. To me some of the best hours are the ones right after midnight, when even New York quiets down and music seems sweeter and makes you think of things that are gone, or might happen, or might have happened if. Last night I laid down about midnight, immediately after my father went off–presumably to make up with Ilse–and went to sleep the way you enter the water when you're coming off a three-meter board.

My father was in his office, Anni informed me, and Ilse had left for the hospital, taking Gustav and Helmut with her. Everybody would be back for lunch. As she brought me breakfast, I asked her if she remembered me now. She gave me a lovely smile.

"*Ach, ja*," she said. "*Du...*" she stopped, and made a gesture of apology for using the familiar form. "*Sie waren Herr Franz's erstes Kind....* You were Mr. Franz' first child, the first-born." She gave the last phrase great emphasis, and accompanied it by a significant look, whose meaning I couldn't read. Yes, she remembered me well. I was *ein hübsches Kind.... a pretty* child, but very *unartig*. From the way she shook her finger and her head and smiled ruefully, she meant "naughty."

How was I *unartig*, I wanted to know.

She stood by the table and thought about it. I asked her to sit down. She shook her head. She would not sit down at the table with me, as she must have done when I was "*die kleine Leni*." I now belonged to the world of adults with prefixes to their name: I was no longer "the little Leni," I was *Fräulein* Lene and she did not sit with her. But she did remember something.

When I was three or four years old, she said, I became fascinated with writing. As she spoke I remembered standing close to my mother, watching her pen scratch effortlessly the small, elegant letters of her handwriting in neat line after line down the page. I felt that it was magical, that it meant something, and although it was as inscrutable to me then as Chinese calligraphy is today, I recalled the feeling–a deep longing to write, to inscribe, like my mother, words on a page. I thought of writing as a special form of speaking, but different from speaking, because words that came out of the pen stayed there, on the white paper, after they were said.

"*Ja*," I said emphatically, "*Ich erinnere mich*." Even as I spoke in the moment, I savored the German verb for remember, which says in literal translation, "I remember myself."

She looked disappointed. "Yes, I said, I remember being–*bezaubert*.... enchanted–with the act of writing, but, I said, I remembered nothing *unartig*, about it. "Ach," she said, nodding her head vigorously, but *she* remembered. She remembered one time when my father came home from a trip and came out of his office with several sheets of his "best" stationery covered with many neat lines of careful, meaningless scribbles–my "writing." Anni imitated him, holding up the sheaf of paper like Justice itself. She told me how he came to my room where I stood, bent over a small child's table, drawing a picture, and threatened to spank me. At this point she started to laugh so much that she could hardly tell me how at this moment–when she was worried for me and was about to intercede, because my father apparently did sometimes spank me (not often, she said, but with *einer schweren Hand*.... a heavy hand)–I did not interrupt what I was doing but swiveled my small behind toward my father and said, while I went on drawing, "*Mach weiter*.... Go ahead." Even though confronted with enough cheek to tempt retribution, my father stopped, laughed, and walked out of the room shaking his head. Anni shook *her* head as she finished the story and as smiling to herself as she went back to the kitchen.

I stirred what was left of my coffee and mused on her story. It lit an aspect of my father's face that was so different from those I had held in my mind for so many years that I could not entirely make it fit. Not that the image I encountered when I thought of him, although faded, was a simple one. That image was of a stern, selfish, handsome, charming, intelligent womanizer who in the end, by not providing my mother with money to leave, consigned us to the mercies of a country that had none for Jews, Lutheran baptisms notwithstanding. Such a man, I had thought, would have been far more comfortable if we no longer existed, so that in the rare moments when such matters arose in conversation, he could shake his head sadly, as he had over the fire-bombing of Dresden, that it was *kläglich....* lamentable–and that would have been the end of it.

The man who laughed and did not spank his errant daughter did not seem at all like the forbidding, uncaring German *Vater* who had occupied most of the images I had constructed over the years. Was that sense of humor still there, I wondered, or had all the years erased that and left only the *Paterfamilias* for whom all stood until he was seated, who deferred to his young wife at home only because he did not concern himself with his household, the private world that was her territory? He had certainly come down on her hard enough when she ventured into his public realm, where the Göring name–his public face–was concerned. I didn't know.

I thought I would wait until my father took his coffee break. But it was still early, so I took my dictionary and found the *Stammbüttler Zeitung* in the living room. I had settled down for the news of the German world when I remembered that it was a weekly. I had read a lot of it—without a dictionary–the night I arrived. I thumbed through the paper to see if there was anything that was interesting enough to go through again, but nothing held me. In those days, politics didn't seem all that important to me personally. Like most Americans, I felt life was basically okay, except for the Russian threat–and we seemed to be holding the line on that. I knew, of course, that things weren't right for American Negroes (we didn't have African-Americans then; there weren't even "Black People" yet), but we were going to make things right for them by seeing that they had their Civil Rights. So I was about to give up when I came across the article about Professor Gross again.

Professor Gross, I remembered, was the teacher on the trip where Hans and Gustav seemed to have something to do with an accident. "*Professor Gross ein Held....* a Hero." I read on, and made out that Professor Gross, who had taught Latin at the local school for twelve years, deserved the thanks of the town of Stammbüttel for saving the life of one of his students, Ernst Toller, the Mayor's son. The good professor had risked his life to save Ernst when Ernst almost fell off a cliff, due to some *unziemliches Betragen....* unseemly behavior on the part of two other students, who had been duly disciplined.

And that must have been what my father and Ilse were talking about last night. Suddenly I felt afraid. Hans' and Gustav's intentions could be far more serious than "unseemly" would indicate. My mind still resisted the thought. But even if the incident in the paper was just the result of thoughtless horsing around, what had they been doing at the top of that cliff with me? Thinking of it, I felt so much vertigo that I leaned back in my chair, dizzy with the sensation of falling.

At that moment my father walked in followed by a tall man about my age. The first thing I noticed was that he had a big nose that supported a pair of the horn-rimmed glasses standard at the time. He was wearing khakis and a sweater over a button-down shirt, looking somehow like an American graduate student. As he entered, he managed to trip over the door sill but he caught himself in time and entered upright, as if this was how he usually came into a room.

Father ignored his entry and introduced him as Wolfgang Herzog, a cousin. Wolfgang took my hand, bowed over it, clicked his heels lightly and said, "Hi. My friends call me Wolf," in an almost perfect American accent. The combination of German body language and American presence startled me. I said "Hi," too and sat back. He laughed, pulled out the chair on my right, and then, looking at Anni coming through the door with a tray laden with the *acoutrements* of a serious coffee break, almost missed the chair as he sat down. But he caught himself, and with a single movement, pulled the chair under him and sat down as if it were a practiced move.

I was thinking impatiently that Father had brought the family clown to entertain me when my father said to Anni, "*Also hier ist dein Wolfi*.... Here is your little Wolf." At the mention of Wolf's name, she beamed at him as she had smiled at me earlier and said, "*Grüss Gott,* Herr Wolfgang."

"So Anni knows you too," I said, putting a question in the statement.

He said, "Anni's sister was my nurse. I was born two weeks before you. We used to play together and you used to beat me up. I think you were bigger than me...then." He laughed and repeated the whole thing in German to Anni and my father–who made appropriate noises–and added, "*Ich bin auch ein Kind von der Anni*.... I am also one of Anni's children."

"Do you have any memory of that?" I asked him. I had none whatsoever. I had played with him. I had spoken nothing but German. I had lived in Stammbüttel and spent days, weeks, several years with Anni. I remembered nothing of that time, except a few dream-like images which were not connected to each other or to anything that I knew.

Wolf smiled. "Not specifically playing with you, but I remember many things from that time, and of course, I remember Anni. Anni often came over, and Gertrude, my nurse, often brought me over to the Görings. Do you remember?"

I shook my head. Father smiled at Wolf. "How are we related?" I asked.

Wolf rubbed a finger behind his ear, causing his glasses to move up and down as he thought. Finally he said that he thought that our *Urgrosseltern*.... our great-grandparents–were sister and brother.

"That makes us third cousins," I said.

Wolf laughed. "That was fast," he said. "I'm a mathematician and I was still working on the problem."

"*Ja*," Father said. "Wolfgang is teaching mathematics at Heidelberg. That is also my university. My brother and my uncle both occupied the chair in mathematics there. We have begun to feel as if it belongs to the Göring family. And I believe that Wolfgang here," he reached over and patted Wolf's shoulder proudly, "will carry on the tradition."

Wolf smiled modestly and said to me, "Uncle Franz has always had great expectations for me." When he saw my father didn't know what he meant, he said it again in German. My father nodded.

"Yes," he said, "Wolfgang has the Göring mind. He will go far." He drank some coffee and took a roll and buttered it as he talked. We did the same. The roll was freshly baked and still warm, separating with a delicate crackling sound as the golden crust crumbled, exposing its soft, white delicately fibered inside. The coffee, too, was rich and fresh, so that the simple food gave off a sense of plenitude, of completeness, that felt like a kind of wealth.

Father said, "Wolf is home for a few days, and he has offered to show you around Stammbüttel. I think this will be very good, because I am very busy right now."

I turned to Wolf and smiled, but I also reminded my father that he had promised me to show me the Verlag–his Press, his offices–and I hadn't seen any of it yet. My father's eyes lit up. "*Ja*," he said. "We must find time for that. Perhaps you will come tomorrow morning, and I will show you everything." He took a last sip from his cup, and with a small wave, went back to his office.

I turned and said to Wolf, "Listen, you don't have to do this." I didn't add that I wasn't looking forward to spending the day with the family clown, math wizardry notwithstanding.

"That is true," he said, nodding and looking at me appraisingly. "But I haven't been in the town for years. Even if you were not so good-looking I would enjoy it."

I was still a fool for lines like that. Even after all these feminist years, I still get a twinge when somebody says something nice about the way I look. I smiled coolly as if people said these things to me only too often and said, "So where did you learn your American English?"

"At MIT." He said. "I spent two years there before I came back here to get my doctorate. I really loved the States. I wanted to stay there. But when I got back here, I realized everything here would be easy. There was already a teaching assistanceship open for me, and one thing led to another." He paused and threw up his hands and said, "So here I am."

"Have you ever gone back?"

"Oh, yes. Of course. I have attended a couple of seminars and conferences, and I still have some friends that I keep in touch with. Only last year I participated in a symposium at the University of Chicago. Everything is so much easier, so much less formal in America...Of course, I should not complain. Things are certainly not hard for me here, but when I get there...But you must know what I mean."

I thought about that. "No," I said, "Actually, I don't. America is really the only place I really know. It's like asking a fish how he likes being in the water. I was brought up there. I think of myself as American. I am American. What happened here was like something that happened in another life, almost on another planet."

"I didn't realize that. When the family heard you were coming to visit, everybody assumed you were coming back–well not to stay, but..."

"But what? What do they think I wanted?"

Suddenly he looked embarrassed. He shook his head and shrugged his shoulders. "Oh, I don't know. People have all kinds of ideas."

I felt both anxious and annoyed. "What kinds of ideas? What do you mean?"

"Well, why *did* you come? After all this time."

"To meet my father. To meet him in the flesh instead of as some kind of mythical figure I've been making up all these years. That's all."

"That's all?"

"Yes. That's all. What else would there be? I have a life. I have my work. I have a profession, I have family, I have friends, I have a swell apartment. What else would I want here?"

He looked at me as if he hadn't seen me before. He said, "You're right. What else is there for you here? Here, you could not easily have all of those." He paused and then he said, as if the idea had just come to him, "Listen, just outside of town there is a wonderful restaurant. Please, come and have lunch with me there and tell me what's happening back in the States. And later, we can see something of the old Stammbüttel."

I protested that Ilse would be back, and would expect me to be there for lunch. He went to ask Anni. As he returned from the kitchen, he stopped in the doorway to tell me that she knew of no special plans Ilse had made, when the swinging door to the kitchen caught him and knocked his glasses off. He picked them up and checked them out. As I continued to try to figure out who he really was, he put them back on and shook his head ruefully. "It is a family joke," he said. "I have always been clumsy." Then he cheered up. "Except," he added, "When I dance, and of course, when I drive, and...." he stopped and smiled.

I let that pass as I thought of Ilse coming back with the boys from the hospital and I realized that I wanted to leave too, and in a few minutes I was in his Volkswagen convertible tying a scarf around my head as we drove through the gate and down the road.

It was another beautiful day, with the sun shining on the grass and leaves that were still new, with the whole summer before them. The town was very pretty, with all those old buildings so neatly kept, and all the streets well paved and all the grass mowed, bushes clipped and flowers planted. I was reminded of those movies where the aliens take over: everyone looked so alike–so white and well dressed, striding purposefully to clear destinations–but I didn't dwell on it. It was great to be with someone my own age who spoke English–American English–and who was, despite his big nose and clumsiness, an attractive guy. I watched him nervously at first, but he drove really well–confidently, as if he were sure he was going to get where he was going–and I relaxed.

The restaurant was in a big wooden house surrounded on three sides by a large garden with a big slate terrace where the tables were set among trees and large bushes. Tables that weren't under a tree had big green and white umbrellas stuck into their middle. The *maitre* took us to a table that was in a nook between two bushes, one of which was a forsythia whose green leaves were pushing off the last of its yellow flowers.

Before we got to the table, however, Wolf managed to trip on the edge of a piece of slate that stuck slightly out of the ground as we followed the *maitre.* He tried to keep from falling forward by grasping a branch that sloped down directly overhead, but he swiveled around as he hung onto it and let it go as he teetered backward, slowly but inevitably, toward the chair of a lone,elegant man. Wolf leaned back on the arm of the man's chair, cradled between his astonished face and the menu. The branch Wolf had released snapped upward in sharp recoil. As it swung back into place, it managed to clip a waiter from behind, so that the instant Wolf fell onto the man's chair there was a huge crash as the waiter and tray, filled with *Getränken, Suppen* and various other solid, liquid and gelatinous creations, fell to the ground and arranged itself like a conceptual piece that had escaped the artist's control. Wolf leapt out of the man's lap with amazing athleticism for someone so clumsy, and without looking back at the man who followed us only with his astonished eyes, hurried me forward to the table between the bushes, from which the *maître* came to look for the cause of the noise.

Wolf held my chair and I seated myself quickly. He sat down opposite me, rested his chin on his hands and looked seriously into my eyes. I started to laugh because I thought he was being funny, but then I saw that the look he was giving me was only superficially cool. After a minute or so he threw himself back in his chair and said, "Sometimes it really gets out of hand. Back in Heidelberg, there is a restaurant that won't even let me in the door."

"You do this regularly? Land in people's laps, do in waiters bearing loaded trays?"

"Well, seldom both at the same time. That is unusual. And the trays are not always so full." He smiled ruefully.

"I don't think I've ever met anyone like you."

"You would remember if you had."

"Is there a name for what you have?"

"You make it sound like a disease," he said, offended.

"No, no," I said hurriedly. I didn't want to hurt his feelings, but I didn't feel I could ignore the situation. "What I mean is more psychological–more like a compulsion...You know, a compulsion to...to make a big entrance, for instance."

He looked at me with annoyance. "I had forgotten that American women are always finding psychological reasons for every act. *That* is what *I* call a compulsion," he said and slapped the edge of the table in emphasis, but then he shrugged and added, "Nevertheless, it is an entirely forgivable one."

"How gracious of you," I said as a shadow fell over the table. It was the shadow of our waiter, a huge man. He wasn't just tall, he was also round from the waist up, and his white jacket hung loosely around his long legs from its button front, which stretched tightly over his enormous belly. Above it rode a large puffy face in several colors, punctuated by a grayish, grizzled Hitler mustache and topped by a lank, grayish band of hair worn Hitler-style over his left forehead. He introduced himself with a small bow that nevertheless overshadowed the table as "*Adolf, euer Kellner.*" We avoided each others' eyes as we took our menus from him, agreed quickly on some beer, and Wolf dispatched him before we started laughing like schoolchildren when the teacher leaves the room.

"Did you see that?" I gasped. "Was he real?"

He shook his head with an amazed expression and said, "Our waiter appears to be real. He is a true 'grotesque.' I think I have seen him before, but never at such close range.

As I thought about Adolph I saw, as a series of flashing images, how this strange man had grown out of an awkward boy. "They didn't hire him as he is now, I said. They hired what he was. I bet he's been here forever." Wolf nodded, and looked at me with new respect.

"Very good. I bet you are right." he said, jabbing an emphatic finger in the air. "Of course! He has been here for so long, they have never noticed how strange looking he has become."

"Listen, Wolf. Here is how it goes. He was a lonely, awkward child, and when he hit adolescence, he really shot up, but even then he had this strange shape, and the children used to make fun of him. Then, Adolf Hitler appeared. Adolf finally saw what an Adolf should look like to get respect, and he did it. For years, no one would have dared to make fun of him. Now, after all this time, no one would think of hurting his feelings." Adolf's shadow loomed over our table again. We both watched him closely as he neatly filled two glasses of beer on his tray from two cold, beaded bottles with exactly the right amount of foam. Wolf asked him to come back in a few minutes to take our order.

"I am certain you have told the story of his life," Wolf said, glancing at his menu but continuing to talk to me. "It would never have occurred to me to do so. I am not sure I should have made such fun of your abilities of psychological analysis." He looked over the menu at me, and his eyes narrowed speculatively. "What I am wondering now," he said slowly, "is: How do you see me? All this time, have you been making a life story for *me*?"

I picked up my beer and regarded the foam as I said, "No. I only do life stories for waiters, and only if they are called Adolf. I have a very limited practice. Do they have Pfifferlinge?"

"How do you know about Pfifferlinge?"

"One of my favorite restaurants in New York is Luchow's, and it's one of their regular dishes. But I don't go there very often, and I really like them. I don't see it on the menu, though."

"I can ask Adolf"–he said the name with a special emphasis, raising his eyebrows and rolling his eyes–"if they have some. But tell me, you have not worked out my childhood, my adolescent dreams, my secret fantasies?"

I looked at him, trying as best I could to emulate Anouk Aimée, one of the most sophisticated Italian actresses of the time, whom I secretly thought in my more optimistic moments that I resembled. "No," I said finally. "At least not yet. You...would require a little thought."

He dropped his eyes to his menu, and said, "I am surprised you have not focused your powers of analysis to bear on Ilse. She should be an interesting case study."

"Wolf," I said, "listen. I'm not the big insightful analyst you're making me out to be. I find people very complicated and difficult to understand. Sometimes, when I think I really know how somebody thinks or feels, I'm just plain wrong. I'm probably entirely wrong about Adolf. He is probably the head of a secret killer Nazi cult that is waiting for the return of Hitler, and that mustache and haircut is *de rigeur*. Alternately, he is an actor and has a role in a comic version of *Mein Kampf*, currently in rehearsal at the local drama club."

I turned my attention the menu. It was not long, but full of large, meaty dishes. *Rindslendenschnitten auf Jägerart....* roast beef hunter's style, or veal goulash with *Nockerl*—little odd-shaped chewy flour dumplings, an acquired taste. I was hungry. I looked up at Wolf. He was still looking at me.

"That was wonderful," he said.

"What was wonderful?"

"The possibilities of Adolf. It is so un-Göring. We are so much more prone to an analytical bent, more pedantic, not so...creative. No Göring I know would ever be able to make up three life histories for a stranger like that."

I laughed. "When I was in college, I hung out with other writers. We never thought of ourselves as writing students; just as writers. We took everything very seriously. We wouldn't just talk *about* writing. We would make remarks in other writers' styles. You were expected to know pretty much what writer someone was referring to, even if you didn't mention his name but only quoted something. And we were always playing with texts and meanings and making the most complex and outrageous puns that were more plays on texts rather than just plays on words." I shrugged. "We were probably obnoxious, but we had a great time. Three lives for Adolf was a piece of cake...though I'm out of practice."

Wolf hadn't taken his eyes off me. "You are different from anyone I ever met," he said.

"Wolf," I said. "That line is no good in New York, and it is probably not much use here. But thank you just the same."

He had the grace to laugh. "*Meine liebe Cousine*, I assure you it is not a 'line' in Stammbüttel. I have never met a *Stammbüttlerin* who was sufficiently different to be remarked on. But I am not going to defend myself further. Your tongue is much faster than mine. What are you going to have...if they don't have Pfifferlinge?"

Adolf was deeply sorry, but the cook only made Pfifferlinge on Tuesdays. He suggested the pike, which was local. Wolf translated for me and we worked our way through a terrific lunch, ending with a childhood favorite, *Kastanientorte mit Schlagobers....* chestnut cake with whipped cream. I had to give up half-way through, but by that time Wolf and I had begun to run out of conversation, not because we were out of words, but because we had fallen into an intimacy which confused both of us, as if all the years between had disappeared and we had known each other all the time.

It was three o'clock when we got up and wandered back to the car. As soon as we got in, Wolf reached to kiss me in a way that would have been incestuous had we been more closely related. I reached up and took off his glasses and kissed him back. I was really enjoying it even as I thought that it was good we weren't Eskimos, noses being what they were.

Chapter 7

We drove back without much conversation–each of us contemplating this turn of events. I thought of Jack. We had been going together, more or less, for a couple of years, but he still occasionally saw his wife–from whom he was separated, not legally and not enough for my taste. I periodically felt passionate about him, but I had learned to cool my feelings because I tended to see less of him every time I said "I love you." Paris had been idyllic, but then, Paris can be; Americans practically feel obligated to be lovers there. It had been one of those occasions when Jack had expressed his intent to get a divorce and marry me, which he did when I got restive, but he had never done anything about it and I was restive now.

I couldn't fathom what Wolf might be thinking; his inner world was foreign territory to me. I stole a glance at him. His nose didn't look as big as it had earlier. I guessed I was getting used to it. It was actually an interesting nose, in that it looked perfectly normal–even somewhat aquiline–from the front, which made it all the more surprising when it was viewed from the side. From the front, he was fairly good-looking; from the side, he was an original. It occurred to me that I didn't know some important things about him–if he were married or serious about someone. It wasn't anything you could ask nonchalantly. You can't say, "Are you married?" sitting in a car with a man who has just kissed you so that you wanted to do it again. I put off the idea of finding out for now. Anni would know; I would ask her.

When I thought about it, all I really wanted was to pursue that kiss further...which was another matter entirely. How, I asked myself, could that be pursued? Back in New York, I could invite him to dinner, with or without other friends. He could stay on after, or not. If we went out, we could end up at my place. I generally preferred going to my place: single men tended to live in dumpy apartments with sheets that had only a cursory acquaintance with detergents and bleach, and kitchens where cockroaches lay in ambush for unfamiliar women making breakfast. In those days, most men would rarely even get as far as making coffee, which in any case was usually black, as any milk in the 'fridge tended to be closer to penicillin than to cows.

"What is your place in Heidelberg like, Wolf?"

"I have rooms near the University. Nothing fancy, as you might say. Just a typical bachelor's home. But I like it. It is comfortable, and several of my friends live in the building."

Well, I thought, that answered a few questions. "Do you like it at Heidelberg?"

"Yes. I like it very much. I get to do what I like, I don't have too many students, I am not so high in the Department that I am involved in departmental politics, I have good friends. It is a good life." He threw a glance at me. "It is, I admit, a little calm sometimes. Very few surprises–other than mathematical ones."

"Are there any women in your department?"

"Two. Both are really like your teaching assistants. There are seldom more than two or three female students in any year. It is not a woman's field."

"Why is that? Because it's hard for women who want to be mathematicians to be taken seriously?"

I really didn't mean to get into a feminist argument, but it always riled me when someone said that "Women are this" or "Women are that," especially if they implied that women are somehow less, or couldn't do something just because they were women.

"Yes. . .well, I don't know. It is not that the Department gets many applications from women and refuses them. It is even possible that most of the women who apply are accepted–there are so few women who major in mathematics, that those who get a degree tend to be quite good. But," he added with a little smile, "they tend"–and he sort of hunkered down a bit to give his words some body language, "to be very 'seeeerious.' None of them ever have ever seemed to have a sense of humor–except one."

Oh, I thought, this is the "she" in his life. "Who is that?"

"Mitzi Dressler. She is married to Kurt, my best friend. She is an excellent mathematician and pretty too. She and Kurt work together. They both work in quadratic equations. Kurt and I always joke about who saw her first. But it is not entirely a joke. I have always been a little in love with Mitzi, but by the time I realized it, she and Kurt were already serious." He hesitated. "I have sometimes been a little shy with women."

"Really," I said.

He laughed. "Yes, really," he said, imitating my accent. "I was always so much teased about my nose–and my clumsiness–that I always waited until I was sure I was accepted. But in the last few years, I don't seem to worry about it so much."

"Something certainly changed. 'Shy with women' is not a way I'd describe you."

He grinned. "I guess not."

"So what changed?"

He frowned. "I have never asked myself that question." After a minute, he shrugged and said, "I don't know."

"Anything special happen in your life in the last few years?"

"Aha!," he said wagging one finger while steering expertly, but very fast, around a curve. "The psychological question. If you are not careful, I will make my observation about American women again."

"If you are not careful, I will start digging into my repertoire of remarks about European males–German males in particular." It was an empty threat. My only non-American dating games were limited to a couple of male French students who were in college with me. I had found them simultaneously more sexually attentive and more intellectually dismissive of me than any American male. "Really, Wolf," I said. I bet something unusual happened in your life a few years ago."

"You know, there was something." He paused. "My father died."

"I'm sorry." I really was. Politeness would have left it at that, but I'm always interested in how people feel about their parents or somebody close dying. It hadn't happened to me then. "Did you like your father? I mean, do you miss him?"

He smiled. "You continue to surprise me. What strange questions. Did I like my father? Yes, I suppose. He was always a little distant, and very serious. A lot like your father. I don't think I knew him very well."

"What did he die from?"

"The diagnosis was gastritis."

"Gastritis! That's usually from food poisoning. How did your father get *that*?"

"Oh, I don't think it was food poisoning. We had all been to Uncle Franz's house for dinner, and no one else got sick, so it couldn't have been the food. It was just before your father married Ilse–a couple of months anyway."

"Wow!" I said.

"Why do you say, 'Wow'?"

"People don't usually die of a stomach problem right after they eat at a relative's house except in the movies–you know, when they've been poisoned."

He sighed. "There was some talk after he died. We didn't hear about it until later–the talk, I mean, and of course, we dismissed it." He frowned.

"So tell me. What was it?"

"A...ach, well, my father, he disapproved of Uncle Franz marrying Ilse. He thought she was only marrying your father for his money and position. Not that we are *that* wealthy–but for Ilse, it is enough. He was very strongly against it, and he tried very hard to change Uncle Franz's mind."

"How did you feel about it."

"I agreed with my father. But I have always had a little special feeling for Uncle Franz, and I know how lonely he was after Adele died. And Ilse took care of everything for him, and looked after him...And we Göring and Herzog men like being looked after." He shot me a sidelong look and a small smile. "And she was pretty and young, and I think after Adele's death, Uncle Franz felt...well...finished. 'Since Adele is gone, I have no life anymore,' he used to say to me. So when he said he was marrying her, I was sympathetic... But I still felt it was a mistake."

"What does this have to do with your father getting sick?"

"Well, he went to that dinner determined to talk your father out of the marriage, but before he could get together with him, he was stricken with these terrible pains...And he never recovered."

"Did he have any history of stomach trouble?"

"Oh, yes. But not serious. He sometimes had indigestion. He couldn't eat some things. And I think he once had an ulcer, but that was not the cause of his death." Wolf sighed.

"What was?"

"Acute gastritis. He fell into shock, and he never recovered. He was not a young man. I think he was more than ten years older than Uncle Franz. The same generation, but different ages." He sighed again.

"You said that you heard there was some 'talk' about your father's death. But your father died the way we expect people to die when they get older. In the States, we get rid of the old by medicating them until they die. If one pill doesn't do it, we add another, plus a third to prevent a toxic interaction among them. You go to the doctor and you say, 'Doctor, these pills you gave me; one of the side effects is death.' And the doctor says, 'Don't worry, there are other, more painful and debilitating side effects that you are much more likely to get before there's any danger of that happening."

"You are a real humorist, Leni. I don't think my father was taking any medication. No, the talk was about Ilse...about the possibility that she had poisoned him."

"No!" I didn't want to deal with I the issue of Ilse and mushrooms. "How could she have done it? Didn't Anni cook the dinner?"

"Yes, she did."

"So how could she have done it?"

He hesitated. "Well, it seems that Ilse would never go into the kitchen. She always said that as long as she was Uncle Franz's secretary, she would not have anything to do with the house. But for this meal, she was in and out of the kitchen the whole time, not only while it was being prepared, but also while it was being served. So between the two things–my father's attitude and that, the talk started. But at that time, it seemed absurd, even though everyone knew that my father was very opposed to the marriage and was expecting to talk Uncle Franz out of it."

"What do you mean, 'At that time'? Did you change your mind?"

He thought about it. He thought a lot, I thought, before he talked. It took control on my part not to assume he hadn't heard me, or didn't understand me, and repeat the question. But I waited for him instead of interrupting mostly because he was a man. I had more respect and patience for men than for women, although I barely admitted that to myself.

Finally he, said, "Well, I cannot say I have 'changed my mind.' Let us just say, I started to entertain the possibility."

"Why?"

He heaved a real sigh. "Last year, something happened to another aunt of mine..."

"Tante Therese? I know about that! But that wasn't serious."

"How do you know about that?"

"Father told me about it."

He negotiated another turn before he said, "I am surprised Uncle Franz described it to you as 'not serious.' I don't think Tante Therese thought it was 'not serious'."

It was my turn to do some thinking. It hadn't sounded that serious when Father had told it, and I wasn't ready to take a position that would make him wrong. "Well," I said, "according to my father, your aunt doesn't remember any of it, and as long as nothing worse happened, I can understand Father treating it as 'not serious.' It's much easier to live with Ilse, treating the thing as 'not serious' rather than as a near miss."

This time, there was an even longer silence. I was thinking that he might be getting mad at me, when he said somberly, "It is not a question that it was what you call a 'near miss.' Nobody thinks that. We are after all civilized people. But it is still a matter of concern."

I thought again about Ilse and Father and the aunt and the mushrooms, and I remembered Ilse in the woods, but I pushed it aside. "Look, I'm just here to visit my father. I can't deal with family feuds."

Wolf pulled up in front of my father's house. He said, "So! We will drop the subject. What time should I pick you up tomorrow for our tour of Stammbüttel?"

"Oh, I better check with Ilse and my father before we make plans."

"I'm sure it will be okay," he said. "I'll call you in the morning."

"Not too early," I said.

"Not too late," he said, and drove off.

I turned the ancient knob of a small wrought iron door beside the big gate and it opened without a sound. I thought how someone must be looking after such things, greasing the hinges. It was still early–only about four. The sun was still shining through the trees along the street, bouncing off the clean, shiny cars parked along the curbs. As I walked toward the door to the house I noticed for the first time that there was another door nearer the gate, marked with worn, carefully serifed lettering, "Göring Verlag." I thought about going in when a man in work clothes, his hands and wrists marked with black, opened the door, the scent of printers ink slipping out around him like an aura.

I was standing so close I startled him, but he immediately bowed and gestured in a courtly way, murmuring something, but I could hardly understand him. I only caught the words "*Fräulein*" and "*helfen*,"–help. I thought he must be speaking with some sort of local accent. I said I was here to see Herr Göring. He motioned for me to follow him and we walked past men poring over chases that contained a mix of loose type, set letter by letter, and linotype, set line by line into poured lead. Loose metal type was a couple of centuries old; linotype was fifty. In a few years it would all be changed: photo-typesetting was less than ten years away; computer-generated pages, less than twenty.

We went upstairs to a small room filled with desks at which a solitary man straight out of Central Casting's supply of newsroom extras, with a cigarette sending a line of curling smoke into one half-closed eye from one end of his tightly closed mouth, jabbed with both forefingers at an old typewriter that responded with loud intermittent staccato bursts. The man didn't look up as we went past him to a door at the end of the room. A desk with stacks of papers on it and a typewriter table with a large old typewriter on it guarded the door, but its occupant was not there. My guide knocked, waited until he heard my father's voice, and then opened it with a small flourish, stepping back to let me enter.

"Hello, Vater," I said in my best German. *"Ich dachte ich wollte dich besuchen....* I thought that I would pay you a visit." As I spoke he took off his glasses and put down a set of galleys. I realized I had not seen him wear glasses before.

For a moment, I wasn't sure he was going to welcome me–he clearly wasn't expecting to be interrupted, but then he smiled and said, *"Aber ja...* But yes. Why not?" And he told me to sit down in a large visitor's chair, a wing chair covered in well-worn leather with brass studs at the seams, the kind that you still see sometimes in older lawyers' offices. Then he leaned back and asked, *"So, wie war dein Nachmittag mit Wolf?...*How was your afternoon with Wolf?"

I told him I liked Wolf–very much–but shook my head. *"Er ist ein..."* I couldn't think of the word for 'dangerous' and started to wave my hands, hoping something would come.

My father frowned and said impatiently, "English!"

I said, "dangerous." He didn't get it. "Danger," I said.

"Erschreckend?" he tried.

I wasn't sure. *"Aber er ist nicht 'schrecklich'....* But he is not 'terrible,'" I said.

He shook his head. "Nein," he said. *"Erschreckend heisst nicht 'schrecklich.'* It doesn't mean 'terrible.' It means..." and then he waved his hand and made an expression similar to mine.

"No," I said. "You mean 'frightened.'"

He nodded vigorously. "Yes," he said in English, "frightened."

"Nein," I said. "*Wolf ist nicht erschrocken.*"

"Ah!" he said. "*Nicht 'erschrocken'; "erschreckend,*'" emphasizing the "d" at the end of the word." Wolf was not frightened, he was 'frightening'!

"*Ja,*" I said, sheepishly, as if the whole thing were due to my being stupid. "*Ein bisschen*.... A little bit." I used '*bisschen*' a lot. I spoke German "*ein bisschen.*" I remembered my childhood "*ein bisschen.*" When offered another piece of cake, I wanted only "*ein bisschen.*"

My father found this very funny. He started to laugh really hard. Finally he wiped a tear from his eye and said, yes, he could see that Wolf was "*ein bisschen erschreckend*, but no one had ever expressed it so...*ganz richtig*.... so exactly." Going anywhere with Wolf, he said, was always an adventure. The miraculous thing, was that he was never really hurt, although many objects had been demolished in his passing. "When you expect a visit from Wolf, one makes sure that there is nothing fragile about that can be easily knocked over." He shook his head. "If I were not so fond of the boy, I would not put up with it. But Wolf has always made me laugh." He looked at the papers on his desk, and put them aside. "Come, I will show you the Verlag."

We went downstairs, where the men were starting to clean up, locking up the chases, most of which were now full pages of type and engravings and line drawings cast in lead. This, he told me, was where the Verlag produced its books. He showed me where the pages would be printed, one by one, to provide reproduction quality images for offset plates. The master copy pages for the books, he said, would be sent out. He did not print his own books. It required far more equipment than he had. But, he said triumphantly, he did print his *Käseblatt*, the *Stammbüttler Zeitung*, right here, on his own press. I followed him through the small, ancient room dutifully, expecting a substantial machine, one that could print a substantial paper.

He strode ahead of me again, through another small, low-ceilinged room and threw open a door. I stepped through and almost stepped back out, because in contrast to the small, medieval spaces through which we had come and which the old combined houses of the Görings represented, there stood The Press, two stories high, silent now, but massive, big enough to chew up and spit out whole blocks of Stammbüttel, with its great print rollers, weighing tons, and glistening wheels and levers, and with its enormous cast steel frame coated with a high gloss enamel in a delicate shade of light green.

I turned to my father, who was standing there, quietly proud. Looking at him, and at that machine, you knew that the press was his baby, and his paper was his heart, and the rest–the books, the Verlag, all of it–were just business.

"How did you do it?" I said. "How did you get it in here?"

He smiled. It was the right question. He showed me how it was set on a thick concrete floor which was poured directly on the rock under the house, and where they had taken out an entire floor above. It must have been a huge undertaking for this part of town, and remembering how he had said that the Town denied him the right to put a picture window in his own office, I wondered how he had managed it all.

"*Die Zeitung kommt zu erst*.... The paper is first in your heart, isn't it?" I said. He looked a little puzzled. I figured I didn't have the idiom right, but the he said, "*Ach, ja*," and then got very quiet. He stood, looking at the machine and not looking at it, and I realized he looked very sad. I thought maybe he was sad that a newspaper was first in his heart when he had a wife and kids and family, or maybe he was sad because once there was Adele who had, perhaps, for a time, even edged out the *Zeitung*.

He looked at his watch and said he had a little more work to do. Ilse would be expecting us soon for supper. He took me to a small door in the back of the composing room. It opened directly into the stairwell of the house, and I paused. Behind me was a whitewashed room full of machines and the scent of printers' ink hovering over it. In front of me was a homey dimness of polished woods and carpets and the smell of cooking food. It was a like stepping through the Looking Glass. I stepped through and slowly closed the door behind me.

Chapter 8

I stood still a while, letting the presence of the house displace the dreamlike vision of that huge machine in my mind. I realized that I didn't know exactly where it was in the house. If you had asked me, at that moment, to draw a map of the buildings, I couldn't have done it. It was as if the machine were in its own dimension, and the rest of the house, in which I now stood, had held onto its space–a truce between creatures of two entirely different worlds.

As I stood, I became aware of the murmur of voices in the dining room interspersed with small explosive interjections–the lower voices of Ilse and the boys and occasionally, Helmut's higher register. The voices were slightly low, engaged in an intense conversation where each exchange was weighed and returned, as if they were passing around something and looking at it very carefully. I was curious to go and see what they might have, but something held me there, and I stopped to listen.

It was stupid, I suppose, since I had a hard enough time understanding what people were trying to say directly to me in simplified German, so all I got were a few phrases, like "*Sie kann nicht*.... She cannot" and "*Sie darf nicht*.... She must not." I gave up and walked through the passage into the room.

As I entered, all of them had already turned to look at the doorway. It was like one of those tableaus that schools used to do at Christmas–with Mary and Joseph, the Wise Men et al, accompanied by the Chorus doing "Silent Night"–where everyone is holding a pose as if caught in motion, although the sight of Helmut in all his beauty like a decadent Carvaggio cherub and Ilse with her slightly overblown good looks reminded me more of the melodramatic painting of the late, late Baroque.

At the time, all this was relatively subliminal. I was more concerned with being regarded with so much surprise, and even suspicion. "*Guten Abend*," I said cheerfully.

Ilse's face immediately took on a more cheerful look, although the others took a while to follow her cue. "Hallo, Leni. Did you have a good time with Wolf?"

"Yes," I said. "He was very nice. And...I stopped to see Father and he showed me the Verlag."

Ilse nodded. "Did he show you the great machine? It is for Franz what my old boss in Nuremberg used to call his automobile. It is his 'pride and joy.'"

I laughed appreciatively. "Yes, you're using that exactly right. It is his 'pride and joy.'"

Hans looked confused. "Pride and joy," Gustav said, like an incantation. "Pride and joy. What is Father's pride and joy?"

"The big press for the *Zeitung*," I said.

Gustav turned to Hans and Helmut. *"Die grosse Druckerpresse! Vati's Druckerpresse! Sie is Vati's 'Stolz und Freude.'"* It must have sounded funny in German, because Hans and Helmut started to giggle, both repeating *"Stolz und Freude, Stolz und Freude"* several times, until all three of them stood up and were chanting it in unison. They started banging on the table, keeping time with each syllable, the table sounding like a drum and their voices rising in crescendo, until Ilse shouted, *"Genug! Genug!"* several times, louder and louder, and suddenly they switched, shouting *"Genug, Genug"* and banging the table with each "ge" and "nug," until all three broke up laughing hysterically.

The boys collapsed back into their chairs, poking each other intermittently, pleased with themselves. It was a better atmosphere than the one I had walked into. *"Wir werden bald essen....* Soon we will eat," Ilse said to them, and told them to go to their rooms until dinner. Hans and Gustav gave Helmut a friendly pat on the shoulder and ushered him along with them, an invitation he seemed pleased to accept, although even now he took a moment to give Ilse a quick apologetic look over his shoulder with a sweep of his long lashes over his eyes, a look that was bound in later years to bind an endless chain of women to him–women who would mistake his practiced ardor for genuine feeling for them, when it would always and forever belong to Ilse–as she had, with unconscious intent, seen that it would. She acknowledged the look with a small, intimate smile, at once giving him leave to go and maintaining the connection between them, the way a fisherman who has hooked his fish will loosen the line so the fish can run itself out, knowing that at any moment he can pull on the line and reel his catch back to him.

"Poor little thing," I thought to myself, the first really kind thought I'd had about the little boy. "Poor little thing, you never had a chance." It wasn't right, I thought, Ilse–any woman doing that to her son, making him unfit for love, really. I had already known men like that, men who were ardent only as long as they were in pursuit and lost interest as the relationship moved into the quieter, deeper waters of intimacy. I had consoled abandoned friends, and showered invectives on the spirits of their departed lovers, but this was the first time I saw the connection with the boys they might have been–assuming, of course, that these men had not left because my friends were just plain hell to live with.

Ilse stood there, watching them go.

"Can I help with dinner?" I asked.

Ilse shook her head. "No," she said. "It is only the children's dinner. We are going out to dinner with the Kurzeldts. They are old friends of your father and want to meet you."

She didn't seem very happy about it. "Oh, that's great," I said. "I'd like to meet some of your friends...and more of the family."

Ilse threw me a slightly soiled look. "The Kurzeldts are not my friends. They are your father's. Dinner at a restaurant with the Kurzeldts is not a 'pleasure' I have had before. And as for the rest of the family...I don't expect you will see too much of them–except possibly Franz's aunt, an old busybody." She paused and gave a short mirthless laugh. "My American boss used to call people like her 'busybodies'.

She sat, looking abstracted. I assumed she meant the aunt who had eaten the psychedelic mushrooms–but then, maybe the family had more than one nosey aunt. However, I was more interested in Ilse's other remarks. About the Kurzeldts not being her friends–well, in the light of what she had told me earlier, that made sense. But the note about not seeing more of the family–I would have thought that they would at least be curious. Here I am, their flesh and blood. My parents had divorced because my mother was Jewish, but that was during the Nazi period. They were civilized, educated people...

Considering my level of sophistication in many other matters, I was still foolish enough, or perhaps desperate enough to say, "And why wouldn't the rest of the family want to meet me?"

"Because you are Jewish," she said without hesitating.

"Really?"

She looked at me as if she were wondering if I were more stupid than she had assumed. "Yes. Of course. Many people still feel like that."

I gave her a hard look. "And you don't feel like that?"

She gave me a hard look back. She was far better at hard looks than I was. "No, I do not. Not the way they do about it. I cannot say I like Jews, or that I would exert myself to do anything for Jews. But I do not feel like Franz's family does."

I thought about her father, the general. "Why don't you feel like they do? After all, weren't you brought up to feel like that?"

"Yes, of course I was. But after I worked for the Americans for three years, it was not so important any more. As a German employee, I could not express any anti-semitism, or I might have lost a very good job at a time when there were almost no jobs of any kind–especially for women. And even though some of the Americans working in Nürnberg sometimes said anti-semitic things, it was very different for them." She paused.

"Different? How? From what?" My mind was juggling everything she said–the family–my father's–not wanting to see me, and Ilse at Nuremberg–of all places–learning not to be anti-semitic–or was it just less anti-semitic?

"Well," she said thoughtfully. She seemed trying to explain something she hadn't explained to herself. "Many of the Americans were Jewish, or partly Jewish–like you–and I had to work with them. But it was more than that. At first, I thought that all Americans were like the English, only more informal, more friendly. But then it became very confusing, because there were many Americans with Italian and Spanish and German and Czech names, and people even seemed to make jokes about it to each other. And some of the Jews were kind to me and some of the...Aryans were very unkind to me. After a while, it stopped mattering so much, who was Jewish and who was this or that. I only worried that I did my job well and was able to live."

I thought about what she said. A part of me appreciated what she had seen. It made me happy that I was an American at that moment, that I belonged to a country where people from completely different backgrounds worked together the way they did in no other country in the world. America was still a good guy in a nasty world and I was happy to be an American. Yet, here I was, unacceptable for nothing I had done or could do anything about. It awakened very threatening feelings. After all, my mother had fled with me for our lives, leaving behind friends and family that she never saw alive, or even dead, again. And I had not been unaware of the terrible threat that once, in a dream, took the form of a great black roaring tidal wave that took the small boat on which I rode and cast it on the very edge of a shore, so that I had to run inland for my life and barely escaped being sucked back into its terminal darkness.

Then, the feeling of belonging safe on the American shore, and the fact that it was time for Ilse and I to get dressed for dinner, folded whatever thoughts I had on the matter back into themselves and I went to my room. I decided to dress as elegantly as I could and picked out a suit which I had brought along for Paris–a Dior knock-off, with a relatively short straight skirt and a three-quarter coat for a jacket, in a big open black-and-gold-on-creamy-white plaid. It might be a bit much for Stammbüttel, I thought, but I decided slightly too much was going to be okay.

When I finally came out ready to go, Ilse's eyes ran over me like an emery board, but all she said was, "It is not a very fancy restaurant." I really didn't care. It wasn't as if I had put on a ball gown for a baseball game. After all, this was what people wore to go out to dinner where I came from. "Franz just came from work. He is getting dressed. We can wait in the living room."

"You know," I said, "I think I'll just go out to the back and get some air before dinner."

I stood there in the early evening light–after the sun had set, but before the light was gone, so that everything was still lit but had a blue cast that deepened minute by minute. I stood in the driveway, which was edged almost its entire length on one side by a flower bed where a dense row of rose bushes had extended new-leaved branches from their cut-back winter stumps. I saw that the first rosebuds were pressing into life and wondered whether these were my father's doing.

The evening light was causing the green leaves of the rose bushes to glow softly, the way light-green leaves do at twilight and in the earliest morning. I had stopped to contemplate them when the door opened and threw a shaft of light across the driveway, turning the leaves it touched a pale, washed-out green as Father and Ilse walked through the doorway in a pair of joined silhouettes.

"*Ich sehe dass du meine Rosen bewunderst....* I see you are admiring my roses," he said as he strolled toward his car.

I said, "*Ja, so viele....* Yes, so many. Are you the gardener?"

My father laughed and shook his head. *"Aber nein!...*But no! The gardener is Tonio, one of my employees," he said as we got into the car. As we drove off, Father turned on the radio. He found some music–it was the middle of Haydn's Trumpet Concerto–and we drove through the darkening streets to the sound of a trumpet being played with such absolute clarity and skill that it shut out all other sounds and made you listen. When it was over and the announcer broke in, my father leaned his head back slightly to tell me we were going to a restaurant called *Die Schwarze Katze*.... The Black Cat. It was a restaurant that was very good and very German, because he thought as long as I was in Germany I should see what a traditional German restaurant was like. I agreed, omitting mention of the very German restaurant where I had lunch with Wolf.

We had left town and were in suburban territory. The headlights swept from side to side as the road curved until it straightened into a small strip of stores and restaurants. We drew up to one with a fairly large blue neon sign that said in script, *"Die Schwarze Katze,"* terminating in a cat outlined in white, with white whiskers, red eyes and a tail that alternately curled up and lay down as one red eye alternately closed to a white line in a relentless wink.

An attendant took the car, greeting my father respectfully by name. It was a little like walking around with a celebrity. I suddenly remembered my mother, in one of our relatively rare conversations about my father, saying that if I had grown up in Stammbüttel as my father's daughter, I would have been 'somebody.' At the time, I had smiled indulgently. I was old enough and hip enough to view the idea that being 'somebody' by birth was not something you bragged about, especially since it would have been 'somebody' in a foreign town–any of which were small puddles in relation to the city where I felt myself to be one of the inner denizens–New York, New York. But now that I walked in Stammbüttel in the company of one of its anointed, I thought about that as we entered the restaurant, where my father was immediately greeted and engaged in conversation by the maître and owner. I thought about how I had grown up in so many places where I was perpetually a stranger, instead of a single, secure and pretty place where I was the child of one of the elect, my schooling and university assured instead of worked through, and in that minute, as I waited with Ilse, who said nothing but watched everything as if she had to keep track to the last nuance, I chose what had happened over what might have been, and found myself for the first time, if briefly, content with the past.

My father introduced Ilse and me to the owner, a Herr Lustigmann. The man seemed to know Ilse, whom he greeted with a small, deferential inclination of the head before he turned to me with a face full of curiosity that held my gaze for several seconds before it fell in a small bow. In those seconds, I imagined how he saw my whole history as he flipped through his files–probably remembering old gossip: 'Ah, yes, the daughter of that Jewish girl he divorced; a youthful indiscretion, long ago smoothed over, and here she is, well that is interesting, from America–Well!'

My father asked after the Kurzeldts–they were not here yet–and we were taken to a table. He turned down one set for six for what was apparently his favorite booth–big enough to seat six closely, but set for four. The backs of the seats were high over the heads of the seated diners, carved into scrolls at the top, closing each booth into an intimate space. The seats were covered with green leather and the table between was covered with a green-checked tablecloth that showed the creases of its starched and ironed state. Each of the four settings had a plate that pictured some eighteenth-century male-oriented domestic scene of German *Gemütlichkeit*: a fat paternal figure in a chair by a fireplace being brought a stein of beer by a small dutiful boy; a man smoking a pipe at a table and petting a dog as a woman brought in a large tray of steaming meat.

The owner was waiting for us to arrange ourselves and I was in the process of sliding into the seat against the wall when the Kurtzelts arrived. The man looked very like my father, not so much in his face as in his figure: his clothes and the way he carried himself–the tweed jacket, the conservative tie, the neatly brushed-back hair, the air of being in exactly the right place–although he looked around him with a much wider angle of vision than my father used, taking in the details of the room, looking at the other diners as he walked toward us. The woman was very different. She was thin and a little nervous, her blonde hair–arranged in waves, possibly natural and cut just an inch below her ears, the gray which must have been there expertly touched away–was partly hidden by an elegant small-brimmed plaid wool hat, the brim slightly tilted over one eye in a style that reminded me of 'Thirties glamour stills. She moved toward us walking just in front of her husband, one shoulder slightly forward as if she were breaking her way through a crowd. Her eyes were on me, but they were unreadable.

As they approached us, her face broke into a smile although the anxious furrows between her eyes deepened. "Hallo, Franz," she said warmly, and added a brief but not unfriendly "Hallo, Ilse."

"*Grüss Gott*, Hannah," my father said, taking her hand and bowing slightly over it. For a split second I thought he might crack his heels together and kiss it, but his gesture was just a shorthand reference to a past when he did the bowing, rather than being bowed to. What was left was a courtly–even charming–gesture to the wife of an old friend.

Hannah shook hands with Ilse and turned to me. "So," she said in clear, accented English with a nervous but genuine smile, "you are Lene. I am glad you have come to visit your father. It has been so many years. You were a very little girl when I last saw you." She stepped back, giving me a friendly but careful once-over, and shook her head approvingly. "You seem to have grown up very well in America. But then, your mother always did have good taste."

There was a small, cold drop in the atmosphere. I understood that mentioning my mother in any real, personal way was akin to having spinach on your teeth and burping at the same time–in terms of its impact on Ilse chiefly and on my father secondarily. I glanced at Ilse, whose face was a shade darker, while my father looked at her and at Hannah and then at the door to the kitchen, as if he couldn't decide whether he should tell Hannah to be quiet, beg Ilse's forgiveness, or make a break for it. I was also ambivalent: wanting to smooth things over by making some socially innocuous remark; wanting to say something nice about my mother, but I stood silent with a half-smile on my face.

It was only a beat later that my father looked over at the man and said, "Hallo, Paul." Paul stepped forward, said, "Hallo, Franz," and shook my father's hand, warmly but casually, as an old friend. Hannah looked over her shoulder and smiled at Paul as if she were happy that he was there, and he put his hand on her shoulder in acknowledgement. I liked them both.

Father directed everyone to their seats. He put Hannah next to me and Paul next to Ilse and sat at the head of the table on a chair that the waiter brought. The menus were gigantic folded cards written in what was for me hard-to-read German script, with long skinny f's for s's and sometimes capital B's for double s's, and w's and m's that were joined at the top and bottom so that you couldn't tell them apart. I asked my father to order "something very German" for me.

"That is an excellent idea," Hannah said. "Paul, *du kannst auch für mich bestellen*.... you can order for me too." Hannah turned to me, and said, "How long will you remain in Stammbüttel?"

"Just until Monday," I said. "I'm going back to Paris for a few days before I fly home."

She looked disappointed. Then she said, "I was hoping that we could spend a little time together." She paused again, and then smiled. "Perhaps your father would not mind if you visited us for a little *Mittagessen*—lunch." She said 'lunch' slowly, lengthening the 'u'.

I started to say how I would have to check with...and I shot a glance at Ilse, but she was listening to Paul and smiling, looking very soft and charming, so that I could see something of her that would have appealed to my father. Then I remembered that I had told Wolf that I would go with him–ostensibly to see Stammbüttel–tomorrow. I'm sorry," I said, "but I have already promised to spend the day with my cousin, Wolf Herzog..."

"Wolfi? Wolfi is in Stammbuettel? I must see him. Of course I know Wolf. My son and he..." She suddenly hesitated and a great space seemed to open up in front of her, but as quickly as it had opened, it closed and she continued. "A wonderful boy." She thought a moment. "Tell me," she said very confidentially. "Is he still..." she sought for a word, waving her thumb and forefinger as if she could pick it out of the air.

"Accident-prone?" I suggested. She laughed. "In a word," I said. "Yes. Very."

"I should not laugh. It is not always funny. But one has to love Wolf even though he might destroy your house." She laughed again, and I joined her. I looked at Ilse. She was giving Hannah a slightly suspicious look, worrying, I thought, that our laugh was at her expense.

"You must come together," she said. "I will call Wolfi in the morning."

The waiter arrived with a tray of beer. Steins for the men; glasses for the ladies. It annoyed me, even though I preferred glasses to the clumsy steins. The meal started with the best pickled herring I had ever eaten. The pickling left a delicate flavor and the flesh tender as fine smoked salmon. We ate seriously, and the conversation slowed to small sound bites, mainly questions about American intentions–as if I knew what Eisenhower was going to do about the Russians; as if anyone really knew what anyone could do about the Russians. Stalin was dead, but Krushchev kept us guessing.

Not that there was much time to talk between courses. The herring was replaced by large plates of *Bayrische Rostbraten*–Bavarian 'roast beef' that was braised rather than roasted, individual rolls of beef filled with ground seasoned smoked pork in a heavy sour cream gravy. After an undistinguished salad, the dishes were cleared and the waiter appeared with a cake on a pedestaled plate and placed it with a flourish in the middle of the table. It was a classic Linzertorte–a raspberry-jam-filled cake made with ground almonds and almost no flour–which Lindy's in New York did just as well, but I didn't say so. After we had all admired it, the waiter took it and cut each of us a large slice delivered with a gob of whipped cream.

After we had finished that, we drank more coffee as my father and Paul had a good-natured argument about Stammbüttel politics. Paul got off a few jabs regarding my father's *Käseblatt.* My father frowned at the use of the phrase on Paul's lips. It was okay, I guessed, for him to use it as an expression of modesty; but not for others, even close friends.

Paul turned to me to explain; his English was as good as Hannah's, although more heavily accented. "Your father and I have always an argument," he said. "I think he should use the *Zeitung* to get rid of the old fools who operate this town like a fief in the Middle Ages. He thinks he should only report the news–which he does very well. We always disagree." He shook his head regretfully.

"Stammbüttel is a conservative town," my father said wearily, as if he had said it before. "*Wenige Leute*.... Few people want it to change. I will not say what no one wants to hear."

"Franz," Paul said, leaning forward slightly, so you could see that he meant it even as he kept his tone light. "*Wir sind uns einig*.... We agree what needs to be done. If you spoke, the town would listen."

My father put one hand on Paul's shoulder and signaled to the waiter with the other. "Paul," he said. "*Es ist nicht möglich*.... It is not possible." He got up.

Paul shrugged. It was obviously an old argument. We slowly moved toward to the door, the men got their coats, and chatted as we waited for the cars. My father's was brought first. As we left Hannah said, "Don't forget: I will call Wolf. Tomorrow."

I nodded, and waved as we drove off.

Chapter 9

We had driven without speaking for a while, sunk into an overfed stupor, when Ilse turned around and said, "What are you doing with Hannah tomorrow?"

"I was going to ask if it was convenient," I said quickly. "She invited me for lunch. But I was going to see Stammbüttel with Wolf anyway..." I stopped. I felt like I was sixteen and asking permission to go out on a date.

"It is certainly not inconvenient, but it is important that you return in the afternoon, because tomorrow evening is the *Mittelball*," she said. "It is a big dance party. Every year it is given by the children's dancing school, a little like a graduation party. Everyone goes. It is quite nice. And of course, we must go."

"Hans and Gustav take dancing lessons?" It was a novel idea. In fact it was pretty funny.

"Only Hans this year. But all the children do. Even your father learned to dance there. *Ist das nicht richtig*, Franz?....Isn't that right, Franz?"

"*Ja, genau. Paul und ich beide.*"

"Oh," I said. "You and Paul were childhood friends?"

"*Ach, Ja. Paul und ich waren wie Brüder*.... Paul and I were like brothers. I was the only child then, and so was he. Then we went to Heidelberg together. I studied literature. Paul became a painter."

"Paul is a painter?"

"Ja. *Wenn du ihn besuchen wirst*.... When you visit him, he will show you."

"Is Hannah from Stammbüttel too?"

"*Nein. Er begegnet ihr*.... He met her during a semester at the University of Munich. I remember, he came back from Munich and said to me 'I have met this wonderful girl!' He was so happy. I thought he would forget her after a few weeks, but he did not. Instead, he asked her to marry him after graduation. His mother tried very hard to stop it." He shook his head, remembering.

"*Warum hat sie*.... Why did she try to stop it?"

"*Zum Teil, glaube ich*.... Partly, I think, because her family did not have very much money." He hesitated. "But mostly, because she was Jewish."

"*Hannah ist eine Jüdin*?" Ilse sounded like it was impossible, that it could not be!

"*Ja*."

I thought about how Hannah had looked at Paul in the restaurant, and how he had put his hand on her shoulder to acknowledge her look. I wanted something like that for myself...Still something after all those years. But many of those years were Nazi years. If she was Jewish...

"*Wie hat Paul*.... How did Paul deal with being married to Hannah during the war?" I asked.

My father didn't say anything. I waited. Ilse was waiting too. She had turned in her seat so that she faced him. I was beginning to think he hadn't heard me when he said, "*Er hat sie verborgen*."

I didn't know what *verborgen* meant. I was trying to figure it out from the conversation when she said "*Wo?.... Where? Wo hat er sie verborgen?*" My father was silent again. Finally he said, "*In seinem Haus*.... At his home."

Ilse sucked in her breath with such a sound of horror that for a second I actually felt my heart stop before it went on beating. I caught from her a feeling of being threatened, as if Paul's hiding of Hannah–for that is what it was: he had *hidden* her–were endangering us all. It lasted only a second, but I actually *tasted* the kind of terror that a revelation like that would once have created. It was a sharp taste, clean and cool, as if my saliva had suddenly gone cold on me, and I shivered.

"*Aber nein! Das konnte er nicht!*.... But no! He couldn't do that!" Ilse's determination to set right this great sin was as powerful as it was meaningless.

Again I had to wait for my father's answer. Finally he said, "*Ja, es war nicht möglich*,...Yes, it was not possible, but he did it."

"*Und du wusstest es?*...And you knew it?"

My father shook his head. "*Nein. Paul hat's mir nicht gesagt*.... Paul did not tell me until after the War."

"*Aber wie*.... But how did he get away with it?"

"*Das ist eine lange Geschichte*.... That is a long story," my father said. "We are nearly home. I will tell you over a glass of brandy."

The house was quiet; Anni and the children were long asleep. Still silent, we entered the dining room where my father went to the sideboard, took out three small brandy snifters and a bottle of cognac. We continued into the living room, still silent. Only after he had handed Ilse and I our glasses did he settle back and tell us the story, with a occasional–and often impatient–translation from Ilse.

One day, he said, after my mother and I were already gone, Paul got the same kind of letter my father had received, warning him that if he did not rid himself of his "Jewish trash," others would, in order to "purify the country." Although there had not been a lot of anti-semitic violence in the area, there had been enough so that Paul knew that something could easily happen to Hannah–and to him, for that matter. At the time, there still seemed the possibility that the whole Nazi era might end soon–in a couple of years, anyway. Some still believed that Nazism was a kind of temporary insanity engendered by economic collapse, and as Germans regained economic security and a place of respect in the world, they would replace the Nazis with a kinder, gentler regime. So Paul thought if Hannah could drop out of sight until that happened, they would live happily ever after.

But where could Hannah go? Her father had died when she was a child, and her mother had died just the year before. Hannah had virtually no family–no brothers or sisters, no uncles or aunts, no cousins with whom she'd kept in touch. When she married Paul, he became her whole life. And although Paul had some modest resources, he could not have taken any money out of the country, or sent any with her: they lived primarily on what Paul made as a teacher, and though Hannah had also studied art, she had never held a job.

Paul had a sister, Lise, with whom he had always been extremely close. Lise was a pianist who hadn't married, partly because she had come home after her studies to keep house for her sick mother. Paul and Lise's father had died when they were still young, leaving only his name. Paul's mother had taught music at the school where Paul now taught painting. When her mother died, that ended the pension she and Lise had been living on. Lise gave piano lessons, but not enough to make a living. Paul and Hannah had discussed having Lise come to live with them, but Lise had put them off.

Paul let everyone know that Hannah was leaving. When asked, he said she was going to stay with friends in the south of France. He was deliberately vague about it, but the few people to whom he mentioned it were more interested that she was leaving than where she went. (And, I thought, perhaps other, more sympathetic listeners did not want to know because they couldn't help.) One day, with a couple of stops to pick up traveling items in Stammbüttel to make her departure a matter of public record, Paul drove her the fifty miles to Hanover and put her on an early evening train for Munich. They said goodbye; she cried.

The next day, Lise moved into Paul's house. It was the most natural thing in the world, since he was now alone. But in fact what had happened was that Hannah had got off the train at the next city. There she went to a cafe near the station that she and Paul had picked out a month earlier, and had coffee. It was, Paul had told him later, like an old spy film. When Paul came into the restaurant, Hannah ignored him, paid her check and left. Paul looked around as if he was expecting someone, waited a while, and left. When he went back to his car, which he had parked around the back in a small, dark side street, Hannah had already climbed into the back seat and hidden under a blanket. Paul drove off. When they got out into the country, Hannah got into the trunk of the car and Paul drove on. Paul told Father that he had never been so afraid in whole life. He drove the whole way without breathing, my father said. He kept finding himself holding his breath and getting dizzy, he was so tense. But there weren't a lot of road blocks in this part of Germany then, and when Paul made it to about ten miles from Stammbüttel, he was just beginning to think he was in the clear, when he came around a curve and there was a police checkpoint.

Paul thought it was the end. Visions of a future painted by a contemporary Hieronymos Bosch veered through his mind. For a split second he even thought of stepping on the accelerator and flying through it. But instead, he stopped. A policeman checked his papers and walked off with them. As Paul waited with alternate routes and possibilities swarming though his mind, the policeman came back with an SS officer. At that moment, Paul told father, he gave up. Paul told him that he will always remember that moment as if it had been the moment of his death. He didn't know how, but he was sure they knew everything and he waited for them to tell him to open his trunk and get Hannah out. Then the officer–who was in his full black uniform with the skull-and-crossbones insignia–leaned forward with a smile and politely asked him in the most casual way if he would take him to Stammbüttel: he had had car trouble and needed a lift.

Paul said that compared to his expectations, driving back to Stammbüttel with an SS officer in the front seat and Hannah in the trunk was a piece of cake–not the phrase my father used, but that was the gist. Paul dropped the officer at a local police station and headed home. When he arrived, Lise ushered a sleepy and confused Hannah into the attic, where she stayed for the next six years.

"*Das ist unglaublich....* That is unbelievable!" Ilse said.

"For all these years, no one even guessed that he was hiding a Jew? He was a lucky man."

"*Ich habe oft darüber nachgedacht....* I have thought about that often since he told me," my father said. "He could not have done it without Lise, but he also did not have to deal with anyone else, in the house or out of it. He lives almost in the forest."

"*Aber hat niemand versucht....* But didn't anyone try to find out what happened to Hannah?" I asked. "Didn't they have any friends who worried about her?"

Both Ilse and my father regarded me carefully. In retrospect, I think they were trying to figure out how to explain the way a person that leaves one's social world tends to sink from sight as if they had stepped into one of the La Brea tar pits in Los Angeles. Those pits swallowed small insects and saber-toothed tigers the same way a person who leaves their job suddenly finds their 'buddies' at their old office no longer taking their calls; the way a woman who separates from her husband suddenly finds that all their married friends no longer have time to talk to her on the phone, never mind inviting her to dinner.

"*Offenbar, nicht....* Apparently no one did. Just as I did not. Paul said she was gone. I knew he cared for her, but he did not seem to want to speak about it, and I did not feel I could do anything. So I did not ask."

I understood something that had been bothering me most of my life. Maybe I wasn't wanted, I had always thought, but I always assumed I had not been forgotten. I had always thought of my father thinking of me, wondering where I was, what I was doing, what I looked like. Now I thought, maybe that none of that was true. Maybe he didn't think of me, or wonder where I was, or what I looked like. Maybe I had dropped into a tar pit in his mind and was a paleontological item in his consciousness, something that only an unusual event or a rare encounter might dig up–until I came back into his life. And when I left Stammbüttel, I would be returned to distant memory. Just as my mother and I had left one day, not to be met at some assigned place and reclaimed despite great danger and cherished at great risk for many years, but instead, consigned to a distant past and forgotten.

I was feeling sorry for myself when I glanced at Ilse. She still had a look of disbelief. "*I kann das nicht glauben*.... I cannot believe that," she said shaking her head indignantly, as if she could turn back the clock and prevent this affront to the security of the Reich.

My father shrugged. Most people, he told Ilse, still don't know. They think Hannah just came back after the War. That's what Paul and Hannah told people when they asked. Most people, he said, did not really want to know. Besides, at the time Hannah 'came back,' people were so involved in putting their own lives back together that they were not even interested.

"*Was hast du darüber gedacht*.... What did you think about it, when Paul told you the story?" I asked.

My father looked at me. I think he understood what I was asking, and in a way, he answered me.

"*Ich bewunderte ihn*.... I admired him. I could not have done that. Where could I have hidden someone? It was not possible."

That was certainly true. On the other hand, I thought that even if he had had a willing sister and a house in the country he would not have done it. I stopped wanting to hear what he was saying, and wished he would just shut up about it. He must have caught the look in my eye, because he took his last sip of cognac, looked at his watch, asked Ilse if she was coming up, and when she said, "*In einem Moment*," said his goodnights and went upstairs.

Ilse sat scrutinizing her glass of cognac with a stern, displeased expression. She opened her mouth a couple of times, but each time she closed it again and went back to inspecting the glass.

I realized I wasn't really keen on finding out what she thought of Father's story. The way she took the news, it was likely that what she thought was not going to endear her to me further. When she finally spoke, all she said was, "We will leave for the Mittelball at six o'clock tomorrow evening," getting up and collecting the glasses. "For this you will need a party dress." She gave my outfit a caustic once-over.

"I think I have something that will be okay," I said.

"Good," she said, stopping at the door. "Everyone will be there, and they will be very interested in how you look." After another long, dissecting glance, tossing back a final *"Gute Nacht,"* she went through the door.

"Gute Nacht," I called after her. I decided to wait until I was sure both she and Father were through with the bathroom before I went up to use it. I looked around for something to read, but everything was in German; I was tired of slogging around in German. I flipped through *Der Spiegel*, Germany's version of *Newsweek,* and looked at the pictures and read the captions. Patrice Lumumba was ripping around the Congo; Hamarskjold was ripping around Africa; DeGaulle was still politicking to free France from its postwar government, and Marilyn Monroe was not yet terminally depressed.

By now it was eleven: I didn't hear anybody moving, and it seemed as good a time as any to soak in a bath with a book–in English. I had brought a couple with me.

When I turned the light on in my bedroom, the bed looked as if someone had been lying in it and tidied it up, but ineptly. I had made it in the morning before I left, and didn't remember sitting on it when I changed for dinner, but I decided I must have, because there it was. The books were still in my suitcase, so I picked it up and lugged it over to the bed. Even though I had unpacked, it was heavy. In Paris I had bought gifts-of-the-traveler-returning for a couple of friends. With a swing, I lifted it up and it landed with a flat and ponderous smack in the center of the bed.

I was about to give thanks that there was no one below and stepped forward to pull the suitcase toward me when something dark and shining came flying off the wall in my peripheral vision with a tiny, crunching sound. It was so unexpected, the house was so quiet, that it caught me completely off guard. Before I could see what it was I let out an enormous shriek, one suitable to a Vincent Price movie with *both* Peter Lorre and Bela Lugosi in full regalia.

The next instant there was a thump and a crunch of glass, as the top of the big heavy mirror over the bed hit the edge of my suitcase and the bottom landed clean across the pillows. If I had been lying there, my head would have been in the way, and my way might have been out of this world. I let out another shriek for good measure and then put a hand over my mouth, stupidly concerned that I might wake someone.

I heard a door slam and my father's voice calling, "*Was ist? Was ist los?*.... What's the matter?" and the sound of his steps on the stairs. I opened my mouth, but nothing came out of it. He came on down and stuck his head in the door. "Leni? *Was ist los?*"

I found my voice. It was cool. "Oh," I said, as if I had dropped a fork while setting the table, "*Es tut mir leid*.... I'm sorry to have disturbed you." I gestured toward the mess on the bed. "I'm afraid this old mirror fell down."

His eyes took it in and widened. He said, "*Gott im Himmel*," staring at the broken mirror as if it were an apparition. Then he said, "Ach!" and turned to me. He stepped over to me and put his hands on my shoulders and said with real concern, "*Bist du in Ordnung?*...Are you all right?"

I nodded without saying anything. It was the first time my father had touched me. I focused on it completely. I felt his hands on my shoulders and I saw him in front of me. I looked at his aging face and the way the dueling scar tucked at the skin of his cheek, his pale blue eyes and thin lips, and a strand of hair that fell in a point to the side of one of his arched, even eyebrows that were raised and brought together in concern for me.

"*Gott sei dank*," he said, dropping his hands and turning to the mess on the bed. Ilse entered and took it in at a glance.

"*Gott im Himmel*," she said–rather faintly, as if echoing my father. Then she turned to me and asked, "Are you hurt?" I shook my head. I was out of words again. I could still feel my father's hands on my shoulder, as if they had left a residue. Ilse stepped up to the bed, and a puzzled look came over her face. "What," she said, "is that?" pointing to a piece of string that had been tied around the nail that had fallen off, and to the picture wire that had held the mirror to the wall all these years.

Now my father's brows came down and knitted themselves almost together over the bridge of his nose. "*Ich weiss nicht*....I don't know." He leaned over the bed and pulled on the string. It went over the top of the headboard. "*Was macht das hier?*...What is it doing there?" He looked at Ilse and then at me.

I looked at the string and shrugged. The feeling in my shoulders had faded. I didn't know. I assumed it had been holding something up. But while everything was sort of old–the paper covering the back of the mirror had cracked and curled with age–the string looked relatively new and clean.

I looked at Ilse. It was as if she were suddenly vibrating to a different frequency, taut and sharp. She looked at the string, at my father, and then at me. Her eyes narrowed slightly. My father tugged at the string that ran over the headboard. It was connected to something at the other end. He shook his head. "*Es scheint mir unsinnig....* It does not make any sense..." Suddenly he stopped and drew in a long breath. He stood up frowning.

Ilse shook her head. "I think it is best," she said, "if we just clean it up so we can all go to bed."

I looked at the mess. It was going to take some doing. "Let me get my suitcase off the bed," I said and tried to pull it away from the mirror. It was stuck. My father stepped forward and lifted the top of the mirror away. It took some effort. The frame was very heavy. As I pulled the suitcase out, a shard of glass shaped like the blade of a long, pointed knife came away with it. It glittered dangerously in the light. I lifted it off gingerly and held it out. I looked at my father and at Ilse. Both of them were staring at it with an open-eyed fascination that was very disconcerting, but my fathers look darkened. I put it back on the bed next to the other shards and put my suitcase on the floor. My father lowered the mirror back onto the bed.

"*Ilse, helf mir....* help me," he said as he stepped forward and untied the string. The knot was tight, but he worked it deftly and delicately until he could pull out the nail and release the knot. He folded the eiderdown around the mirror, glass and all. I tried to help but Ilse was already there, and the two of them carried it over to the window where they laid it down on the floor, the broken glass tinkling with deceptive innocence.

Ilse checked the pillows for more broken glass, wrapped the mysterious string into a little coil and pushed it over the top of the bed so that it fell behind the headboard. She gave a satisfied nod and said, "I will get you another eiderdown. There is one upstairs." She turned to my father and put her hand on his shoulder. "*Komm, Franz. Wir werden das morgen besprechen....* We will sort this out in the morning." My father shook his head.

"Nein," he said, hitting his left hand with his right fist. "*Das kann nich warten....* This will not wait." He left the room and Ilse followed him out.

I sat down on the chair. I didn't feel anything, but when I looked down, my hands were shaking. When Ilse came back, she was carrying a clean sheet and another eiderdown, wrapped in an immaculate cover of old white linen with a row of buttons on one side. I helped her put them on the bed. She surveyed the bed with housewifely satisfaction and then looked up at the pale outline left by the old mirror. "Now nothing more can fall down on you." There was no emotion in her voice.

"*Gute Nacht*, Ilse," I said in German. Ilse said, "Good night, Lene," and went back upstairs.

I closed the door and looked at the bed. I wasn't too eager to sleep in it. I lifted up the eiderdown and poked it. The mattress rustled slightly. An old horsehair mattress, I thought. I put my hand between the mattress and the bed's heavy side frame. There were two fairly thin mattresses, and when I lifted them, there was an old coil spring underneath. Without thinking too much about why I did it, I lay down and looked under the bed, a space of about six inches. It was dark, but it wasn't very dusty. I reached out my arm and felt around for the string. When I touched it, my heart jumped and my hand jumped away too, scratching itself on the open underside of the spring. I didn't really want to find it. It was like touching a bug or a snake that you suspected might be there but hoped that it wasn't. I sucked on the scratch on the back of my hand and reached back in and ran my fingers along the string to where it was attached. I lay there as my eyes became accustomed to the low light, and I could see where it was tied to one of the coils.

I stared at the tied string in the dimness. I understood, even though I didn't want to: the mirror was rigged to fall down when I got into the bed. But my next thought was: How stupid can those boys be? I was not a cartoon. Didn't they realize that the mirror would do more than give me a bump on the head? But what could I do? I was a guest in my father's house. What would he say if I claimed my brothers were trying to kill me?

I was going upstairs to the bathroom, when through the closed door of the boys' room I heard Hans say loudly over the full-volume sobs emanating from Gustav, "*Wir wollten nur*.... We only wanted her to leave."

"*Gott im Himmel*!" my father shouted. "She will leave Monday, and while she is here, she is my daughter and our guest. These pranks must stop. That mirror could have killed her!"

There was a silence. I stood at the top of the stairs and thought I should get out of there, but I couldn't move. What could they say? I had to know. There was a silence, then I heard Gustav speak, but he mumbled. I couldn't understand anything but the word "*Geld*.... money."

"*Was*!?" My father almost barked the words. "*Was sagst du*?...What are you saying?" Then his voice softened. "*Wo hast du*.... Where did you get such a crazy idea?"

One of the boys mumbled something. I started to take a step when my father said incredulously, "*Deine Tante Ilse*?...That is utter nonsense!"

There were sounds of protest from both boys and then my father's voice was suddenly nearer, as if he were about to open the door. I heard only, "*Ich will nicht*.... I will not listen to such nonsense," before I was released from the spell and darted into the bathroom, closing the door as fast and as quietly as I could behind me. I closed the toilet seat and sat down with my head on my hands.

Even though I knew they didn't like me, it still came as a shock to learn that they really were concerned that I was after money. I had been so intent on my emotional relationship to my father that I hadn't even considered an economic one, let alone determine that I had any actual rights in the matter. I had to agree with my father. The idea that I could take their money even if I wanted to was nonsense, although the exchange did shed some light on the conversation he and I had on the road to Stammbüttel: he *had* been concerned that I would have financial expectations, and he tried to tell me he had obligations he considered more important than the one he might have to me.

Now Ilse's pointed conversation of the first night, when she told me of her expectations for her children, and her children's children, made more sense. She had warned me not to stand in their way. Still...I shook my head. The boys may be disturbed, having lost their mother and all, but I still couldn't see Ilse inciting them to...kill me. I got up to brush my teeth but I felt ill. I was scared. I sat down on the side of the tub. Maybe I should leave. Now. But then I thought, No. I'm not finished...and I'm not scared enough to run.

My father, I thought as I finally brushed my teeth, was on my side–although I should have begun to wonder what that counted for when the rest of the family was arrayed against me. The reason I didn't, I think, was because–like my father–I was unwilling to believe that it would go any further. Now that they had laid out their cards for him, I thought, my father would bring all of them to their senses and protect me. Even now, I think Ilse was not participating in the boys' schemes. Rather, they were mining the vein of paranoia she had planted with her belief that I was out to corner the Göring "fortune" or any part of it. It was, after all, something she would do if she were me. She would not have believed–ever–that it was not something I had in mind, and if she ever had believed that, she would have thought me a complete fool for not pursuing it.

Chapter 10

The next morning, I overslept. I woke up to hear Anni knocking on my door, calling my name. When I answered, she said Wolf was on the phone. I followed her into the living room where she pointed to a small black telephone that must have dated from before the war. When I said hello with a yawn, Wolf laughed and said, "So. You are sleeping on this beautiful morning?"

I looked outside. It was another clear, sunny day and I was about to make some joke about sleeping late when I remembered last night. It took the shine out of the sun for a moment. "Well, I had a rather exciting evening," I said.

"Truly?" he said. "I love Paul and Hannah, but I have never thought of them as 'exciting'."

I gave a short laugh. "I'll tell you later," I said in a low voice. In a more cheerful tone I said, "So Hannah's already called you."

"Yes. She has invited us to lunch. I said I had other plans, but I allowed her to 'twist my arm.'" He used the term as if he were taking it out of mothballs. "I hope that will be all right with you."

On the one hand, I really looked forward to going to the Kurzeldt's–in a way, I was ready to move in if they asked me. On the other–before I was nearly killed by the mirror–I had envisioned a day with just Wolf and me, getting, at the least, better acquainted. "Sure," I said. "You can twist my arm. I'll go quietly."

"Not too quietly, I hope," he said in real sweet way. "Being quiet is not your most endearing characteristic."

I went to get dressed. As I walked in, I saw the eiderdown folded around the mirror, lying under the window. The sun shone innocently on the damn thing, which had taken on such a sinister cast in my mind that I didn't even want to look at it.

As this was the late 'fifties, even lunch in the country was a blouse and slacks and makeup. When I was done, I shut the door behind me and went out to find coffee and a roll waiting for me. I had forgotten about breakfast, but Anni hadn't. I was drinking the coffee and was halfway through the roll when Wolf arrived.

As he came in the door looking very energetic, I looked at him carefully. I hadn't remembered that his hair was light brown and slightly curly, which showed because Wolf wore it longer (longer than men did in the States back then, where half-inch sides with a longer flip at the top were the almost military norm) and combed back into waves from which a couple of curls escaped onto his forehead. He was as tall and as thin as I remembered, and he wore the same tweed jacket he'd worn yesterday, except his shirt, starched collar and all with two faint wide ocher-colored lines running repetitively over its ironed whiteness, was open at the neck, his tie loosened into a careless pendant below the first button. His nose–when he turned his head sideways–was as big as I remembered.

But I saw that even as he was walking in, greeting Anni, accepting an offer of coffee and sitting down–almost without mishap except for catching his toe on the chair as he pulled it out as anyone might and lifting his foot out of the way at the same moment as he sat, so that he sort of launched himself down into the chair rather than merely lowering himself into it–even as he was doing all these things he was checking me out too, seeing if the person he remembered from yesterday, the person he was clearly looking forward to seeing again was the same person who was now looking at him and sort of smiling while trying to swallow a piece of roll and return his "Hello" with her own.

"Having breakfast," I said, as if he'd asked me.

"So I see," he said. "We are not expected at the Kurzeldts until half-past twelve. So we can take our time–and you might even have time to digest it." Annie brought him coffee, touching him lightly on his shoulder as she put it down in front of him, so that he turned and seeing her tender, smiling face looking down on him, gave her a radiant smile back from which she immediately turned away into herself as if it were more than she had a right to expect, but looking pleased all the same. And for a moment I thought of her with an entire life spent on other people's lives, and wondered if she had ever even for a little while had a life she could call her own in the way we think we call our lives our own–even as we spend them almost entirely following routes that have been laid down for us.

"What do you know about Anni?" I said to Wolf as she disappeared through the kitchen door.

"What do you mean?" Two sharp vertical furrows appeared over the sharp, narrow bridge of his nose. With his glasses, it gave him an owlish look. "Anni has always been...Anni." He sat back in his chair as if that settled it.

I smiled, full of overbearing wisdom and feminine insight. "But that's just what I mean. She's just `Anni' to you. But what about her personal life; you know, the life she has apart from taking care of everyone in this family–everyone who'll let her, anyway."

He smiled and shook his head. "Leni," he said, using the diminutive form of my name which made him sound instantly older and wiser, "Leni, you are talking from another world, another planet. Anni does not have a 'personal life' in the way that you mean. She came to the Görings from an orphanage. She was trained as a children's nurse and housekeeper."

"Just like Jane Eyre."

He looked blank again. "*Jane Eyre*," I said, "is one of the classics of English literature, and Jane is an orphan who is trained as a children's governess. Of course, the lord of the manor falls in love with her and marries her in the end–after various vicissitudes. But it is hard to believe that this was still happening in the twentieth century."

Wolf had started drinking his coffee, but now he was laughing so that his coffee cup just made it to the saucer before he spilled it. "Leni, Leni," he said, still laughing, "one moment you are so sophisticated, so, so..." He waved his hand in a circle to catch the word he wanted, but it came up German–"so *weltlich*,...so worldly, and the next, you are..."–he made the motion again–*weltfremd!*"

"World-strange," I said. "You mean unworldly–right?"

He nodded. I never knew what to say when people described myself to me. I really wasn't clear enough about myself to set him right if he was wrong, or to agree if he was right. Growing up in too many places can do that to you. What had been right in Stammbüttel had been dead wrong in Edinburgh where my mother had stopped in her flight to America, and what had finally been right in Edinburgh had been a disaster in Wilton, Connecticut, my first American foster home. It had taken a lot of fine-tuning to get most of it right so I could move through the world without stumbling.

"So!" Wolf said, changing the subject. "What happened last night that was so exciting?"

I must have winced. "What's wrong?" Wolf said. "It can't have been that terrible."

I heaved a large sigh. "Wolf, it really was. I could have been killed. The mirror over my bed fell on my pillow. If my head had been on it…" I put my head in my hands. It suddenly hurt.

"That is terrible. How fortunate that you were not lying down." He sighed too. "These are very old houses. I suppose, finally, the…"

He stopped, because I was shaking my head. "No, Wolf," I said. "The nail that had held up the mirror all these years did not let go all by itself. It had help. And I'm afraid I know who helped it."

"What do you mean, 'It had help?' You mean someone in this house did this…deliberately?" I nodded.

His expression became a little wary. I could see him thinking that he might have been wrong about me, that I was after all crazy. He decided on a reserved listening stance and said, "Why do you think that?"

I was about to launch into a detailed description of the entire event, when the way he was looking at me–as if I might, after all, really be a paranoid case, a crooked offshoot of the Görings that should have stayed three thousand miles away after all–got to me, and I said, "Wolf, you've got to see this for yourself. Come on," and headed for my room. He looked at me doubtfully, but he followed me. The mirror in its wrap was still under the window. As I folded back a part of the eiderdown, the shards tinkled with a sinister music that gave me a chill. I covered it up again, strode over to the bed, and knelt down. "Come on Wolf. Stop looking like that and look at this." I lay down on my back and looked under the bed. In the daylight, the string and its knot were clearly visible.

Wolf knelt down gingerly and without lying down lowered his head to the floor and turned it sideways to follow my arm. "What is that?" he said.

"It's a string, Wolf," I said, the way you say it when you imply that someone is an idiot. "Let me show you," and I pulled out the other end of the string neatly coiled with the nail still attached. He still looked doubtful, so I stood up and took the string and ran it over the headboard. "If you loosened the nail that held the mirror so that it was hanging by a crumb of plaster, and then you ran a string from the mirror to the bed spring…"

"Anyone getting into the bed would depress the springs and pull on the nail and..." He looked at me with the light dawning. When I told him about throwing my heavy suitcase on the bed and triggering the trap, he took both my hands and said, "Ach, Leni. I am very sorry. It was very difficult to believe what you were telling me. But you are right..." He closed his eyes as if they could shut out what he thought.

"Yes," I said. "I think those boys are in serious trouble. I don't think anybody realizes how much their mother's death must have affected them. Do you think there's any possibility of their getting into psychotherapy?"

Wolf had listened sympathetically, still holding my hands until I got to "psychotherapy," and then he dropped them and a bewildered grin crept over his face. "Psychotherapy?" he said incredulously. "A Göring in psychotherapy? It is most unlikely. I think this is something your father will handle without the assistance of learned doctors of psychiatry."

Coming as I did from New York, where nearly everybody had consulted a psych-something at sometime in their lives–not necessarily with much success but with faith in the process if not in the practitioners–this was a strange attitude. "Wolf," I said. "This isn't a matter of a spanking, or something. These kids are out of their minds."

"Ach!" said Wolf, looking at his watch. "We must go. The Kurzeldts' house is almost thirty kilometers from here."

We were on the road in minutes. We passed from the old town as Wolf's car hummed over well-paved roads into farm country, through hills and woods and more farms, and drove without speaking for a while. I was glad for the silence, but I realized I had to tell Wolf what I knew, so that he would know I knew. It was like a secret, keeping other people out, so I said, "Wolf, my father told me last night about Hannah and Paul–during the War."

"Good," Wolf said. "I am glad. I was thinking about telling you, but I did not know where to begin."

"Ilse didn't know about it."

"What did she say when your Father told her?"

"She was in a state of shock. It was as if hiding a Jew in the middle of Nazi Germany violated her basic beliefs."

Wolf nodded. "That is Ilse," he said.

"But you knew?" I said. "You were little. How could you know?"

We stopped in silence to let a large herd of sheep cross the road, baahhing and bleating, noting the small lambs amid a crush of gray woolly sheep keeping together around a shepherd carrying a crook out of a biblical illustration, as several dogs ran around and barked staccato commands. Wolf turned off into a well-packed dirt road that turned tightly as we climbed through a dense wood.

As we drove out of the wood into a large high meadow of delicate green grasses scattered with flowers, Wolf blew his horn twice. I saw at the far end of the meadow a fair-sized two-story house with a wide roof that peaked over the front and sloped almost to the top of the ground floor. The roof was gray slate; the walls were wood and stucco, the wood beams breaking the stucco into clearly defined triangles above ground floor windows that looked out over boxes of newly flowering geraniums. As we approached it, the front door opened and a woman stepped out and waved. It was Hannah. The horn must have been an old signal between them, I thought.

She waited as we drove up and parked at the side of the house under a large tree that spread its freshly-leaved branches over a great shaded circle interrupted only slightly by the leaves. As we walked over to her, she looked at us fondly, including me as if she had known me all her life.

"Leni," she said, smiling and shook my hand. Then she turned and said "Wolfi!" and gave him a big hug, which he returned in a loose, slightly bashful way that seemed left over from younger years. She motioned me into the house and took Wolf's hand to bring him in, asking him small personal questions as we entered.

We came into a big room, dim in the darkness to our unadapted eyes, gradually brightening as I looked. The front of the room reached to the eaves and spread to the sides of the house under the exposed rafters. In the rear, the room yielded to other structures, at the top of which was a railed walk, leading, it appeared, to bedrooms upstairs. In the center, toward the back, was a huge stone fireplace where the makings of a fire had been set on oversize andirons that extended out into the wide stone hearth. Several large comfortable-looking and well-worn leather upholstered chairs of Bauhaus vintage sat around it, along with several small tables stacked with books, newspapers and magazines. On the left, there was a large desk and worktable covered with stacks of papers. A long refectory table with an embroidered runner down its center, surrounded by eight side chairs of varying but related styles, stood to the right. It was set for four at one end, with large heavy-looking stoneware plates and hearty-looking goblets and plain, modern silver. Several well-worn oriental rugs of different Near-Eastern provenances were laid among these three islands of the Kurzeldts' life. On the walls were several small paintings of flowers in old-fashioned carved gilt frames. I wondered if they were Paul's.

"You like the house?" Hannah stood beside me. She had on a large, white apron over a white blouse and dark green slacks.

"It's beautiful," I said. It was.

"Komm," Hannah said, motioning to me. "Wolfi, go to the studio and get Paul," she said to Wolf. "The lunch is almost ready."

I followed her past the dining table into the kitchen, where a youngish, heavy-set woman was preparing a salad. As Hannah introduced her to me as Gertrud, she gave me a short, expressionless nod. A small cake glazed only on top with a hard layer of very dark chocolate sat on a cake stand in the middle of a large, heavy kitchen table. There were several covered pots on the big old cast-iron stove with an oven on the side. The air swam with the smells of cooking.

"Here is the wine," Hannah said to me. "You can put it on the table. It is a little cold, but it will be just right by the time we sit down to eat." She laughed. "It always takes Paul at least twenty minutes to get out of the studio–more sometimes. He is like that. It takes him a long time to start, and it takes him a long time to stop." She laughed again. "But Wolf knows. I have sent him often to get Paul."

As I opened the wine–it was an Alsatian *Spätlese*–I thought about Hannah's laugh. For somebody who had spent seven years hiding in an attic in fear of her life, she seemed very happy. At the time, I wondered about it. I wondered if you had something terrible happen to you and you survived it intact to enjoy the world again, did that make you more capable of happiness than someone who had never looked at their life as something that was almost lost and then regained? Now I know that this is not the way people are. Some who never got more seriously lost than being unpopular in school go around forever digging up their old unhappiness so that nothing else can ever grow, so the world they walk on is perpetually mud and dust. Some people came back from Dachau and they raise their face to feel a spring rain, and they smile–like Hannah. Which is not to say they ever forget. But when they were in Dachau, they were in Dachau. And when they are making lunch for friends in their beautiful house, they are making lunch for friends on a late spring day. I think, now, that doing it is partly a gift and partly a choice. Then, however, I just wondered how Hannah managed it.

Wolf appeared at the door and announced that Paul would be along shortly. Could he, Wolf, help? At which Hannah put her hands on her hips and gave Wolf a mock command not to return until he got Paul out of the studio. Wolf smiled at me, shrugged and went back to retrieve Paul.

Hannah shook her head. "Wolf *knows* that Paul will take even longer if he does not wait for him." She took up a small tureen and started to ladle a wonderful-looking stew into it. I was about to ask her what it was when she said, "It is goulash." She handed the tureen to me and picked up a bowl filled with tiny new potatoes, golden with butter, each potato carefully peeled after it was boiled to keep its original smooth shape. We had put on all the other dishes–a heap of slender asparagus, a quarter of a huge loaf of a gray-beige rye, a crock of pale, sweet butter that looked like it had just been made–when Wolf and Paul came in, and we all sat down to eat.

We spent some time serving and getting served and eating. The food tasted like it had smelled, hearty and subtly flavored at the same time. The asparagus, Hannah said, came from her garden. The wine was light and slightly sweet with a dry aftertaste, and fitted perfectly with the dinner. We were working on the second bottle and finishing the food on our plates when Hannah patted Wolf's arm and said, "It is so nice to have you here again, Wolfi."

"Yes," Wolf said, putting down his glass. "It has been almost a year, I think." Then Paul and Hannah beamed at Wolf fondly.

"How do you all know each other–other than living in the same town and knowing the same people? I mean…" It seemed like an ordinary question, but as uncovering nests of yellowjackets seemed to have become my specialty since I arrived in Stammbüttel, I realized from the stillness that dropped over us that I had stepped right onto one.

Chapter 11

The affectionate silence we had been sitting in became charged with meaning I could not fathom. Paul and Wolf exchanged significant looks; then both of them looked at Hannah, who looked away from them to me and then to her glass. I mumbled, "Look, if it's a long story, you don't have to tell me now."

Hannah shook her head. "No, Lene," she said. "It is all right, your question. It is just that the answer is full of difficult memories." She was silent again. The two men sat still, their fixed, blank faces like manikins as she spoke in a calm, even voice that had something of the schoolteacher patiently explaining a complex equation.

"Before the war, Wolf and our son, Rainer, were best friends." She paused and looked at me. "Actually, you knew Rainer, Leni, when you were a little girl in Stammbüttel. You did not see him often, but your mother and I were very friendly, and I often visited your parents with him. And also, Paul and Franz had been best friends since they were boys."

I cleared my throat. "Last night..." I hesitated. "Father told me about you...and Paul. During the War."

"*Wirklich?*–Really?" Paul said, clearing his throat as if he had just found his voice.

"Yes," I said. "He told me about it, but he didn't mention you had a son."

"No?" Paul said. "Hmmm." Suddenly Hannah got up.

"I will get the salad," she said.

I started to get up too. "I'll help," I said.

"No, no," Hannah said. "Gertrud will get everything else," and she went into the kitchen carrying the tureen. In a moment, Gertrud appeared and cleared the table, returning finally with salad plates of clear green glass, followed by Hannah bearing the salad itself in a smooth, dark wooden bowl.

Where was their son? Something terrible had happened. Sitting in that frozen torrent of feelings I had uncovered, I wished I could fold time back to before I had spoken.

When she had served us salad in the silence, Hannah said, speaking in a voice that was heavy and slow, "About Rainer, Wolf can tell you later. But about Wolf, I can tell you more," and she essayed a small smile at him.

"About 1943, it was, I think, Paul received a telephone call from Thomas, Wolf's father. Wolf and his family were living in Heldeschweig, and the Allies had begun to bomb the factories there. Wolf had often stayed with us before the War. He knew that Paul was living here with his sister, Lise, and he asked Paul to let Wolf stay with him for the summer, to get him out of the bombing. This, as you can imagine, put Paul in a very difficult position. Paul, of course, tried to…*Ausflucht nehmen*," Hannah turned to Wolf.

"Make excuses," Wolf said.

"Yes." Hannah folded her hands, one over the other. "Paul, of course, tried to make excuses." "But the more Paul said 'No,' the more Thomas insisted. As Paul said when he told me, it was the most natural thing for Wolf to come here. He and Rainer had been such good friends, and we and the Herzogs had always been very friendly. And now, here was Wolfi in danger and Paul apparently without a son. Paul was afraid that if he refused, Thomas would get suspicious. So finally Paul said, Yes, Wolfi should come in the summer as soon as school was over."

"Would Wolf's father have betrayed you?" It was strange to ask such a theatrical question and have it mean something concrete and personal, like 'Would he have turned you in, knowing you would be murdered, or worse?'"

Hannah looked at Paul with the question in her eyes. Paul said, "You know, I don't remember asking that even from myself. Even now, I don't know. I know we did not think we could risk it." He did not look at Wolf. Wolf frowned and looked at the table too.

Hannah spoke again. "When we knew Wolf was coming we were full of panic." She leaned her head wearily on the tips of her fingers and rubbed her forehead as she talked. "You must understand that at the time German children were good little Nazis: they loved their Führer, and Wolf was not an exception. But we did not believe we could keep the secret of my presence from him for very long. Already it was a miracle that we had not been found out, or even suspected. A miracle." She shook her head in wonder at the memory.

"Hannah is right," Wolf said. "We were all good little Nazis–and not such nice little Nazis either. When I arrived, I was upset, because my mother had not let me wear my Hitler Jugend shirt that day–out of deference to Paul, of course, but I could not be told that. I was also annoyed that my father was sending me to this farm, when all the red-blooded German youths who were too young to serve '*unser lieber Führer*' in the army wanted to be where the action was–at least, where bombs were falling. Fortunately, my father prevailed."

I vaguely remembered my own brief, juvenile swim in the tide of passion for 'our dear Leader' and waited for one of them to continue.

"We went on as we were, as if everything was normal, except of course that Hannah, who would come and stay with me after dark, now stayed in the attic," Paul said. "It was difficult for Wolf at first, because our life was so quiet for an active little boy who was used to a very stimulating time"–he threw Wolf a teasing glance–"preparing to conquer the world during the day, ducking bombs at night. Nothing we had or did was right. We would have to do things differently, he kept telling us, when the New Order got to this remote farm. And fortunately–as it turned out–there were no other children his age in the area."

"It took me a while, but it was not so bad," Wolf said. "You see, Paul is an amateur mathematician."

"Really?" I said. "Art and mathematics don't often mix."

"Like oil and water?" Paul smiled. "I suppose that is true, but for me, mathematics..." he shook his head. "For me it is not the elegant, creative mathematics that Wolf does, but the problem-solving kind. Mathematical puzzles. You know, like they have in your magazine, *Scientific American*–those I enjoy. And Wolf and I spent a lot of time together doing that. Already then he was so fast to see a solution. It was wonderful. And when I painted, he would draw. He has a certain graphic talent, our Wolfi," he said and patted Wolf's shoulder in a very fatherly way. "So," he finished, "we spent the summer together and became very good friends." He looked at Wolf fondly again.

"And Wolf...did he find out about Hannah?" I asked.

"Strangely enough, he did not," Paul said, shaking his head as Hannah had done before. "Not that summer, anyway. A few times, he almost did. But by that time, we had undone a little of the brainwashing that made Germany's littlest Nazis masters of suspicion. Wolf and I had many 'man-to-man' talks..." Paul and Wolf exchanged amused glances. "Wolf trusted us, so when we explained away things like noises and extra plates of food, we were able to convince him that it was all right. It was not until the next year, when Wolfi visited us again, that he found out."

"Yes, I remember," Wolf said. "I was very angry that you had not told me about Hannah before. All I could think of was that you had lied to me. I had trusted you and you had lied." He scowled and looked angry, remembering.

"Wolfi," Hannah said, reaching out and taking his arm as if she still needed to convince him. "How could Paul have told *dem kleinen Nazi Herzog* that he was hiding a *Jude*? What would *der gute kleine Nazi*.... the good little Nazi have done?"

Wolf gave a small, shy laugh. "You are right. You are right. Of course you could not have told me. But it took me a long time to understand. Paul had to talk to me again and again, isn't that so, Paul?"

Paul sat with his chin in on his fists and nodded and said, "But that was much later." Hannah rose and started to clear the table with Gertrud and asked Paul to bring the coffee. Wolf and I, cautioned to remain where we were, sat silent with our thoughts, half in the mundane world of cups and saucers and cream-and-sugar; half in imagined and real memories of war and betrayal and the danger of death.

Hannah and Paul settled down at the table amid the aromas of coffee and chocolate and the smell of the tiny, delicate wild strawberries that Hannah heaped onto the whipped cream she mounded on each piece of the cake. When we had tasted and appreciated the dessert, I wanted to ask about everything: just how Wolf had found out about Hannah? Where was Lise? What had happened to Rainer? But all I asked was, when had Wolf returned?

"Ah," said Paul, apparently relieved at what was a relatively simple question, "that was late in the War, when the Allies were halfway into Germany. Thomas asked us to take Wolfi again. The bombing of Heldeschweig was almost constant. The German cities were grim. Every day was like the last day on earth. I told Thomas that we were afraid here too. But Thomas said he was less afraid of the Americans than of the bombs. I could not disagree, although to myself and to Hannah I worried how we would explain to American soldiers that we were not their enemies?"

"How did you do that?" I asked.

"Lene, Lene," Paul said, waving my question away and laughing. "You will have to come and visit us again and I will tell you. But not today."

"Okay," I said. "But how did Wolf find out about Hannah?"

"It was rather strange," Hannah said. "Wolf was with us only a few weeks then. It was a difficult time. The Americans were moving toward us quickly. We were both hopeful and afraid. Every day the bombers flew over us on their way to a target, and one day–one cold, sunny afternoon, a plane dropped several bombs on that field."

Paul pointed to the flowered meadow we had passed as we approached the house. "It must have been an accident," he said. "We were very lucky they did not fall on the house. But it shook the house so hard I thought we were hit. I rushed upstairs to get Hannah. The whole house was shaking like in an earthquake!" His eyes were open wide, so that the whites made a ring around his pupils as if they were seeing the field go up in great geysers of dirt while the world shook.

"But I was already running down the stairs," Hannah said, "and so in the middle of this terrible bombing and Paul and I ran into each other and we reached out to each other, so..." she opened her arms and embraced the air. "And Paul, also, reached out to me, so..." and she embraced the air again. "But the house was shaking and we were both running and–*unglaublich!*... unbelievable!–we lost our balance and fell down the stairs together!"

Both Paul and Hannah started to laugh hysterically, as if they were telling an ordinary, peacetime story. I had been so involved with the life-and-death aspect that they caught me by surprise. I looked at Wolf. He was also looking from one to the other as if they and we were on totally different wavelengths. But then the picture of them–in the middle of all this awfulness–taking an ordinary pratfall...well...I love slapstick, and I started to laugh too, and so did Wolf and the four of us were covering out faces and holding our sides, and Paul kept thumping the table with his fist, and Hannah kept hitting her chest just under her collarbone as if to make herself stop, but she only laughed more, until we were all wiping our eyes and giggling and snorting and Paul said, "I did not think I would laugh that hard again before I died. I must thank you, Lene."

When we were quiet, and when Paul had poured us more coffee, I asked, "Were you hurt?"

"That was also very funny," Paul said, with a big smile. "We were not hurt from the bombs, but from the fall down the stairs!" He started to point to his arm, but had another fit of laughter.

"Pauli, genug–enough!" Hannah said, laughing too. "When we got up from the bottom of the stairs, Paul could not move his arm. He had broken it! It was not a serious break, *Dank Gott!*–but it took many weeks to heal."

Paul wiped his eyes again and took a sip of coffee. "But that was not the biggest joke that *der lieber Gott* played on us at that moment, because as soon as Hannah and I realized we were all right–except of course for my arm–we remembered that Wolf and Lise had gone for a walk. We were having terrible thoughts when the door opened and both of them ran in. You cannot imagine that moment. It was not one moment, it was many moments at once. You see, we were all so happy to see each other and to see that everyone was alive and in one piece. But then all of us realized that here were Wolf and Hannah–in the same room! *Mein Gott*! What a moment! None of us knew what to say!

We were all looking at each other, waiting, you know, for lightning to strike, to find something to say. Then, suddenly, Wolf said, 'Tante Hannah! *Du bist zurück gekommen!*...You have come back!' He looked at her, very surprised. And we all looked at each other again."

"Lise recovered first," Hannah said. "She came over and embraced me and told me how glad she was to see me again. Then Wolf looked at me and said, 'Where is your coat?' But I was very calm and said, 'I took it off. What has happened to your face?' And in fact, Wolf had scratched his face running back to the house. So I made a big fuss over Wolf, and we did not tell him the whole story until many days later. By then the Americans had captured our village, everything was confusion anyway, so everything ended happily–at least then." Then she said, "Wolfi, why don't you and Lene go for a walk in the forest a little. You can visit Paul's studio when you come back. It is already so beautiful and it is warm."

Wolf looked at me. I looked back. "Sure," I said, and we went out.

I followed Wolf behind the house to a path padded with dead leaves and patches of pine needles that led into the wood. The path went gently upward through columns of warm sunlight that rose through the softer coolness of the darker air under the cover of the trees. We didn't speak. From the moment we stepped onto the path, all my questions had disappeared, as if the light and air of the wood had blotted them up, leaving only the actual process of walking and breathing a new, unfamiliar atmosphere.

But while I was taking in everything I could absorb with my eyes and nose greedy for this new forest, I was intently aware of Wolf walking in front of me. For someone who was so uneasy in object-filled houses, constantly avoiding small entanglements with furniture, things and structural presences–like door frames–he moved easily along the path, so that, after about twenty minutes of walking, it was I who tripped on a root and went sprawling ungracefully into what was fortunately a nest of pine needles.

As I turned myself over and sat up, dusting myself off, Wolf knelt down beside me and I looked up directly into his face which hovered close to mine with a really sweet expression of concern, so that when he leaned even closer and started to kiss me very slowly and gently there really wasn't anything else that I could or wanted to do but kiss him back in the same way. I realized that I had been waiting for him to do this ever since he had kissed me before and I had wanted to see where the kiss was going. So we kissed like that for a while, just with our lips, very much like kisses I tasted years before but without clumsiness and confusion, and as we kissed I breathed in the sweet male scent of him and then our tongues touched, and we followed that until Wolf pulled away just a little bit and ran the tip of his tongue over my upper lip, and that was it, that little gesture lit up my whole body with a slow green flash. I raised my arms, and at the same time he lifted his arms and drew my body to him so nothing was holding us up and we fell down lying against each other and kissing and of course by then we wanted nothing so much as naked skin, but there we were, fully dressed in the some outpost of the Black Forest. I was running my hand down his neck to his back when there was a soft rustle above our heads and we both looked up to find ourselves eyes-to-eyes with a formidable-looking snake.

In my next second of consciousness we were standing up. Not much else had changed: the snake was still there, laid out in a long black waving line with a yellow pattern following the line down its back to its mean, shiny head with its golden eyes and its golden tongue flicking in and out, and Wolf and I were still body to body, his arms still around me. My hands were gripping his shoulders, and both of us were eyeing the snake, who was keeping his slanty eyes on us, his dim, reptilian brain snaking its way to making the choice between fight and flight.

I was hoping for the latter, when Wolf, without moving his head, said in a very soft voice, "Don't move. It is a viper. It is poisonous."

My feeling about snakes is very akin to my feeling about high, unprotected places: I can deal with them, but I prefer to avoid them. I just stood there, hoping the damn thing would go away. It took some more time, thinking its reptile thoughts. I became aware again of Wolf's body against mine. I relaxed a little and leaned against him. He tightened his arms round me slightly. As we stood there the snake–bored, I think, with the lack of entertaining movement–turned and wove away into the underbrush.

We both sighed and stepped away from each other. Wolf brushed the pine needles off his jacket and tucked his shirt into his pants. I brushed the pine needles off and tucked my blouse in. In a switch on the biblical version, the snake had lain in the way of temptation.

"Are you all right?" he said, after a minute.

"Yes," I said with a sigh of relief. "I'm okay. How about you?"

He laughed. "You might not believe it, but we German mathematicians are made of strong stuff. We spend a lot of time hiking and climbing around in the mountains around Heidelberg–unlike our American counterparts who prefer indoor sports, like drinking and eating. Snakes…"

"Oh, come on, Wolf," I said. "Don't carry on. You were not exactly ready to pet the animal yourself."

"You are right," he said smiling and took my hand. "But I was preoccupied. Come. We have time, I will show you my favorite place," and I went with him, walking for a little way holding hands until the trail narrowed again and I walked behind him in silence. At last we stepped out into a clearing to look for miles over a design of neat farms and small patches of woods threaded by roads and streams that occasionally flashed silver where the sunlight brushed them.

The last stretch had been fairly steep. I was a little out of breath, so I was glad when he took off his jacket and threw it down in front of a big granite boulder that had pushed its way out of the mountain as a convenient backrest and said, "Come. Sit here," and sat down himself. I sat down and he put his arm around my shoulder and we leaned back against the rock and looked quietly at the world below us for a long time.

Years later, I still wonder at that time we spent on the mountain, hardly knowing each other at all and yet perfectly in tune, breathing together as if we had been together a long time. We just sat and watched the world lie still under the late spring sun, letting our eyes rest on the hazy mountains that formed our horizon, until slowly my thoughts coalesced and wandered back to our lunch and the missing pieces of the conversation.

But it was Wolf who cleared his throat and said, "About Rainer," and sighed as he gently pulled his arm from my shoulders and hunched forward, wrapping both his arms around his bent knees as if to contain himself more. I braced myself as if against a cold wind, leaning back but folding my arms across my chest.

"It is a terrible story." He stopped. It was a good minute before he continued. "When Hannah 'went away,'" he said, emphasizing the words so that they carried all the connotations that were involved in the act itself, "she took Rainer with her."

I looked up surprised. "But my father never mentioned..."

"That Rainer was with her? Yes. I can't explain it, but nobody ever speaks of him. I spoke once to Uncle Franz about Hannah. We started to have a conversation, but when I mentioned Rainer, he stopped talking. He started to say something one or two times, and then he just shook his head and said, '*Schrecklich, schrecklich....* Terrible, terrible.' And that was the end of the conversation."

We were silent for a while. I thought I understood. Hannah survived, and that made a good story. But Rainer's fate left a radioactive zone of guilt around him.

"Rainer was never very strong. I remember that sometimes I could not visit him because he had a cold, or an earache, or something like that. It never stopped him from doing everything when he was with me, but...he wasn't naturally strong. The first winter...almost right after Hannah and he started hiding, he became ill. He became steadily worse. They tried everything. To cover up for the medicine Paul bought for him, Lise would pretend she was ill whenever anyone visited. But he still did not get better. Finally he got pneumonia. It was before antibiotics–even before sulfa. There was nothing they could do."

"Wasn't there one doctor they could trust?"

He turned to me and put his arm around my shoulders again. "Leni, Leni, you ask that? Then Germany was the country of the good Herr Doktor Mengele of Auschwitz and all the other doctors who participated in all kinds of experiments on human beings. Even if Paul and Lise didn't know about those good doctors, they knew they couldn't take that kind of risk. Paul said to me, when he told me, he said he would have been glad to die if it would have saved Rainer, and so would Hannah, but they knew…" His voice was bleak and flat as he talked, and as he spoke the first chilly breeze blew over us. "They knew enough," he said. "They knew that if they were taken, even if they lived, Rainer would be taken with them–perhaps taken away, and they would be powerless to help him. So.."

"My God," I said. "You mean…" and I covered my face because I did not want him to see the horrible expression that was seizing it, "…you mean they just had to watch him die?"

"Ya," Wolf said, almost wearily. "Yes. I think it almost killed them both. Lise too."

We sat for several minutes, me with my hands over my face, Wolf with his arm around me, both of us silent. Then I lay my head against his shoulder and he put his arm around me again and we both sat there, looking out over a landscape that had lost its charms, peopled as it was with those who would let a child die for the most stupid and primitive of reasons–because he belonged, they thought, to another tribe. And I knew as well that if I had not been lucky enough to have a mother that got me out, the child that died could have–would almost certainly have been me as well. At that moment, I loathed everything German more than I had loathed them during the war and more than I had loathed them after the war, when the evidence of their evil spilled out into the world in films and photographs of the camps. I began to hate the fact that I had German blood running through my arteries, although strangely enough I did not worry about the very German blood that was running through Wolf's.

Which was just as well. Now it is after Cambodia, after Yugoslavia, after Rwanda…and there is always Mylai. Monstrous as the Germans were, the Beast that rose in them is always just under the skin, waiting, waiting for another Hitler, another Pol Pot, another Milosevic to call it out to club and torture and kill even the smallest child in the name of tribal otherness, satisfying itself in the meantime with morsels of daily cruelties bestowed by one person on another. But even then, leaning as I did with my ear to Wolf's chest and hearing his German heart pump his German blood surely and evenly through the arm that held me, I swore a sort of oath in my heart that I would never allow the Beast to use me against anyone…even Germans.

Chapter 12

Wolf and I turned to look at each other, and we kissed, but it was a very different kiss from before. It was a kiss that was about everything that had been said and felt between us, a lost-and-found kiss, more serious than anything that had passed between us yet, as if knowing all these things had connected us. So he kissed me tenderly, and I kissed him tenderly back. As I rested my head on his shoulder, I opened my eyes and saw that the sun had moved much further than my eye expected.

"Wolf," I said, pushing myself away. "Wolf, look at the sun. I've got to get back and be ready by six."

"Why?" he said, as if I were making a completely unreasonable demand.

I said, "Because tonight is the Mittelball, whatever that is, and I have to go!"

Wolf looked at his watch. It was after four. We were about half an hour from Paul and Hannah's house, and the house was at least half an hour from my father's house, which would, if I was lucky, give me barely enough time to get ready.

Wolf heaved a regretful sigh that echoed my feelings. "Okay," he said, getting up and picking up his jacket. "But Paul will be very offended if we do not visit his studio, so we will have to go fast," and set a pace I just barely kept up with down to the Kurzeldt's. Just before we reached the end of the path where it opened onto the back of Paul and Hannah's house, Wolf stopped suddenly and turned. He grabbed me and held me and said, "Listen. I *have* to see you again."

I said, "Definitely. Tomorrow. But now you've got to get me..." I paused an instant because I almost said, 'home,' but I said, "get me back," instead. I gave him a fast kiss, but pulled away before it could get meaningful. He didn't insist, but kept his arm around my waist until we reached the back door and went in.

Hannah was in the kitchen. "Ilse called," she said with her eyebrows raised as she chopped parsley.

"What did she say," I asked.

"She wanted to know if you remembered the *Mittelball*."

I looked at Wolf and we both laughed. "Yes," I said. "I remembered the *Mittelball*. But I'm afraid if Wolf doesn't drive fast I will be late."

"Ach," she said and wiped her hands on her apron. "But you must go to the studio to see Paul." She smiled and shook her head regretfully but firmly, to say this was not something we could sidestep. "Wolfi, take Leni. Paul is expecting you."

Wolf took my hand, which he held tighter than was necessary, and led me to a door under the stairs, down another stair and through a hallway to a door that opened onto an artist's studio. It had been a two-car garage, with a wall of windows that looked out on the field where the bombs had fallen. Now the field was green flecked with white and red where daisies and poppies wavered in the soft wind of the late afternoon.

Bare stretched canvases leaned in stacks against the wall as did canvases in various stages of completion. A rack held finished paintings ordered by size, with the largest ones about two by three feet, the smallest barely a foot high. There were shelves of bottles of solvents and mediums and boxes of oil paints in tubes. A heavy wooden easel at center stage held the current canvas, a very nice painting-in-progress of flowers in a vase on a table, done in a loose, Expressionist style. Having spent Tuesday evenings hanging out at gallery openings on Tenth Street where Abstract Expressionist painters like Jackson Pollock and Franz Klein were holding forth against representation in Art, the work looked timid and old-fashioned.

Being used to an artist's environment in which expressing an opinion was often more important that having an original idea of one's own, I felt a little tense. Not that you were expected to give a critical evaluation of the artist's work–far from it: the idea was to say something knowledgeable and meaningful that would in one phrase indicate you were hip to the ideas the artist was supposed to be "struggling with" ("I really like the way you have those red brush strokes pulling forward against the blue ground") while being neither effusively complimentary or at all negative. At the same time, I was partly relieved of responsibility because I was a woman. In that very male chauvinist period of contemporary art, being a woman lowered an artist's expectation of me more than the fact that I wasn't an artist, because the greatest expectation a woman could have in that world was to be an Artist's

Wife. I was expected to know what I was talking about only the way women in an earlier time were expected to play the piano–as an ornament that increased their mating value.

I looked at Paul's paintings, trying to think of something appropriate to say that would belittle neither him nor me. As I dashed around in my mind like a cook checking her pantry for something to serve unexpected guests, Paul stood there cleaning one of his brushes, waiting, so I just said, "Paul, that is lovely." It would not have done on Tenth Street, I thought snobbily, but Tenth Street would never know I said it. Then, however, it turned out to be exactly the right thing. Both Paul and Wolf beamed.

"You like it?" Paul asked. I nodded. I did like it, despite what I saw as its flaws. "Your mother was always very enthusiastic about my flowers." I doubted that. My mother held no regard for modern art of any kind; her taste ran to the polished restraint of David. On the other hand, she would have had fewer pretensions about art than I did then, and felt freer to praise a friend's work simply because he was a friend. "Actually," Paul said with a small smile, "the two paintings in your father's living room I gave to her, more than to your father. But she had to leave them."

"I will have to look at them again all the more carefully," I said sincerely.

"Good, good," Paul said. We were silent for a moment, watching him think, until he spoke. "I will name the painting for the occasion," he said, tapping the air with his right forefinger. "Let me see," he said as he put down the brush he was cleaning and scratched the side of his neck with the other hand, leaving a small brown smudge. "I will call it 'The Visit.' Do you like that?"

"Oh, yes," I said with genuine enthusiasm. I liked the idea that the painting would hold something of my life in it as long as it lasted. Although the work of people without worldly reputations sometimes lasts no longer than they do, Paul's local reputation would enable "The Visit" to escape oblivion much longer. I imagined the painting hanging into the Twenty-first Century in a home in which I might not even be welcome, a closet memento of this visit.

"Good, good," Paul said again. "You have helped me. I did not have a name for this painting."

"In New York, the artist would name such a painting 'Untitled,'" I said. "Or, if he felt very traditional, he might call it 'Flowers in a Vase.'"

Paul laughed and shook his head. "Yes, yes," he said. "I of course read about what is happening in New York. It must be a very exciting place for a young artist."

"Their work is very different from yours," I said doubtfully.

"Of course. Of course it is," he said. "But I was trained in another time, in another world, really. I am too old to change, and I cannot even say I fully understand what the American artists are doing. But I can understand how they must feel! To be a young artist, trying out new ideas! It is wonderful!"

Wolf had listened quietly throughout this conversation, but now he looked at his watch. "Leni," he told Paul, "must be taken home to prepare for the Mittelball."

"Ach," Paul said. "So that is tonight? Summer is coming soon. That is what I remember. The Mittelball is always held at the edge of summer." He sighed. "I hated them. I was not a bad dancer, but there were never as many boys as girls, and we boys would have to dance with homely girls who were taller than we were, and I remember that it was embarrassing." He saw Wolf looking at his watch again. "Yes, yes, I know, Wolfi. This is not a time for memories. Come, I will go with you to the car."

We didn't talk much most of the ride. Wolf occasionally took his eyes off the road to look at me, and when our eyes met, I gave him my best Mona Lisa imitation–something in smiles that was not too warm, not too cold. It wasn't that I didn't want to see him as soon as possible and pursue the possibilities that were unfolding between us: it was that the Mittelball had grown in my mind to a grand affair where I would be presented by my father to the rest of the little world of Stammbüttel, and I wanted to be ready for the occasion.

I looked out at the countryside moving by, slowly in the distance and quickly up close, the sun lower now, the shadows longer. We were already nearing the town when I remembered Paul's sister, Lise, and I asked Wolf what had happened to her.

A bemused look came over his face. "Lise," he said. "Yes, of course. Actually, that is a very nice story."

"I'm glad there's one nice story in all of this, Wolf. I didn't dare ask. I was afraid I would disinter another horrible memory."

He gave me an appreciative little smile. "That was very thoughtful of you. But fortunately it is not necessary."

"So," I said, "tell me what happened."

"Right after the end of the War," Wolf said, "when everything was still terrible, the first soldiers were coming back, and–I remember this–the sight of a German soldier walking down the street was not the best sight. You must remember that we were defeated. Totally and terribly defeated. And some soldiers came back to nothing: their homes destroyed, their families dead. And those few who had survived Russian camps, many of them came back half-crazy from the experience. At that time also, groups of soldiers had formed gangs, and some of them were living off the land, like bandits. So when you saw a man you did not know still in his uniform, you approached him cautiously if at all."

"However, one day Paul was in the big room when he heard a knock on the door. It wasn't a 'police knock,' as Paul said to me, but it wasn't a neighbor's knock either."

We stopped at a traffic light. "Paul looked out the window," Wolf continued, "but there was no car. And he looked sideways, and saw the back of the man, and he could see that the man was in Wehrmacht uniform. So he got his gun and asked who it was. A man's voice said, 'Leopold Schnitzer.'" Wolf was really getting into the story, and I regretted to see we were close to my father's house.

"Come on, Wolf," I said, laughing. "Who *was* Leopold Schnitzer?"

I will tell you," Wolf said, rolling his eyes and waggling his eyebrows comically as we stopped at another light. "Paul knew who it was: it was a man that Lise had been engaged to before the war! Apparently *die Gute Lise* had been quite a flirt when she was young, and she and Leopold had had serious quarrels. And during one of those quarrels, Leopold spent one night too many with another maiden and had to marry her, and not Lise. Apparently Lise had never got over it, or at least she had never married anyone else. Now, it happened that when Leopold dutifully came back to his home in Braunschweig, his house and family were gone–kaput–everybody killed in a raid!"

"How long did it take Leopold to find Lise?"

"I do not believe he hesitated one minute! Apparently he had–how you say–'carried the torch' for Lise all this time, and knew where she was. When the opportunity offered itself, he went straight to Paul's house."

"What did Lise say?"

"Paul only told me that they have not been apart one day since that day."

"You mean they never gave another thought to wife number one and his child?"

"Yes, I am sure they did–but probably not until later. I think from what I know now, with all the death Leopold must have seen, that it was not as shocking to him as it would be now. Now they are married. They live not far from here–happily ever after, I think." As he finished, we stopped in front of my father's house.

I jumped out of the car, waved goodbye, and ran through the gate. It was twenty-five to six. When I entered the hall, I could hear Helmut small, piercing voice in the dining room. Ilse heard me too. "Is that you, Lene?" she called.

I stuck my head in. Ilse was wrestling with Helmut. Gustav was watching expressionless. Next to him sat Hans, dressed in a dark suit with an immaculate white shirt and conservative tie–the Stammbüttler *Bürger*, youthful version–dressed for the Mittelball. "Yes," I said hurriedly, "it's me. I'm late, but I'll be ready in a few minutes."

"You *are* late. We have been waiting." Reproof and guilt–Ilse excelled at this unbeatable combination.

I made a dash for my room and shut the door. Once inside, I rolled my eyes to heaven and found myself in a state of *deja vu,* placing me back to a time when I got home late from a date and had to field my mother's questions. I took a ninety-second shower and put on a red silk dinner dress with a relatively deep vee neck. I just had time to draw in my eyeliner and flick on some mascara before Ilse was knocking at my door.

"Lene, it is six o'clock. We must leave now."

"Come in," I said to buy an extra minute.

She came in, eyed the clothes tossed on the bed with disapproval and said, "Your father is getting the car. We must go."

I looked at my watch. It was one minute to six. I felt as if I was going to a military operation, not a party. My thoughts had no effect on Ilse, who was scrutinizing my dress. I never knew what she thought of it because at that moment Helmut gave a shriek followed by a crash, and she dashed out of the room.

When I came out, Helmut's wails were at full volume, although Ilse's words of comfort seemed to rise over the din. Helmut was shrieking, "*Er kneifte mich....* He pinched me," over and over, while Ilse kept repeating "*Ruhe, Liebchen, ruhe....* Hush, darling, hush," alternating, in an altogether different tone, "*Welcher von euch hat's getan?...*Which of you did this?"

Ilse stood with Helmut in one arm, with the other raised, looking with her stern mien like a Statue of Liberty brought forth for a new version of the Judgment of Solomon. Hans and Gustav huddled together at the other end of the table like criminals waiting for sentencing. Helmut was holding his left upper arm with his other hand. As I entered, he turned to look at me and dropped his hand, revealing a red welt. That was a real pinch, I thought.

If Ilse's eyes could have flashed lightning, they would have. "*Gott im Himmel!*" she shouted at them, What did they think they were doing? Who did they think they were, the sons of a *Schauspielerin....* an actress!" She spat out the word.

Hans' face, which was dark with confusion, became even darker with anger, and Gustav clenched and unclenched his fists. I thought for a minute they would do something drastic, like throw something at her, but they kept their defensive position at the other end of the table, and even backed off a step when she took a step toward them as she talked. At one point, Gustav opened his mouth and said, "*Sie ware wenigstens nicht eine....* At least she wasn't a..." but he didn't finish. I thought he was going to say 'secretary' with the same venom with which she had said 'actress,' but he knew he was outclassed, outgunned, even out-manned, to all intents and purposes.

I was uneasy about them myself, but I felt for them. I threw them a sympathetic glance, but they ignored me. I felt that even now, they hated me more than they hated her.

But Ilse understood and stepped forward again, her index finger pointing down at them from her raised right arm and punctuating each phrase as she said that they had better watch what they said and did. It was she who had their father's ear and it was she who would let *Him*–she said it with a capital H–know what *bösen Buben....* wicked boys.... they had become.

Helmut's cries were decreasing in volume and duration. She turned to him and cooed, "*Und warum haben deine bösen Brüder....* And why did your wicked brothers pinch my good little boy?"

Helmut put his head down and put his hand against his mouth and said, "*Weil*.... Because."

"*Weil warum?*" his mother said. It was just like getting information out of a small child in English: "Because why?"

"*Weil.*" Helmut didn't want to say. I looked at Hans and Gustav. They were both shifting uneasily from foot to foot.

Outside, my father leaned on his horn. Ilse looked at a clock on the sideboard: it was almost ten after six. She started to put Helmut down. He clung to her. "*Weil*," he said quickly, intending to keep her there, "*Ich wollte soeben sagen*.... I was just going to say..."

"*Was sagen, Liebchen?*.... Tell what, darling?"

Helmut hesitated. He turned to look at the boys. I followed his gaze. Both of them were looking at him intently. He glowered back, but he could see that Ilse's ear was focused elsewhere as my father leaned on his horn a little longer. In the Land of the Father–the Fatherland–the sound was not to be ignored. "*Ach*," Helmut said resignedly, "*dass du mich am liebsten hast, Mutti*.... That you love me best, Mama."

"*Ach so, Liebchen*.... But of course," she said, giving him a parting hug and kiss as she called Anni and handed Helmut over to her. Hans and Gustav continued to stand there, watching us sullenly. As I went ahead and held the door for her, Ilse turned and said to them, "*Und keine weiteren Streiche*.... And no more mischief from you two, understand?"

Gustav kicked the floor and said, "*Ja, Tante Ilse.*" Hans said nothing.

"Hans," Ilse said sharply. "*Hörst du mich?*"...Do you hear me?"

"*Ja*," said Hans giving the floor another kick. "*Ich höre.*"

"*Gut*," Ilse said, heading for the door and gesturing to Hans. "*Komm*, Hans," she added and proceeded to shoo him along in front of her. "*Ich werde morgen*.... I will talk to you two in the morning."

I was still holding the door as she walked out. I looked back to see Gustav looking at me, and I didn't like the way he looked at me at all. I began to understand that if Ilse was beyond the reach of their anger, I was fair game. But how could I ask my father for help from a danger he could not see?

When I followed Ilse out the door, she had opened the car door on the passenger side and was talking to Father. Hans was getting into the back, and as I walked up, she motioned me into the back too. As Father drove, he and Ilse were arguing: she complaining about the boys; Father telling her she spoiled Helmut. I looked at Hans beside me. He threw me a lizard glance and settled himself deeper into the corner. I wondered how I would get to talk to my father with Hans there. But then, as it was his Mittelball, Hans would have to dance a few waltzes.

At that point my father glanced at me over his shoulder and asked me if I liked to dance. I did, I said, very much. "Gut," he said. "You will have many chances to dance tonight."

"Me?" I said. I thought this ball was for the students.

Yes, my father said. Each student had to ask the ladies to dance. That was the rule. And of course, my father added, he would have to dance with both Ilse and myself as well.

That, I thought, was still a different angle. It was one of several that the evening would take.

Chapter 13

My father turned in to a wide driveway marked by an opening in a stone wall over which a wrought iron arch held some lettering I could not read, topped by a Teutonic cross. As we stopped just short of the entrance to a large building, both front doors of the car were pulled open and held by two spit-and-polished boys who clicked their heels loudly and bowed us out of the car. One of them was about to drive the car off when my father raised an imperious hand and opened the trunk. Ilse took out a basket covered with a white napkin while Father gingerly lifted out a second, smaller basket in which three bottles of red wine reclined. Keeping them level, he carefully closed the trunk.

Father and the wine led the way onto a flagstone path that wound toward a screen of trees beside the building. As we approached, the sound of a waltz filtered through the leaves, and the outline of an enormous tent threaded through the branches. At the end of the path, some wooden steps led up to a wood platform that stretched under the tent and supported some forty tables arranged in four tiers, two on either side to define a dance floor. At the far end there was a tuxedoed band whose members looked as if they were assembled by the same agency that used to send out high school and college bands all over the States until most of them were replaced by ambitious local rockers.

About half the tables were still empty, their accompanying chairs waiting around them in neat precision. The other half were covered with tablecloths, mostly white, laid out with abundances of breads and cold cuts and salads and fruits and glasses of wine and beer and mineral water being consumed by assorted families.

As we arrived on the platform, a man in a tuxedo rushed up to my father with an air of eager expectation and rendered a slight but respectful bow. My father introduced me to Herr Hohenruf, the *Tanzmeister*–the dancing master and head of the school. The teacher bowed slowly to Ilse and gave a perfunctory bow to me before he spun on his heel to usher us to a center table. From the way people were arranged, it appeared that Herr Hohenruf had a pecking order in mind, and as usual, my father was high on the list. The tables in the tier away from the dance floor were only separated from ours by a low wall rising about ten inches above the table like the partitions in a coffee shop, but they were clearly in another territory, where the inhabitants had to approach the dance floor through designated aisles. And as we arrived at the table, those on either side greeted my father with easy familiarity, while the men of the families on the other side of the divide rose slightly from their chairs to give my father obligatory bows of recognition.

In the midst of these greetings Ilse was busy with the table. As Hans resentfully held the basket, she shook out a white linen tablecloth embroidered with a finely cross-stitched blue border, transforming the table by this gesture into a personal island among the other islands floating around us in hierarchical order. As she took out several wineglasses carefully wrapped in white linen napkins, my father submitted one of his bottles to the scrutiny of a neighbor. It was an estate-bottled Bordeaux, twelve years old. The man nodded with grudging admiration and handed the bottle back to my father. After cutting the foil neatly around the top of the bottle, my father drove and old-fashioned corkscrew precisely down the center of the cork and withdrew the cork smoothly. He poured himself a small sample and sipped it, and poured a glass for the man and for himself. Then both sipped the wine in a ritual of male communion.

Throughout the last of this ceremony, we three lesser beings stood and waited as the ambient light darkened into early evening and brought into relief the lights that were strung along the top of the dividers and around the poles that held up the tent. Each table had one or two tall glasses with candles in them, elegant makeshift hurricane lamps that cast a flickering light on the faces around each table. Ilse lit ours before she took out our supper: bread, cold cuts, a bowl of *Gurkensalat*–a salad of finely sliced and slightly crushed cucumbers–and a small basket of fruit. Then, with Hans gazing into the basket as if it were a bottomless pit, Ilse took out knives, forks and glass plates and finally released him. Hans moved away into the back, where he joined the other boys whose silhouettes formed a frieze of male adolescents posing in their dress suits against the blue evening light.

I looked back at my father, who was pouring wine into Ilse's and my glasses as he said in English, "A little wine, ladies?" "Yes, thank you," we said in English with a small laugh.

As the tables filled, the dancing master was dancing as fast as he could, directing everyone to their destined tables with a finesse that would have served him well as Chief of Protocol at an embassy. As I watched him seat each arriving party, almost all of them nodded and went to their tables as if to their destiny. Only one man, who regarded everything with a gloomy expression that spoke of a grievous event that would overtake us all and was accompanied by a woman who clung to his arm as if that event was about to transpire–only this man, who was taken to a front-rank table, but the last in the line, back by the edge of the tent–looked at his assigned place and at the dancing master as if some mistake had transpired. And apparently, his was a borderline case, because the host immediately pirouetted and took him to a table two places nearer the center, which was deemed satisfactory.

I never noticed what happened to the family that was destined for that last place because my father called my attention back to the table. A tall, good-looking, well-dressed man who had grayed elegantly around his temples, stood beside him looking at me in a calculating way–the way you might view a horse you are considering for your stable. "Herr Kammenberg, *meine älteste Tochter*,...my oldest daughter. Helene, this is an old friend, Otto Kammenberg." As the man bent forward slightly, his eyes on mine, my right hand, of its own volition, extended itself, and he took it in his and brushed his lips so fleetingly across the back of it that it was not a kiss as kissing goes, but as hand kissing goes it seemed pretty professional, even considering that my hand had not been kissed before (at least in public)–and while he was making this gesture, he gave his heels the slightest click and straightened up with a half-smile, as if he had somehow satisfied himself and had the better of me. He held my hand a second longer, pressing his forefinger into my palm softly but firmly so that I could not easily pull it away until he released it. When he finally did, our eyes still locked, I was split in two: one part, which shyly withdrew her hand and returned it to her lap, was charmed; the other wanted to get up and smack him.

"I am pleased to meet you," he said in English.

"Otto," my father said, "travels often to New York and speaks very good English, much better than mine."

"No, no," Otto protested. "*Nur durch Übung*.... Only from practice."

"You have business in America?" I asked.

"Yes," he said, "I have business." The phrase closed the issue, as though I could not possibly be interested in what he did professionally. He turned back to my father. Refusing an offer of wine while giving the bottle an approving tap, he and my father fell into a rapid discussion that I couldn't follow.

Throughout this conversation both Ilse and I sat watching the crowd. Gathered behind the tables across from us were the girls, dressed in longish dresses in pale shades, holding small posies wrapped in lace doilies and tied with long red ribbons.

The girls interested me enormously. It would have been as one of them that I would have appeared here, dressed like them by my mother in a stiff dress that I was not accustomed to wearing, and little heels that all of them seemed to be wearing for the first time. There were, of course, the exceptions–the tall, pretty, slender girls with pale hair that stayed in place, falling to their shoulders with a small swoop, their complexions undimmed, their waists already narrowed, waiting now with self-possessed smiles. I would not have been one of these. Nor would I have been one of the fat, ugly or truly awkward, but one of those–and there were several–in-between: those pretty enough and athletic enough and bright enough, but also those whose hair would not stay smooth, whose complexion periodically failed them, whose nails broke, who were not sure, and who waited, therefore, in an agony of conflicting expectations as to whether they would be one of the last to be chosen for the dance.

I found one to root for–a girl of about fifteen, pretty but with a few pounds of pre-teen fat still on her, her long brown hair falling too much over one eye, standing in a pose that was still more girl than woman, at once wishing to be somewhere else and wishing to be the belle of this little ball.

Just then the band stopped and the dancing master rang a small silver bell. Within a few seconds the entire tent was silent, so that Herr Hohenruf could speak almost without raising his voice. "*Gnädige Damen und Herren....* Gracious ladies and gentlemen," he began, and launched into a rapid-fire speech which I would not have followed in English, let alone German. Instead I looked around me, at all the families who appeared to be giving him their polite and undivided attention; at the boys, who had gathered into a neat group to his right and stood at attention too–Hans looking surprisingly at ease among them–all clearly aware that they were the cynosure of the moment; and at the girls, standing in an equally neat but decidedly less self-possessed group to his left.

With a flourish, Herr Hohenruf announced the first dance: a foxtrot. I waited anxiously for my stand-in to be chosen quickly, but all the dancers assembled themselves on the floor with prescribed partners. The dancing master and an assistant who appeared from the sidelines (a young, earnest and slightly balding man) took up the slack with the surplus of girls–the fattest going to Mr. Hohenruf, the assistant taking on an ugly duckling with protruding braces, a bad complexion and glasses, for whom I sent a prayer to heaven that she would come back from college as a swan.

The foxtrot was followed by a tango, a rhumba and other Latin variations, with pauses for bows to the audience, bows to partners, changes of partners, enthusiastic applause, and then by a break in which three couples who clearly represented the more advanced–or at least more adept–students, did a Charleston. They were more politely acknowledged, with only a few tables–partisans of the dancers–showing enthusiasm. This was followed by a variation of the foxtrot and–an apparently daring innovation–a Lindy hop, into which the dancers put serious energy and enthusiasm. In the States we were doing the twist and Elvis and Chubby Checkers were already moving us into rock-and-roll, but in most small towns of the western world, this was still the repertoire.

The Lindy finished to mixed applause. The dancers stood smiling and pleased with themselves as the dancing master announced the grand finale–the waltz. The band, who had played enthusiastically throughout, now seemed to double their efforts in a vigorous Blue Danube. The dancers, still pleased with their performance of the lindy, stepped into it with fluid energy. As I looked for my personal choice, she danced past us and I realized with a small shock that she was in Hans' arms.

Both were transformed. With her head slightly thrown back, she looked up at him, the movement of the dance catching her lanky wave into flowing tresses, her face luminous with excitement, her lips slightly parted in a small, charming smile, while he–bent over her with his hand firmly holding her back at the waist, cradling her right hand in his upturned palm–was transformed from a gangly, clumsy, sullen adolescent into a young man in control of the moment as he guided the girl smoothly across the floor in enthusiastic circles.

During the dances, night had fallen and the dance floor was more shadow than light, so that the tent was now lit primarily by the small lights and candles on the tables, with only a soft glow from the small lights strung along the aisles. As the waltz came to an end, everyone stood up and applauded. My father clapped too, smiling at the happy dancers who bowed to each side of the room and to each other. They remained standing as Herr Hohenruf, wiping his forehead, strode to the bandstand and thanked everybody, congratulated the students, and invited everyone "to show the young ones how to do it right"–a toady to those who paid the bills.

After another burst of applause, the dancers headed for the familial tables and Hans returned to ours. For the first time I saw him pleased with himself and I smiled at him. For a second he started to respond, but Ilse spoke to him and his face sobered as he turned to answer her. My father interrupted. "Hans, *du hast sehr gut getanzt....* you danced very well," he said. "Sit down and eat." Hans walked behind me and sat down next to me as if I weren't there. I suddenly remembered my resolve–forgotten in the action of the ball–to talk with my father about Hans and Gustav. My heart sank. Not only was it going to be tough to talk to him alone, I didn't even know how I was going to bring it up. Sophisticated as my father was in some ways, I began to think Wolf was right: it was doubtful that Father had ever thought of Freud-and-company as other than a bunch of Jewish troublemakers with eccentric ideas. Suggesting that his own sons might need help from such a quarter was probably more likely to raise doubts about my psychological state than theirs. On the other hand, staying on in a house with two angry and possibly demented teenagers without saying anything to anyone seemed equally untenable.

I took the plate Ilse gave me and stared down at it. My father asked me if I were tired. "*Nein, nein,*" I said hastily, forcing a smile, and lifting my glass to him. "The wine is wonderful." He smiled. I looked at my plate which Ilse had heaped with good food and I flashed her a smile too, for good measure–which she returned in lesser but adequate measure–and focused on eating. After a short break, the band started to play again, the music skittering over the clatter of silver on plates and the tinkle of glasses. Father gave Hans his choice of wine or beer; he chose beer. When he had poured it, we toasted him. He seemed pleased, but a couple of times I saw him look at me, and then his eyes glowered like spent coals brushed by the wind. He only smiled when my father teased him about his energetic waltz. We finished eating in silence as the band played over the murmur of families at supper.

When the band launched into a foxtrot, my father stood up and asked Ilse to dance. She shook her head. Not now, she was tired. She would dance a little later, she said. "So, Lene...I must dance. Please," he said, and bowed.

I got up feeling flustered, like a teenager asked to dance by the class throb. We started off badly. I was so nervous I stepped on his foot, and saw my excessive apology brushed off. He was not concerned with my feelings, but it seemed to me that it took a great deal of *sang froid* to present a daughter who belonged in the eyes of his peers to a Pariah class, without the slightest note of unease or social apology. As a man who had his place in the world, as long as that was not threatened, he could please himself. He had pleased himself when he sent my mother and brother and me away; he pleased himself when he presented me to the town at the Mittelball, because as far as he was concerned, his daughter could not expect anything less. With all these other issues on my mind, the dance was over before I realized that he was really a pretty good dancer, and that I had also blown the only chance I would probably have to talk to him alone that evening.

As we walked back to the table, I saw that Ilse and Hans were in close conversation. Ilse had reached out so that her hand grasped his arm and she was speaking intensely, urgently. Hans looked sullen and stubborn, but at the sight of his father, he sat up straight. Ilse gave another pat to his arm and I heard her hiss: "*Merk dir*.... Remember, nothing rash."

My father took a sip of his wine and looked at Hans fondly. Like any adolescent gazed on by a parent, Hans pretended not to notice, and buried his nose in his nearly empty glass. My father poured him some more beer from the open bottle, telling him with a smile that that was going to be it. As I was watching the exchange, there was a sound like a small pistol shot from my left and I looked up to see a slightly perspiring boy bowing to my father after clicking his heels. When my father acknowledged him with a nod, he turned to me and repeated the maneuver, muttering a fast "*Gnädiges Fräulein*."

I threw a questioning look at my father, who smiled and said, "*Er bittet dich*.... He asks to dance with you. It is customary."

It was a foxtrot, which the boy, who was about Hans' age, did in a workmanlike manner, with his eyes focused sternly at an infinity that lay just beyond my left ear, probably praying that I wouldn't try to make conversation or patronize him. I asked him his name, which was Sigmund, and left it at that as we went once around the room, trying to keep both my eyes and my smile neutral so that I would not embarrass him. When we returned to the table, he deposited me with another shot from his heels and a bow before departing to find other required dancing partners.

It looked like Siggy was the first one to go on a dare, because *apres* Siggy it was *la deluge*. One boy after another appeared, shot off his heels and bowed, and I proceeded to waltz, tango and foxtrot repeatedly around the room. None of them looked directly at me at any time, keeping their gaze in the distance (apparently the correct eye position for dancing with older women). The only exception was a boy who caught me for a tango and who thought he was really hot stuff, holding me closer than was necessary and dipping precariously on the turns while he locked eyes with me with a boldness that was undoubtedly fueled by the presence of peers and a couple of beers. It probably ruined him for life by encouraging his machismo, but I eyed him right back and gave him a sexy half-smile; he stood his ground, reddening only a little, and finished the dance, his eyes sliding back to infinity as he escorted me back to the table. I thought the whole thing had been real cute; but I was about to get another view of the Mittelball.

When the spate of student dancers had abated, my father looked at his watch and said, "Ach," he had to go speak with an acquaintance, Hans Leibnitz, and walked away. As soon as he left it was as if some sort of energy field had been withdrawn. All three of us leaned back in out chairs and relaxed. Even Ilse tended to sit up and lean toward him when he was sitting next to her, and to lean back when he left.

I looked across the table at Ilse to find her regarding me through half-closed eyes, with a cold expression. I gave her a small social smile. She responded in kind. I was sitting there trying to think of something to say when Otto Kammenberg came to the table. He greeted Ilse politely, ignored Hans, and gave me a little bow. "May I have this dance?" he said as more of a statement than a question. I had no intentions of refusing; he was saving me from having to deal further with Hans and Ilse.

As Kammenberg led me to the dance floor, there were many couples dancing, both older people dancing together and older people dancing with young ones. We started off well. It was a foxtrot to some kind of pop love song–the kind Father's second wife used to sing. One of the members of the band had abandoned his instrument and was gripping the mike in a moment of bandstand ecstasy, his eyes closed, crooning the words in a passable baritone. Kammenberg danced well and took a strong lead, and we danced for a while without saying anything, and I stopped thinking of Hans *et al* and stayed with the pleasure of dancing. Then Kammenberg said, "You live in New York? In Manhattan?"

"Yes," I said.

"Do you live with your mother or do you have your own apartment?"

I said tentatively, "I have my own apartment," holding myself back from a wild urge to add, "You're looking for a place to stay?"

"Where do you live?"

I couldn't see where this was leading, but I told him I lived on West Ninth Street.

"Ach," he said, looking very pleased. "That is in Greenwich Village, yes?"

"Yes," I said. He executed a neat turn with a slight dip. I followed, waiting to see where he was leading.

"Ach," he said, looking down to me with the faint hint of a leer, "Greenwich Village. I have been to Greenwich Village. To the night clubs. The girls in those shows..." He heaved a sigh. "Just like Paris. The Latin Quarter. It must be a very.."–he paused significantly—"interesting place to live."

Christ, I said to myself, he thinks I live in a red-light district. Next thing he'll want to know what I do for a living.

"You live alone?"

"Yes."

He closed his eyes and nodded. I was meeting some expectations. "And you work?"

"Yes," I said, but I didn't want to keep this up. "I am a writer," I said. "I write..." I decided I'd had enough and was about to give him a short resume before the conversation got out of hand, but he cut me short.

"A writer!" he said. "An *artiste.* Yes, there was always in your father that artistic side." He made 'artistic' sound risqué. "Tell me, do you write poetry or do you make up fiction?"

For an entirely different reason than the one he was operating on, he moved me right from offense back to defense. I was about to tell this man about how I was a respected professional science writer who made a very good living at what she did, when he said the magic words, 'poetry' and 'fiction.' Now in the world of writers there is definitely a hierarchy that is not based so much on fame and money (although fame and money always get their salutes) as it is on those who write fiction and those who write fact, and despite everything, those who write fiction are always one up on all the others, so that the writer of the American novel, even in its most pedestrian version, has a certain status that the successful writer of non-fiction does not. Though my dancing partner knew nothing of this, I felt at a disadvantage, so when I stammered that I did neither, that I wrote about science, he was merely amused.

"How interesting," he said. "But it must be very difficult. As a publisher, I know that people are not interested in that kind of thing–unless, of course, it is written by a professional–and even then..." He paused, and looked at me sympathetically.

"I make a very good living," I said.

"I am sure you do," he said, shaking his head as if humoring me and repeated, "I am sure you do."

The dance seemed to be taking a long time, and I listened for the end of the song only to realize that the singer had shifted directly into another piece: we were being treated to a medley. I thought briefly of making an excuse, but the alternative was not charming enough to induce me to avoid a few minutes more on the dance floor with a man I would never have to see again. We danced on.

"I will be in New York next month," he said. I didn't say anything. "I will be there for a week."

I said, "Really."

He took that as encouragement. "Yes," he said, flashing a smile and doing fast turn followed by an exuberant dip. "I will, of course, be doing business, but I will have some time for amusement."

"Like Greenwich Village night clubs," I said.

If he heard the sarcasm, he ignored it. "No, no," he said. "I was taken to the night club by a business acquaintance. He wanted to show me what he called 'a good time.' He meant well, of course, but...my amusements are more in the opera and the theater, both of which are excellent in New York."

"Yes," I said dryly and waited for his next turn when it came with another dip as the singer shifted into what I hoped would be his last song.

"Perhaps when I am in New York you will have dinner and go to the theater with me?"

I opened my mouth to say I was seeing someone, and that it would be impossible, when he struck his head in a theatrical gesture and said, "Ach, but how thoughtless of me. You perhaps have a...boyfriend?" He leered slightly as he said the word.

"Yes," I said. "Exactly. I have a boyfriend."

"Ach," he said. "Of course. You have someone to take care of you. 'Writing about science.' Now I understand."

I was getting really annoyed. I remembered my impulse to smack him: it had been right. "No," I said, trying not to be as rude as he deserved. "I don't think you do understand. Jack does not support me, and he does not pay my bills." I was about to add that Jack was my lover, not my keeper, but I stopped.

"Ach," he said. "Then that is all right." I was about to ask him what was all right when he continued. "So perhaps you can help me."

"With what?" I said warily.

"Perhaps you can recommend a hotel."

"A hotel? If you go to New York all the time, you probably know the hotels better than I do."

"Now, that is not so. You see, I have not stayed at a hotel in New York for some time. For some years, as a matter of fact."

I wasn't sure about what was coming next, but I was leery about catching it.

"You see," he said, looking for a split second as if he was going to be shy. "I had," he said, lowering his voice so that it came out dramatically, "a little friend, *eine Kleine*, with whom I always stayed."

Although I had known men who kept mistresses, I was not used to have one of them leaning on me, but I only said, "What happened to her?"

He sighed. "Unfortunately, she is getting married."

"Good for her," I said. Then I thought that even though his story wasn't all that interesting, I was surprised he was telling it to me, here, on his own ground, and my father's.

He was unfazed. "Not so good for me," he said. "I was very fond of her. She was very intelligent. I tried to reason with her, but she would not even keep the apartment, although I offered to continue to pay the rent if she would just see me occasionally." He paused and shook his head. "It shows that common prejudices are wrong."

"Which prejudice?" I asked, thinking he was referring to fallen women and the like.

"Elaine was a Jewess, like you," he said. "But she was not concerned only about money."

To this day, when I think back on that moment, I continue to be amazed at the way an ordinary conversation–or even a lightly un-ordinary one–could blow up on me just on the issue of what both sides have referred to as "The Jewish Question." It is of course the same question as "The Palestinian Question," "The Black Question," or in Rwanda, "The Tutsi" or "Hutu Question," which are not 'questions' but stories that one group makes up about the other. But at that moment it clarified for me just why this stranger was so willing to say what he had said: he could tell me everything because I did not matter, because even though I was my father's daughter, the taint of Jewish blood was stronger than the power of my father's because I was, after all, just the result of my father's dalliance with one of Them. As my feet continued to follow his I was numb. There was nothing I could say to him that he would understand. He was in a dream where Jews were this and that, and the departing Elaine and I had our prescribed roles.

"Otto," I said, "let me tell you something. Hitler did me a big favor: he got me away from here. Now please take me back to my father's table."

He gave me a long look. "Of course," he said. "You are tired." As we neared the table, he stopped. "You will not speak of this to your father," he said, with only a hint of a question.

"No," I said. "I don't think he would appreciate it."

Chapter 14

When I woke up the next morning I felt slightly fuzzy–the familiar sensation of a mild hangover, occasioned by my father and I finishing the last of the three bottles. An unfamiliar bird was singing in the garden. The sky out the window seemed faintly overcast, neither blue nor gray.

The house was quiet except for a small clatter that came from the kitchen. Something tugged at my mind, and I remembered: Wolf was coming to pick me up–to show me Stammbüttel. I had a feeling that Wolf's idea of a tour was not going to be particularly extensive, but I did want to see the church where I and apparently a lot of Görings had been baptized, and the old palace of the Grand Duke whose current descendant had called in some markers and saved the area from being a part of East Germany after the war.

As I started to get up, I remembered Otto Kammenberg, which cast a faint pall on my thoughts, as if the sky had suddenly become more gray than blue. What had hurt was the way Kammenberg had made it clear he could tell me things because I didn't matter, and my not-mattering was a tender subject–especially here, because it made me feel I didn't matter to someone to whom I had once wanted to matter more than anything in the world, for whose mattering I would once have been willing to immolate my tiny being if it could have made a difference; people have died for much less.

And now, despite the fact that I was here, in my father's house where I had once belonged, that earlier time might as well have been in another life. I did not plan to stay: I could not have stayed if I had wanted to. I belonged nowhere. My deepest connection was to my mother, who had established herself in New York where she had landed, but she had not survived by sending down roots–connecting herself to other relations and to a society, the way most people did. She settled herself the way an epiphyte settles itself on a tree, feeding on the prevailing air: it may bloom into an orchid, but it never connects itself to the earth, and its seeds do the same. I had an apartment, work, friends, but only vague connections to family other than my mother, and none to Place. I was born here, but I couldn't even speak the language well. I was American, for sure, but there was no place I could go back to where anybody would know my name.

But I would not stay if I could. I had told Kammenberg that Hitler had done me a favor when he got me out of Stammbüttel and that was true. Had I stayed rooted in this small, secure world, I would also have been its prisoner. If it hadn't sucked me down into its conventions, I would have rebelled against it, and I knew from friends who had rebelled against their family that they had merely entered an anti-prison where they had to live out what their family did *not* represent: they ate the foods the family didn't eat; wore the clothes they didn't wear; held to beliefs the family didn't hold to. Out of the necessity of my rootless state I had found a kind of freedom–there hadn't even been anything strong enough to rebel against. I had pretty well made myself up. I had floundered; I had done many stupid things that a settled, formal upbringing would have averted. But I could pick and chose what I kept and what I passed on.

Now, years later, I know that was just a story I told myself, a pep talk that got me out of the Slough of Despond. Now I know that I walk a path that follows all sorts of rules my father, my mother and sundry other mentors, anti-mentors and peers and fashion magazines have laid out for me, diverging from it only by the most stringent effort. But then I only knew that I was okay without my Göring roots, and it was enough to get me out of bed in a reasonably cheerful frame of mind.

As I finished brushing my hair, I heard a crash that terminated further contemplation. I found Wolf on his hands and knees, picking up the pieces of some china. Anni stood above him, looking down, holding an empty tray with one hand and rubbing her forehead with the other.

"*Was ist passiert?*.... What happened?" I said. Anni just looked at me and shook her head as Wolf looked up and gave me an big but slightly embarrassed smile.

"*Es ist nur Herr Wolfi*.... It's just Mr. Wolf," she said, gesturing with her tray toward him, as if that were all the explanation that was needed. Wolf appeared to have made one of his wild entrances, managing to whack Anni with the door as she was bringing a tray through it.

I shrugged and gave him a big smile back. "I'll be right out," I said, going back to my room, "but I've got to have some coffee before we go."

I checked myself out in the mirror over the dresser. I was wearing a really pretty blue cotton Liberty print dress with a tight bodice and a full skirt. I thought I looked okay–as good as I ever thought I looked, which was always short of what I felt I *should* look like. Like most women, I measured myself against the lean and elegant models in magazines, prepared for their images by staffs of experts. Nothing has changed, except that the models are now leaner, younger and electronically retouched–putting them even more light-years away from comparison, as if a dream of traveling to Mars had been stretched to a wistful desire for a cruise to Alpha Centauri.

Wolf was ensconced with a cup of coffee, talking to my father. An empty cup and a roll sat waiting for me. As I was stirring milk into my coffee, my father asked me if I had slept well.

I looked at him before answering. So much had happened in my thoughts since I first awoke that I had to think back to answer him. "*Ja, danke*," I said. "Very well."

My father turned to Wolf and started to tell him about the Mittelball, twitting me about the wine, implying playfully that I liked it so much I had drunk a great deal of it.

I threw him an amused glance. "I had willing company," I said.

My father crinkled his eyes in a attractive way and nodded, "*Jawohl*," he said, "that is true."

"Where is Ilse?" I asked.

"*Sie ist zum Arzt gegangen*.... She went to the doctor–for her migraine. You will probably not see her until this evening."

I was about to say politely I was sorry to hear it when Wolf pushed his chair back and said, "It is after eleven. I think we should get started."

My father looked from Wolf to me. "*Wohin geht ihr?*...Where are you two going?" Before either of us could answer, he turned to Wolf and added with an inquisitive smile, "*und warum hast du es so eilig*.... and why are you in a hurry to fetch my long-lost daughter away?"

Wolf opened his mouth, but only said, "Ah." I couldn't say anything either. The term "long-lost daughter" had seized my heart and caught my tongue. I took the phrase and held it to myself where it matched exactly what some long-forgotten part of myself had held to all these years. His long-lost daughter. At some time that had been the totality of me, and probably never more so than when I gave him up forever. I lost myself then, I lost the round-faced, short-haired little girl who spoke childish German, whose letters the person I am now can barely read, letters written by my father's long-lost daughter. Not by me, the tall, long-haired American woman who was just visiting him.

Wolf said, *"Aber Onkel Franz,*...But Uncle Franz, you said that I should show Lene Stammbüttel."

My father regarded Wolf with the same quizzical smile with which he had called me his long-lost daughter. Then he said, *"Aber das war vorgestern....* But that was the day before yesterday. Tomorrow I want to do that myself." As Wolf looked at him with concern, my father turned to me. "My old friend, Herzog Friedrich," he said to me in English, "invites us to lunch."

It was Wolf's turn to be surprised. "I didn't know that you and the Count were still friends."

"Aber Ja," my father said, nodding. *"Wir waren Brüder...*.We were brothers in the same fraternity." He turned to me. *"Diese Schmiss ist von meiner Einweihung,"* he said, pointing to the scar on his face.

"The scar is from the fraternity initiation," Wolf said.

"Yes, I know," I said.

There was a momentary silence. Wolf quickly suggested that he could instead take me for a drive into the mountains.

When he mentioned the mountains, my father and I looked at each other. "Lene," he said to Wolf, *"hat schon....* has already had an adventure in the mountains. I don't know if..."

"Aber Vati," I said, the endearing form for 'father' slipping from my mouth unimpeded. *"Ich möchte in die Berge....* I want to go to the mountains with Wolf. I would like that. And today, Ilse has a migraine and you must work."

I got no further than *'arbeiten....* work' when my father looked at his watch and jumped up. *"Lieber Gott!"* he said. "I am late for an appointment." He started toward the door and stopped. *"Mach was du willst....* Do what you want. But tell Anni, please, when you are coming back," he added, and rushed out.

I leaned my chin on my hand and looked at Wolf with a small conspiratorial smile. He looked back at me with a level gaze and said, "Are you ready?"

Yes," I said, standing up. "I just have to get my bag. Why don't you tell Anni while I do that?"

When he came out of the kitchen, I heard Anni say, "*Ich werde*.... I will tell Mrs. Göring."

"*Nur wenn*.... Only if she feels better," Wolf called over his shoulder as he waved me out of the door in front of him.

"*Jawohl, Herr Wolfi*.... I understand."

"I think she does," Wolf said to me. He heaved a sigh of relief. "*Gott*, I thought I would never get you out of there."

"The best-laid plans of mice and men.... ." I said.

"What about them?" Wolf said, opening the car door.

"Gang aft agley."

"What does that mean?" he said, as he got in on his side.

"It means, one never knows," I said, leaning forward and kissing him. But I cut the kiss short: I didn't want to be seen kissing Wolf in front of my father's house.

"Where are we going?" I said, starting to repair my lipstick in my compact mirror.

"Leave it off," he said.

"Why would I do that?" I said, applying it anyway.

"Don't be coy, please," he said. "It doesn't suit you."

"I think it's more likely that it doesn't suit you," I said, putting my lipstick away.

"It does not. We are going to a small house one of my friends keeps in the mountains. He goes there to hunt and ski, but he is not there this weekend. I have the key."

"You have this all worked out."

"Does it not please you?"

"Sure," I said slowly. "Sure it does. It's just..." I couldn't say that I was realizing that I was having strong feelings toward a man I hardly knew, who I had no idea I was going to see again, and here we were, rushing through the German countryside to get into bed with each other as quickly as possible. But it wasn't just having sex. I had done that far more...at least more casually than this, with a few men I didn't know all that well. It was this powerful feeling with which my whole body reached out toward him that was suddenly causing me to lean back, the way you lean back from the edge of a cliff as if the chasm at your feet were pulling on you, drawing you over–and down.

"Just what?"

I took a deep breath. "Just," I said, "the way things have been going at my father's." I was dodging, but I wanted to talk about that.

"Oh?" he said, throwing a questioning glance at me as he guided the car around a turn.

"You drive beautifully. Like breathing."

He relaxed and smiled, and his right hand started to move toward my left thigh. I caught it and gently put it back on the wheel. "Not at 85 miles an hour."

"I don't drive miles," he said with a laugh. "I drive kilometers." He threw a glance at the odometer. "But you know, you are about right–About the speed."

"Intuitive math. It's the only kind I do."

"Don't laugh at it. It is essential to all mathematics."

"That's like saying the icing is essential to the cake. But it's not."

"No. That is not a correct analogy. If we are talking about food, it is more like yeast is to bread. Unleavened bread is the bread of poverty. Isn't it used in some Jewish ritual to express deprivation?"

"Wolf, don't ask me. I was brought up Presbyterian."

He glanced at me with genuine surprise. "Is that really true? Your mother..."

"My mother has nothing to do with Judaism. If she had any interest in religion at all, I think she would become a Catholic. She likes the ritual. I'm sure it was she who saw to it that I was baptized."

"You were baptized?"

"Yes. In Father's church. I expect he's going to take me there tomorrow."

"Ach, that will be die Michaelskirche. That is where I also was baptized."

We drove on in silence. I wondered if Wolf was thinking, as I was, about the way our lives started in the same world, and how we met again as strangers–but with such a strong connection! But could we have bridged it, I wondered, if Wolf had not spent so much time in the States?

We were still driving along the highway. The road was fast, wide and beautifully tended, with long sweeping curves between increasingly high hills with huge shoulders of stone pushing their way out of the green slopes, and occasional rock walls sloping steeply up from the verge.

"I think..." Wolf said finally, "we go out this exit," and we took a long, tight turn and slipped under the highway to come out on the other side on a road that cut directly into the hills.

"Well," I said. "What else do you think?"

"About what?"

"About Gustav and Hans and my father and Ilse and..." I said.

"...these childish attempts on your life?"

"Childish!" I said angrily. "Wolf, these attempts are not 'childish.' They are serious!"

Wolf heaved a large, impatient sigh. "Leni, Leni," he said. "There is no question that the boys must be punished for how they have behaved, and it is not just possible but *probable* that Ilse thinks that you are a threat to the family wealth–although I must tell you that I think the size of the Göring fortune has been greatly exaggerated. And it is even possible that Ilse said something in front of the boys. But now that your father knows about it, it will stop. Your father is a good man. He would not let them harm you."

"My father was not such a good man when he did not help my mother to leave. If he had really wanted, he could have helped with money, to make sure we were at least safe."

"I really do not know about that time, Leni, except that I have heard that the people who left were not allowed to take anything out of Germany–no money, no jewelry, nothing of value. So what could he have given your mother?"

As he said that, I remembered more about the story my mother told me about an SS officer on the train when we were leaving Germany. He saw the tiny gold angel pendant I wore on a chain–a typical child's necklace–and was about to tear it off my neck when I burst into tears, and he retreated. I don't remember it. It may have been the same man who dazzled me with his black and silver uniform, but in any case, Wolf was partly right: if my father had given us money for the journey, we might not have been able to take it. It was a confusing thought. Had my father done all he could then? Would he do all that was needed now?

The road became steeper, the rock walls taller, the trees closer above us, so that we often drove in shade, thin beams of sunlight flashing down into the woods around us. It was a beautiful day. I opened my window wide so that the sound of the road rushed through the car and the wind blew my hair back and cooled my neck. The scent of leaves and evergreen and earth poured into the car with it.

"How about some lunch?" I said, eyeing a sign for a small inn that whipped by on our right.

"Lunch," Wolf said with a grin, "is taken care of–and possibly dinner as well."

"Oh, so you have this all planned."

He smiled and ignored my question. "Our housekeeper prepared a picnic for us–all my favorites, she said."

"And what are they?"

"Let me see," he said, rubbing his chin thoughtfully. "Champagne, caviar?" He waited for my reaction, but I didn't say anything, so he shrugged and said overdramatically, "No, I do not think so. More possibly, sandwiches with Cervelat–you know what that is?"

"Yes, a little like salami," I said. "My mother used to buy it from a really good store in the German section of New York City. It was always a special treat."

"I am glad to hear your mother did not abandon all German things when she took you to America. Or was it the opposite? When I was in the States, many of the *emigrès* I met were always regretting. Talking to them, one would think everything had been better here."

"No, she didn't do that. In fact I remember once she actually said to me that everything was better in America–except the fruit. 'You have never really tasted an apple,' she would say."

He laughed. "Yes, I can understand that. American apples are so much more beautiful than ours, but so disappointing to eat. But life is easier in many ways."

"Unless it is already set up for you here."

He nodded, with a shorter, more rueful laugh. "Yes. You are right."

"Do you sometimes think about coming back to live in the States?"

"Not 'coming back'," he said, laughing again. "I `come back' here."

"Right," I said. "But I didn't know mathematicians were into grammatical nuance."

"It's not a grammatical nuance. It is...relativity. I observe the world from here: the United States is *there*. So I can only 'come back' here. But you, *liebe* Lene, are free to chose: you can 'come back' to either place."

It was true. Even if my remaining here was tactically impossible, it was still, at least in fact, the place I came *from*. I belonged in America as much as I belonged anywhere; but I was connected to this part of Germany by blood, and for this moment, sitting next to Wolf whose blood I distantly shared, I felt for the first time connected to the landscape I was passing through, and as I looked at Wolf I was swept by a feeling of tender gratitude, so that I reached out my hand and traced the perimeter of his ear. He smiled a small smile and took a sharp breath, but kept his eye on the road, which had narrowed and was winding steeply up a mountain. Wolf was still going at a good clip, but he handled the car smoothly, accelerating gently through the turns so that the car cornered flatly.

"How much further?" I said, speaking softly into the tension that was growing between us.

"Less than a kilometer, I think," he said, speaking softly too. "There should be a narrow dirt road on the left."

The road was not easy to see, but it would have had to be a particularly clever road to elude us at that point. It turned out to be little more than an overgrown two-wheel track, hard-packed and rocky, so that it was drivable but slow. As we entered it, Wolf braked abruptly. He took a deep breath as if he was going to say something, and then he grabbed me and kissed me long and roughly, and I closed my eyes and kissed him back and only opened them when he pulled away and shook his head and frowned as if he were angry. "Since I saw you two days ago, I cannot think of anything else." And then kissed me again–a short, almost bitter kiss—before he put the car in gear.

Chapter 15

As we bounced along the rutted track, I realized that the intensity of Wolf's feeling was more than I was ready for. I had been assuming that both of us were on the same course–of attraction and lust, but not more than that–not yet, at least. And as I thought about it, I felt myself withdrawing from him. I wanted to go where we had been going. Farther than that, I wasn't ready to go.

The track ended in a wide clearing. Wolf got out and took an old wicker basket out of the trunk. I followed him as he entered an opening in the brush that turned into a narrow path. When we had walked about thirty yards I finally saw the house–a simple chalet-style cabin with a door and two small windows facing the path with trees on either side. As we got closer and I could look through the trees, I saw that the land fell away in back of the house; it was on the top of a steep hill. When we got to the door, Wolf took a large, old-fashioned key out of his jacket pocket and unlocked it.

The cabin was open, divided into two spaces by a wall that only rose to the roof's hip, with a door standing ajar. The inside walls were of the same weathered wood as the outside. A large stone fireplace held the remains of a very large log, the ends tilted on a pair of heavy andirons shaped like stags' horns. A bank of almost uninterrupted small-paned windows through which the sunlight was slanting opened the room to an amazing view. I put down the basket and saw mountains folded behind mountains, and behind them, more distant mountains that faded into a soft blue haze. Far below us, the midday sun poured down on the tops of trees that formed a green cascade down into a deep ravine from which a formidable slate-black wall rose to form the base of another mountain that ended in a jagged ridge in the near distance.

I sank down on the window seat, turning sideways to keep the view in front of me. "Oh, Wolf," shaking my head in wonder, "this is...a perfect place."

He sat down close beside me and put his arms around me. "I am so glad you approve," he said, his voice muffled as he nuzzled my neck. I drew my breath in sharply, turning my head toward him as he moved up to my ear. As I turned, I saw first his large nose, and I thought fleetingly that his nose had become more endearing than strange, and some small part of me that was not yet completely caught up in the run of small steps that first-time lovers take to get to bed, smiled to acknowledge the power of desire that somehow makes all aspects of the beloved desirable, and that it was not surprising that people have, from time to time, believed that magic potions can create desire, not understanding that the reasons of desire brew the necessary chemicals in our veins.

"Wolf," I whispered and ran the tip of my tongue down the edge of his nose. He gave a short moan as we started to kiss and pulled me up. "Come," he said, taking a deep breath and then with a half smile he pulled me to him and picked me up and carried me to the other room.

I was surprised at the ease with which he had lifted me, but before I could think about it any more he put me down and started unbuttoning my blouse–impatiently, so that I finally unbuttoned it myself and took off my clothes as he took off his, and we fell onto the bed almost without looking, just knowing there was something to lie on. But the moment we lay there, naked together, all the tension went out of both of us. It wasn't that the wanting was gone; it was that we suddenly had time, and we spent it luxuriously.

Later, as we lay there in that state where the sweetness and intensity are still ebbing but the backflow is already building the next wave, I started to say something, but couldn't really talk.

"Wolf," I whispered, my eyes still closed, my mouth against his neck, and stopped.

"Hmmm," he said. I said his name again, adding a slight emphasis, but all he did was slide down a little and plant his mouth on mine, so that other more powerful sensations took precedence, and it was not until the shadows of the windows across the floor had already begun to lengthen that I sat up and realized I was hungry.

"What about this great lunch you had prepared?" I asked.

"*Ach, ja*! The lunch." he said, "I am hungry too." And with one gesture, he vaulted over me and picked up his shorts, putting them on as he headed toward the other room. I leaned back and watched him go, thinking what a nice body he had–thin, but entirely muscular, the body of an athlete, not a mathematician.

I found myself more than a few questions down the road of wanting, really, to know *him*, to *know* him, the way you know somebody you have known intimately for a long, long time. You can, of course, know someone that way for a moment–for a flash–when their whole being suddenly becomes transparent for you, as if you have known them always. But that moment passes, and they become opaque again and only a long intimacy can reveal them to you bit by bit, like a great territory that you explore. Even then, they can suddenly reveal to you something you hadn't known–a gesture, an attitude, a thought–that makes you realize the vast expanses that elude even a truly searching heart.

Now that the warmth of his body was gone, I shivered, feeling a cool edge to the air of the cold mountain evening coming fast. I put on my blouse and panties and wandered into the other room, holding myself against the chill. Wolf had the basket open and was unloading it on the table.

"How about a fire?" I asked. "Is there any wood?"

"Ach, you are cold. Ja, sure. But it is outside."

"I'll put the food out," I said. "Why don't you get some."

I started setting the food out on the table. Wolf's housekeeper had prepared enough large, overstuffed sandwiches for several appetites beside ours. There were pickles in a large jar on which the cover was sealed with wax and string. Just then the door swung open, pushed by a gust of wind that rushed through the room and the still-open window just as Wolf entered, his arms filled with wood. The wind was still blowing strongly so I stepped around him and closed the door, and had just turned to start unloading some of the split logs from his arms when the door, which had apparently not caught its latch, swung open again with even greater force and hit Wolf in the back. It was a heavy old solid door and it hit him with enough force to throw him forward and knock the wood from his arms so that the pieces of wood went spinning around into the room. As they fell, Wolf tried to catch them like a mad juggler whose mountain of balanced objects has collapsed, but he only succeeded in scattering them even further, losing his balance all the while, so that in the end both he and I and several pieces of wood hit the floor at once in a miscellaneous pile, swept by an unremitting wind that continued to flow over us from the door and out the open window.

I raised myself on my elbows and surveyed the damage. Wolf, put his head in his hands moaned several *"Lieber Gott*'s." The wood lay scattered about us. The wind blew my hair and tousled Wolf's as he lay there. I started to laugh.

"*Bitte*, Leni,...don't laugh!" Wolf said, without moving. "*Wie kannst du so grausam sein?*"

I sat up and started to put the pieces of wood to one side, still giggling. More than anything, I wanted to shut the door and stop the wind, but I asked: "*Grausam?* What does *grausam* mean?"

"Ach–what are we doing? We don't even speak the same language. It means...cruel. Cruel! If you had any feeling for me you would not laugh!"

"I am *not* cruel!" I said indignantly. "The door hit you. We fell. The wood fell. The wind is blowing and we are lying here." I started laughing again. "It is goddam funny!"

Wolf continued to lie there, his head in his hands, shaking his head slowly from side to side. "No," he moaned. "It is *not* funny. If you had spoiled half of your life falling down at every possible occasion, it would not be funny to you. Everything was perfect–until now."

I looked down at this man who had been, up to now, a wonderful lover–not because he used any sophisticated sexual legerdemain, but because he somehow answered me–as I seemed to be able to know him: mood for mood, touch for touch. Now, there he was, sulking in a pile of wood in a gusty wind.

I said sharply, "What the hell do you mean we don't speak the same language? We speak English–in fact we both speak American English, and we speak it just fine!"

My change in tone seemed to stop him. He took his left hand off his face and rolled over on his side to look at me, leaning on his right arm. As he did so, I saw that he had scratched his left side, probably on the wood as he fell, so that several uneven, delicate red lines of seeping blood were drawn upon his skin. He followed my gaze and saw the abrasion, and started to reach toward it when I swiftly got up on my knees and stopped him, holding his hand away from it.

"No," I said in a commanding tone that surprised me even as I spoke, and with one swift motion I leaned forward and slammed the door shut with my free hand as I bent over and started to lick the wound. For a second he just lay there, not resisting, which felt like a goad, feeding my anger and making me want to take it even further. I pushed him on his back so that he fell off his right hand and I heard his head hit the floor as I reached my hand into his shorts and grabbed his penis. His whole body tightened and he raised himself and grabbed my arms and pushed me away as he hissed, *"Miststück!.... Bitch!"*

I didn't know what it meant, but I just smiled at him and hung on because I could feel him becoming erect, which was what I wanted, making him answer to me, making him stop lying there and feeling sorry for himself. But now he was angry too. "*Lass los....* let go!" he said sharply and shook me.

He held me firmly, but I still felt powerful. "Sure," I said, gently stroking its now considerable length before I let it go. He shuddered, but at that moment Wolf reversed everything with one strong move, so that I was on my back and he was on top of me. I wanted to fight him, but I was too busy moving pieces of wood out from under us, so that he had pulled my panties aside and entered me before I could do anything about it, and by then I didn't want to, even though he kept his tight hold on my arms and didn't kiss me until he said to me, "Say 'Uncle,'" which I did–and gratefully kissed him back.

Much later I awoke with a start to darkness broken by wild flashes and the hiss of lightning as thunder shook the bed. It was only Wolf's body against mine that reminded me where I was. I sat up and said, "My God, Wolf, what time is it?"

"After ten, I think," he murmured sleepily. He sat up and put his arms around me and tried to pull me gently down again. "Lie down," he said. "Lie down."

"No, Wolf, we have to go. My father will be worried."

"Your father will be much more worried if you are killed by lightning."

"Stop kidding around. We have to go." I started to climb over him, letting the blanket slide off my body. It was really cold.

"Leni, Leni," Wolf said more forcefully, pulling me back against him and covering us with the blanket, a coarse and scratchy old wool blanket that didn't smell very clean. "We cannot leave until this storm stops. It is too dangerous. You father knows that."

"My father doesn't know we're still in the mountains and being careful. He is undoubtedly thinking that we are in the Stammbüttler lowlands and are dead."

"If Anni told him what I told her to say, they do not expect to see you until they get up in the morning. There is only one thing we can do..." As he spoke, the lighting and thunder were almost muffled by the roar of rain on the roof and the windows. I felt so sleepy and the darkness and the noise of the rain blended with the feeling of his kisses and his hands moving on my body so that I cast off the moorings of my filial obligation and floated off with him again.

When I awoke again it was to silence and that faint lightening at the end of the night that turns the world into a blue-edged image. Wolf was sleeping deeply next to me, his long, slow breaths fanning my cheek. He lay on his back with his head turned toward me, his left arm thrown over his head, his right hand still under my left side. I watched his chest rise and fall with his breathing as the light gathered itself to show the shapes of his body under the blanket while his face on the pillow remained in shadow. Watching him, I felt like one of those pagan deities in baroque paintings who watches a naked woman sleeping, desire for her written on him the way it lay for Wolf in me. And yet, even as I wanted to touch him, I felt a tenderness that wanted him to stay undisturbed, to stay as he was: quiet, slow-breathing, deep asleep.

As I wavered between those feelings I thought vaguely, wordlessly, about us–about the 'us' that had come out of the hours since we had fought on the floor. I thought about it as the dark blue light slowly brightened into a deep cobalt haze, although I thought about it the way you watch a film, remembering it only as it was, not thinking about what it had meant into words.

We had spent the rest of the afternoon and early evening alternately eating and making love. I use the term 'making love' carefully. It was different after that struggle amid the pieces of firewood than it had been before. It has only been over the years that I have understood what happened to us, that in those moments we had shown ourselves to each other without reckoning and had moved to a place, at least for that night, that could have taken us months, even years to reach, if we had reached it ever.

But understanding would not have changed those moments in the earliest morning, because as soon as I slid my hand over his body he woke up and reached for me, and I could no more have reminded him that we had to go than I would have listened had he reminded me. But as soon as I could bring myself to put any distance between us, I sat up and said, "Wolf, I have to wash. I can't go back like this…"

"Okay, Leni. We will go. But it will take time to make a fire and heat some water."

"What time is it?"

Wolf looked at his watch on the table. "It is just after five o'clock."

"How long will it take us to get back?"

"At this time on a Sunday morning, just a little over an hour, I think. Don't worry, we will be in Stammbûttel before breakfast. No one will be awake—except Anni."

"Wolf, I am not worried about what Anni thinks–or even–later–what my father will think. It's just…I came all this way, after all these years, to see him. I don't want to complicate the one day I can really spend with him by having him wake up and think I'm dead—or something."

"Or something," Wolf said with a grin. But he got out of bed, threw on his shirt and went into the other room. I pulled the blanket around me and followed him. He had opened the small wood stove and was putting in kindling, so that in a few minutes a small, hot fire was crackling in it.

"Watch the fire, Leni," he said, "and put in some of those. I will get water."

Before I could add anything to the fire, he was back, carrying an old bucket filled almost to the brim. He poured some into a large chipped enamel basin and put it on the stove.

"My friend has a cistern. There is no ground water up here," he said, "But always, rain."

"We had plenty of that last night."

"*Ja*," he said. "We had plenty of that." A silence fell between us. I stood there, hugging the old blanket around me. Wolf stood barelegged in his shirt, his hair tousled, looking at me intently.

I looked away, around the room. "Where can I wash?"

Wolf's eyes crinkled with amusement. He pointed to the door. "Out there."

"On the porch?"

He shook his head. "There is no bath."

Wolf went back to the corner where he had gotten the basin and returned with a dubious looking towel and an chipped oval dish in which resided a large piece of luxurious-looking soap. "I think you will like the soap," he said.

"I'm glad to find you are also a comedian," I said, giving the towel a lethal look. I turned to look through the windows. The rising sun had turned the distant mountains a glittering orange and tinted the lower slopes with flashes of gold. "Oh, Wolf, look," I said.

"Yes," he said. He stepped over and put his arms around me, gathering me against him, both of us looking out at the riot of the dawn.

When the water was lukewarm, Wolf and I took turns and washed quickly. While Wolf finished dressing, I folded the blanket. I looked at the sheet; Wolf and I were not the first people to use it. My heart sank. I looked at Wolf and pointed to the evidence. "Are these your tracks?" I said sarcastically.

Wolf rolled his eyes with mock exasperation to the roof. "No, they are *not* mine. This is Herman's house. I have never before been here with anyone else but Herman and other friends, when we go hiking–or skiing in winter. Herman does not usually 'loan' this house to his friends. This is Herman's house, it is his `nest' to which he brings his '*Vögelein*'–his 'little birds'–and I can tell you, it was only with the greatest difficulty that I persuaded Herman to let me bring you here—and a little luck."

"A little luck?"

"Yes, it was his grandfather's eightieth birthday, and he had to spend the weekend with his family."

I regarded Wolf carefully. When it really matters to me, I often have trouble knowing when people are telling the truth. I was torn between wanting to believe him and fearing that he was lying and wanting so much not be fooled, not to be a fool in the end. I looked at Wolf. The little smile behind his eyes was gone. He looked intently back at me, as if what I would say really mattered. I wanted so much to believe him.

Suddenly, I was crying–not just tears, but big sobs that I couldn't hold back, that came out of me so roughly that they hurt, and Wolf was holding me so that I was sobbing into the hollow beneath his shoulder, and I was soaking his shirt with my tears, and that somehow mattered. But even as I was thinking this, I became aware of Wolf's voice, and he was saying, over and over, "I love you, I love you, I love you."

In all the day and night that we had been lovers, neither of us had ever declared anything about our feelings for each other at all. When we did talk, we kidded around, or told each other about our lives or about ourselves. Now that it was my turn, the silence opened like a dark space at my feet that widened every second that I kept quiet. It would have closed completely if I could have said "I love you too," but I couldn't.

It wasn't that I hadn't said it before. I'd told Jack I loved him–when he pressed me; I had told my first serious boyfriend that I loved him–and at the time I had thought I did–or *did*, as much as I understood about love, then.

I'd had times when possibilities of loving had seemed momentarily to appear, though it was like a glimpse of great truth read over a stranger's shoulder in a subway from a book that you don't know, which he closes as he departs at the next stop before you can gather yourself to ask the book's name. But at the same time, my mind leapt forward to what seemed, then, like the impossibility of it all: I was leaving; he was staying in Germany. If I said, "I love you," I would have given him a part of myself that I might not have been able to retrieve. If I said, "I love you," where would that have taken us? The chasm opened over three thousand miles of hopeless distance. It wasn't after all a time like now, when transcontinental spaces can be bridged by the flip of a credit or calling card which can be paid for later–somehow. Even in the late Fifties only the naive, who didn't know what they were getting into, and the rich, who could afford it, embarked on transcontinental love affairs.

I was neither, but I teetered there at the edge of falling in love with Wolf. When Wolf and I woke that morning we had drawn so close together. Sometimes I think it was because we shared genes that already connected us. If blood *is* thicker than water, it might create connections that transcend consciousness.

But all of that happened on the level of feeling. On another level, Wolf and I knew none of this. So that even after Wolf repeated his declaration in German like a confession of truth to which I should have to reply, all I did was reach up and say "Oh, Wolf," and kiss him so that nothing more would be said on the subject until I said, "We've got to go," and pressed away from him.

He held onto me a second longer and then he said resignedly, "Yes. You are right," and we left the house. By the time we got to the car, which stood beaded and glistening in the early morning sun that shot through the trees, it was almost six. As soon as Wolf started the car, he turned and reached for me. I pulled back, but he said with great seriousness, "The engine has to warm up," so I smiled and kissed him, relieved to find that my body was quiet, and presented no arguments to ending the kiss.

But Wolf kissed me hard, with that mixture of hunger and anger with which he had kissed me only yesterday, before we got to the house. I knew that in a way the reason was the same, but it felt completely different, and suddenly there was the possibility that he could take his feelings away from me. The edifice of subliminal rationalizations that I had built crumbled, leaving a vague anxiety in its place.

When we reached the road, Wolf turned to me and said, "Now I will get you back to your father in a hurry." The car lurched forward, and he took the first turn with the tires on a high note. I braced myself against the floor and took a sharp breath. He took a quick glance at me and smiled to himself. He skidded a little on the next turn and slowed down slightly, but not enough for comfort.

But when we were on the straight road of the highway, he reached out and put his hand on my leg with a firm touch that held more affection than desire. I took a deep breath and put my hand on top of his. As I touched him, he turned his hand to grasp mine so tightly that his arm trembled. Holding it tightly, I lifted his hand and kissed it tenderly and felt him relax although he didn't let go, and we stayed that way until he needed both hands to turn off the highway into Stammbüttel.

It was almost seven when we pulled up in front of the house. By this time, all my anxiety of finding my father up and around had returned. All I was thinking of was how to get in the house without seeing him first. I had started to open the car door when Wolf grasped my arm. I smiled and slid out of his grasp and waved as I ran through the gate.

The courtyard was empty except for Father's elegant blue Audi, which stood gleaming in its splendor against the rose bushes. When I got to the door, my heart suddenly leapt into an extra beat as I realized that it might be locked. But when I turned the handle, it opened quietly.

Quietly, I closed it behind me and started for my room. The floor creaked, and I stopped, but I only heard the water running in the kitchen. Anni was up. I moved quickly to take advantage of the running water to cover my steps and had the door to my room open when I thought I saw the kitchen door swing out. I had the wit not to pause and slipped into my room, shutting the door behind me.

I undressed quickly and changed into my pajamas, which would give me cover to get into the bathroom. I put on my robe and started toward the door, when I caught sight of myself in the mirror over the dresser. There was nothing about me that suggested a night's sleep. The remnants of mascara that edged my eyes and the patch on my right cheek where Wolf's incipient beard had roughened it spoke of other venues.

I hurried up the stairs and claimed the bathroom, filling the tub and getting into it as fast as I could. I was shaving my armpit when I remembered how fascinated Wolf had been by what he called its "nakedness." Shaving your armpits, Wolf had explained later, was slightly "naughty"–something a prostitute might do, but not a respectable woman.

"Didn't you see a lot of 'naked' armpits when you were in the States?" I had said.

"Oh, sure," he had said, "but I never got used to it. It was always exciting." And I was remembering how ticklish I was when Wolf insisted on kissing my armpits and how I had laughed and struggled with him, when there was a soft knock on the door and I heard my father's voice.

"Hans? Gustav?" he said.

"Nein, Vater," I said. *"Es ist Leni. Ein Moment, bitte."*

There was a short pause. *"Ja, Ja,"* he said, and I heard his footsteps go back down the hall.

I felt like a teenager caught *in flagrante.* The bath water felt suddenly cool. I jumped out and dried myself hastily. When I stepped out into the hall again, no one was in sight, but the air was full of the small stirrings a household makes as it edges its way into the day. There was a faint tinkle of dishes from the kitchen, a murmur from one room, a soft step in another. I made it just in time, I thought, as I went down the stairs and into my room, which was full of the sunlight that threaded through the trees in front of the house.

Chapter 16

I didn't have to decide what to wear. It was another Liberty print dress I had bought the year before for more money than I usually spent. It had looked so simple and elegant and casual at the same time, the way I always imagined clothes looked when money was no object.

Without really making the point explicit, my mother had always imbued me with an idea that one could belong to a class of ineffable good taste, good manners and infinite *savoir faire*–and that it was in fact the class to which she *expected* me to belong. This Code–unwritten but clear–was reinforced by the idea that this ineffable class was in fact the one to which I was entitled by birth. But for me, the grand abilities required by this Code were to be exercised without much money. How one was to gain any degree of *savoir faire* when hopping around among refugee homes and occasional foster parents? This was not discussed. I handled it as well as I could as I grew up by gleaning miscellaneous hints from such diverse guides as Charlotte Bronte, Ayn Rand, *Harper's Bazaar* and of course, the movies. Nevertheless, the Code, if unfamiliar to the generally working-class world in which I often found myself, wasn't all bad. It included fidelity, stoicism, bravery and maintaining a sense of humor in the face of disaster. The combined effect was to make me a snob with strong proletarian sympathies.

Over the years, I have tried to weed the ridiculous out of these rules, to think less about my self and more about what I actually did, but it is still hard. Our early decisions enclose us like a mold in which we comfortably fit; any decision to change opens cracks through which our very soul threatens to escape and leave us a stranger in our skin. It is always hard.

While I often doubted my ability to sustain grace under all pressures, I felt I looked the part that morning. But as my father was the judge before whom my standards were currently set, only his approval could determine if I was right, so when I entered the dining room that morning and he set his cup of coffee down and said, "*Eine sehr nettes Kleid*,...A very nice dress. Very elegant," it was a very good thing we are not wired like lightning bugs; I would have gone into permanent short circuit.

But I only muttered "*Danke*" and added, "You too. Very elegant," which he was, even at that time in the morning, in his white shirt open at the neck to a silk paisley cravat, and his jacket of a rough and lovely old tweed.

I sat down as Ilse entered from the kitchen, bearing a plate of sweet rolls from which still rose an occasional wisp of steam. When Ilse saw me she said coolly, "You are up early."

"Not very," I said as casually as I could.

"You were out very late," she said. "I was beginning to worry."

"Oh, I'm sorry," I said paying very close attention to pouring my coffee. "But we got caught in an electrical storm in the mountains and had to stay under shelter until it was over." I hadn't really worked out a story, but it came out smoothly.

"Under shelter?" she said, repeating my phrase as if it were somehow incomprehensible.

"We were walking near a hut in the mountains that belongs to a friend of Wolf's. Wolf knew where the key was, so we waited there."

Ilse raised her eyebrows as high as possible while looking at a point beyond the end of her nose. My father, who was reading a large newspaper–it looked like a German Sunday *Times*–had looked up at my mention of an electrical storm and made "Tsk, tsk" sounds. We both looked at him expectantly, but all he said was, "*Ach, die Stürme in den Bergen*.... the storms in the mountains are very bad, very dangerous."

"How fortunate," Ilse said, "that you were so near the hut when the storm broke."

"Oh," I said cheerfully, "I don't think it was luck. Wolf and his friends hike around that area. He knows it well."

"*Was meinst 'hike'*?" my father asked. He was apparently listening behind his paper.

"*Wandern*," Ilse said.

"*Ach, ja*." My father nodded, turning a page and folding his paper to read something at the bottom. "*Weisst du, dass Wolf*.... Do you know that Wolf is also a mountain climber?" Although he was looking at his paper, I understood he was talking to me. "He has climbed some difficult peaks."

"*Wirklich?*" I said. Wolf hadn't mentioned any particular prowess in this area.

My father looked up and grinned and said, *"Ja, das würde man nicht....* One would not expect that from our Wolfi, would one?"

"Wolf's...." I said, and stopped. I didn't know the words. "Ilse," I said, turning to her. Her look reminded me of a teacher who is expecting the wrong answer. "Ilse, how do you say, 'Wolf's clumsiness seems to be very selective.'?"

She turned to my father and repeated the statement in German. Her tone expressed impatience. I had worn out my welcome with her, if I had ever had any. But my father just laughed and said, *"Ja, genau....* Yes. That's true. He is, for example, an excellent driver, isn't he?" I nodded. "I believe," he said, tapping his temple with his forefinger and narrowing his eyes as if he were about to impart a great insight he had achieved after much contemplation–"*dass es für ihn eine psychologisches Problem ist....* that it is for him a psychological problem." He paused significantly. Then he said quickly, "But not serious."

I looked at my father. Could I take that remark further? I thought, but I only said, "I believe you are right."

"Und weisst du," he continued, "And do you know that Wolf was one of the best dancers at his Mittelball?" I shook my head. My father nodded his emphatically. *"Ja.* Aber wenn er hat.... But when he brought the girl back to her family's table..." Here he stopped and put down his paper. He shook his head and started to laugh. Wolf's accidents seemed to provide him with a great source of entertainment. With considerable relish and large gestures, he told me that the tablecloth used by the mother of the girl was too large for the table, so that it hung onto the floor, and Wolf apparently managed to get caught in it and dumped a bowl of *Gurkensalat* into the father's lap. "It was very comical," he said.

I looked at Ilse. Her face was a blank. I turned to my father. *"Es muss sehr schwer....* It must have been very hard for Wolf."

"Aber ja," my father said more soberly, *"er war sehr verlegen....* he was very embarrassed." He was about to continue when Gustav and Hans came through the door with curt *"Morgens."* Both of them were in pajamas and bathrobes, but neither looked at all sleepy. They looked keen, as if they had been up for hours.

Father smiled at them and said *"Guten Morgen, Buben....* Good morning, boys. You look very awake for Sunday morning."

I thought from the way he looked at them that he really must love them. But for me, it was hard to feel any kinship. I found myself tense just being in the same room with them, and they didn't look at me at all.

"Wir haben an einem Projekt gearbeitet.... We are working on a project," Hans said. As he said it, he looked very pleased with himself, but I saw that Gustav shot him an angry look.

"Ein besseres als das letzte Woche.... One better than last week, I hope" my father said, chuckling. "No bombs in the house, please."

He turned to me and started to say, *"Letzte Woche....* Last week, the boys mixed some chemicals..."

Gustav said quickly, *"Oh, nein, Vati. Keine Bomben im Haus,"* with a conspiratorial smile as if he were acknowledging Father's wit, but the way he said it did not rule out a universe of other possibilities.

"Und kein Lärm oder Gestank.... And no noise or stink." I was not happy to see that my father's tone was more teasing than severe. The boys smiled smugly and nodded. I wished he would begin to understand that there was a *"psychologisches Problem"* here too, and that it was a lot more serious than Wolf's, but he only smiled back at them and asked Ilse where Helmut was.

Helmut had a little cold this morning, and went back to sleep, she told him. She looked at her watch. "Ach, he will be awake very soon, I think." She took a sip of her coffee and said to me with an almost casual smile, "You are leaving tomorrow, yes?" It was the first time she had addressed me directly this morning. The boys looked at me as if they had just discovered I was there and assumed a listening attitude.

"Yes," I said, measuring my words as if I were releasing state secrets to the enemy. "I believe there is a five o'clock train from Hanover, and I was thinking of taking that."

My father looked up from his paper. *"Du fährst aus Hanover?"*

"Ja, Vater. By train at five o'clock. Can you take me there?"

"You are going by train?" Ilse said with a frown.

"Yes. I like traveling by train."

"You do not like to fly?"

"No. I love to fly, but I also like to travel by train and see the country." I turned back to my father, but he was consulting his coffee cup. I had planned to discuss my travel arrangements with him when we were out together.

"You are not going back to New York?"

"I am going to spend a few more days in Paris and catch my plane back to the States from there."

"You have friends in Paris?" Ilse's questions had the quality of interrogation, but I smiled, less because I felt friendly than because it was beginning to feel like a tennis match when you try to anticipate where the next ball is landing.

"Yes. A couple I know just moved there. I am going to stay with them and leave Thursday night."

"You are expecting to come back to visit us soon?" Ilse gave me thin smile.

"Not soon. In a few years, perhaps." I had no intention of visiting my father again before "the boys" were grown and gone.

There was silence. The boys looked at each other and both of them looked at Ilse, who was consulting her coffee.

"But you will 'keep in touch,'" she said. It was a statement. It was not a statement meant to encourage me. She didn't mean, "so we can keep in touch." She meant, "so we will have to deal with you."

I wanted to make a joke of it, to say, "Don't worry, Ilse. All I'll send is a Christmas card." But all three of them were looking at me as if they were hanging on my words, so I said the only thing I thought I could say, which was, "Of course."

Both Gustav and Hans' stony faces crinkled into deep frowns as they both turned to Ilse as if to say, "I told you so." Ilse returned to her coffee. I was wondering how soon I could get my father to leave for our tour of the town when he looked up and said, half in English, "*Ja, Ich werde dich*.... I will take you to the train."

"*Danke, Vater*. And when are we going out today?"

"*Ich dachte*.... I thought we would leave at eleven o'clock. The Count expects us at one."

It was nine-thirty. It was going to be a long hour-and-a-half.

"Excuse me," I said, standing up. "I think I'll go and read a while." I smiled at everyone and went back to my room.

I was glad I had insisted on making my own bed, so I didn't have to muss it up to pretend I had slept in it. Nevertheless, I inspected it carefully, rearranging the pillow so that it wouldn't look *exactly* like it did yesterday, when Anni might have dusted the room. Then I realized I had retreated to my room to secure myself against those I saw as my enemies, but I decided it was better not to underline the situation. I took a book and went into the living room.

I tried to read, but other images crowded in front of the pages. Even though I thought I finally understood my situation, I still couldn't guess what my position really was in the minds of Ilse and the boys. I was worried that the boys would try something again, and I was concerned that her fears were egging them on, and that Father's blind eye to the operations of his venal offspring gave me no protection from his side.

And then there was Wolf. What was I going to do about him? It wasn't that I didn't want him. If we had had any future I could visualize, I might have been thinking very hard about Wolf. I had just spent what I still remember as a very romantic night with him. But the more I thought about it, the more I drew a blank. Wolf's life as a mathematician was a university life. From the few things he'd said to me, it was highly unlikely that he was about to toil in the vineyards of corporate engineering, using math to configure exotic guidance or information storage systems. He had already given his heart to pure mathematics, and there was no other venue that tolerated such romantic pursuits, any more than a corporation would have paid Einstein to work out the equivalent of $e = mc^2$ without a waiting list of known applications.

Then, if Wolf's life were to be a university life, there was Heidelberg, but I was not about to join him in Germany. As I sat staring at my book, I was pushed by thoughts of what it was I *was* prepared to consider–with or without Wolf. They were disturbingly vague. I had a great feeling for the style of the life I wanted, and to some extent, lived, but the substance escaped me. I wanted a life of beautiful clothes, a really nice apartment, fine food with great wines, all conducted in the company of smart, accomplished, amusing men, and sex as often as possible within this context. On the one hand, I had all the makings of an accomplished courtesan. On the other, I mixed all of this up with a fierce commitment to being economically and emotionally independent. It was perhaps rooted in a commitment made early in my life, when in a moment of childish rage over a deserved or undeserved punishment–it did not matter–I had sworn a real oath that when I grew up, *nobody* would ever tell me what to do. Oaths are different for children; they really mean something, so that later, when they are long forgotten, their power still rules our lives.

I confused matters further by being full of artistic aspirations: beneath my (I hoped) *soignè* exterior beat the heart of what I believed to be a wonderful (and possibly great) writer. It was fortunate for this self-image that it was not seriously put to the test. Making a living and living in a manner that supported the rest of this complex, rickety structure took up most waking hours.

And it was into this structure that Wolf had stumbled. He had many of the right attributes for me: he was smart, accomplished, amusing and seriously and sweetly sexual. He was not particularly sophisticated, but he was no hick. If he had been living in New York, I would not have hesitated to take off on a serious and exclusive affair with him–kissing Jack and any lingering others a hurried goodbye–as long as we were not talking about marriage. In those years, I was as shy of marriage as any cowboy that ever rode into the sunset, and for much the same reasons. I was much less afraid of being alone and being lonely–things I had more or less control over and that I saw at the time as temporary and remediable conditions–than I was of the idea of committing to walk a road with someone where I could no longer make solo decisions or turn off onto enticing side ways. It was a childish position, and impossible to hold even in those relationships I entered, where I often gave more than I should have because I didn't dare incur the commitment that asking involved. But it was the only position I understood at this time, and one that I held to for dear life.

What would I say to Wolf? I didn't want to hurt his feelings. I comforted myself with the ideas that he would get over me quickly, that he would come to the States for some kind of math conference sooner or later, and I would see him then. None of them worked; despite all my notions, I had fallen at least twice (but not recently) for men who cared for me less than I cared for them, and it had been incredibly painful. On the other hand, it hadn't been fatal. I had gotten over it. And this wasn't the first time I would turn away someone who had more feelings for me than I wanted to contend with. But it left me upset and confused.

I must still have been staring hard at the book when I heard Wolf's voice. He was greeting Anni and my father; he was being invited to have coffee, he was accepting and sitting down. My feelings about him went into a wild cascade of affection, indignation, desire, annoyance, fear, and joy. As time went by, annoyance won out. Minutes passed and the conversation in the next room continued, ebbing and flowing, but Wolf did not come to look for me. I could not hear the words, only the voices and intonations, the clink of silver and china, the kitchen door opening and closing as Anni went back and forth.

I tried to go back to reading, but the words on the page could have been in Hungarian: they held no meaning. The annoyance shaded off into indignation. Had he even asked for me? I read on, but the words would not gather themselves into coherence. More time passed and indignation started to shade into anxiety. Maybe Wolf had thought the better of it. Maybe he would leave and I would not see him again. I thought back to last night, and closed my eyes. I was back in the house on the mountain, lying against him. We were kissing...I fell asleep.

I became aware of a tickling sensation in my palm and opened my eyes to find Wolf holding my hand and nuzzling it with his eyes on me. When he saw my eyes were open he said in a low voice that was almost a whisper, his mouth still on my hand, "Your father asked me to tell you that he is ready to leave."

I sat up. The book slid to the floor and I leaned over to pick it up. I could not reach it because Wolf held onto my other hand. "Wolf, let me go," I said in a low voice.

"Never," he said, holding onto my hand.

I turned to look at him and said in my most serious voice, "I have to go to the bathroom."

"Okay," he said, releasing my hand as we both started to laugh.

I picked up the book and leaned over and kissed him on the mouth, stepping back as he reached for me and turning toward the door. I stopped cold, because Helmut stood there glowering at us. He was still in his pajamas, a vengeful cherub, his beautiful small face twisted in a scowl of disapproval.

He raised his little arm with Jehovian authority. "*Ich sah euch*.... I saw you."

I looked at Wolf. He looked worried. I looked back at Helmut. He hadn't moved. "Gut," I said. "*Erzähl es der Mutti*....tell your mother."

He lowered his arm and looked at me with such simple childlike confusion that I was prepared to give him the benefit of the doubt, but he scowled again and ran out of the room.

"I better go," I said.

"Leni," my father called from the other room.

"*Sofort....* right away," I called back.

"Leni," Wolf said.

"I'll see you tomorrow," I said, letting my mind slide over the fact that I was leaving as I ran out of the room and went upstairs. When I came down, Wolf had gone. "*Ich sollte dir von Wolf 'so long' sagen,..*.Wolf said to tell you, '*So long*,'" my father said, emphasizing the American phrase carefully so that it sounded like "Zo longe."

"Oh," I said casually, "*Weisst du....* Do you know what he meant?"

"*Ja*," my father answered smiling broadly, "*er sagte das....* he said that because he will see you soon."

"Oh?" I said, raising my eyebrows in a question. As we walked out to the car, my father explained that he had to come back and work in the afternoon, and that Wolf had offered to finish showing me Stammbüttel. He was meeting us at the fountain in the Burgplatz after lunch. When I turned and saw a half-smile on my father's face, I began to wonder if he had some idea of what was going on and was not entirely displeased.

We were out of the gate and driving down the road when he spoke again and straightened me out. Wolf, he reminded me, was his favorite nephew. He understood that I enjoyed his company; he was an exceptional young man. He hoped soon that he would marry, and the family had always expected that he would marry the daughter of his father's best friend, Martina Wessel. A wonderful girl, very pretty. They had grown up together.

"*Wirklich*," I said.

"*Ja*," he said. "*Es ist am besten wenn Leute ihre eigene Sorte heiraten....* It is best when people marry their own kind." When I didn't say anything he added, "Marriage between people from different backgrounds is very difficult."

"*Ja*," I said. "*Ich bin sicher....* I am sure you are right."

I knew he was speaking from experience. His marriage to my mother must have been no picnic; remembering my mother's descriptions of their differences, I cannot imagine that they understood one word of each other's thoughts and feelings, and bad sex was probably not the least of it. But I thought his reference to Wolf and me was probably partially right too. If Wolf and I ever settled down together, we would probably find plenty to disagree about once we got out of bed.

At the same time, the remark made me angry. Wolf and I did have different backgrounds, but we also spent our first five years in the same one, and several generations back, we shared blood. As we had discovered last night, we were not strangers to each other; we understood each other very well on a real gut level. And Wolf was a grown man; I thought he would marry whom he would marry; not someone his family expected him to.

But I could say none of this, although I planned to ask Wolf about it when we met in the afternoon. Once again, I was thankful that I had *not* grown up in my father's venue, with all the expectations pressing me to follow roads that were not mine.

So as my father and I were thinking our very different thoughts, we drove through streets which were becoming marked by familiar sights where I had passed before. My father started to point things out–this building, that statue, this fountain, that park, until we came to a large, nondescript church with one tall and one truncated tower, the Michaelskirche, St. Michael's Church–the church, he said, where I and all the rest of the Görings had been baptized, and to which the family still belonged.

Chapter 17

We entered one of the church's tall carved doors. It opened into an antechamber where my father opened a second, smaller door and ushered me into the sanctuary. The church smelled the way all western churches smell: old wood, old fabric, candles and cleaning compounds blended in coolness and a silence immanent with echoes of sounds long since gone. We stopped as I took it all in with a deep breath and breathed it out again. As we walked slowly down one of the side aisles, my father pointed out the carved wooden pews and wood paneling that climbed above the choir to wrap around the base of the rough marble columns that fanned into vaulted arches high above. The original church on the site dated back to the eleventh century; the church in which we stood was built upon the Romanesque foundations in the late fifteenth century, a nice example of late Gothic, restrained by Lutheran piety on the one hand and decorated on the other to meet the princely demands of a nobility whose patronage had made it (and of course Lutheranism itself) possible.

There were very few worshippers in the church, except a couple of elderly people and a girl of about twenty who seemed to be very upset. A thin, pale man wandered around the altar, dusting and rearranging things in an abstract way, as if he were not really present, as if he didn't need to be present to do what he had always done. My father spoke in that quiet voice we use when we don't want our words to carry, and this, combined with the fact that I constantly had to extrapolate the meaning of words from their context, made me lean toward him, my head bent in a posture of acquiescence.

As we walked farther back into the church, a small area like a miniature chapel unfolded from the gloom to reveal, behind a wrought iron fence with open double doors, a large marble basin–the baptismal font. We stopped in front of it and I looked down at the empty bowl. The edges of the basin were polished and smooth, worn by countless hands and arms holding infants surprised by the rush of cold water on small heads still delicately covered by the first growth of baby hair–myself included. Yet the child who was held here had only anecdotal connection to a present self: we only knew that we had been here because we had been told so, and because we had an official paper, our *Taufschein*–our Baptismal Certificate, a very important form of identification in the Germany into which I was born–to attest to that. I stood there, trying to connect myself to this place. I could not.

I had attended the baptism of the children of friends and I knew that it was a time when you invited all your friends and made the baby's place in the world somehow official, and if you didn't feel official about it, it was, anyway, a celebration. I tried to think what it must have been like–with me, the child, no doubt dressed in a long white embroidered linen Christening dress and a white cap that was removed so that, when my mother–no doubt still young and pretty with her bobbed dark brown hair covered by a hat, holding me in a white blanket–leaned over, my head would be over the font and the minister with his silver pitcher of holy water would say the words that would bring me into the then apparently safe circle of the Christian community and out of the dark and dangerous world of being a Jew, from which she had fled.

My father spoke out of the silence of the church into which his voice had fallen as we approached the font. *"Es war ihr sehr wichtig....* It was very important to your mother, your Christening."

*"Und nicht für dich?...*And not for you?"

"Aber natürlich, für mich auch.... But of course, for me too," he said quickly. "But if your mother had not wanted it...I would not have insisted on it."

"Warum nicht?.... Why not?" I knew the answer, but I wanted him to say it.

He didn't say anything for a minute, and I thought he was going to let it pass, but finally he said, *"Denn...deine Mutter war eine Jüdin....* Because... your mother was a Jew."

I nodded.

He sighed. *"Ich bin ein Mann mit freien Ansichten....* I am a broadminded man. If your mother hadn't wanted it..."

We walked in silence back down the aisle. I looked at the church. The girl was still there. Now she was crying, holding a crumpled white handkerchief to her face, red and wet with tears. Was it a broken heart, or had someone died? She might be pregnant; she might have lost her job. I couldn't guess what mattered so much to her.

My father touched my elbow and I turned away to follow his pointing gesture to one of the tall stained-glass windows, donated, he whispered, by a distant ancestor. In brilliant primary colors it depicted the story of the talents, showing Christ with two haloed servants displaying their coins and the third servant–haloless–with his shovel, being sent away–the punishment for not investing–an odd, mercenary, and very Calvinist tale despite its dimension as a parable, and a telling choice for a church window here. We looked at it for a minute, and then I followed him out the door.

We walked slowly around the church. A slight overcast had given way to sun and blue sky alternating with large clouds that cooled the air and made you look up to find the reason for the sudden darkening. An impudent wind came and went, now from the front, now stopping, now blowing my hair across my face from the side. We looked at the foundation. Nearly a thousand years old. It was impossible to conceive. I couldn't even grasp the extent of my short life. I knew the little girl called Leni had existed, although thinking even of that was like thinking in terms of having had a previous incarnation.

As we rounded the nave we came upon the minister's house. Between them lay an extensive rose garden, where rows of tagged rose bushes had little to show but leaves and fat buds.

"*Ach*," my father exclaimed with the warmth one usually reserved for favorite pets and long-lost friends, "*die Rosen von Pfarrer Lessing*!...Father Lessing's roses!" And he started to walk among them with great interest, examining each one as if it might be an old friend or a new guest, and as he did so, a man who I assumed was the minister stepped out of the door and greeted him. As they fell into conversation, I stopped and waited. To my eye, roses had awkwardly angled branches, long thorns and sparse leaves–all in the service of a capricious plant that might produce a few exotic and heavily scented flowers if enough time and devotion were expended on it, and tended–as now–to be either before or past their prime when I got to see them. I liked more ordinary flowers–banks of daylilies, thatches of dandelions in the spring, summer fields soft with daisies, cornflowers, and Queen Anne's lace amid the seeded grasses–found flowers, growing where they found themselves as best they could.

But my father and the minister had stopped and were bending over a low bush on the other side of the garden. My father stood up and called me over. He introduced me hurriedly. The minister acknowledged the introduction with a small nod.

My father said eagerly, *"Seh dir diese Rose an, Leni....* Look at this rose, Leni. It is remarkable!" He was pointing to a single rose which had begun to blossom, its heart still furled but its outer petals open, arching slightly at their edges. *"Bemerkenswert!.... Remarkable!"* he repeated, shaking his head in disbelief, *"Und so früh....* And so early." We stood and looked at the flower, its pale gold color gleaming with light, its flawless, velvet petals suggesting a perfect object for the sense of touch. My mind's wild lilies wilted in its presence.

After another reverent minute, my father said goodbye to Minister Lessing who acknowledged me again with another perfunctory nod and walked back into his house as we continued around the church, walking a little faster. It was already after twelve, my father said, we must hurry a little.

We got back in the car and drove to the end of the town, taking a road that took us past a large park to a huge wrought iron gate in a wrought iron wall whose sections were linked by tall, carved stone posts. A sign on the gate said, "Schloss.... Castle." We drove along a winding, graveled road that ended at the castle in a large area covered with a fine, pebbled white gravel that must once have been filled with carriages and horsemen but was now a parking lot to some half dozen cars. The castle itself was late Baroque, with a formidable entrance surrounded by at least a dozen bigger-than-life-size statues, figures in classic draperies standing and lounging on every possible projection and platform under their sooty coats. The facade stood three tall stories behind them, with only slender pilasters between tall windows. Above the third story the castle rose into intricately decorated dormered roofs where odd windows hinted at higher stories. We walked through a pair of great carved doors into an enormous high-ceilinged hall in whose center a marble stairway rose, divided in two, and curved away into the dimness.

At the entrance we were greeted by a man who looked less like a footman or butler than a museum guard, which in fact he was, as half the castle was now a public museum, my father said, and his friend, the Count, lived in the other half. We still had time and would take a look at the museum first. We wandered through antechambers and chambers, ballrooms and dining rooms, bedrooms and sitting rooms. They looked the way most buildings look that were once functioning houses and are now only for show: slightly seedy and forlorn. It took an effort to see the women in their elaborate dresses trimmed with masses of handmade lace and the men in their ornate costumes, belted and buckled and still carrying thin swords used less in the defense of the realm than to bully each other to prevent slights to an honor that was becoming ever more ephemeral. What remained were their portraits, the damasked wall coverings, the florid ceiling murals, the carved marble and plaster columns and moldings, and the carved and gilded doors and furnishings, with only the electrified chandeliers giving away the fact that they were all dead and gone, and most of them entirely forgotten.

We were in the antechamber to the Countess' original bedroom when my father looked at his watch and started us back to the entrance. We lost our way a couple of times, taking what my father thought were shortcuts down back stairs only to find ourselves in unfamiliar territory. We moved around more and more quickly until we opened a door and stepped back into the central hall.

Another man was standing there, half turned away from us, talking with the guard. He was heavily built but not fat, and his gray hair was combed and pomaded back from his receding temples around what was probably once a handsome face. Looking sad and slightly serious, he jabbed his right forefinger into his left palm for emphasis as he talked. He was dressed very much like my father except that his tweed jacket was belted and he wore a sweater over his shirt and tie. As we walked toward him, I could see that the sweater was old. The jacket had leather patches at the elbows.

When he saw us he broke into a genuine smile that made me like him immediately and walked toward us, throwing up one arm in welcome and exclaiming, "*Franz, du alter Fuchs! Wie gehts?*. . .you old fox! How are you?" They clapped each other on the shoulders, exchanging greetings. Then both men turned to me and the other man said, "*Und das ist deine Tochter, nicht wahr?*. . . And this is your daughter, isn't it?" My father introduced me to Graf Walther Rainer von Friedrich by my full name. The Count took my hand, but turned to my father with surprise and then looked back at me.

"Gelbart?" he said in very British English, "is that your married name?"

I laughed, partly because the question was both natural and dead wrong and partly in surprise at his almost perfect English accent. "No," I said, "my mother changed our name when we got to America. As you might imagine, emigrating when we did, Göring was not the best name to have there."

"Ah yes," he said, smiling warmly at me and nodding, holding my hand in a friendly grasp. "Of course." He paused and looked at me carefully, stepping half a step back as if to take in my whole person. "But you seem to have done well, despite everything."

I wasn't quite sure how to take this, and so I said, in a slightly confused way, "Oh, yes, well…"

The term, "despite everything," threw me. It covered, in two words, the separation from my father, the schools, the homes, the War itself. He meant it, and I took it, as a compliment, but it was something I did not want to take that way, it made everything seem so much simpler than it had been, as if I had come to an old-fashioned Hollywood ending where all loose threads had been neatly tied, while my life was still a tangle.

The Count and I continued to smile at each other–he, waiting for me to finish my sentence; I, finding no coherent words to do so. As I looked at him I understood that he did mean it as a compliment, that he thought I looked okay, that I looked like I had come up to whatever standards he might have set for his friends' daughters, and I understood that those standards were probably my father's too and any incoherent objections I might have at this time had no place in the conversation.

"Yes," I said, "You are right. We have done well in the States."

He laughed. "The States…After the war, I was working with the Americans. I had a clerk, an American soldier, who used to call it that. He was very amusing, always making jokes. Let me think: his name was Bob Johnson. Such an American name for such an American young man." And talking in this way he ushered us through one of a pair of large doors in the side of the room. The door was marked "*Privat. Eingang Verboten….* Private. Entrance Forbidden," so much more forbidding than the American, "Do not enter." But that was German signage, full of "*Achtung's*–Attention's" and "*Verboten's*," often followed by an exclamation mark.

We entered another huge room filled with settees and chairs and a variety of tables. The walls between the dark wood moldings were covered with a pale green satin damask whose pattern shimmered in the light that made it through the heavily curtained windows. The damask looked fresh and new behind the portraits and landscapes that hung over it, in contrast to the several oriental carpets that looked still lovely, but old and worn and in need of repair. Similarly, some of the chairs had been recently upholstered, while others were faded and showed their years.

The Count stopped and said, "We are gradually bringing the house back to its proper state. It is a big job."

"I can imagine," I said. Is that green damask like the original wall covering?"

He smiled. "No. It was entirely my wife's choice, although I think it an excellent one. We are not constrained by the historical preservation laws inside our part of the *Schloss*. The outside, and of course the eastern wing, is taken care of by the State, but here we can do as we wish." He held up a cautionary finger,–"although I expect we would cause a small storm if we were to change the room to say, Bauhaus style." As he laughed and slapped my father on the shoulder, as if it were a great joke, I looked over his shoulder and saw the portrait of a young woman that startled me. At first I couldn't put my finger on what was so unexpected about it. It was an amazingly informal portrait compared to the others: the woman–she was just past being a girl–wore her dark, wavy hair down over her shoulders, with just a trace of a braid at the sides to hold its fullness back from her face. The simple dress was blue with a white lace collar, gathered into fullness at the waist and sleeves. She stood in a three-quarter pose, looking over her shoulder at us as she held a ribbon-trimmed straw hat down in front of her with both hands. Behind her was a landscape. But what was most remarkable was her direct, uncomplicated gaze, clear as a child's, her face with its long straight nose, wide blue eyes and small, straight mouth looking at us without any stance at all–with none of the hauteur or self-possession of the other portraits hanging around her.

But there was more to the portrait than the gaze. In the moment that I stopped to look at the picture, as the men turned around and followed my gaze, I realized that what had surprised me was that the woman in the portrait had an exceptional resemblance to my mother.

The Count looked at me and smiled and then looked back at the picture. "You are admiring my ancestress, the Baroness Mathilde. It was painted by David when her father was an ambassador to the court of Louis Seize.. According to the family story, she was taken up by the young Marie Antoinette and her coterie. As you can see, it was the period when the young women of the court played at being milkmaids and shepherdesses. I understand her father, an uncle, heard something about a flirtation and ordered her back to

Stammbüttel over her vigorous protests. It caused a scandal, according to the story, not because anything actually happened, but because she tried to defy her father and was locked in her room for a year before she gave in.

I shuddered. "What a horrible story," I said. "Did they really do that to her?"

"Oh, yes. I am quite sure they did that. It was unheard of. It is hardly heard of now. Good German daughters still follow the father's wishes. Although they choose their own husbands, they rarely choose one of which a father will disapprove. I would not have expected my own daughter to marry someone...unsuitable."

He cleared his throat. I thought it was because he had become aware that he was wading into deep water. He was, but I was to learn that the water was even deeper than I knew. I said, "She is very pretty," trying to decide whether I could mention her resemblance to my mother.

"Yes," the Count said, "and what was very interesting is that my younger sister, Marthe, used to look very much like her. In fact, the resemblance was so strong, it was quite uncanny." Then, as if he had thought of something, he turned to my father, slapped him on the shoulder and said, "*Ist das nicht so, Franz?*" and laughed suggestively.

My father shook his head. "*Ach, Walther, das war lange her....* that was long ago."

But the Count was not letting my father off the hook. "Your father was very fond of Marthe, and," he said, nodding with his eyes half-closed to emphasize the truth of his observation, "I think she was very fond of Franz." He looked at my father, who looked at the floor as if waiting for this to be over. "But," he continued, "my sister was not a Mathilde in spirit. My father had chosen someone else to be her husband, and she married him while Franz and I were still at Heidelberg. That was the year Franz went off to Munich. *Nicht war*, Franz?...Isn't that so, Franz?"

It was startling information, but I could not be sure that my father and the Count realized what they had just told me–my father had met my mother on the rebound–had probably been attracted to her because she so resembled the woman he really wanted. I looked from one to the other, but neither of them seemed to be involved in anything more than that my father had lost out on his first choice. My father only looked at the Count with pained patience. "*Das ist erwürdige Geschichte....* That is ancient history. Isn't it time for lunch?"

"*Ach, natürlich, Franz und.... Lene.* I am sorry. Let us go to our lunch!" And he held out his arms so that his right arm pointed to the door and his left invited me to pass by. My father turned and headed toward the door and I went to follow him, and as I did, the Count took my arm firmly above the elbow in a gesture that was both polite and intimate and we walked chatting about the rooms and passages through which we passed until we came into a room that was like an enormous greenhouse. It had a stone floor and was full of trees and plants that breathed a green smell as we entered. Near the wall of windows a table had been set with exquisite linen and silver and crystal and china and flowers for three.

"What a beautiful room," I exclaimed. "And what incredible plants. Those trees must be decades old," I said, gazing at a number of trees in huge wooden containers that were growing happily in the early afternoon sun.

"Yes," the Count said, smiling fondly at them. "They are from before the war. Maintaining them is my wife's 'project.' It is modeled after the English style—" he looked at me with a question. I blinked and shook my head slightly to say I didn't know what he meant. "The Victorians," he continued, "built greenhouses onto their large country houses to grow the exotic plants that they brought from parts of their Colonial Empire. These morning rooms were generally used for the family breakfast and by the mistress of the house. My wife added the room shortly after we were married. She kept most of the trees alive through the last winters of the War, when there was no fuel to heat the living quarters, and certainly none for a greenhouse. I don't know how she managed it. Please sit here," he said, pulling out a chair for me, pushing it in deftly as I seated myself, the heavy metal garden chair scraping over the stones. I barely noticed the sound, because I was wondering where his wife was. I decided to wait until there was a context for the question.

The Count waited until my father seated himself too and had pulled the large stiff white napkin across his lap before he rang a small silver bell with a clear, beautiful tone. Immediately a door opened behind us, and before I could turn, a footman rolled beside me a small cart with a tureen on it, whisked off the domed lid and set it down. The tureen was large and elegant, a pink scene of some sort glazed over crenellated sides that rose from a pedestaled base, but the soup it contained was thick and brown and smelled warm and homely, turning out to be some beef broth with barley that the footman ladled into my plate with a short bow.

As the man served my father, I said to the Count, "Your English has no accent at all," trailing the statement off into a question.

He smiled, leaning slightly to his right to allow the servant to take his soup plate, and said, "My mother was English, and I spent the summers of my childhood in Sussex with my grandparents."

"Wasn't that very unusual?"

"It was not as unusual as you might think. The German and English genealogies are very intertwined, and a substantial part of the English nobility was very sympathetic to Germany until very late in the game. And of course," he said in a grimmer tone, looking down at his plate, "there were those of us that were hoping we could avoid war with England entirely."

"Oh," I said. "You must have felt very ambivalent."

"No. At the time, things seemed very clear. There was sentiment, and there was duty. My duty was to my family and to my country. I could regret, I could hope that the England I knew and loved would survive. Before we were at war I could–as did your father"–he nodded toward my father who looked back at him expressionless–"express–privately–our dismay at the rise of the Hitler rabble. But once we were at war...I was an officer in the Hussar Thirteenth Regiment, my father's regiment and my grandfather's before him. No, I was not ambivalent. Not at all. *Nach Kriegsanfang.... Once* we were at war, it was only God and Fatherland, wasn't it, Franz?" He sighed and picked up his soup spoon.

My father sighed and picked up his spoon as well. "*Jawohl, Friedrich, du hast recht. Dann war es nur Gott und Vaterland.* One did not have a choice."

We ate the soup in silence. I was full of questions I wanted to ask this charming, civilized man who had spent all those years working for the Devil. Did he really think that all this cant about God and country absolved him? On the other hand, I was a well-brought-up girl; I could not ask him such impertinent questions at his own table. The longer I thought about it, the more difficult it became, so I was surprised when at the point I was about to give up and retire into safer territory he said, as if his thoughts had been running silently alongside mine, "But of course the matter of the concentration camps was entirely different. Not acceptable. Not acceptable at all."

Again, I did not know what to say. In one way, I understood it was an acknowledgement made for my benefit, in its way an apology from a man who was probably not used to apologizing. In another sense, it seemed such a feeble statement, like my father's description of the Holocaust (although that term was not then in general use) as a "great tragedy." I looked at my father. He looked back at me intently and then lowered his eyes. I felt he was asking me to drop the subject, because he was uncomfortable with it. The concentration camps were–and still are in Germany–a *declassé* topic of conversation. When I get bitter over this, I have to remind myself that the wounds we inflicted on Indian and African people are not favorite topics of the American table conversation either.

The servant cleared our soup plates and reappeared with his cart and a loaf-shaped roast glistening with a sour-cream sauce and sprinkled with dill. The Count proceeded to cut the roast expertly into several thin, even slices. As the footman held my plate, the Count deftly lifted the slices onto it. When the Count had served my father and himself, the servant offered us two covered bowls: one contained tiny roast new potatoes; the other held a pile of thin young asparagus. I remembered Hannah's was home-grown. As I wondered where this came from, the Count said, "It is from our garden. We have always kept a large vegetable garden, even when I was a child. My mother thought it was important for our health, and my wife kept the garden going during the war; at first, I think, for the children, and then, when they were gone, she would give to friends."

"Where did the children go?" I said. My eyes caught my father's, which flashed a warning. It was too late.

The Count had picked up his knife and fork, but he put them down again carefully. "Then," he said, emphasizing the word, "we sent them to schools in the country to keep them away from the bombs that we thought would fall on Stammbüttel. Now they are both dead."

"Oh, God," I said quickly. "I am so sorry."

"My daughter was at a convent that was overrun by the Russians. You can imagine what happened there. My son was, unfortunately, a dedicated Hitler youth. In the last days of the war and against his mother's express orders–I was of course away–he joined Hitler's call for all men over the age of thirteen to fight to the last man. His body was never found. It probably lies in one of the mass graves in a suburb of Berlin. My wife has never recovered from the shock. My brother died on the Russian front, as did my brother-in-law. My sister has no children. I have no heirs. When I die, the other half of my *Schloss* will go to the State and the von Friedrich name will disappear from the Earth. You see, my dear, life is not so simple." And he picked up his knife and fork and started to eat.

I looked at my plate. I could not look at my father. I was full of tears, but I could not allow myself to cry. Partly I knew it was that the tears would not have been only for him; they were for all the bereft who were cut much more than their share of loss. In less than ten years, at the Auschwitz Trials in Frankfurt, the men indicted for running the camps, who were personally responsible for the death of some three million people including throwing living children into furnaces to meet death quotas, would be out on bail and would sit dressed in expensive suits in the courtroom beside their lawyers, ducking out between sessions to make telephone calls to check on the progress of their business enterprises. Some of them did a little time; none of them were condemned to know that their children died alone and afraid. And here I sat with a man who had done what he thought was right, who had certainly participated in the catastrophe but had not done–at least I believed not–anything remotely as evil as the men on trial, but had, it seemed, been more severely punished than if we had hung him, the most severe punishment we meted out at Nürnberg for the worst Nazis of all.

And I, who had been sitting in judgment on everyone, suddenly found myself looking back at what Ilse of all people had rightly said were merely the little disturbances of my life. My childhood griefs had shrunk. I wasn't writing them off; I would not have wished my childhood on anyone else. But here I sat in front of a future full of possibilities–and American possibilities to boot. None of this grief and loss was mine any more.

I picked up my knife and fork and began to eat, thinking of the train that tomorrow would take me away.

Chapter 18

After a few minutes, the Count lifted his wineglass. Caught up in all that he had said, I had not noticed the wine being poured. It was, he said, a Burgundy from a case that an old friend had sent him, the first one since the War. His voice was even and pleasant, as if the deep, dark well from which he had called to us did not in fact exist, although the shadows of its depths still hung about us, and shreds of its darkness become visible whenever I recall his cry, the way concentration camp survivors' stories darken the light when we remember them.

"*Prosit*!–To you health!" was all he said.

It was not until the table was cleared for dessert that the conversation returned to its original tenor. I wondered if the Count smiled a great deal because it helped him ward off his grief. He spoke now mostly to my father, and mostly in German, mostly about the several businesses in which he seemed to be engaged, throwing in an occasional translation out of politeness so that I should not be left out. He was, as I had first thought, a nice man, a thoughtful man.

As I watched the two of them together, so alike, and clearly such good friends, I wondered if Ilse had been to visit. From what she had said, I thought not, except perhaps to large occasions–like a Christmas party. It made me wonder, though, why I had been invited. I wouldn't have been invited as a favor to my father–although I thought the Count would have done that–because my father would not have asked.

It is possible he invited me just so he could say what he did, perhaps seeing me as someone who had lost–as he saw it–everything to exile as he had lost everything to war, perhaps that was what he thought, or perhaps inchoately felt. It is also possible that his telling me what he did involved some sort of attempt at rapprochement, as if for him I represented all Jews, all those people dispossessed by the madness of the German Reich. Or perhaps, after all, he was just curious, and what he said spilled out of him the way large feelings breach even high social walls.

At that moment, I would not have thought that there was more to know about the Count's personal life, but we had just started dessert when another layer unfolded. Dessert had come as a piece of delicate pound cake topped with whole raspberries in a thin Kirsch-laced syrup, and of course, *Sahne.* The raspberries, too, were from the garden, the Count said–last year's crop—preserved in his kitchen. And then the coffee in a tall, bellied white pot whose sides were laced with a delicate green pattern that twined up the graceful arched neck of the spout.

"Echter Kaffee!.... Real coffee!" the Count said, putting his cup down with a satisfied sigh after the first sip.

"Jawohl, echter Kaffee," my father echoed in the same tone.

I looked at them curiously. "You must understand," the Count said amused by my incomprehension, "that one of the great subjects at dinner tables all through the War was '*der schreckliche Erzatz Kaffee....* the terrible imitation coffee.' We Germans had to drink it all through the war, because of course we could not import from your allies in South America. It was," he added with a rueful smile, "a great source of German discontent at all levels of society."

I laughed. "Of course. In America we also consider a good cup of coffee an essential right. If the government tried to interfere with coffee drinkers, I don't know what the political consequences might be." My father and the Count nodded appreciatively as the door opened and the footman brought a tray of bottles on the cart.

"Schnapps, Franz? Und Helene?" the Count said, looking inquiringly at each of us. We both nodded and smiled. The Count had just reached over to select an impressive looking old cognac when the door across the room opened and a thin pale, gray-haired woman in a gray lace dress entered and looked at us hesitantly.

Both men stood up quickly. I joined them, but more slowly.

"Lotte!" the Count greeted her. *"Liebchen! Ich bin froh dass du hier bist....* I'm glad you are here. We are just having coffee." He turned to me. "Let me introduce my wife, Charlotte, the Countess von Friedrich." I bobbed my head and felt my knees give a slight bend in an involuntary curtsey. The Count turned back to her. "My dear, this is Helene, Franz's daughter, visiting from America, and of course, you remember Franz. Please join us," and he gestured to the servant to make a place for her.

The Countess remained standing just inside the room, moving only her eyes from one to the other until the Count introduced me. Then she seized me with a fierce gaze as she walked slowly toward me. Beside me, the servant hesitated and looked from the Count to her and back again.

She came up to me and took my hand in both of hers. Her hands were extremely cold and soft. Her pale aquamarine eyes gazed into and through me as if I were far away, as she spoke in elegantly accented English. "My dear," she said, pressing my hand as if she were placing into it an urgent, secret message, "you have finally come back to your dear father. He was such a fool to let you stay away for so long. You must not leave him again." She stopped and continued to look at me. "Ach," she said, softening her hold on my hand and taking half a step back as if to get a better look at me, "you must be just the same age as my Hedwig. She has been away a long time also. But she is coming back soon."

She stepped back and regarded me fondly as she let go of my hand. Then she turned to her husband, and said, with a half smile and a slight, regretful inclination of her head, "Nein, danke, Walther." She turned to my father and then to me with the same small smile and said, "Please excuse me. I am very busy. The children will come back and their rooms will not be ready for them." She turned and went out the door which she had entered and closed it softly but firmly behind her.

I looked at the Count. His eyes were still on the door through which his wife had just returned, looking with a longing like that which Orpheus must have felt after his backward glance had drawn Euridice back to Hades. He closed his eyes and shook his head and sighed. When he opened them, he was back as our genial host, gesturing to us with both hands: "*Bitte, bitte, setzt euch wieder. Karl, Cognac und Zigarren.*"

We finished our lunch in silence that was barely disturbed by my father's appreciative noting of the cognac and the cigar. It wasn't until my father mentioned that I had still to see the Cathedral that the Count became animated again. He waved the half-smoked cigar and said that the Dom was an excellent example of early German Gothic, that I must pay particular attention to the vaulting, it was especially notable, as were the woodcarvings in the Karlkapelle, the chapel in the north transept that was built in honor of one of his ancestors, a Knight Templar who had died, apparently heroically, on one of the Crusades.

"Your family has a long history of military service," I said. In the Nineteen-Fifties a long history of military service, even in the German army, was not, per se, suspect.

He looked surprised. "My dear Helene, the men who established duchies and their heirs were warriors by necessity. He who did not have the respect of other knights could not call on them to help defend his realm and did not hold it long. The Middle Ages were not a time for the rule of law, but of force. And of course," he said rising, for lunch was over, "the rule of law is, as one of my English cousins used to say, a sometime thing."

I turned and said to him, "I hope not. I hope this time, the rule of law will last." I expected a warm assent, but instead he and my father exchanged inscrutable glances.

My father finally said, "I am sure it will, Leni, at least for some time. At least in Europe, and in America. As for the rest of the world..." He shook his head ruefully and we walked back through the grand rooms until the Count kissed my hand goodbye at the door to the great hall and we left.

My father looked at his watch. *"Lieber Gott,"* he said, *"es ist fast drei!....* it is almost three! We must hurry: Wolf is waiting at the church," and he hurried out to the car, leaving me to rush after him.

I was not in a mood to rush. The visit with the Count had unsettled me, not least because it had ruffled my notions of 'them' and 'us,' but only briefly. Even now, when Cambodia, Serbia and Rwanda have given them serious competition in the annals of evil, no one has quite replaced the Nazis in sheer scope of their entries into that record.

When we arrived at the cathedral, my father pulled the car up to the stone steps that ran across the front of the facade. Several small tour groups were standing there, and it was not until one of them moved that I saw Wolf, who was sitting on one of the lower steps with his legs akimbo, his elbows resting on his knees, his forearms hanging down as did his head, so that he seemed to be gazing intently at the step in front of him.

I moved to get out of the car when my father said, *"Ach, ich hab's fast vergessen....* I almost forgot. Ilse is making a small formal dinner for you. My old aunt and your cousin Rudi, my brother's son, will be there."

This was interesting news. I would have liked to ask how this had come about, but my father had clearly wedged its announcement into a no-question zone. *"Es wird um halb sieben sein....* It will be at six-thirty, but please come back earlier."

I nodded, and got out of the car as I called and waved to Wolf. When he saw me he started up and ran across the stairs toward us. Wolf took my right hand in his and shook it, saying, "Hello, Leni," in a casual voice to which I answered "Hello, Wolf," in the same tone, and then he transferred my hand to his left hand and opened the car door further to lean in and greet my father. I hardly listened, because the entire time he held my hand so tightly that his grip almost hurt, and I could feel his hand over mine trembling. Then he closed the car door and my father drove off as both of us waved with our free hands.

When my father's car had turned a corner, I looked questioningly at Wolf, but he just turned and I followed him through a small side door into the great dark gothic shadows of the nave.

The church was empty except for the scattered few who sat quietly with their thoughts or prayers in different pews, but the air was filled with music from a vast organ whose pipes rose in serried ranks across our heads. The organist must have been practicing because he occasionally stopped and repeated a phrase, but for the most part, he played on with abandon that felt as if he were getting a lot of pleasure in making this great sound to fill this ancient arched and vaulted space.

Wolf took my hand and led me through a side aisle to the transept, where we turned and walked on. There were two small chapels on either side that were closed off by beautiful gates of wrought iron shafts topped by ornate gilded points. We went on through another door to a large empty hexagonal vestibule where a single hanging lamp illuminated the entire area with a dim, golden nocturnal glow that left shadows in every corner and the high ceiling in darkness. The grand volume of the organ faded to a distant, musical hum. Wolf drew me over to a wall and pulling me close to him began to kiss me tenderly but firmly and hungrily, and we kissed until his hand on my breast and his erection pressing against me made me remember where we were.

"Wolf!" I said, pressing my hands against his shoulders. "Wolf! Please. Let's stop."

Still holding me, he looked around him and said, *"Ach, ja,"* and sighed deeply. He looked at me with a look that was full of sadness and said in a whisper, "Only let me hold you," and I nodded. As he pulled me back to him I slid my hands inside his jacket to put my arms around him too and I felt him shudder slightly. A sadness rose in me from the knowledge that he had fallen very hard for me, much harder than I had for him. The sadness which was both for him and for this unborn thing between us was mixed with a selfish concern about how I was going to get out of this situation.

So even as I was leaning against him, and enjoying intensely the feeling of being held, the sheer feeling of yielding and yet holding so that you are giving back the holding at the same time, I was thinking about things that I might say to him that might start to ease me away, when he tightened his grip around me and said in a strangled voice, "Leni, I love you so much. It is terrible, terrible..."

I didn't know what to say. I wasn't clear what he meant by "terrible." I suppose any fool who has been really in love would have immediately understood, but then I had spent more of my life avoiding love than running after it, except when it was pretty clear that it could get away. So for all my sophistication about the ways of the world, about where to eat and what to wear and what to say and the intricacies of painting and literature, when Wolf said that loving me was "terrible" all I could do was to wonder what he meant. Now I understand that he meant that it was terrible to feel something so intensely that it was almost like pain; that it was terrible to need to actually touch someone even when they were not there; that it was terrible to feel that your life depended on someone being around who was not likely to be there for more than another day. But I didn't really understand, so when Wolf shook his head and said, "Let's just go for a drive, okay?" I said, "Sure, but first you have to show me the Cathedral. My father will ask if I saw it."

Wolf sighed and took my hand as we walked back through the doors into the heart of the cathedral. His hand still shook a little as it held onto mine, but he seemed composed, if a little abstracted. We walked slowly into the back of the church where a series of tall, narrow stained glass windows about forty feet high were flooded with afternoon light so that their gaudy colors dressed the figures in tawdry magnificence. The mottled sunlight from the windows painted us in their colors, so that when I turned to look at Wolf he seemed as if he were changing like a chameleon before my eyes, and he mistook my look for the tender gaze of the eyes of love and squeezed my hand again so that it hurt me. I winced, and he relaxed his grip and lifting my hand to his mouth gently kissed the inside of my palm.

I didn't expect him to do that and I snatched my hand away. "Wolf!" I said with exasperation–because with every gesture he seemed to undo my resolve to undo this situation with some kind of grace–"Wolf, how does a German mathematician. . . ." I stopped. What could I say?

He looked at me quizzically. "How does a German mathematician do what?" he said, gazing at me searchingly as I held the hand he had just kissed as if it had been burned. As we stood in the aisle of the cathedral, I looked past him the length of the nave that stretched a couple of hundred feet to where the massive rosette window glowed a deep, quiet red. "How does a German mathematician do what?" he repeated, kissing me just below my ear, making me catch my breath. I stepped back.

"Do *that*!" I said, putting my hand to my neck.

Wolf looked at me with an almost calculating expression, and then he smiled. Suddenly it was he who seemed to be in possession of himself and I who was unsure. He put his arm back around my waist as we started walking slowly down the aisle.

"I will tell you a very personal story. I have never told all of it to anyone."

"Oh," I said. "I hadn't thought of you as a man with a past."

"A past?"

"A secret history."

He gave a small chuckle. "I suppose, in that sense, I have a past." We stopped walking. Wolf continued to hold my right hand, rubbing his thumb gently across the back of it as he spoke.

"When I was eighteen," he said, "and had just finished Gymnasium, my mother, who has always done a little drawing, decided we should go to Wesenbad, where there is a small artists' colony, for the summer. I was not enthusiastic, but I didn't have any other plans, and with one thing and another, we went. At first I felt very lost. None of my friends were there, and as a kid with a funny nose who was famous for embarrassing incidents, I was not particularly popular. So I had resigned myself to taking long walks and doing some climbing.

"I was feeling very sorry for myself and one day when I was walking along a steep path, I came around a large rock and there was a woman sitting in front of an easel, drawing. She had her back to me, and I stopped and watched her. She was working with so much concentration that she didn't notice I was there. I saw she was wearing this peasant blouse and it was cut low so I could see her back, and it was covered with fine hair like golden down on her pale skin, and she was sweating a little, so there were tiny beads of sweat that shone in the sun. I still remember that all I wanted in the whole world was to touch that back, and of course I knew it was *verboten*, but I almost did it anyway, when she must have sensed me and turned.

"I think we were both surprised then, but I was as embarrassed as if I had really done something, and it was worse, because she was not a girl, she was a much older woman, nearer my mother in age. She told me afterward that I turned very red, but she thought it was because I had been spying on her drawing, and she invited me to sit down and watch her. She drew beautifully and easily, and she talked to me. She talked to me as if I were her equal, and before I knew it I was telling her all about myself, and she told me about herself, and she invited me to have lunch with her at her cottage, which was nearby, all by itself and away from the town."

"And she seduced you?"

He laughed. "Not that day. Nor for several days. And I could not say that it was entirely she who seduced me."

We walked on again a little ways and I saw that to our right there was a worn, partially gilded sign that said, 'Karlkapelle,' which the Count had mentioned.

"Let's look at this," I said, but I was still imagining Wolf with this woman. "Was she beautiful?"

"No, not really. But she had the most beautiful skin I have ever seen, what you call 'peaches and cream.'"

"What did you tell your mother?"

"Nothing, of course."

"I mean, didn't she ask you where you were going every day, and all that?"

"Well, you see, Elise made all that simple. The first day we met, we talked a lot about drawing, and she offered to teach me. So I told my mother I was taking drawing lessons. And for a some of the time, I really was. She was a very good teacher."

"Yes," I said dryly, "I know."

"Of drawing," he said.

"But not only of drawing."

"No," he said, "not only of drawing."

The chapel was only lit by candles on the altar and large tapers on wrought iron stands. Between us and the altar was a stone sarcophagus on which the figure of a knight holding a shield and sword reposed, revealed only as deep shadows and highlights under the flickering light. "This must be the Count's ancestor," I said.

"The Count?" Wolf said.

"Yes, Count von Friedrich. Father and I had lunch with him."

"Ach, Graf von Friedrich. Yes, of course. I have only met him once myself, when he came to school and awarded the prizes at my graduation."

"Did you get a prize?"

"Yes. I did."

"What for?"

"Mathematics."

"Not for 'drawing'?" I said.

"Not for drawing," he said. "That came later."

We stood in the dark chapel amid the flickering candles. I remembered the Count's mention of the vaulting, and I looked up, but I could barely make out the traces of the arches that formed the ceiling in the dim light. I knew that I wanted to know more about Wolf and the woman, Elise. The notion of the two of them together intrigued and repelled me at the same time. Older men and younger women, well, they were somehow acceptable. But an older woman and a much younger man seemed somehow reprehensible.

"So how did it happen?" I asked. "I mean, one minute you're taking drawing lessons and the next minute you're in bed with her. How did it happen?"

Even as I was asking him, I was asking myself what business it was of mine. I had never discussed the details of sleeping with a particular lover with anyone else. I think I was not just curious about Wolf's past; I was after something that has always puzzled me–the way people make the transition from being casual to being intimate. It's a transition that I have always found difficult, sometimes missing the moment and turning away when I needed most to step forward. But Wolf said, "Leni," stopping and shaking his head, "I can't talk about that."

"Oh, 'gentlemen don't talk.' Is that it?"

He hesitated. "Yes," he said slowly, "that is part of it. But..." He stopped and we stood in the aisle facing each other again, Wolf holding my hand as he had done before. "It is not only that. She was...my friend. She gave me...a great deal."

"You mean she made a man out of you."

He ignored the sarcasm in my remark, and shrugged. "Yes, you could say that. But not in the way you mean it. It was not that she made me *männlich*.... manly. When I met her, I had only the crudest ideas about sex, you understand, very crude and impossibly romantic at the same time. Later that summer..."

"She saved you a great deal of pain."

He shrugged again. "Yes, you could say that too. But again..."

"Again, that's not it. Were you in love with her?"

He smiled with a faraway look that was at the same time a little impatient and didn't say anything for a minute. We resumed walking and started down the long aisle toward the front of the cathedral, hand in hand. "Yes," he said finally in a whisper. "I thought I was. I was crazy about her." He shook his head ruefully. "I wanted to marry her."

"What did she say to that?"

"She made me promise not to speak of it again. She sat down with me and reminded me that our 'special friendship,' as she called it, was forbidden. No one must ever know."

"Did anyone ever find out?"

"Almost...A couple of times. I think, in the end, one of my mother's friends suspected, but she never did anything but make innuendos. My mother was having a wonderful time with her artistic friends and was happy not to have me around all the time. My father was only there for short periods–he was very busy that summer. But in the end, we got away with it–*Gott sei dank*."

I realized that Wolf's story had a powerful effect on me. "And here I thought it was my charms that gave us such a great night together," I finally said. I had meant it as a small joke, but found myself feeling slightly hurt.

"*Ach, du lieber Gott, Leni!*" he said, stopping and turning to face me. "That was eight...almost nine years ago!" Wolf put his arm around my shoulder and tried to hold me back. "Leni, with you it was...I do not have to tell you." He took me by the shoulders and turned me toward him. "It was the same for you. I know that."

I didn't say anything. I felt full of feelings that were making lies out of each other. We had come a long way down the side aisle of the nave where the outer section of seats ended, and we were standing in front of the confessional, a small, ancient wooden hut with two sections, with well-worn red velvet curtains on each side. Suddenly Wolf seized me and shuttled us into the right-hand section, where the darkness, tinged a faint red, enveloped us.

"Wolf!" I whispered, "we can't stay in here," but he pulled me back and pushed me against a narrow seat so that I was entirely held up by Wolf's arms, and he was kissing me on my neck and my ear and then his mouth found mine and I was caught in the rush, forgetting entirely where we were until right beside us I heard this great "Harrumph!" of someone clearing his throat.

Then a voice, speaking softly and matter-of-factly, said, "*Erzähl es mir, mein Kind.*"

It was the voice of the priest waiting to hear the confession of a sinner who was sitting fully clothed and full of truth on our side of the panel. I straightened up like a folded table leg that snaps into place and pushed Wolf away. His right arm was still around me as we both made for the front, but the red curtain which had seemed fairly flimsy as we entered wrapped us in its heavy, velvety embrace. Finally Wolf found its edge and pushed it aside as we stepped out. "Leni," Wolf said urgently, "Come. This way."

We ran out of the door, down the steps and around the corner, Wolf still pulling me by the hand until we came to Wolf's car and jumped in it like movie villains fleeing a bank with loot. In seconds we were rolling away from what felt like the scene of a crime.

Chapter 19

I leaned back in the seat. My heart was beating very fast and I was still breathing hard from running. Wolf didn't seem to be short of breath, but he was concentrating on driving. At a stoplight he turned to look at me, and I gave him a conspiratorial smile, as if we were a couple of kids on the lam from the teacher. He looked away but I could see he was fighting a smile as he turned into the next side street and pulled to a fast stop. Suddenly we were both laughing too hard to stop. "I wonder what the priest thought," I said, which sent us off again as if we were twelve–or less.

Finally Wolf leaned over me and looked at me with his eyes full of tenderness and said, "I don't think life with you would ever be dull."

I looked at him. We were back at the same impasse that I had been dodging since this morning: he opening his arms and wanting me to rush into them and even though I wanted to run into them and do that "Yes-I-will-yes-yes-yes" Molly Bloom thing, I just looked back at him fondly and with what I thought was a worldly-wise look and said, "How about moving to the States?" knowing I was playing a dirty game. "You could get into trouble with me anytime you wanted to."

He rubbed his fingers of his right hand against his temple and looked thoughtful. "Do not think I have not been considering this," he said, getting very serious. "It is just difficult to see how to do it. Mathematics lecturers are not hired on the moment."

I understood what he meant. It was June. The fall semester at most universities was already written in stone, on a time frame that was more suitable to plants than people. Even though there might be some twenty colleges close to New York City, it would be no more than an off-chance that any of them would have even a mediocre opening next year. I knew enough of the academic world to appreciate what he was up against, and I had enough respect for someone's life's work that I wouldn't consider asking him to leave it. I tried to look at my watch, but my watch arm was wedged between his right side and his seat.

Wolf rose to the occasion. "Almost five o'clock."

"God," I said. "Ilse is fixing dinner for my last night. Probably a celebration–that I'm leaving, I mean. But I have to get back to the house and dress for it."

"Yes, I know," Wolf said. "I have also been invited–this morning, when I visited. Your father said that old Tante Therese had been asking about you and wanted to meet you. Apparently, her curiosity about you is bigger that her feelings about Ilse, so she is coming too."

"And it is apparently bigger than the taboo against acknowledging relatives that are Jewish–if only by marriage. I wonder if mushrooms are on the menu," I said.

Wolf smiled. "She said that she is making Hühnchen. I do not know what they are called in English."

"Squabs."

"Squabs? It is such a funny word."

"Not as funny as some German words."

"For example?"

"How about Schmuck? Does that sound like jewelry? Or how about Rundfahrt? In English, that's a bad smell, not a tour of the city."

Wolf started to laugh. "I never heard it like that," he said, "with an American ear. That is funny."

"We've got to go," I said, pulling my arm out from behind him.

"One more kiss, to last me the evening," Wolf said, reaching for me again.

"It's going to have to last both of us," I said, suddenly regretful, as I started kissing him back.

On the one hand, it was hard to believe we had known each other only a few days; on the other, it was very understandable that the sheer bodily hunger we had developed for each other was still voracious. In a minute Wolf's hands were working their way up my thigh when there was a loud knock on the window behind me.

We jumped apart like magnetic toys whose polarities had been suddenly reversed. I looked over my shoulder into the eyes of an outraged matron brandishing an indignant finger. I felt my face assume an apologetic smirk that was immediately replaced by an angry scowl. I was about to say something to Wolf but he was starting the engine, and with the moral outrage of Stammbüttel on our tail, we roared off.

"Oh, Wolf," I said. "I can't stand this being chased around like a teenager with no place to go."

"Yes," he said angrily. "I feel the same way. There should be something we can do, but I must be back at Heidelberg to teach tomorrow afternoon. I should already have driven back today. I only came home because it was the anniversary of my father's death."

"I didn't know that."

"I did not tell you. And I have been shamefully neglecting my mother."

"What has she said about your 'shameful neglect'?"

"Amazingly little. She seems to be more...amused by my interest in you, than anything else."

"You told her about us?"

"Not exactly, of course. But she is not stupid."

"Does she expect you to marry Martina too?"

We had arrived at the house and he braked the car sharply in front of it. Then he turned to me with an incredulous look and said, "How do you know about Martina?"

"My father straightened me out. He told me you were going to marry Martina and that people were better off if they married their own kind. Speaking, of course, from bitter experience," I added. "Just in case I was getting ideas about marrying you myself."

Wolf shook his head. "I cannot believe that they still expect me to marry Martina."

"Why not?"

"Martina." He stopped and shook his head. "Martina and I have known each other since we were children. We have never been lovers. It would be like being with my sister."

"My father is not stupid either. Why does he still have the idea that you're going to marry her and live happily ever after."

"I think I can explain that," he said. "When I visit home, we often go out together–sometimes with Hermann and other friends. It is like when we were much younger."

"And she is not married."

"No. She was engaged, but she broke it off."

"And you're not in love with her?"

He put his right hand on my neck, running his thumb slowly along my jaw and up below my ear. "Do you care?"

I shook my head free. "Certainly. I didn't want you to have been telling me lies." I turned and opened the door.

He grabbed my left hand and brought it to his mouth. "No lies," he said, kissing my hand. "No lies." He let go of my hand and got out too, and we went into the house together.

The air in the house was filled with the smells of the roasting birds. Anni was in the dining room setting the table for ten. I counted heads. "*Wer wird kommen....* Who is coming, Anni?" I asked.

"*Die Kreutzelten, ihres Vaters Tante, und Herr Rudi....*your cousin by your father's brother," she said counting her fingers silently as she added the rest of the family.

"My father's brother? Then he's my first cousin," I said to Wolf. "I didn't know I had any...on my father's side, anyway. Well! I guess curiosity did overcome the fear of contamination."

Wolf heard the contempt in my voice; he looked at me with concern. "Leni," he said, "I understand how you feel, but this is not America, where everyone talks to everyone else, at least in theory. This is not easy for them. You must be polite."

I laughed. "Wolf," I said, "you think I'm much freer than I really am. I am often polite to people who don't deserve it. I would be polite to them even if this weren't my father's house. Don't worry about it." I went to my room.

When I shut the door behind me, I realized how glad I was to have a few minutes to myself. I thought about the coming evening. I was curious about this Tante Therese. She seemed quite a character; I found myself actually looking forward to meeting her. And this cousin of mine...*His* father was sending Rudi to look me over. I wanted to tell them all they were just a bunch of cowards and bigots. But revenge was not what I really wanted. I wanted a chance to spend more time alone with my father–like lunch for just the two us, or a walk in the woods. Why, I asked myself with a panicky feeling, hadn't I tried to get him to spend more time with me earlier, rather than going off with Wolf? At the time I didn't understand that my father had arranged as much time as he could manage with me, and I had accepted as much time as I could manage with him, and the sudden and intense affair with Wolf was heaven-sent for the three of us. But the question of Wolf remained. If I were going to deal seriously with him, what about Jack? Suddenly, that seemed to answer itself: I was finished with Jack. Thank God, I thought, that's really over! For a moment, it was a relief.

I wandered over to the bed and sat down, still making a quick check of the mirror, but the ghost of its outline was all that remained. I thought about why I had stayed with Jack all this time. I ran over all the reasons I had been giving my friends: he was at least as smart as I thought I was, he was sophisticated, we were great in bed, I was in love with him. In retrospect, I didn't really acknowledge one of the most important items: I liked who I was with him. I liked the couple we were, I liked the prospect of a life that was interesting, amusing and comfortable, and that was something that Jack had, however impermanently, delivered.

Looking at Wolf on the same scale, Wolf came up short, even though I was ready to give him credit for a number of unknowns. Would life with Wolf be as interesting, as amusing? I didn't know. On another hand, Jack was twelve years older than I was–half a generation–and it showed in the way he looked at the world. For Jack, there were already fewer surprises. He treated my willingness to still be amazed by the world with tolerant amusement. With Wolf...

I was brought out of this reverie by the sound of several shrieks that spoke distinctly of Helmut. I opened my door to check the lay of the land; everybody seemed to be in the living room. Through the doorway I could see my father holding Helmut in the air like a large doll and looking at him with a fatherly frown. Helmut was sobbing.

When I entered the living room, Helmut's storm had subsided and he was looking angelic on Ilse's knee, playing with a voracious-looking toy nutcracker of the tin-soldier-with-shako variety. An old woman in a very full blue paisley silk dress was sitting in the large leather armchair, my father on a chair across from her. Wolf sat at the other end of the couch looking bemused as my father introduced me to Tante Therese.

I went over to her and extended my hand. She slowly extended hers, hardly looking at me, barely brushed my fingers and dropped her hand again. As we touched, I genuflected slightly, and she closed her eyes and nodded. When she opened them, I saw they were a pale but piercing blue that looked directly at me with a gaze that was a little like Helmut's in its uncompromising directness. I waited for her to speak, but she only motioned to me to sit on the couch next to her.

As I sat down I noticed Wolf was holding a glass that looked like scotch with some ice in it, and my father asked me if I would like some, or would I prefer some very good dry sherry? I was about to ask for scotch when I caught sight of an exquisite cut crystal sherry glass half-filled with a golden amber liquid on the table next to me. I decided if Tante Therese was drinking it, it would be a good move to drink it too. It was. "*Franz hat immer die besten Weine*.... Franz always has the best wines," she said as she scrunched out a small smile.

I took the beautiful glass and ran my eyes over its glittering facets. It caught the light and shot it back brilliantly with a faint iridescence. When I looked up again, everyone was watching me, so I tasted the sherry. It was dry and warm with that edge of fruitiness that even the driest sherry never loses. I nodded and smiled and everyone nodded and smiled back. I looked at Ilse and gestured toward Helmut and said, "What happened?"

"When Anni tried to give him his supper, he became very upset because he wanted to 'Come to the party,'" Ilse said.

I understood how he felt; I had a vague memory of having to eat early and go to bed while the sky still held some light. I gave him a sympathetic smile. He looked away. "What has made him happy again?" I asked.

"*Er wird an seinem kleinen Tisch*.... He will sit at his little table," Ilse said, looking at him with Madonna eyes. "*Bei seiner Mutti*.... Next to his Mom–and be very quiet. Won't you, darling?"

Helmut didn't look at her, but he nodded and put her finger in the nutcracker's mouth. She removed it dexterously just as he closed the pincers, with a timing that she must have developed from earlier encounters. As the nutcracker clacked shut, Tante Therese cleared her throat and said, "*So du kommst den ganze langen Wege*...So, you have come all the way from America just to visit us."

The statement hung in the air over me the way a stone the Roadrunner is dropping on the Wolf hangs in the air before it nails him into the ground. If she had been here earlier in the week, I would have answered with Juneallysonian innocence, thinking she was merely passing the time of day. Now I assumed she was asking me how much I expected to get out of my visit.

I felt a great need to set her straight. A panicky feeling rose up in me when I started to answer her as all the thoughts I had on the matter tried to get out at once, the way the passengers on a sinking ship might jam together in a door leading to the deck. I had just succeeded in pulling one item out of the horde of my thoughts when I remembered that I had to express myself entirely in German, and for a moment even the modest German I had deserted me. Throughout these long, extended seconds everyone gazed at me with what seemed like great expectation that I would illuminate and set at rest the entire subject.

Finally I said somewhat lamely, "*Ich kam meinen Vater zu besuchen...*" I turned to Wolf. "How do you say, 'I came to see him in the flesh instead of as a memory'?" I knew that the only word I knew for 'flesh' could translate as 'meat,' but humor was not what I was trying for.

Wolf cleared his throat. "*Ich glaub du musst sagen 'in Fleisch und Blut.'*"

I was so startled to have him address me in German that I couldn't understand him. I looked at him blankly.

He gave me a little smile and said in English, "You can't translate 'in the flesh' into German. You have to say, 'in Fleisch und Blut—in flesh and blood.'"

"*In Fleisch und Blut?*" the aunt said, looking puzzled. My father, the subject of all my efforts, seemed only mildly interested, looking from one to another as if he were watching tennis. I decided to try again.

"*Ich wollte mein Vater in Fleisch und Blut besuchen....* I wanted to visit my father as a real person, instead of always thinking of him as a memory."

The sentence lay there, embarrassingly shopworn with all the handling. I looked at Wolf, who had the flicker of a smile hovering around his mouth, and a gave him a threatening look that despite my best effort landed less as a threat than an acknowledgement of our connection.

The aunt was onto it in a flash. "*Ich sehe,*" she said with a nod heavy with the knowledge of years, "*dass du und Wolf....* I see that you and Wolf have renewed your friendship."

"*Ja,*" I said, giving him my best cousinly look, "*das ist richtig....* Isn't that right, Wolf?"

Wolf smiled and said, "*Ja, Tante,* wir sind.... we are friends again."

It suddenly occurred to me that Tante Therese might remember a part of my life. "*Erinnern Sie sich an uns....* Do you remember us playing together?"

She nodded, smiling broadly. *"Ja, genau. Ich erinnere mich, wie Wolf....* I remember once, how Wolf was your horse, and you rode him." Everyone laughed, including Wolf and me, although I wasn't at all sure I liked the image. I looked at Wolf to see how he felt about it, but he had turned to Tante Therese and said with mock anxiety, *"Ich glaube nicht....* I don't think I want to hear this."

I threw a quick glance at Helmut. His cherubic mouth was open and his eyes were darting from Wolf to me to the aunt and back again. He was getting the sense of what was going on. Even if he missed details, it belonged in his little sphere and fascinated him.

"Und ich erinnere mich.... And I remember how when you rode Wolf, you beat him with a stick!" And she whipped her closed fist in front of her with a triumphant look and immediately broke into girlish giggles, covering her mouth daintily with her fingers.

I said indignantly, *"Nein!"* as if it were necessary to defend my infant honor. *"Ich hätte das nie getan....* I would never have done that!"

"Ach, aber ja!" the aunt said, nodding emphatically. *"Du hast das getan....* You did that and more. You made him cry. I saw it." She gleefully shook her finger at me and added with an expression of great satisfaction: *"Du warst....* you were a real little she-devil."

I turned to my father and blurted out, *"So, Vati....* what do you think of that?"

My father, smiled and cleared his throat. *"Leni, Tante Therese hat es ganz richtig erzählt....* Aunt Therese has told it exactly right: you were a little devil. I often had to spank you," he said as he leaned back with a look of genial amusement.

My childish feeling of embarrassment changed to one of surprise. They weren't talking with disapproval; they remembered me as one hell of a lively child. At the moment this was confusing, but later I came to understand how my penchant for jumping into new situations, for being willing to try new ideas, new venues–all came from this. My father might have spanked me for what I did, but there was an undertone of admiration for my temerity, an attitude usually reserved for boys, and it had conditioned my approach to life.

Ilse set Helmut down to go to kitchen. He began to protest, but my father told him to sit beside him, which he did with surprising meekness, casting a mournful glance at his mother as she went out the door.

"Wo sind die Buben?...Where are the boys?" my father called after her.

I heard her call them upstairs, but there was no answer. She appeared in the door and told my father that he would have to fetch them, because only God knew what they were up to up there.

I said a quiet 'Amen' to that, casting a quick glance at Wolf who merely gave me a reassuring smile. My father only said, *"Ja, sofort,"* and went on sitting with Helmut in his lap. As the kitchen door swung shut, everyone turned to look at the door behind me.

I turned too and saw one of the most beautiful men I have ever seen. His looks were so startling that it took me several seconds to see the Kurtzelts standing behind him. His were not the kind of looks that had made Robert Redford or Gary Cooper cinema icons. It was more like the kind of beauty that you occasionally see in a woman's face, except there was nothing effeminate about it: he exuded a kind of confident male sexuality that was almost arrogant. He was probably not more than eighteen, but he was old enough to have learned that all his features were perfect and in the right size and place: the large blue eyes that were checking the room, and the straight nose that ended about the right distance above the small smile that played on his lips. And even more startling was his dark, almost black hair and eyelashes that gave his marvelously even skin a preternaturally pale cast.

He took a step into the room, bowed and clicked his heels, once to my father and once to Tante Therese, and then he took another step and repeated the maneuver beside my chair, looking into my eyes. The combination of his looks and the gesture threw me off. I just sat there like the proverbial mouse before the snake, waiting, until he said *"Rudi Göring, Fräulein Helene."*

The *'Fräulein Helene'* broke the spell and I said, *"Nicht 'Fräulein Helene' Rudi;*...Not *'Miss* Helene' Rudi; our fathers are brothers. You must call me Lene."

He gave me an odd look. I think he was surprised less by what I said than how I said it–maybe my accent, or maybe because he didn't expect me to speak German, or maybe because he expected me to speak it better than I did. In any case, it was just a flash, and then that strange and lovely face went back to that small, secret smile which it seemed to bear like armor against a curious world. He bowed and clicked his heels again and said in English, "But certainly, Cousin Lene," which gave him the last word on the matter.

Then the Kurzeldts had greeted my father warmly, and turned, with more respect and distance, to Tante Therese. She was regarding them with a look that edged curiosity with suspicion. My father said, "*Tante, das sind...* these are my old friends..." And as he introduced them with the subtle implication that she really did know who they were but was not acknowledging it, each of them stepped before her–Hannah with a small nod of her body that acknowledged the aunt's age and status, and Paul with a full bow and a kiss of her hand that seemed to be somewhat over-graciously extended.

My father had gone over to small table that served as a bar and provided Hannah and Paul with scotch-and-sodas. Hannah chose to sit between Wolf and me on the couch, while Paul took a chair beside my father who made room for Helmut beside his crossed legs.

"So," said Hannah to me in English, "you are leaving us tomorrow. I am sorry you could not visit us again before you left."

"*Bitte,*" my father said to Hannah, "*meine Tante....* my Aunt speaks no English."

"*Bitte, Entschuldigung....* pardon me," Hannah said with a smile to the aunt as she repeated her words to me in German. "*So, du fährst....*you are going directly back to New York?"

"*Nein,*" I said, "*Ich werde....* I will spend a few days in Paris with friends."

"*Ach, wunderbar,*" Hannah said enthusiastically, "*Ich seit vor dem Krieg nicht....* I have not been to Paris since before the War."

"*Wirklich?...*Really?" Tante Therese said in a tone of astonishment that caught everyone's attention. "*Ich dachte....* I thought that you had spent the War in Paris."

The room fell silent. Hannah looked worried, which didn't surprise me: it wasn't worth telling the truth, but it was hardly worth a lie. Hannah looked at her hand and my eyes followed hers to her wedding ring.

Just then, Ilse stuck her head into the room and said with some annoyance, "*Wirklich, Franz....* Really, Franz. You must get the boys. They don't answer."

"*Komm, Helmut,*" my father said good-naturedly as he got up, offering his hand to a complaisant Helmut who took it and followed him out of the room. All eyes immediately returned to Hannah who was just clearing her throat, when we heard my father say loudly, "*Lieber Gott!....* Good Lord! Where have you been?" which was answered by mumbles.

"*Ball gespielt?*...Playing ball? With what, a piece of coal?" There was a moment of silence. Then he said "Ach!" with an expression of such deep paternal disgust that I imagined the boys shriveling slightly, although it was more likely they were relieved that no thunderbolts were launched at them that moment. Then he added, "*Geh hinauf and wasch dich*.... Go up and wash. Quick! Quick! Five minutes! Clean clothes and clean hands and faces." There was a small thunder of feet on the stairs.

"*Was haben die Buben gemacht?*...What were the boys doing?" Tante Therese asked.

My father sat down, rearranged Helmut beside him and took a sip of his drink with almost theatrical relish in the delay before he answered. "*Sie sagten sie haben Ball gespielt*.... They *said* they were playing ball, but they were as dirty as chimney sweeps." He shook his head ruefully with an indulgent smile on his lips. "*Ich weiss nicht*.... I don't know. Boys will be boys," he said with a fatherly sigh.

"*Ja*," Paul said agreeably, welcoming, I thought, the change of subject. "*Du hast recht, Franz*.... You are right, Franz. We were boys once too."

At this point both of them started laughing and clicked glasses. Then they had to repeat the process with Wolf and Rudi. I looked at Hannah. Without another word, we both raised our glasses to Tante Therese, who gave us a small smile as we clinked them together and I said, "*Zu Frauen*.... To Women!" and we drank.

But immediately, my father laughed and raised his glass too and said, "*Aber ja, zu Frauen!*" and everyone was drinking when Ilse entered and called us to dinner.

Chapter 20

Ilse sat us down in traditional order, allowing for the scarcity of women. She avoided not only putting Wolf next to me, but also seating Paul next to Hannah: after marriage spouses are

always seated at a distance on the presumption they have nothing more to say to each other. I had to make do for both Paul and Rudi. The boys, who came down looking unusually washed and sullen as usual, sat on either side of Ilse at the table's other end.

Helmut sat on a chair stacked with pillows, sharing Ilse's place. He seemed aware of his special dispensation and sat rosy-cheeked and silent, watching the proceedings with enormous attention as if some special, secret rite from which he had been hitherto excluded were about to be revealed to him. It reminded me of the way the young hero of *Swann's Way* approached his first ball at the house of the fashionable Duchesse de Guermantes, although Helmut was to leave much less disappointed than Proust had been.

We had just seated ourselves when the aunt leaned over to my father and addressing him as "Lieber Franzl" in a lowered voice, asked to change seats with Paul, claiming that she was having some sort of problem with her right shoulder or her right elbow, as she rubbed her upper arm with dramatic intensity. As this new arrangement was executed, Ilse came back from the kitchen and regarded us balefully, shaking her head at this wanton disturbance of her careful arrangements.

"*Warum spielt ihr....* Why are you playing musical chairs?" she asked Tante Therese with a preemptory tone. I was surprised: it seemed excessively rude. "*Warum kann Sie nicht....* Why can't you sit at Franz's right?"

There was an audible sniff of indignation from Tante Therese, but before overt hostilities could get under way, my father raised his hands like a blessing and interceded with Ilse, who accepted defeat with small grace. As she turned on her heel and went back to the kitchen, the aunt hissed in my ear, "*Diese Frau ist unerträglich....* This woman is insufferable. I cannot understand your father."

Not wishing to be in the middle of this ongoing war, I opted for a weak smile and a nod and said, "*Sie* kann *schwierig sein*.... She *can* be difficult," casting at the next moment an apologetic smile at my father. Tante Therese gave a satisfied nod and my father only raised an eyebrow, accompanied by the twitch of a smile as he turned to answer a question from Paul.

As soon as she saw that my father was engaged, Tante Therese leaned toward me and said softly, "*Was hoffst du zu erreichen?*...What do you hope to gain? She will not let you have any of your father's money. She will kill you first."

As she spoke she helped herself from a large plate Anni held out to her, on which a salad of pickled herring lay in gelid folds within a garnish of parsley. As Anni presented it to me, I found myself concentrating closely on it for a minute, but it nevertheless remained a cypher. I had lost the thread of the ordinary reality that told me what should be done with the plate. I looked back up into Tante Therese's eyes, which were glistening with anticipation. I decided she *was* slightly crazy. It seemed a logical way to deal with the situation: the aunt was crazy, Ilse was crazy, the boys were out of their minds, my father chose to be oblivious to the whole thing–and I was leaving tomorrow. I helped myself to some of the herring and watched Anni move on to Rudi, who was engaged in entertaining a worshipful Hans and Gustav.

I turned back to my plate and stole a glance at the aunt. She had turned her earnest attention onto the herring: eating was serious business with Tante Therese. I looked at Wolf; he was working on his herring and talking to Hannah. As I started to eat mine, I realized that nothing was settled. Why had I imagined that Tante Therese was crazy when all she had told me was what I suspected anyway: that Ilse might be willing to kill me rather than let me touch a *Pfennig* of her children's inheritance?

"*Ich fahre morgen ab*.... I am leaving tomorrow," I said to the aunt quietly.

She swallowed a piece of herring and impaled another on her fork. "*So ist es am besten*.... It is best," she said, and put the herring in her mouth.

I felt I had to contribute more to the conversation, and swallowed first. "*Mein wirkliches Problem*.... My real problem has not been with Ilse," I said *sotto voce*.

She swallowed and said, "*Nein?*" with an astonishing lift of her eyebrows, which hung high on her forehead and then dropped with a slight quiver.

"*Nein*," I said. "*Mein Problem*.... My problem has been with the boys," asking myself how I could even have raised the issue with this elderly woman with an odd reputation. Perhaps I was more desperate than I realized.

"*Die Buben*," she said as she lifted her fork the way a conductor raises his baton at the start of a performance, "*Sie hat sie ganz verdorben*.... She has completely spoiled them." And she brought down her fork with a swoop to impale another piece of herring.

"*Wirklich?*" I said, stabbing a morsel.

"Aber ja," she said, waving the herring like a small trophy. "*Diese Buben waren wirklich gute Buben*.... Those boys were really good boys until *she* became their mother."

"*Wirklich*," I said again. The vision of Hans and Gustav as model children stalled my imagination.

"*Ich habe deinem Vater gesagt*.... I have told your father: he must reestablish his authority over his sons," she said.

"*Was sagte er dazu?*.... What did he say to that?" I said and restrained myself from suggesting that he said, "*Buben werden Buben sein*," by putting a piece of herring in my mouth.

"*Ich fürchte*.... I am afraid that Ilse has turned him against me," Tante Therese said. He is always polite, but he does not listen to me."

Just then my father turned from Paul and said in a joking way, "*Wer hört dir nicht zu?*...Who doesn't listen to you? I listen to your every word."

"Franz," she said as she speared the last, large piece of herring with her fork and held it in front of her. "*Du hast nie* wirklich.... You never *really* listened to me, and *now* you don't listen at all."

My father smiled patronizingly. "*Tante, das ist nicht wahr*.... that is *not* true. I always listen to you."

She held her fork with the herring on it like a fencer holds his *epee* before he thrusts it forward. "Franz," she said indignantly, as the herring quivered on the tines, "*Ich will nicht*.... I will not let you patronize me. You know that I worry about your sons. You must take them by the hand again."

My father looked concerned. *"Liebe Tante, du darfst dich nicht aufregen....* You mustn't upset yourself. Remember your heart. *Denke an dein Herz,"* he repeated.

I looked up at her face and saw that she had become very red. Her hand shook.

"Wirklich," I said before she could answer my father. "You mustn't excite yourself."

She turned to me with a look that laced indignation with *hauteur. "Junges Fräulein, es ist nicht dein Platz....* Young woman, it is not your place to caution me," and turned back to my father, adding, "and it is not yours, Nephew." She laid her fork back onto her plate and looked like she was ready to stand up and stalk out.

My father became extremely respectful and conciliatory. He dropped his voice and addressed her with an edge of urgency in his tone, flattering her with a mixture of compliments, calls on his need of her, references to old family intimacies. In a space of a minute he touched all bases and made a home run. He even told her how right she was about the boys and only the press of business...If it was not entirely sincere, I remember it as pure virtuoso, and I loved the entire performance.

In the meantime I had ignored the rest of the table. I looked around. Wolf was still talking to Hannah, but he caught my eye and gave me an intense, intimate look before responding to Hannah's words. She caught the look as he spoke and looked at me and smiled. The boys and Rudi were laughing loudly to my left. Even Helmut, whose little frown made it clear that he hadn't understood much of what was going on was chortling and hitting the table with one hand to be in on the party.

My first instinct was to turn away again and stay out of it; it didn't feel as if I could find myself a place in their conversation. But the fact that I would be leaving tomorrow and leaving with all this bad feeling in place suddenly began to irk me, so I said, *"Was ist so komisch....* What's so funny?"

Their laughter stopped abruptly as they all turned to look at me. Helmut's hand stopped in its descent and hovered an inch over the table as he stared at me, his frown deepening. Hans and Gustav started laughing again. Ilse rose with a disapproving look, but with a small smile tugging at her lips, as if she too found the joke funny against her better judgment, and went into the kitchen.

Only Rudi turned to me with a friendly look and said, "Ach, Cousine Leni, I'm sorry, but it was just a dumb joke–to entertain the boys," he added in English. "Unfortunately, it is in slang. It would be impossible to translate," and he looked at me regretfully with his clear blue eyes with their long dark lashes. For an instant I was caught up by that face, suddenly so close to me; it felt a little like looking at a work of art, but I was torn from its contemplation by loud guffaws from the boys and Gustav saying, "*Ja, genau!*...Yes, exactly! It is impossible! Entirely impossible!" as he burst again into laughter which Hans and Helmut joined.

They stopped suddenly when my father raised his voice. "Hans! Gustav! *Genug!*...Enough! What is this racket? If you want to sit with the grown-ups, you have to behave like one."

The boys reduced their laughter to exchanges of small snorts, and everybody went back to their conversations. I still sat half-turned toward Rudi, who continued to incline his head toward me politely, so I said to him, "So, Rudi," intending to ask him about himself, when he interrupted me and said, "Please, can we speak English? I must practice."

"Oh," I said. "Sure. What are you practicing for?"

"To learn English of course. It is necessary now for everything. I think, sometimes, when America conquered Germany, she conquered the world."

"Well," I said, unwilling to restrain myself, "it was better than the other way round."

He seemed to draw a blank at that, so I said, "Well, it *is* 'slang,' but it *is* translatable. 'The other way round' means 'the opposite.' I could have said, 'It was better than the opposite.'"

He smiled. "Ja, I see what you mean. Maybe not better for us, but better for you, yes?"

"No," I said with relish. "I think better for Germans, too. The world under the Third Reich would not have been a nice place, even for most Germans."

"Why do you think that?" he said with small indignation, frowning a little. The small puckering of his forehead made me realize how little he changed his expression, as if he were saving his face, for something–perhaps for itself.

"If Germany had won," I said, "there never would have been any real peace. You would have been too busy killing all your enemies and every country you had conquered would have continued to fight you. And because of that you would have stayed at war, and you would always have been looking for enemies at home, so you would always have had to be careful, even in your own country, and so you would never really have been free and at peace."

"Like in Russia?" he said and I answered, "Yes, something like that."

That was the end of our political conversation, and I was asking him about his life when Anni came around and collected our herring plates. I had only found out that he had just completed his first year of college–at Heidelberg–("*Aber natürlich*," I said), when Anni returned, with Ilse proudly behind her, bearing a huge silver platter on which a covey of small stuffed birds lay in glistening splendor among a field of buttered and parsleyed potatoes. My father and Paul exclaimed loudly over it as it was placed in front of my father for serving.

Ilse continued to hover behind him. She handed him a pair of large silver tongs and pointed to the platter as she whispered into his ear. He turned to look at her and then looked back at the platter and shook his head resignedly. "So," he said, pointing with the tongs to the bird that lay nearest us. "*Ich fange mit diesem an?*.... I start with this one?"

She nodded, and he lay it decorously on the top plate in the stack in front of him, as Anni, standing beside my father, placed several potatoes at its side and put it in front of Tante Therese.

But Tante Therese was sitting very straight, looking down at her plate as if a spider had just crawled onto it. I could not see anything wrong. If anything, it was a perfect bird, its skin golden-brown and crinkled; the stumps of its legs and wings neat and symmetrical. She looked back at me and shook her head. For a second, I didn't understand what she might be getting at, when I remembered that her last dining experience might have given her grounds for concern.

I looked serious and gave a little shake of my head and said *sotto voce*, "*Aber gewiss*.... But I'm sure that is a really perfect squab."

As she gave me an annoyed look, I felt a little tap on my left shoulder. It was Anni, coming to set my plate in front of me. I turned back to the aunt to find her eyeing my bird as if there were gold in it. Before I could say anything, she said, "*Willst du tauschen*.... Will you change your plate with mine?"

"*Sicher*.... Certainly," I said, and before I could give her a hand she had switched our plates. I looked up to see whether anyone had noticed, but only Hannah–who raised her eyebrows and rolled her eyes upward–seemed to have followed the action. I looked at what had been mine and was now Tante Therese's bird. Its only distinction was that one of its legs seemed to be shorter than the other, as if the bone had been slightly trimmed. But even though I did not believe that Ilse would *actually* poison anyone, especially in front of the whole family, I felt an uneasy relief that the aunt and not I had that particular bird, and with mentally crossed fingers I wished Tante Therese *bon appetit.*

When everyone was served, my father introduced the wine, which, he said, was an *echt deutscher Wein*–a truly German wine, one that was not even exported–served, he said, in my honor on my last truly German evening. When everyone's glass was filled (including the older boys', although theirs was only filled part way), my father rose and called for a toast. The men rose enthusiastically and the boys followed. Then my father raised his glass to me and said "*Auf meine Tochter, Helene, Gesundheit und Freude*.... health and happiness." He looked at me warmly, even affectionately, I thought, as he said it, and everyone repeated "*Gesundheit und Freude*"–even the boys, after a look from my father. Transformed by my father's warm glance the moment remains a memento that even after all these years I keep as slim evidence that in some secret corner of his heart he cared for me.

They drank, and when I had sipped my wine and acknowledged the toast, my father asked me how I liked the wine. "*Anders als die französischen Weine*.... Different from the French wines you are used to, isn't it?" I nodded and smiled. It was a Gewürztraminer, and although it leaned to my Francophile taste too much toward sweetness, it went wonderfully with the birds, which turned out to be filled with a really good bread stuffing in which thin slices of a small mushroom and flecks of parsley blended with the birds' delicate taste.

The table fell silent, only the small plinking sounds of silver on porcelain marking the time. Then Father cleared his throat and said, "*Wir müssen*.... We must drink to Ilse...To the chef!" We raised our glasses and made enthusiastic sounds of agreement. Mine was entirely sincere: the birds were tiny masterpieces. Tante Therese went at hers with expert gusto, dissecting the limbs with panache and lifting the meat from the bones with the finesse of a maître d', so that only a small pile of bones and a carcass remained. It was an impressive performance.

When we finished the main course, we were served salad in what my father observed was the 'French style,' although the salad, a lightly-dressed melange of thinly sliced cabbage, cucumbers and radishes, was not particularly French. As we ate it, I looked up to see Wolf looking at me. I gave him a smile, which he had just started to return when I heard a strange sound next to me and saw Tante Therese grasping her throat. She had turned a dark red and looked like she was choking. The sounds she made were as unnerving as the way she looked; they were deep animal noises, frightening, intense and strange in this over-civilized setting. I didn't know what to do and for a moment that seemed far longer than it really was we all sat there staring as if we were taking part in a horrible tableau.

Suddenly my father leapt up and hit her on her back with the flat of his hand, and the strange sounds stopped. For an instant there was silence, and it startled everyone into action. Ilse, Hannah and Paul jumped up and rushed to her side. They started to talk at once, calling her name. She continued to sit there with her hand on her throat, the mottled red of her skin turning into patches of purple. Then, in another moment, everything stopped again as without a sound she collapsed forward so that her face fell directly onto her plate as her head hit her glass and sent it glittering and twirling across the table in a macabre dance.

In a second, Hannah and my father had lifted her up again, Hannah brushing the pieces of salad from her face with her napkin as my father started to hit Tante Therese on the back again. Paul shouted that he was going to call a doctor and rushed out, only to rush back in and ask which doctor to call. Rudi rushed out after him, shouting that he would fetch the doctor. My father was still slapping the aunt on her back and shouted at Paul to call Doctor Kenner, and Paul rushed out again.

Hannah kept calling to her, "*Frau Göring, bitte, versuchen zu husten....* try to cough," but it seemed pointless. My father stopped hitting her on the back. It was finally Helmut who asked the question, "*Ist sie tot?...*Is she dead?" Everyone whirled around and shouted at him that of course she was not dead, she was only ill, although it must have been clear to all of us that if she wasn't dead she was in danger of dying, and none of us were of any use.

Ilse went to pick Helmut up, but he ran away from her, keeping his eyes on the aunt even as he darted in and out of the scattered chairs. When Gustav caught Helmut as he went by him, he started to cry loudly, but his howls seemed appropriate to the setting. Ilse carried him protesting through the door, taking the boys with her, which they did with less fuss but with the same reluctance, looking over their shoulders as they backed out of the room.

As they left, Paul and Rudi returned to say that the doctor was coming and had called an ambulance. By this time the aunt was lying back in her chair looking horrible, held up by Hannah's arm around her shoulders. The purple color was fading in patches and her face was slack.

I was wondering if Helmut had been right about the aunt's condition when Hannah said, "*Sie atmet!*...She is breathing," and then we could see a faint rise and fall of the silk gathers that lay over the aunt's large breasts. A sudden, intangible feeling of relief swept through us as if a window had suddenly let in a gust of cool air, although the white curtains that covered them did not stir. I got up and pushed my chair over so that Hannah could sit down in it as she held Tante Therese's inert body. Then a silence fell.

My mind was just beginning to pick at the tangle of possibilities when Hannah asked, "Franz, *glaubst du*....do you think it is her heart?"

My father said with a worried frown, "*Ja, es ist möglich*....it is possible. I think it is very possible."

Wolf, whom I had almost completely forgotten, now came over and we both sat down. I turned to him, acknowledging his presence and the situation with a small *moue* as I put my elbows on the table and leant on them. He leant his elbows on the table as well, with his right elbow against mine, turning to me with lifted eyebrows to acknowledge that there was nothing more we could say under the peculiar circumstances.

We sat in silence, casting occasional glances at the tableau of the aunt in the arms of Hannah, with my father standing over her as Paul and Rudi hovered behind him. Hannah and my father exchanged glances and whispered.

My mind started again to toy with the cause of Tante Therese's sudden collapse, but the pressure of Wolf's arm distracted me. I heard the subtle sounds of the house: our breaths and small coughs; Helmut's small, complaining voice upstairs; Anni's kitchen noises and the creaking of the old house. Into this suspended silence, my father suddenly stamped his foot and said exasperatedly, "*Lieber Gott! Wo ist der Doktor?!*" and sent Rudi to look out for his arrival.

It was probably only a couple of minutes later that we heard car doors slamming, house doors opening to the sound of footsteps. Rudi came into the room with a small, serious-looking man with gray hair and a short, full mustache, close behind him. The doctor walked in quickly and pulled my father's chair up to Tante Therese's her inert body. He took out his stethoscope and started to examine her, asking Hannah and my father short, intense questions.

A few minutes later Rudi was back with two men and a stretcher. The larger of the two men–a solidly built man so pale that his thinning hair and eyebrows were hardly visible–went to take the aunt from Hannah's arms as the other slipped an expert arm under her knees. When the pale man had hold of the aunt's shoulders, he pulled her over to the right. As he did so, the aunt's full weight shifted suddenly to the men, and immediately both of them were on their knees, cradling the woman's large, cheerfully clad body in their laps like a bizarre *Pieta.* After a second, they regained their balance and maneuvered Tante Therese over the stretcher. They laid her down on it gently as Hannah tucked her skirt under her.

"*Macht schnell!*...Quick, quick!" the doctor said to the men, making shooing motions with his right hand. The men moved quickly and deftly out through the door, the doctor close behind them, followed by my father.

"*Bitte,*" Rudi said rushing after them, "*Ich möchte mit ihr fahren*.... I want to go with her."

My father hesitated, but when Rudi said insistently "*Sie ist auch meine Tante*.... She is my aunt too!" he turned and Rudi followed him out.

When they had gone, the four of us looked at each other. Anni came out of the kitchen and asked, "*Wollen Sie Kaffee?*...Do you wish to have coffee?"

Paul sighed deeply and rubbed his hand over his face. *Nein*, danke Anni," he said. "*Ich glaube wir brauchen Schnapps*.... I think we need some brandy."

When Anni brought glasses, Paul poured a generous amount of cognac for each of us. As he set the bottle down carefully, we picked up our glasses and stopped for a bare instant, as if waiting for a toast. Then we drank in silence.

Chapter 21

In the silence, my mind kept returning to the moment when Tante Therese exchanged plates with me. I looked at the others. Paul and Wolf were still studying their cognacs, but when I looked at Hannah, she looked up at me and said, "I saw her take your plate."

I nodded. Paul and Wolf said, almost at once, "She took your plate?"

I nodded again. I was trying not to cry.

"Yes," Hannah said. "I saw. When the *Hühnchen* were served, she took Leni's and gave Leni hers. I thought, at the time, it was just silly."

Wolf reached over and took my hand. The gesture at this moment, when I felt so alone and at the same time so responsible for the old woman's condition broke the last filament of my resolve not to cry, and I held onto his hand and put the other over my face as it folded into terrible, hard tears, while all the things that had happened this last week broke over me.

"Oh, *Liebchen*," I heard Hannah say, and in a moment she had drawn up a chair and put her arm around me. It was comforting even as I had the fleeting thought that I would have preferred it to be Wolf's arm, but still keeping hold of his hand, I let my tears well out of my eyes and run over my face.

"I know it is terrible, but there is nothing you could have done," I heard Paul say.

I looked around for a napkin to wipe my face. Hannah seemed to understand my look, because I she said to Paul, "Paul, *dein Taschentuch*.... your handkerchief," and he reached into his pocket and handed it to me.

I took it and wiped my eyes. "I shouldn't have let her take my plate," I said.

"Ach, Leni. It was stupid of me to refer to that." Hannah was patting my back as she spoke, the way one comforts a child.

"It is meaningless. Frau Wiedemeier has a weak heart. It was not what she ate."

"I am not so sure," I said. My voice was still breaking, and I realized that they knew nothing of what had been going on with me all week. Only Wolf knew, and I was not sure how much he really believed–not so much as to *what* happened as to why it happened, or anyway, whether it was all really intentional or just a dangerous kind of horseplay. But I turned to him, as if he could somehow in one breath explain it all.

"Wolf," I said, dabbing at my eyes. "Ilse collected a lot of mushrooms when we went to the woods." As soon as I said it, it sounded so inadequate and paranoid that I was embarrassed.

"But Leni, Ilse always collects mushrooms. Everyone knows that." Paul's voice was patronizing. I began to feel desperate.

"Wolf," I said, "tell them what has been happening. Please."

Hannah took her arm off my back and pulled her chair around so she could see me. "What do you mean?" she said.

"Well," Wolf said diffidently, as if he wasn't sure how far he wanted to take it, "Leni has had some frightening experiences since she arrived here."

They looked at me with so much surprise that I realized that even as I trying to become accustomed to the idea that the Göring family ambience ran to dementia, it wasn't part of the common knowledge of Stammbüttel.

"Yes!" I said–more impatiently than I meant to as I dried the last of my tears. "First the boys tried to push me off a *very* high cliff, then they tried to break my skull with a very large mirror that hung over my bed, and God only knows what they'll up to before I leave tomorrow."

As both Hannah and Paul looked at me like I was losing my mind, Wolf looked at me with an expression that said, "See, it will be impossible to get anyone to believe you."

"What," said Hannah, looking as if she was trying very hard to take me seriously, "What makes you think this has been done deliberately?" while Paul was saying, "Why would they want to do such terrible things?"

As I looked at them, I could see how unprepared they were to hear anything I might try to say, like trying to explain sex to a pair of celibate ecclesiastics. "Because," I said very seriously and deliberately, "they think that I came here to take my father's money away from them when he dies."

"But is that true?" Hannah said. "Could you do that?"

"I don't have a clue–I don't have the faintest idea." I was beginning to feel exasperated. "I'm not even sure my father has enough money to make such an idea worthwhile."

The moment I said that, all three of them gave me a very long look, and I realized how cynical I must have sounded. "Oh, no." I protested. "No, that's not what I mean. When I took this trip money was the farthest thing from my mind. I mean, it still is. I make really good money. I don't need my father's money. All I wanted to do was meet him and get to know him. I didn't even know there was enough money to fight about–and I wouldn't be surprised if there wasn't any–at least not much. That's what I meant." And I started to cry again, this time more out of frustration than anything else.

"You know," Paul said quietly, "there is a possible explanation. There are old primogeniture laws that may still exist, although I would think they usually specify the 'first-born male'," he said. "Of course, that aspect might be voided by the issue of sexual equality. It is entirely possible that Ilse may have somehow got the idea that the laws would apply to Leni. If that were really true, Leni could receive Franz's entire estate just by making a claim for it. It would supersede everyone else's claim–including Ilse's."

We all sat there without saying anything for a minute. Paul's explanation could explain a great deal–if it were true, I thought. I found myself wondering if Ilse would have checked this out or whether she would have acted just on the *possibility* of my having any rights of inheritance. Even then I had lived long enough to understand that fear and passion for control feel like justification: when you claim you are protecting you and yours, you are right and the other is wrong. Any tribal text will do.

"Ilse told me, the first evening I was here," I said, "that even though people may snub her personally, she knows that her children will be accepted, and that her grandchildren will marry into the families that snub her now in Stammbüttel. She also told me that she will allow *nothing* to get in the way of that. She was very emphatic."

I found myself recalling the conversation as if it were still taking place, sitting in the next room with Ilse, except now I thought I understood exactly why she was telling it to me. It took me a couple of seconds to hear Hannah asking, "But even so, how does that explain the behavior of the boys?"

"Yes," Paul said," I do not understand why they would be involved. And it is unthinkable that she would involve them, no matter how worried she might be."

I sighed. I felt very heavy. It seemed like the effort of trying to convince Paul and Hannah of all that had been going on had too much weight for me to carry it into words with enough sense to move them to my side. I wiped my tears away and wanted to blow my nose, but Paul's handkerchief seemed too pristine for me to use for that so I just dabbed discretely and snuffled as they sat, like good people everywhere asking, "Why would anyone *do* such a thing?"–wanting to believe that money wasn't enough reason to do serious harm.

"Well," I said, catching my breath, "maybe it's unthinkable, but the minute I arrived Helmut screamed at me that I was an evil witch and gave me a royal kick in my shin, and the boys were anything but friendly, even then."

"But that is terrible!" Hannah said, looking shocked. "You must have been very upset."

"Actually, no," I said quickly. "I was so busy trying to get everyone to like me and making excuses for them that I just didn't take it seriously."

"What was this about being pushed off a cliff?" Paul sounded like he was trying to work it out in a reasonable way. I told him briefly what had happened.

When I finished, he was still looking at me expectantly, as if I hadn't finished the story, so I added, "Apparently it's not their first try. They almost killed a schoolmate recently."

"Ach, ja!" Paul said. "I heard about that. It was almost impossible to believe that such a story referred to Franz's sons."

He was silent a moment and then he said, "It is difficult to know what is the right thing to do about what Frau Wiedemeier ate. Franz is my oldest friend. But I think I have a solution. Bibo Rotenberg is also a very old friend and he is a doctor at the hospital. Perhaps if I call him, he can do something. I can ask him to be discreet about it." I suddenly felt hopeful. But he still waited. It occurred to me that he might be hoping that we would tell him not to do it. But when no one said anything, he got up and went to the telephone.

When Paul started speaking and I heard him say, "Bibo," I felt as if the phone call might undo everything that happened tonight. Paul spoke in a low voice with a lot of pauses. I realized I was listening more to the tone of his voice than his words–now sounding diffident, now precise, now urgent. I was surprised, then, when Paul hung up the phone and stood there rubbing the back of his neck, smiling with a quizzical look.

"Pauli!" Hannah said almost sternly. "*Was gibts?*...What is it?"

Paul shook his head in disbelief. "Once he understood what I wanted, Bibo laughed!" Paul's voice was full of disbelief. "He actually laughed."

"He laughed?" Hanna repeated it as a question, mirroring Paul's astonishment.

Paul walked back to the table and sat down and poured himself more cognac, with an odd, half-humorous look on his face. "He laughed," Paul said, and took a sip before he continued, "he laughed because he says that this sort of thing happens all the time. People come in with various illnesses, and someone discretely points out that just before he fell ill, the patient ate some wild mushrooms, and although they are sure it is not possible, perhaps the doctor might want to look into it–of course, without embarrassing the family, or the host, or whoever..."

"You mean he thought it was no big deal?"

"Ach," Paul said. "Almost exactly so. My friend treated it almost as a matter of no consequence."

"What is he going to do?" Hannah asked.

"He is calling a colleague at the hospital and he will 'suggest' that perhaps he should check the contents of Frau Wiedenmeier's stomach–especially for mushrooms. He said his colleague will understand, and will be discreet about it."

"So you see," Wolf said to me. "Now you don't have to worry. The doctor will take care of Tante Therese. If there is a problem with the mushrooms, he will find it."

Paul looked at his watch. "*Lieber Gott*," he said. "It is almost ten. Yes, certainly, let us go. Franz will not be expecting to see us here when he returns."

"I wonder where Ilse is," Hannah said, looking toward the door.

"I expect she is still trying to calm down Helmut," I said. "He watched the whole thing. It made his day." I must have become so used to thinking defensively about my half-siblings that I didn't even hear the cynicism in my words, but Hannah did.

"I think," Hannah said with a reprimand in her voice, "that it must have frightened him. The poor little boy will probably have nightmares. Ilse will have her hands full."

I was about to say that I thought that Helmut would take it all in stride, but there was no question that Ilse would have her hands full, so I just nodded and said, "Yes, I'm sure you're right."

"And I wonder," Hannah said, looking around, "where Gustav and Hans are. It is not like them," she said with a smile, "to be sent to bed early without even a *small* protest."

Hannah was right, I thought. Gustav would probably have been curious enough to come down and talk to Wolf about what had happened. As I look back on it, I should have had at least a dime's worth of suspicion left in me, but the shock of seeing the old aunt collapse apparently limited my capacity for paranoia. "They probably have a 'project' that is keeping them busy," I said, as if the 'project' could not possibly concern me.

"Good," Paul said, getting up too. "Then we will go."

Hannah bent over and kissed me on the cheek. "I am glad we saw you again before you left, Leni." she said. "Please be sure to write us."

Paul reached over and shook my hand. "Yes, Leni," he said. "You must write us."

"I will. I will," I said, and meant it. A minute later, they were gone.

Wolf had walked with me to the door to see the Kurzeldts off, and came back with me. I looked up the stairs. I heard Helmut's small plaintive voice and Ilse's muffled answer. There was no sound from the boys' room. I dismissed them from my mind as we returned to the dining room where Anni was almost finished clearing the last things from the table onto a tray. She had left the bottle of cognac and our glasses, and asked if we still wanted them. We both shook our heads, no. Anni said *"Gute Nacht"*, and returned to the kitchen.

When the door swung closed behind her, I suddenly felt very tired. "Wolf," I said. "I want to sit down."

He took my hand and pulled me into the living room. "Come," he said in a very sweet way, and let me over to the couch. When I sat down, he sat down next to me and put both his arms around me, so that my head was on his shoulder. I just relaxed into him and closed my eyes. It felt so good just to sit there that I stopped for a minute and just let myself be there without any thoughts at all, so that I became aware of the rough tweedy wool of his jacket against my cheek, and as I breathed in the smell of the wool I also became aware of the scent of Wolf's skin, and still without thinking and my eyes still closed I raised my head–more, perhaps, to satisfy my nose that he still smelled as I remembered him than for anything else, but immediately I felt his mouth on mine and we just kissed, sitting there, his arms around me and my arms still in my lap.

It was a wonderful kiss, full of tenderness and familiarity, and after that terrible evening, it seemed almost like a kind of coming home, a safe-harbor kind of feeling, and I wanted it to continue but I pulled my head away slightly and raised my hand to stroke his hair. As I touched him he drew his breath in sharply.

"Leni," he said. "Leni." His voice was thick and the hand he reached up to my breast shook, and as if it carried some kind of electric current that started to flow though me as well. We kissed again, but the kiss was now very different, full of sex and need. "Come," he said as he stood up and pulled me up too, and pulled me by the hand through the door, heading for my room.

I stopped as if the next step would take me against a wall. "No!" I said in a hoarse whisper. "Not here!"

"No one will know," he whispered back and pulled me against him, kissing me below my ear and running his lips down my neck as he repeated, "No one will know."

"This is my father's house," I whispered, trying desperately to gather enough resolution out of the feeling of impropriety of having sex *here,* of all places–to uphold some idea that this, my father's place, was not a place where I could do anything but behave exactly as my father would expect, and as I was struggling feebly with these ideas, Wolf suddenly tightened his arms around me and said with a low voice that sounded as if he were out of breath, "Just let me hold you. I just want to hold you."

For an instant his words broke the tension, so that I laughed. "You just want to hold me?" I said smiling, trying to gain control.

He looked back at me with his eyes slightly narrowed as if he were measuring me, and then he tightened his arms around me again and said in the same low tone in which I'd spoken, "Yes, you can believe that. At this moment, all I want to do is to hold you, preferably in a bed, preferably naked, and preferably right now," and as he spoke he started to kiss me on the neck again so that his words fell as soft puffs of air against my skin, and as I felt the hard muscles of his arms through the fabric of his jacket hard against my ribs I also felt my concern over having sex in my father's house entirely overwhelmed by wanting to be held.

As I said, "Okay," we both turned at once and slipped quickly across the deserted dining room into mine, closing the door behind us. There was an old-fashioned key in an old-fashioned lock under the door knob, and as I turned it, it clicked closed with a satisfying sound.

I turned to see Wolf already out of his jacket and untying his shoes. As I stepped out of mine, I said, still talking in a whisper, "And how are you going to get out of here without running into somebody?"

He pulled off his tie and said, "Through the window." Then he smiled. "It won't be the first time." I had forgotten about the window, which I had left slightly ajar, but it was screened from the street by thick bushes and a white curtain.

"Christ," I said, walking over to him and starting to unbutton his shirt, "you're a veritable Don Juan, aren't you?" but he ignored me and concentrated on unbuttoning my dress. We finished undressing in silence and in the dark and in a great hurry as if we had no more time at all, but as if he needed to keep his word, he held me, and still in silence except for the sound of our breath we kissed and caressed each other and he didn't enter me until almost the very end.

We lay in the center of the deep, soft mattress. I felt very sleepy, but I could feel Wolf still awake beside me. His right arm was still around me while his left wandered slowly and thoughtfully over the left side of my body, his fingertips slipping over the ridges and hollows of my flesh as if recording a topological memory. "Stay," he whispered. "Stay. Don't leave tomorrow."

I breathed a deep sigh and lay still for several seconds. "Right now," I whispered, "I don't want to think of leaving you either." At that moment, lying next to Wolf in that soft bed, I meant it. "God, Wolf, I really mean it," I whispered as I kissed him and slipped into sleep.

I don't know how much later it was when a thump or a crash of some kind woke me. It was a metallic sound, like the sound of a heavy can or bucket being knocked over, and had I remembered that my father's house was not a safe place for me, instead of being lulled into an illusion of safety by lying in Wolf's arms, I would have known it came from the basement directly below me, where my father's new, modern gas-fired hot water system had only recently been installed.

"What was that?" I said, trying to sit up. I felt heavy and light at the same time, as if I were slightly dizzy.

"Probably a cat," Wolf murmured sleepily. He spoke slowly with a slight slur, as if he were talking in his sleep. A small breeze stirred fresh, cool air over us from the open window. When it stopped, the air in the room had an odd, metallic taste. I knew what the taste was, but my mind refused to name it, even though it should have set off alarms. In full consciousness I would have noticed the smell, rather than the taste, and would have immediately understood that the air of the room was full of ordinary cooking gas.

My mind was trying to know *something*, but unable to grasp it, it just kept toying with this unidentifiable *something*, when Wolf reached for me and started to kiss me, at first slowly, sleepily, and I kissed him slowly, sleepily back. As I kissed him, I slowly ran my fingers over his shoulders and down his back, sleepily savoring the simultaneous feeling of touching his smooth, lean flesh and having his hands slipping over my body, touching me, and all this time I had this strange, slightly giddy feeling of sliding along the edge of consciousness, so that half awake my hand slid over the curve of his buttock and almost as if I were skating I slid along the inside of his thigh.

I don't remember any transition from this drifting, dreamlike state, but suddenly Wolf's body was tautly arching over me, and with one move he had lifted me and impaled me and even as one part of me knew exactly what we were doing, we were also riding a galloping horse under a dark sky, and gradually our horse's leaps became longer and longer, and higher and higher, and just as we went up for ever I heard a great noise–a huge explosion–and I felt the both of us lifting, lifting and not coming down at all, and I hung tightly on to Wolf, and started to slide into a kind of blackness when suddenly we crashed down hard, and I woke up on the floor, on top of Wolf, half-covered by the eiderdown, with the smell of singed wood all around us and a wind from the now fully open window blowing fresh air across the bed.

Chapter 22

I sat up, leaning on my arm because the lower part of me was still entwined with Wolf's. I moved my legs and ran my hand over my body. I was okay, I decided. I somehow understood that there had been an explosion, but I felt nothing, no fear, no concern.

"Wolf," I said. "Wolf." There was no answer. I reached for his shoulder and shook him. He didn't respond. I thought, "Oh, God. He's dead!"

I started to shake and my breath went short. I was edging into hysteria when Wolf sat up and said, "*Was ist geschehen?*.... What happened?" I was so relieved that I tried to throw my arms around him, but I only succeeded in knocking both of us back down. We seemed to be lying partly on the bed and partly on the floor. As we fell, Wolf yelled and cursed in German. Then he put his hand on my arm and said, "Stay, Leni. Do not move. I think it is dangerous. I will try to see if the light is working," and very slowly he started to climb across the bed.

The bed groaned and shifted and for a second it seemed as if it were going to fall apart, but then it stopped making noises and Wolf climbed up and across it toward where the little table with the lamp had been. I heard him fumbling and the light came on.

It dazzled me, but in a moment my eyes had adapted and I could see Wolf above me holding up the lamp, looking like something out of a Mannerist painting. He was hanging onto what was now the upper edge of the bed, which sloped toward me at an acute angle that made it clear that the entire bottom corner had sunk into the floor. As I looked around at the edges of the light I could see that it glinted on the shiny teeth of nails sticking out of the ends of some of the wide floor boards that had come loose.

Wolf took a look around. "*Lieber Gott!*" he said in a low voice, shaking his head slowly from side to side. "I think, Leni, maybe the heating must have exploded."

I tried to think clearly, but my brain still wasn't working too well. I had just started to get up when I heard footsteps. A second later the door handle clicked and I heard my father shouting, "Leni! Leni! *Was ist los?....* What's happened? Are you all right?"

For a second Wolf and I just stared at each other. Finally I called out, "*Ja, Vati.* Ich bin okay."

My father rattled the door again. "*Bitte, Leni....* Open the door!"

"*Ein Moment, Vati,*" I said. "It is very dangerous walking in here." Wolf and I exchanged another long look. I think we both felt torn between assuming our right as adults and feeling our old places as children before the German paterfamilias. In a second, the German paterfamilias had won. Wolf slid off the bed and gingerly began to pick his way around, holding the lamp high, but as he did so, I saw the lamp cord tighten.

"Watch out!" I whispered. "The cord." Wolf lay the lamp gingerly on the bed. It stayed lit as my father called me again. "*Was ist los?....* What is going on?"

"*Moment, Vater,*" I said, "*Ich darf....* I have to put on a robe." As I spoke I was watching Wolf make his way carefully around the periphery of the room, where the floor was more or less intact. In the process, he had to pass the door behind which my father was standing. As he passed it, my father rattled the door again and Wolf jumped.

"*Ach,*" my father said impatiently, "*dass ist nicht nötig....* that is not necessary. *Bitte, Leni!...*Open the door! Immediately!"

I wasn't about to greet my estranged father in my current birthday suit, considering that the last one he had seen me in wouldn't even have qualified for Lolita. He, of course, assumed that I was covered by at least a nightgown and was being unduly modest. Little does he know, I thought, as I watched Wolf reach the place where our clothes had been so hastily dropped.

"*Ich komme, Vati,*" I called as I stood up gingerly, trying to see a way to the path that Wolf had taken. "*Es stecken viele grosse Nägel....* There are many big nails sticking out of the floor."

"*Lieber Gott,*" I heard him mutter. "*Ja, ja*" he said impatiently, "*Ich verstehe....* I understand. Be careful. But hurry!"

I took another few steps and was almost at the door when I looked up to see Wolf, who had put on his shorts and undershirt, standing with his clothes over his arm and one foot out of the window. He threw me a kiss with a gallant wave, and when I stopped to return it, he responded with an even more extravagant gesture and leaped–like a half-dressed d'Artagnan–through the window.

It appeared, however, that he had miscalculated the distance to the ground below and the location of the bushes. He disappeared from sight as if he had been sucked out of the window, his exit followed by a crackling and snapping of branches and a stifled cry.

"Leni!" my father shouted, starting to shake the door violently, and I thanked its age and strength as I made a final dash to the window, looked out to see dimly that Wolf was picking himself up from a broken bush, found my robe still hanging from a corner of the bed and put in on before I made as much of a dash for the door as circumstances permitted.

When I opened it, my father took a step into the room and stopped. His jaw literally dropped and hung there, resisting his efforts to pick it up as he repeated, "Ah, Ah, Ah," several times. It was then that I became aware that the definite, now-familiar smell was still in the air, and this time I had no problem identifying it.

"Vati!" I said, sniffing the air. "*Es ist Gas!*...It is gas! Can you smell it?"

My father gave the air a thoughtful sniff. "*Lieber Gott!*" he exclaimed. "*Du hast recht!*...You are right! But how is that possible?" He shook his head and pressed his hand over his eyes. "I must go downstairs," and he turned on his heel and went out.

I didn't want to spend another moment in the demolished room, and followed him through the kitchen to a small, low doorway that led into the basement. I was aware of Anni standing in her nightgown in a corner of the kitchen, her hand to her mouth, still in shock. My father stopped at the head of the stairs. I saw that his hand was on an old light switch, but he didn't throw it–which was good, considering that the basement still smelled of gas. He turned, frowning, went out into the hall, and returned with a large flashlight. "*Öffnet die Fenster*.... Open the windows," he said to Anni over his shoulder, as I followed him carefully down the stairs.

My father stood on one of the lower steps and slowly moved the light around the room. In its bright, wide swath, the first thing we saw was a tangle of boxes and buckets and odd pieces of furniture, all thrown in a jumble against the walls. I was surprised to find myself breathing fairly easily: there didn't seem to be much gas in the air. Then the light picked up a pair of legs that were slowly moving from side to side. It was Hans, who was sitting like a cast-away doll jammed between a bin and a large cylinder. There was soot all over him, and his nose was bleeding. When the light reached him he opened his eyes and looked up without moving his head.

"Hans!" father almost shouted. "*Was ist hier passiert?....* What's happened here? *Lieber Gott!!*" He dropped on his knees beside Hans. Hans groaned. As I looked around, I wondered at the way Hans seemed to have a cat's ability to survive certain death. With the light from the kitchen and the light from my father's lamp, my eyes had adapted and I could see that the cylinder to Hans' right had a small nozzle or spigot on it. But what really caught my attention was a long, thin hose of rubber tubing that looped across the room. At that moment I also saw that the other end of the tubing had been stuck into a hole in the floor of what had been my bedroom.

"*Vater! Sieh das an!....* Look at that!" I said.

He looked around and he *must* have understood what it was, but all he said was, "*Ja, Ja. Bitte....* Please ask Ilse to call the doctor." I turned to go, but remembered that Hans was only half the story.

"*Wo ist Gustav?*" I asked.

"*Ja*," he said, starting. "*Wo ist der Bub?....* Where *is* the boy?" as he ran his torch across to the far wall of the cellar. Halfway across it lit Gustav, who was sitting hunched over on an old couch which turned out to have saved his life by catching him and absorbing the impact of the explosion. He was in better shape than Hans: he looked dazed and dirty, but there didn't seem to be a scratch on him.

"Gustav," my father said to him sharply. "*Bist du in Ordnung?*"

"*Ja, Vati*," he said in a low voice. "*Ich bin in Ordnung....* I'm all right."

Still crouching over Hans, my father shook his head and said in a low, urgent tone, "*Wie ist das passiert?....* How did this happen?"

"*Es war der dumme Hans.*" Gustav's voice was full of exasperation. "It was that dumb Hans. When the hose fell off the nozzle, he lit a match!" His voice rose a quarter octave, quavering with disbelief. "He lit a match!...So he could see better!"

"*In Name Gottes, was habt ihr mit dem Gas gemacht....* What in the name of God were you doing with the gas in the middle of the night?" My father looked at Gustav with incredulity. He still didn't want to see what they were up to, but I did, and I felt a darkness hovering over everything. The strange smell and the drifting feeling...If I hadn't had the window open, both of us might have been dead before Hans put an end to it.

At that moment, Hans groaned again and said haltingly, "*Ich konnte....* I couldn't see."

"*Dummkopf!*" Gustav said to him harshly. "*Du hast alles verdorben....* You've spoiled everything. Look!" he said, pointing at me. "She is still alive! She will take everything!" And he put his head in his hands, his elbows resting on his knees, in a gesture of complete despair.

I looked at my father. He had sat down on the floor and was sitting with his hands on his head and his elbows on this thighs, almost as Gustav was sitting. "*Lieber Gott!*" he repeated over and over. "*Lieber Gott!*" I stood there, not sure of what I could say or do, except that keeping my eyes fixed on him prevented me from looking at Gustav's construction. When Hans groaned again and tried to sit, my father helped him up. I turned and went back up the stairs to get Ilse and a doctor.

As I passed through the kitchen, Anni turned from the stove where–as a reflex, I suppose–she was making coffee. She gave me a long, strange look, something between sympathy and reproach, but she didn't say anything. When I got upstairs, I realized that I wasn't really sure whose room was whose–except the boys', and that was at the far end of the hall. At the other end, a door stood ajar and I looked in. It contained a large, beautiful bed with a great carved oak headboard, dark with patina, making the white sheets shine starkly against it under the single bedside lamp. Through the window across the bed, the outline of a tree showed black against the first faint paling of the night sky.

I had assumed it was my father's and Ilse's room, but I saw that only one pillow in the center had been slept on, and Ilse was not there. I listened, hoping that some sound would show me where she was, but I heard nothing. Considering that the house had nearly blown up, I began to wonder why she hadn't shown up downstairs. I knocked softly on another door to my left. When there was no answer, I hesitated, but when I opened the door, all I found was another empty room where the light from a lamp shone on a narrow, old-fashioned bed, with the whiteness of the bedclothes broken by a pale green-striped blanket cover. A dressing table in the corner made it Ilse's room. I shut the door.

Only one door close to the head of the stairs remained. I knocked on that and waited. My hand was just moving toward the handle when it opened, and Ilse, her face wan with half-sleep, looked at me with a blank look that took several split seconds to move to recognition. When it did, she raised her forefinger to her mouth in a gesture of silence so that I understood that Helmut was sleeping in the darkness over her shoulder before she stepped through the door and closed it behind her.

"What has happened?" she whispered.

I looked at her. How was I going to describe what had happened: I couldn't: it was suddenly obscene. I looked at Ilse. She looked back at me expectantly. I felt that she knew and didn't know. I said, "Hans has been hurt. Father says to call the doctor." She opened her mouth. I know she wanted to ask me what had really happened, *how* Hans had been hurt, but she must have caught some kind of look from my face that she didn't want to deal with and closed her mouth again.

"*Ja*," she said. "I will call the doctor," and started down the stairs to the phone in the living room.

I stood at the top of the stairs looking after her, an aimless feeling drifting over me like the early morning fog that lazed over the ponds and meadows of the country around Stammbüttel as the night sky blued toward morning. I looked down at my robe. It had a small tear near the hem where a nail must have caught it. The smell of coffee was drifting up the stairs.

I would shower and get dressed, I thought, and started down the stairs but stopped again, the prospect of entering my room repulsive–like a visit to a cell where an execution had taken place. I looked down the hall through the open door of my father's room and saw again through the window the dark tree against the glowing cobalt sky, and thinking that its blue color was one of the beautiful colors of the world I turned and walked toward it again, standing at his window, absorbing myself into its liquid blueness.

As the blue transmuted itself by imperceptible shadings from its nighttime self, something in me seemed to be changing wordlessly yet perceptibly, so that a part of me watched the changing sky and another deeper part seemed to stand by and watch a different alteration in my self, as if the deep blue yearning for my father's unconditional recognition were fading. I think it was in that moment that I began to see that my German roots, cut so long ago, would never accept the graft of my irreducibly American self. I began to feel that my self was already complete without any roots; I did not need my father's blessing. I was all right; I had always been all right. I had been caught by the insistent call of tradition, the culture sustaining itself by demanding that I be incomplete until I belonged–to my father, to the Göring clan, to Stammbüttel–to anything to which I could attach my primitive limpet longings. But as the blue transformed itself into the dawn, I began to cast off my old hopes and pretensions, leaving me for that moment as light as an object in free fall, so that I caught my breath, unable to feel the difference between being free and falling. I whispered, "I'm all right, I'm all right," and it felt less like a reassurance than a statement of fact, and although I understood the feeling was temporary, I would never entirely forget this moment in the blue light, even though I could not hold onto an instant of its being as it faded into the ordinary loveliness of a morning sky.

I walked quickly downstairs to my room. The full morning light jarred its destruction into complete focus in all its nastiness. The bed leaned like a prop in a bad Cubist stage set; the carpet had sprouted nails like an art work by Lucas Samarras. I tried to comfort myself with the thought that one day the description of the room would be part of the story of a wild and crazy filial visit that would amuse my friends, but I couldn't get hold of the funny edge of it. I still haven't.

The light of the lamp which still lay incongruously suspended in its shade on the bed had paled to a small golden circle. Moving carefully, I picked my way toward the dresser and wardrobe, which stood as if nothing had happened. I took out some things and went back up to the bathroom.

I came back downstairs to the sound of low voices. Ilse and my father were interrupting what sounded like the doctor's careful instructions with tense whispered questions, the rising intonations of their endings ascending almost to a level where the words came clear.

I returned to my room, thinking that the best thing would be to pack and get my things out so that I would never have to enter it again, when I remembered that I had put my suitcase under the bed. I wasn't certain that the floor around the bed would hold my weight, but it looked like there was a narrow path to the suitcase, which looked intact. I got on my hands and knees and moved toward it, like a fox testing thin ice. I reached forward over splintered wood and had just grabbed the handle when one of the joists beneath me groaned and started to give way. I felt the floor descend under me as if it were going to swallow me whole, like something out of a Vincent Price film.

But I hung onto the suitcase, which had become enmeshed in my mind with the idea of escape as the floor sagged a couple of inches and stopped. In one motion, I yanked the suitcase out from under the bed and jumped back, dragging it across the broken flooring, which made a few threatening creaks, but held.

But the suitcase was a lot lighter than I expected it to be. When I looked down, half of the bottom had been ripped away, and what was left of its contents looked like they had been chewed. I have heard people say, "My heart sank." My heart really did. How, I thought, would I ever get out of there if I didn't have a suitcase? I had put so much meaning into packing it that I sat there like a child, pondering what seemed for the moment an imminent defeat.

Finally, reason returned: I had to get a new suitcase, and quickly. I picked it up again and made my way back into the dining room where Ilse, still in her robe, was sitting down to a cup of coffee.

"Have some coffee," she said, as if it were some kind of medicine which would cure the situation.

"I will, thank you," I said, speaking very formally. "But I think I had better do something about this as soon as possible." I held up the suitcase, bottom side out.

"Tsk, what a pity," she said. "We will get you another one. Your father needs a new one too. His old suitcase is worn out, although he does not want to admit it. After breakfast, we will go to Strohmeier's in Salzgitter. You will not find better luggage in New York."

"When can we go?" I asked.

Ilse looked at her watch; I looked at mine. It was a little after seven. "I do not think Strohmeier opens before 9:30. If we leave then, we can get there by ten. Then I can give Helmut his breakfast and..." she paused.

I knew the "and" referred to "the boys," and for a moment I was glad she hadn't mentioned them, but curiosity got the better of me, and I asked, "Is Hans...all right?"

"To everyone's surprise, including the doctor's, Hans is not very hurt. He has many small cuts and several bruises. After all that has happened to him, it is quite amazing. The doctor fixed him up, as you would say, and sent him to bed. They are both sleeping."

I nodded dumbly. As I poured myself coffee, my father entered, and Anni brought in some rolls. I looked at my father, who was dressed immaculately for this crazy morning, his white shirt with its starched collar gleaming against his silk rep tie and tweed jacket, but his manner was preoccupied as he nodded to each of us in turn with a brief "*Morgen*" and sat down.

"*Die Buben schlafen?*...The boys are sleeping?" he asked, pouring his coffee.

Ilse nodded, but he was looking at the coffee pouring into his cup and didn't see her. When he finished pouring, he looked up with a questioning look and she said, "*Ja, sie schlafen–das hoffe ich*.... Yes, they are sleeping–I hope."

I didn't like the addendum. My father noted it too and frowned. "*Ja*," he said grimly. "*Es wäre besser*.... They had better be sleeping...and making no more trouble." He sighed. "*Ich habe es mir überlegt*.... I have been thinking that this next year I will send them to the St. Pauli School in Wiesbaden. My cousin is the principal there."

Ilse cast him a quick glance and didn't say anything. I wasn't clear where her opinion lay in the matter. There was a knock on the door. Anni answered it, and came back with the paper, which she brought to my father who took it with a grunt of thanks. It was the *Zeitung*.

We ate in silence, sifting what had to be similar thoughts through different screens, coming up with different residues that probably bore little resemblance to each other. My father was absorbed in his coffee and paper. I looked at his still-handsome, intelligent, intent face; his elegant hands with their long, slender fingers that ended in neat, short, manicured nails. "Well, anyway" I thought, "thanks for the genes." It wasn't a bad deal, really, accepting the fact that there would never be a complete paternity package. And if I had had any doubt about the benefits of growing up American, my visit had confirmed that the original package came with serious disabilities. Life had clipped even my father's wings. My heart was still extrapolating what he must have been like when he could still fly, when he looked up and caught my speculating eye. He responded with the shadow of a smile and rose, folding up the paper and laying it carefully back on the table. "*Die heutige*.... Today's," he said. There was pride in his voice.

I said, *"Danke,"* and smiled to acknowledge that I appreciated his feeling. He nodded and had started to go when he stopped and clapped his right hand dramatically against his forehead.

"Lieber Gott!" he exclaimed. *"Mit allen diesen Störungen....* With all these disturbances I completely forgot: the poor Aunt. I talked to her nephew and he is coming here today to discuss the..." he waved his hand, searching for the word "...situation."

*"Was für eine Situation...*What 'situation?'" she asked sharply.

My father stopped and gave her a long, exasperated look that had a such sharp edge of real anger to it that it surprised me. *"Mit ihrer Krankheit....* With her illness."

So Tante Therese was still alive! That was a relief. But what was the 'situation,' what was the illness that was bringing her brother to see my father? And why did my father seem so angry? I looked from one to the other, but they were unaware of me.

Ilse ignored the my father's undertone. Looking into her coffee cup, she said casually, *"Aber ja....* But yes, of course. I will have coffee and cake for them. And please don't forget that it is Helmut's birthday and his friends and their mothers will be here."

I suddenly felt very tired. "I'm going to lie down in the living room until we leave to get the suitcase," I said. She nodded without looking up. I went into the living room and sat down on the couch and pulled a pillow toward me. I don't even remember lying down, but it was half-past-nine when Ilse called me from the doorway and said she was ready to leave.

Chapter 23

I was still a little groggy when Ilse and I drove away, but her road style hadn't changed. At the first swerve I found myself wide awake, backseat-driving with my mouth shut. It was a cloudy day, with big gray-and-white clouds moving over the farms and green hills, suddenly opening to let loose celestial shafts of sun, only to close again and leave the landscape looking more gloomy than it had before.

In the half hour it took us to get to the store, I had time to wonder at the way Ilse and Father were taking the destruction in the basement. My father's apparently casual return to work seemed strange. I would have expected–at the least–a covey of repairmen who would be pulling on their lower lips, frowning, to assess the damage–not to mention a few officials taking notes. But when I followed Ilse out the door, the house was much in its usual late-morning state, with the table partly set for lunch as Helmut's small piercing voice held forth at length in the kitchen to Anni's shorter, softer replies. Hans and Gustav were not in sight.

We parked in a vast underground garage that would have been the envy of any of the malls that were yet to pave America the Beautiful and mounted stairs that led directly into the store. I asked Ilse, if so many ordinary things were still in such short supply, where did the money come from for such elaborate construction?

"Probably from the Marshall Plan," she said dryly. "As for the construction, Salzgitter was heavily bombed during the war. When they rebuilt it, they rebuilt for the future. I think it probably cost less than rebuilding the old town."

It made sense, but as we climbed the stairs I wondered to myself what folks back home would say to all this American-dollar-funded German construction. I wasn't thinking so much of my friends, most of whom would just shrug–Germany was not a really interesting place to think about then, when American art and writing seemed the center of their world, and for the politically minded, the Civil Rights movement kept the focus back home. But what I pictured was the "Average American," who at that moment was still beset by a McCarthian paranoia and a mistrust of everything that wasn't red-white-and-blue. The Cold War was going full tilt, and while West Germany was our ally, America was still having some tough times, too tough for us to appreciate that this well-appointed commercial center of our former enemy was paid for in great part with our money, while back home, complexes like these were a decade away.

But when we got into the store, there wasn't much in the way of goods to back up the impressive structure. There were barely half a dozen suitcases to choose from, and only two in the size I had lost. It seems foolish now, but without hesitating I chose one that was made entirely of leather, beautiful but heavy, turning my nose up at the one with nylon sides, a light frame and synthetic trim–now the quintessential travel bag of the airborne poor and rich alike.

As soon as I pointed to it, Ilse turned to me and said, her voice holding an edge of weary irony, "You are certainly your father's daughter. It is what he would choose. I myself prefer the newer style, but your father will never agree to carry anything but leather," and she told the clerk to get her another one. He returned with a twin. A few minutes later, after an exchange of what looked like an enormous number of Deutschmarks, Ilse and I headed back to Stammbüttel.

When we got back to the house, I saw that the door to my room was ajar, and that the repairmen, at least, had come. From the "*Lieber Gott's*" and "*Schrecklich's*", I understood they had just entered and were still trying to grasp the situation. Ilse took one look, put down the suitcase she was carrying, and went into the kitchen. I wasn't ready to answer any questions about the damage either, so I went into the living room to hide my thoughts in some magazines, telling myself I would just concentrate on getting out of Stammbüttel in one piece.

When the men were gone, I started to go upstairs to wash. In the dining room, my father was standing near the table in a thoughtful pose, his chin in his hand.

"*Was haben die Männer gesagt?*.... What did the men say?"

He smiled ruefully. "*Sie sagen, 'Schrecklich,'*...They said, 'Terrible,' several times and not much else," he said with more humor than I would have expected. Then his expression became more serious. "*Aber es wird viel Geld*.... But it will cost a lot of money to repair the house."

He looked over to me as I stood on the first step of the stairs. Even allowing for the difference in levels, he looked smaller than I remembered him. I had always thought of him as being taller–not huge, but a great deal taller than I, who was not quite five-eight. I stepped down and saw that he was no more than an inch taller–at most. I was taking this in when I saw him look at me questioningly and realized he had spoken.

"*Bitte?*" I said.

"*Du scheinst ganz wohl zu sein,*...You look all right," he said. It was more an assertion than an inquiry.

"*Ja,*" I said in the same tone. "*Ich bin ganz in Ordnung.*... I am all right," and added "*Danke,*" as if he had asked about the state of my health.

He nodded and started for the door, putting a hand into his vest pocket as if searching for something he had put there, and stopped. "*Und der Koffer.*... And the suitcase...?"

"*Ilse kaufte ein neuen für mich.*... Ilse bought me a new one...and also for you...the same. Very nice. All leather."

He frowned but then nodded with a resigned smile. "*Ja,*" he said. "*Sie hat das schon lange gewollt.*... She has wanted to do that for a long time," and left.

I stood for a moment listening to the sounds of Anni and Ilse in the kitchen. Neither of them were talking much; there was just the occasional sound of two people working together. It struck me that it was the sound of two people working companionably, a description I wouldn't have expected to use for the two of them even yesterday. But then I remembered how frightened Anni had been in the kitchen after the blast. Having Ilse stolidly around was probably preferable to having to think about the craziness that seemed to have seized the boys she had raised.

Against this mundane background I wondered how the murderous intent that lay behind all that had happened was still being swept aside. No one was addressing it. No word had been said that even acknowledged that the boys had tried, had even *said* they tried, to murder me. But even as I thought about it I couldn't see any possibility of doing anything about it at all. I couldn't see my father going to the police or any other civil authority. And bringing in the rest of the family seemed also out of the question.

The sight of the suitcases standing in the hall reminded me: I could pack. The bags were a perfect match. .I picked one up, took a deep breath as I reached the door of my former room, and went in. After I maneuvered around the room's edge, it didn't take me long to throw everything into the suitcase, jam it shut, and take it into the living room. I spread my things out on the couch so I could pack it right. It wasn't until I had the whole thing done and closed that I remembered that there were some cosmetics sitting out on the dresser. .I looked at my watch. It was almost noon and despite everything, I thought, lunch would be on time. I would deal with it later, before Helmut's party arrived. But it didn't seem right with visitors coming to leave the suitcase in the living room. I took it back out into the hall, but now the other one wasn't there.

As I put it down, Ilse came out and saw me. "Ach, you are packed?" he said. I nodded. She sighed. "I am packing your father's also. He is leaving on a business trip early tomorrow morning." She went upstairs.

My father came in for lunch. "Hans und Gust'l don't want to eat," she said as she went to her place at the end of the table. "I told them they can stay in their room. It is probably best."

I silently said 'Amen' to that as we sat down. It was my last meal at my father's house, but I wasn't feeling nostalgic about it. We ate in silence. My mind wandered over the last few days and I realized I hadn't really thought much about Wolf since he had made it out the window. As the meal went on, I began to think more about him. What a sweet guy, I thought. I would miss him. I hadn't had a boyfriend my own age for some time. Most of my men had been older than me–some, like Jack, considerably older. It had suited me. They were men established in their professions, and I enjoyed being treated like their peer. I had told myself that men my own age were too young, not really mature, not sophisticated enough. Looking back on my time with Wolf, my argument felt less solid. I couldn't imagine any of them letting themselves get emotionally involved in such short order. They *were* more mature, more sophisticated, and they wouldn't have fallen for me virtually overnight if their lives had depended on it.

As I thought about Wolf, I understood that he had literally *fallen* in love with me. By the time Anni brought our coffee, I had begun to toy with the idea that I might, after all, have fallen in love with *him* as well, and at that moment, the way these things often happen, the phone rang and it was Wolf–Ilse said dryly when she returned from the living room–and he wanted to talk to me.

I picked up the phone and said, "Hello."

"Leni," Wolf said. There was a long pause.

"Where are you?" I asked.

"In Heidelberg."

"In Heidelberg? How did you do that?" I was surprised, as if he had driven from New York to Atlanta in a morning.

"I drove down after I left you. Distances are not so far here as they are in America. And the Autobahn has no speed limit."

"I know," I said, remembering. "By the way, are you all right?"

He laughed. "Yes," he said. "Only a few scratches. And I was in time for my class, although I am not so sure I taught very well today."

"Well," I said. "I guess I won't see you, then."

"Actually, I have an idea."

"Yes?" I said, and waited.

"Leni," he said, "why don't you come and stay with me just a day or two at Heidelberg? I only have a few classes to teach and we could spend a lot of time in the mountains, and in the town. You would enjoy it. It is very beautiful."

"Sure we could," I said, "but would we?"

"Would we what?"

"Spend time in the mountains and the town."

He laughed. "Yes," he said. "I promise you. We will spend some time in the mountains and in the town."

"My ticket is Hanover to Paris."

"The train stops in Frankfurt in any case. You can get the ticket changed there for a small fee."

"Does the train go to Heidelberg?"

"No. I will meet your train in Frankfurt. It is only an hour away from here."

"I don't know," I said. I didn't. Seeing Wolf again was appealing, but my friends in Paris were expecting me.

"There is not much time to think," he said. I could hear his voice slipping into disappointment. I remembered again how it felt–loving and not being loved. "Are you sure I can change my ticket?"

"Yes," he said.

"Well, I'll see if I can arrange it," I said. "But only for a day. I still want to spend time in Paris." This time without Jack, I said to myself. Just going around Paris with my friends. Even as I stood there, talking to Wolf, it was like a new idea–to go somewhere on my own, not being with, not really looking out for, a man. It was not an easy idea, but it was suddenly full of possibilities, a momentary vision of a kind of freedom.

"Yes," he said, "of course," but I knew he hoped to keep me in Heidelberg as long as possible, and I wasn't all that sure I would find it that easy to leave once I got there. My "Okay" didn't have a lot of enthusiasm, and the moment I said it, I wasn't sure. "Wolf," I said, trying to figure out how to say so, but he was already speaking.

"Wonderful," he said, sounding hurried all of a sudden. "I will meet your train in Frankfurt," he finished, and hung up. I dropped the receiver into its cradle, feeling frustrated that I couldn't be clear about what I wanted, and went back to the table.

Lunch was quiet: the boys stayed in their room; Helmut ate with Anni in the kitchen without any fuss because he could keep an eye on his party cakes, Ilse said, sounding pleased. Apparently some of the *grandes dames* of Stammbüttel were allowing their sons to play with Ilse's.

A very large man, tall and almost fat, entered and was introduced as Emil Wiedemeier, Tante Therese's nephew. When he limply shook my hand, he gave me a very long, impersonal look, the sort you might give an interesting specimen. He was trailed by a tall, very thin, very tidy woman–his wife, Theodora.

They were followed by a girl in her teens, in a white-collared dress that was too young for her but which she was probably condemned to wear because it still fit. She was somehow familiar; I realized that she was the girl who had danced with Hans, the one I had half-mindedly chosen as my earlier alter-ego. I gave her what I meant as a friendly look; she gave me a curious glance and looked away. She had that non-committal look that teenagers have when they are with their parents–of being with them but not of them.

My father stepped forward and introduced her to me as Liesel, their daughter. She gave me the shadow of a curtsey. Her parents nodded to me; nobody extended a hand.

We stood there for an awkward moment, and then Ilse said, "*Die Wiedemeier wollen mit deinem Vater sprechen*.... The Wiedemeiers want to talk with your father. Meanwhile, perhaps you and Liesel would like to..." She had no particular idea of what Liesel and I would want to do together, and I didn't either. She made a small suggestion of throwing up her hands, and then pointed at the living room and said, *"Anni wird euch Kaffee und Kuchen bringen....* Anni will bring you coffee and cake." And she returned to the kitchen.

Liesel and I looked at each other; I raised my eyebrows and shrugged: she put her hand to her mouth and giggled. As we entered the room, she turned to me and said, "Please let us speak English. I must practice."

"Sure," I said. "Whatever you want. It's easier for me. I'm leaving on the five o'clock train."

"You are leaving?" she said. She looked surprised. "I did not know that," she said. "I think you will stay much longer."

I sighed. I wasn't going to address her real question, so I said, "My visit to my father is over," speaking as clearly as I could. "I am going back home."

"Ach! You go back to America." I nodded. She looked pleased for a moment, but then she paused, unsure again.

"My visit to my father is finished," I said, and waited. Then I said it in German: *"Mein Besuch ist beendet."*

"No," she said. "I understand that. But I do not understand why you go. Everybody says you have come to live here with Uncle Franz."

"Everybody is wrong," I said, wearily. "My friends, my family, my job, my apartment–it is all in America. Not here. I don't need my father."

"Every person needs a father," she said indignantly. Anni came in with a tray and we helped ourselves to pieces of a golden cake moist with the dark halves of blue plums that stained the cake around them.

"No," I said. "Everybody can *use* a father–but they don't have to have one." As I spoke, I realized it was still a novel idea for me too. All my life I had felt I was one father short, and that it was not a situation to be recommended.

She ate her cake thoughtfully. "I cannot think how it will be if I do not have a father."

"Well," I said, "it's harder without one than with one, but it is not impossible. I mean, I am here, and no father helped me grow up."

"But Uncle Franz would have helped you if he could have." She was very certain about it.

Her certainty aggravated me. "Well he could have, but he didn't."

"But he thought you were dead."

The possibility that my father thought we had died had never occurred to me, and I was about to entertain it when I remembered how he had seen us on our way to England via Paris. "No, he didn't. He knew we were alive. He may not have known where we were, but he knew we were alive."

She looked at me indignantly and said very carefully, "That is not possible. He told us you were killed in an air raid in Wien."

"No," I said firmly. "We were not in Vienna. We were on our way to England when my father last saw us."

I felt at once angry and wearied by this new erasure of my existence from my father's life. As I spoke, I saw that disbelief was chasing belief across her face. It was obviously important to her that Uncle Franz remain a nice guy. I sighed and said, "Let's not talk about Uncle Franz. What do you do when you are not in school?" I wanted to know what it might have been like to grow up Leni Göring of Stammbüttel instead of Helene Gelbart of New York City.

She looked at me warily. I ran on: "I mean, do you study a lot, do your have a boyfriend, what do you do on weekends?" Even as I said it, it sounded a little inane. I heard the voices of women and the piping sounds of small, excited children. Helmut's party had started. I looked at my watch. It was a little after three, getting close to train time. I still had to collect things from the bomb site and I was running out of time.

I turned back to Liesel, who was still looking at me with a frown of concentration, working out an answer to my questions. "Liesel, please excuse me. I still have something I must pack. I'll be back in a minute. Please have some more cake," I said and went out.

A small crowd of women were tugging at a few little boys. There were only four of them besides Helmut, but they seemed like more, all amazingly well-dressed by American little-boy-party standards, with starched white shirts tucked into a variety of short pants with suspenders. They all wore white socks and highly polished leather shoes. Their hair had been brushed and slicked down, with only rebellious cowlicks testifying to any resistance to the relentless polishing they had undergone. When they saw me, everyone stopped for a heartbeat, and Helmut, who had been dashing from one to the other, stopped and glowered at me. I nodded to everyone with a stiff social smile and slipped into the remains of my room. It took me only a few minutes to find my things. Some of them had been scattered, but most of them were still on the dresser. I took a last look around and eased out of the door.

If I had hoped to escape attention, I had hoped wrong. All four little boys were huddled together at the other end of the dining room, looking at me with replicas of Helmut's hostile expression. The four mothers were standing and talking in the doorway with Ilse. I said, "*Hallo, Buben*–Hello, boys," the way I might have in a similar situation back home.

But the moment I spoke, one boy–the littlest one–opened his mouth wide and started to cry. Then pale blonde boy next to him pressed both his fists to his mouth as if he were trying not to scream; another assumed a Sugar Ray Robinson pose and started hopping around; and the fourth–who was the heftiest of the group–started flailing his arms wildly in a sort of windmill motion and in the process elbowed the blonde boy, who let out a shriek. Only Helmut was quiet, alternately regarding me and checking out his party mates with cool interest. I stood there trying to make up my mind what to do. As the mothers rushed toward them, all the boys started to point to me, calling me "*Die Hexe*–The witch."

I smiled weakly at the mothers, trying to suggest that this was just a kids' thing and we adults could get on with other things, but it was no good. They only looked back suspiciously, taking a protective stance slightly in front of their children. The whole phalanx stood between me and my suitcase, which also reminded me that it was not long to train time, and my father was still talking with the Wiedemeiers. As I headed toward the clump of milling children, their mothers were frowning and shaking their heads and glancing at me as if I really were the cause of it all. Behind them Ilse had her hands on the shoulders of Helmut, who stood demurely in front of her.

As I picked up my suitcase, it felt heavier than I remembered. Back to the living room I excused myself to Liesel, put everything in my cosmetics bag and stuffed it into a corner of the suitcase without really opening it. I looked at my watch. It was rounding toward four.

Behind me in the dining room the eating part of Helmut's party had begun with the mothers and Ilse hovering in attendance. I heard the door open and Father and the Wiedemeiers came in. I looked out. Emil Wiedemeier and my father were still talking, their heads bent toward each other as they walked, ushering Frau Wiedemeier in ahead of them.

My father walked to the table and made appropriate paternal comments on the party. I saw how all the little boys suddenly came to polite attention, all ten eyes riveted on my father, the living symbol of all their future fatherhoods in their Father Land. They already understood that their *Muttis*–their moms–were okay as comfort stations, but the real power lay with the men, and the men they would become.

Frau Wiedemeier was looking around rather vaguely. I guessed she was looking for her daughter and got up to motion her into the living room. Liesel was sitting looking through a copy of *Modernes Leben*, which looked like Germany's answer to *Redbook* or any number of other women's magazines. As we entered she shut the magazine quickly as if caught in some forbidden act, although I couldn't imagine any magazine that the staid German society in which my father and Ilse moved could have anything worth hiding in its pages.

My father and Emil Wiedemeier entered the living room, still deep in conversation. I heard Mr. Wiedenmeir say, "*Es wird eine lange Konvaleszenz....* It will be a long convalescence, a long while before she can be home again. We are very grateful for your help."

I wondered how Tante Therese was and what had happened to her. It wasn't until after I returned to the States that I learned from a letter from Hannah that the doctor Paul knew at the hospital had called him a few days later. The doctor told him that the mushrooms Tante Therese had eaten appeared to be harmless, although there was more than one species and he couldn't be sure he had found all of them. What he was sure of was that Tante Therese had had a mild heart attack, probably brought on by choking rather than any toxic mushroom chemicals. But she was a tough old lady, the doctor said, and would recover.

Chapter 24

The Wiedemeiers refused coffee and cake, gathered up their daughter, and left. As I waited for my father, I watched the boys play a game that seemed to have a lot of rules which their mothers policed like Los Angeles traffic cops while the boys created as many violations as possible. Every breech of the game's law was nevertheless stringently re-enforced, and the game was constantly stopped to correct the boys' moves. It surprised me how coolly the boys took all the interference with what should have been their game, protesting only occasionally and then with less annoyance than I felt. Watching them, I began to wonder whether even at this early age they might actually be humoring their mothers (as they might later humor the women they would date and marry) the way people humor children and dogs that can't be ignored but are not equals.

That brought me back to Wolf. After all, it was his world I was watching unfold the way a fragment of a hologram contains the entire holographic image in itself. I felt how peripheral women were to the real life of my father's world and felt grateful again to whatever the operative powers might be that I had left it at an early age. The possibility of getting more entangled with Wolf receded further, even as I understood that the change in my feelings wasn't really Wolf's fault, and that it would be cruel of me not to at least talk to him while the train stopped in Frankfurt. That was why, when the time came and I knew I had twenty-two minutes before the train left Frankfurt again, that I hurried down the platform to meet him.

But he wasn't there.

After a short while I decided that he might be waiting for me at the counter where he expected me to change my ticket, but when I found it, Wolf wasn't there either. By then I realized that a good fifteen of the twenty-two minutes were gone and that I had better get back to the train before it left with my new suitcase. The distance was further than I had expected, and I ended up at the right train but on the wrong side. It was only luck that I found a conductor who showed me an open door on that side and got me back on the train. But finding my compartment when I had lost my bearings wasn't easy, and I reached it just when the train gave that little jolt that trains give before they start rolling.

I looked out the window and caught my breath because there was Wolf running all out down the platform toward me. I opened the window and leaned out, but he was still some distance away, running in the same direction as the train was moving. As it gathered speed, I thought for a moment he would catch it, but just as he reached for the handrail by the steps at the end of the car near me, he ran full speed into a porter who was jockeying a heavily laden handcart of luggage as a serious, *bürgerlich* couple watched. The result was an explosion of bags, one of which must have fallen open, because my last image was of Wolf trailing something long and silky and running a losing race with the train.

But that was still in the future when my father returned and said that it was time to say goodbye so that we could go. I quickly stepped into the kitchen to speak to Anni. "Anni," I said a little hesitantly, not being sure of where I stood with her now. "*Anni, ich muss jetzt zum Zug*.... I must leave for the train, but I want to thank you for everything."

She cocked her head to one side as she wiped her hands on her apron, and said in a kind voice, "*Da ist nichts zu danken, Fräulein Helene*.... You don't need to thank me." I was about to try to find words to express what I was thanking her for when she added in a completely different and darker tone, "*aber bitte, passen Sie auf sich auf!*...but please, take care of yourself!" and then, as if she had said too much, she turned back to the stove. I hesitated a moment, but there seemed to be nothing more to say and I left the kitchen.

In the outer room the game had ended and the boys clumped together in what seemed to be peripatetic wrestling groups, ignoring their mothers' shouted instructions. My father and Ilse were standing by my suitcase in deep conversation. As I waited, the mothers gathered up their sons in a communal sweep and paid their respects to Ilse and my father, prodding their sons through miniature heel-clicking bows. Suddenly they were all gone.

I turned to Ilse and said, "Thanks for..." but words literally failed me, so I stuck out my hand and she shook it after only a fractional hesitation. I turned to my father; he looked at his watch anxiously and said we had to hurry. He picked up my suitcase, and we left.

We got in his car. Shortly after we pulled away I looked back and saw Gustav running out of the gate. He stopped short and looked quickly right and left. When he caught sight of the car he raised his hand and screamed something, but the car was just turning the corner and I wasn't about to ask my father to turn back, so all I saw was Gustav waving his arm and screaming and running toward us as we turned out of sight. I was just relieved to be in the car with my father on my way to the train, and it wasn't very long before we were on the highway, driving fast toward Hanover.

We didn't speak for a while. I felt full of things I wanted to say that didn't at that moment have any words connected to them. Finally he said in his slow English, "I am very sorry that the boys behaved so badly. When I learned you would visit, I was hoping that you and they would become friends."

"Well, I'm sorry too," I said.

"Possibly, when they are older, they will behave better," he said. I looked at him to see if he was serious. He was.

"Well," I said, "I don't expect that I will be visiting you again very soon."

He nodded. "Yes," he said. "But of course. You are in New York."

"Yes," I said, feeling as if I were following a badly written script, "and you are in Stammbüttel."

He sighed and looked sad. "Yes," he said. "It is a great distance."

"Maybe one day you will visit me in New York," I said. I wasn't improving on the script.

He gave his head a quick nod to the side. "Ach," he said. "I would like once to visit America. But," he added, "it is very expensive. Perhaps in later years, when the children have finished at the University."

"Well," I said, "be sure to let me know if you are coming." The script was so bad I wanted to cover my eyes, but I felt as if I had to follow it. At each line, I searched for something else to say, something that would mean something when I looked back on my time alone with him, but nothing came to me.

Talking about this later in Paris with my friend Isabelle, she said to me, "But of course you couldn't find what you wanted to say. You wanted to know, 'Why did you send me away? Didn't you love me? Why didn't you try to find me when the war was over? Do you love me now?" I looked at her. I had not articulated even one of those questions to myself. But she was exactly right: those were the questions lying untouched in my heart the whole time.

I said, "Well, excluding the last one about now, why didn't I ask them?"

"Because you were afraid of the answer."

"What answer?" I said indignantly. "That he didn't love me? That he didn't care? I know that. At least I assume it."

"Yes," she said, "you *assume* it, but you don't know. Somewhere you probably have this little bit, a shard, perhaps,"–and she held up her thumb and forefinger together to show how small that shard might be—"a little bit of hope that he did everything to avoid your going, that he really cared, that he has always cared somewhere in his heart. But if you asked, even if he didn't give you a straight answer, you would have known from his voice that he probably didn't give enough of a damn to count."

I had protested again that I was quite aware that my father was indifferent–had probably always been indifferent–to my fate, to which she shrugged, stood up, and patted me on the back as she walked toward the kitchen to check on dinner. Although I didn't acknowledge it at that moment, I thought she was right, and it wasn't until long after that I understood that asking if someone loves you is a bad question: showing that you are either too emotionally stupid to know how the other person feels or too needy for reassurance and therefore somehow unworthy, and in any case, you are committing the cardinal sin of demanding that another person acknowledge dangerous feelings that they may not be ready to lay out for you, and rather than acknowledge the feeling and put themselves at risk, they may withdraw that feeling from you altogether.

But in a way, my questions to Isabelle had already been partly answered. My father had brought the new issue of the *Stambüttler Zeitung* to the station so that I could read it on the train. As I thumbed through the pages between Hanover and Franfurt, the first thing I saw was a center spread about the *Mittelball*–pictures of everyone, it seemed, who was there, including the obnoxious Otto Kammenberg; Hans turning a graceful corner; and my father and Ilse at either side of the table, smiling, facing the camera, glasses raised in their hands as if toasting the photographer. I searched through the twenty-odd photographs to see whom I could recognize. It was not until I started to look through the whole lot again with the feeling that I was looking for someone that I realized that I was looking for myself, and that I wasn't there.

I was able to hold off the implications for just a moment before the meaning of it made my heart fall again with an almost audible thud. I remembered that the photographer had taken several pictures that included me, including one at the table with my father and Ilse, but my father had clearly not seen fit to print that. I was not there. I had not been there. I had never been there, in his life, in his world, and when I left, I would become one of those subjects of which a polite visitor would not remind him.

I recognized the feeling in my heart; I had known it often in all its black, unredeemable bitterness. It was the feeling you get when you realize that someone you still love deeply and passionately no longer loves you; that he is gone; that even if you see him again he isn't coming back to you; that you are utterly and completely alone and it seems for that moment impossible ever to be loved again.

The image of my small self on the train suddenly came over me almost like a hallucination so that I was both on this train and on that early one, watching the tracks that were leading me forever away from my father, watching those tracks crossing and uncrossing beside my window as I heard the creak and felt the sway and tilt of the train passing over them–then and now. And sitting there, older and so young all at once, I understood in some chaotic, feeling way that the feeling in my heart now was the feeling I had then, when my small heart in its wisdom knew that it couldn't hold so great a grief and had stashed it away, the memory of the moment on the train marking the place where it had been left, returned now with its full force.

I slid into that nostalgia where the sweet pain of loss enshrines old wounds, making the present fade like a rerun on an old black-and-white set. But before I descended into those feelings I caught myself as I had earlier in the blue light. I understood that this was no longer about love; I had lived without my father most of my life. Whatever was gone was gone long ago. I wasn't missing anything. I did not need to have my picture in a local German newspaper, not even my father's. It would have been nice, but it wouldn't have changed the years before. Nothing ever would, but nothing was missing. It was a strange feeling. Not nearly as romantic as mourning love lost. More solemn, quieter, solid. As the train passed out of a tunnel back into a flashing of green trees, I turned my thoughts to what had really happened, to my father's last goodbye.

In Hanover, my father and I, still having said nothing of importance, arrived at the Station and parked. As we entered the Bahnhof, the great sounds of railway stations everywhere surrounded us. Destinations, hours, minutes, arrivals, tracks, warnings darted through the air with the authority of information emitted from loudspeakers, all of it echoing from the tall ceiling above us. My father insisted on paying for my ticket, although I made a small and meaningless protest–somehow thinking, perhaps, that he might think better of me if I paid my own way. At this point the train was only some fifteen minutes from leaving, so we hurried down to the track. My father found me a compartment with a seat by a window and put my suitcase on the overhead rack, admonishing me not to forget it in a sudden parental gesture.

I look back on our conversation and remember how we stood there so coolly, playing the roles of father and departing daughter even though the parts weren't entirely familiar to us, unaware that we had just escaped being blown to bits.

It wasn't until the train had pulled out of Frankfurt and I looked in my suitcase for a sweater to find that, except for my cosmetics case, its contents consisted entirely of shirts, ties, and other male overnight stuff, that I understood that in Gustav chase after the car he had been trying to let us know we had the wrong one. Had I carried the suitcase myself, I would have known before we left the house because mine was a lot heavier than my father's, but it was my father who carried it and stowed it in the rack. At that moment I was really upset about not having my clothes and things when I was just heading to party my way through Paris with my friends, but that was nothing to what I felt when I finally reached my father by phone two days later.

I haven't put all the pieces together, but I think my scenario is as good as any: Convinced that I was not only after but *entitled to* the entire family "fortune," Gustav decided in one last desperate measure to save it by blowing me up. More than one bright child with a precocious interest in chemistry and access to a few innocent and ordinary chemicals and an alarm clock has created an explosion big enough to kill someone. When I finally reached my father after the phone lines in the Verlag were repaired, it was clear that a bomb had exploded there and that bomb had been in my suitcase. The disappearing suitcases had apparently been the alternate product of Gustav taking mine to be rigged and Ilse taking Father's to be packed.

But there were a couple of things I can never be certain of. One is why my Father's suitcase was downstairs and mine was not. Perhaps Ilse had brought his back down for some reason, while Gustav (or more probably

Hans) had taken mine back up for some reason, not realizing that it would miss the train.

Another thing I don't understand is why the damn thing went off at almost five o'clock, moments before the train was to leave. Gustav could have found out that my train would not arrive in Paris until six in the morning and set the clock to blow me up at five a.m. when I would still have been with my suitcase on the train. But something went wrong. My bet is that Gustav, as he had done often before in some kind of neurotic need to put the kybosh on his ventures, had left the final clock-setting to Hans.

Of course I tried to call my father about the suitcase as soon as I got to Paris. When nobody answered the phone after my fifth try, I called the Stammbüttel phone company who could only tell me the phone was not in order. When I finally reached him, my father sounded very strange–at least his manner *seemed* strange until he told me what had happened. He was still in a state of shock: mine didn't come on until after I hung up.

You have to give young Gustl credit: it was one hell of a bomb. My normally reticent father, once he started talking, couldn't seem to stop, so I missed a lot of the details as he spoke only German and I didn't feel I could, under the circumstances, ask him to tell me in English. But the gist of it was that the bomb went off in front of the house–fortunately after Ilse, Hans and Gustav had gone back inside–probably trying to figure out how to get me and it back together. The bomb wrecked the entrance and blew out the front windows–including the one in my father's office that he wanted to replace. The stairs were open to the street; the front door was in pieces, but had apparently prevented the blast from doing more than knock Ilse and the boys to the floor, from which they arose with nothing more than a few scrapes and bruises.

I was listening intently until I heard my father use the word, accident, to describe the scene. "*Was meinst du, Vati? Es war kein Unfall!*...What do you mean, Daddy? It was no accident!" I said. There was a long silence. "*Vater?*" I said tentatively, wondering if he was still on the line.

"*Ja...Ja,*" he said slowly. "*Du hast recht. Es war vermutlich nicht ein Unfall*...You are right. It was probably not an accident." There was another long silence.

"*Was meinst du, vermutlich nicht?*.... What do you mean, probably not?" I said. I understood that he was there and I wasn't; that he had almost lost his wife and his children, and I was demanding he toe the line of truth. But I didn't want to let go of it: I wanted to engage him, have him acknowledge what really happened: not only the truth about the boys, but also about Ilse and what had gone on during my visit. My father's denial of that seemed like his denial of everything that had gone on through the years.

But then, after another pause he sighed and said, "*Leni, du muss verstehen....* You must understand. Hier es ist nicht möglich.... Here it isn't possible to make such private matters public. *Sogar wenn Jeder weiss,...*Even when everybody knows, one doesn't speak of it. Possibly it is different in America, but here..."

I suddenly felt tired, and as his voice trailed off again, I decided to drop it. He was far away; I wouldn't be visiting soon. I had tried my best to make contact with him. I was not big on causes, and I was even smaller on hopeless ones.

"*Ich nehme an, dass nichts übrig bleibt....* I guess that there's nothing left of my things?"

"*Ach! Aber natürlich, deine Sachen!*" His voice brightened slightly. "*Alle deine Kleider!...*All your clothes! Terrible! I will send you money!" I started to protest, that it wasn't necessary; money wasn't the issue, but then I thought of all my favorite dresses and all the things I had already had to buy, and after some waffling he suggested a figure, and anyway, he was so eager to do it, to do something for me that I could actually use, that I couldn't say no, so I said yes, and we worked out a transfer to my friend's account in Paris which of course didn't happen until after I left, communications being what they were in those years, but eventually, about a month later, it caught up with me in New York, and I was glad to have it.

With that it felt like the call was over, but I suddenly thought to ask after Anni. She was, my father said, all right; she had apparently been in her room when the suitcase exploded and she was shaken up, but okay. The wall to her room had cracked–loudly, she had told my father, like the crack of doom–but it had held. As he spoke I realized that the whole time I had stayed in the house I had never knew exactly where Anni lived. She just seemed to be eternally *there*, like the table and chairs, an integral part of the house.

"*Ja*," my father said thoughtfully, "*Gott sei Dank, sie lebt....* Thank God she is alive."

But knowing all this was still in the future when my father and I stood on the platform to say goodbye. We spoke a little about Paris, which he said he had always liked. *"Ich hab's sehr gern....* I'm very fond of it," he said with a faraway look in his eyes, and I remembered that he spoke fluent French, so I asked him why he didn't visit it more often and he shrugged and said he didn't have time to travel except on business.

And so we passed the few minutes before the train left slowly, one by one, since the things that were on our minds we couldn't say and the things we said were not on our minds, until suddenly my father took a step toward me and embraced me, pressing his cheek to mine and then quickly releasing me and stepping away again before I could raise my surprised arms and embrace him back. Then he motioned me into my compartment, but I stopped on the lowest step and turned back to him. He stood by the open door, looking down the platform as if at some distant view that was unfolding itself to him, and though I looked hard where he was looking I just saw a Renaissance perspective of tracks and roof beams converging toward large arched exit ways through which the trains came and went. Finally my father said in a low voice so that I had to lean toward him to hear him over the thousand sounds of the great station: *"Ich habe viele grosse Fehler gemacht....* I have made many great mistakes."

I wanted to hear him say it again, but in the face of it–it was such a small offering and such a great offering all at once–I couldn't say I hadn't heard or hadn't understood. For a minute I just stood there, not knowing what to say. I couldn't after all disagree, and to agree with it would have been like sitting in judgment on him, which I wasn't prepared to do either, even though I had sat in judgment on him many times in my mind. But he stood there looking hard still at the distant view and I wanted so much to at least acknowledge the offering in some way that would fit, but finally, as the porters started the "All aboard!" and the sound of doors slamming shut punctuated the station's ambient noise, I said the only thing I could think of, and to this date I still can't think of anything else I might, under the circumstances have said.

"Niemand ist perfekt.... Nobody's perfect!" I said.

And I guess it was the right thing to say because he shook his head and closed his eyes momentarily and looked sad, as if he were in perfect agreement with it. I stepped into to my compartment. He was still looking away as he closed my door and stepped back.

As the train made its first starting sounds and moved away, I leaned on the half-open window in the door and looked at him. He turned and looked at me with a sad charming smile and raised his hand to say goodbye. He stood that way as I slid away down the platform and I saw him become smaller and smaller until he disappeared altogether.

www.ingramcontent.com/pod-product-compliance
Lightning Source LLC
LaVergne TN
LVHW091042080826
845145LV00002B/598